Levi p[...]at fun." He accentuated the word with a suggestive lift of his eyebrows.

She seemed to consider the proposal. "So that's it then?" she finally said, giving him a skeptical glare. "We have a summer fling, no strings attached, then go our separate ways in July."

"Exactly." He said it as though they'd completed a negotiation, though he had no intention of sticking to it. To close the deal, he snaked his hand up her thigh. "I promise I'll be the best fling you'll ever have."

"You'll be the only fling I've ever had," she corrected boldly, but she didn't brush his hand away.

That was a good sign. "So when can I take you out?"

Cass hesitated. "Maybe next week?"

"Perfect." That'd give him plenty of time to plan the most epic date she'd ever been on…

ACCLAIM FOR SARA RICHARDSON

COMEBACK COWBOY

"Richardson's empathy for her protagonists shines through every page of her second Rocky Mountain Riders novel, making their long-awaited reunion into a sweet tale that will easily win readers' hearts."

—RTBookReviews.com

HOMETOWN COWBOY

"Filled with humor, heart, and love, this page-turner is one wild ride."

—Jennifer Ryan,
New York Times **bestselling author**

"An emotional ride with characters that come alive on every single page. Sara brings real feelings to every scene she writes."

—Carolyn Brown,
New York Times **bestselling author**

"This will satisfy Richardson's fans while welcoming new readers to a sweeping land of mountains, cowboys, and romance."

—Publishers Weekly

MORE THAN A FEELING

"Ruby is the kind of heroine you can't help but love and root

Fall in Love with Forever Romance

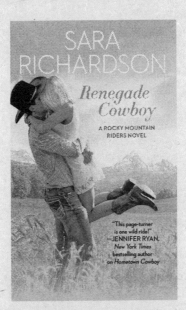

RENEGADE COWBOY
By Sara Richardson

In the *New York Times* bestselling tradition of Jennifer Ryan and Maisey Yates comes the latest in Sara Richardson's Rocky Mountain Riders series. Cassidy Greer and Levi Cortez have a history together—and a sizzling attraction that's too hot to ignore. When Levi rides back into town, he knows Cass doesn't want to get roped into a relationship with a cowboy. So he's offered her a no-strings fling. But can he convince himself that one night is enough?

THE HIGHLAND GUARDIAN
By Amy Jarecki

Captain Reid MacKenzie has vowed to watch over his dying friend's daughter. But Reid's new ward is no wee lass. She's a ravishing, fully grown woman, and it's all he can do to remember his duty and not seduce her...Miss Audrey Kennet is stunned by the news of her father's death, and then outraged when the kilted brute who delivers the news insists she must now marry. But Audrey soon realizes the brave, brawny Scot is the only man she wants—though loving him means risking her lands, her freedom, and even her life.

Fall in Love with Forever Romance

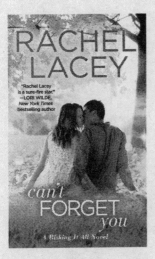

CAN'T FORGET YOU
By Rachel Lacey

Jessica Flynn is proud of the spa she's built on her own. Now that the land next door is for sale, she can expand her business...Until Mark Dalton, the man who once stole her heart, places a higher bid on the property. Mark doesn't want to compete with Jess. But as he tries to repair the past, he realizes that Jess may never forgive him if she learns why he left all those years ago.

BACK HOME AT FIREFLY LAKE
By Jen Gilroy

Fans of RaeAnne Thayne, Debbie Mason, and Susan Wiggs will love the latest from Jen Gilroy. Firefly Lake is just a pit stop for single mom Cat McGuire. That is, until sparks fly with her longtime crush—who also happens to be her daughter's hockey coach—Luc Simard. When Luc starts to fall hard, can he convince Cat to stay?

Fall in Love with Forever Romance

New York Times Bestselling Author

JILL SHALVIS

Simply Irresistible

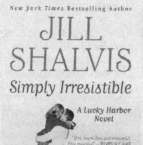

A Lucky Harbor Novel

SIMPLY IRRESISTIBLE
By Jill Shalvis

Now featuring ten bonus recipes never available before in print! Don't miss this new edition of *Simply Irresistible*, the first book in *New York Times* bestselling author Jill Shalvis's beloved Lucky Harbor series!

NOTORIOUS PLEASURES
By Elizabeth Hoyt

Rediscover the Maiden Lane Series by *New York Times* bestselling author Elizabeth Hoyt in this beautiful reissue with an all-new cover! Lady Hero Batten wants for nothing, until she meets her fiancé's notorious brother. Griffin Remmington is a mysterious rogue, whose interests belong to the worst sorts of debauchery. Hero and Griffin are constantly at odds, so when sparks fly, can these two imperfect people find a perfect true love?

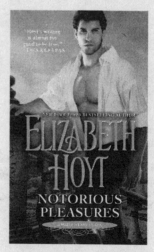

"It's not like he's a prize," she said, turning to address them all. "He's a technology consultant, for God's sake. Not Chris Hemsworth." Not that she knew what being a technology consultant meant. But it'd sounded good when she'd met him after she found his stray puggle wandering downtown six months ago. Peabody had pranced right up to her on the street and peed on her leg, the little shit. Now, Jessa was a dog person—an *animal* person—but that puggle had it out for her from day one.

When Cam had come in to retrieve his little beast from the shelter, stars had circled in her eyes. He was the first attractive man she'd seen since all those bull riders had passed through town three months ago. So unfair for those smokin' hot cowboys to gather in town and get the women all revved up only to leave them the next day.

In all honesty, Cam was no cowboy. Though his slight bulk suggested he spent a good portion of every day sitting in front of a computer screen, his soft brown eyes had a kind shimmer that instantly drew you in. He'd been good to her—taking her out to fancy restaurants and buying her flowers just because. Also, because she'd saved his beloved varmint from the potential fate of being mauled by a mountain lion, he'd made monthly donations to the shelter, which had kept them going.

Now he was gone.

"I can't believe this. How could he break up with me?"

Everyone around her had gone back to their own conversations, either unwilling to answer or pretending they didn't hear. So she turned to Big Man. "I guess you're happy about this, huh? Now the seat's all yours."

He didn't even look at her. "Nope. I'm good right where I am, thanks."

Oh, sure. After all that, now he didn't want to sit by her? "Fine. That's fine. It's all fine." Raising the glass to her lips, she drained the rest of her wine in one gulp.

"You know what?" she asked Big Man, not caring one iota that he seemed hell-bent on ignoring her. "I'm done." This had to stop. The falling in love thing. It always started innocently enough. A man would ask her out and they'd go on a few dates. She'd swear that this time she wouldn't get too attached too soon, but before she knew it, she was looking up wedding venues and bridal gowns and honeymoon destinations online. She couldn't help it. Her heart had always been a sucker for romance. Her father had said it was her best quality—that she could love someone so quickly, that she could give her heart to others so easily. He got it because he was the same way. Her mother, of course, labeled it her worst quality. *You're simply in love with the idea of being in love*, her wise mother would say. And it was true. Was that so *wrong*?

"Hey, Jessa."

The gruffness of the quiet voice, aged by years of good cigars, snapped up her head. She turned.

Luis Cortez stood behind her, hunched in his bowlegged stance. Clad in worn jeans and sporting his pro rodeo belt buckle, he looked like he'd just stepped off the set of an old western, face tanned and leathery, white hair tufted after a long ride on his trusty steed.

"Hi there, Luis," she mumbled, trying to hold her head high. Luis was her lone volunteer at the shelter, and he just might be the only one in town who loved animals as much as she did. He'd also been her dad's best friend and since she'd come back to town last year to settle her father's estate, she'd spent a lot of time with the man.

Maybe that was part of her problem with finding the love of her life. She spent most of her free time with a sixty-seven-year-old man...

"You all right?" Luis asked, gimping to the stool next to her. Seeing as how he was a retired bull-riding legend, it was a wonder he could walk at all.

"Uh." That was a complicated question. "Yes." She cleared the tremble out of her voice. "I'm fine. Great." She would be, anyway. As soon as the sting wore off.

"Thought you and Cam had a date tonight." Luis shifted with a wince, as though his arthritis was flaring again. "Where is he anyway? I was hopin' I could talk him into puttin' in his donation early this month. We gotta replace half the roof before the snow comes."

Cam. That name was her newest curse word. *Cam him! Cam it!* Feeling the burn of humiliation pulse across her cheeks, she turned on her phone and pushed it over to him so he could read the text. "Cam broke up with me." Luis had obviously missed the little announcement she'd made earlier.

He held up the phone and squinted, mouthing the words as he read. The older man looked as outraged as she was, bless him. "Man wasn't good enough for you, anyways, Jess. He's a damn fool."

"I have a knack for picking the fools." Just ask her mother. Every time she went through one of these breakups, Carla Roth, DO, would remind her of how bad the odds were for finding true love. Her mother had never married her father. She didn't believe in monogamy. *One person out of six billion?* she'd ask. *That is highly unlikely, Jessa.*

It might be unlikely, but the odds weren't enough to kill the dream. Not for her. Neither was the lack of any significant relationship in her mother's life. Jessa had grown up being shuffled back and forth—summers and Christmas in Topaz Falls with her father and the rest of the year with her college professor mother who didn't believe in love, secretly watching old romantic classics and movies like *Sleepless in Seattle* and *You've Got Mail* with wistful tears stinging in her eyes.

"Don't worry, Jess," Luis said in his kind way. "You'll find someone."

Big Man snorted.

Before she could backhand him, Luis gave her shoulder a pat. "My boys ain't married yet," he reminded her, as if she would *ever* be able to forget the Cortez brothers. Every woman's fantasy.

Lance, the oldest, had followed in his father's footsteps, though rumor had it this would be his last season on the circuit. He trained nonstop and had little time for anything else in his life, considering he left the ranch only about once a month. The thought of him married almost made her laugh. Over the years, he'd built quite the reputation with women, though she had no personal experience. Even with her father being one of his father's best friends, Lance had said maybe five words to her in all the years she'd known him. He seemed to prefer a woman who'd let him off the hook easily, and God knew there were plenty of them following those cowboys around.

Then there was Levi. Oh, hallelujah, Levi. One of God's greatest gifts to women. She'd had a fling with him the summer of their sophomore year, but after that he'd left home to train with some big-shot rodeo mentor and rarely came home.

There was a third Cortez brother, but Luis didn't talk

about him. Lucas, the middle child, had been sent to prison for arson when he was seventeen.

"Sure wish I'd see more of Levi," Luis said wistfully. "He ain't been home in a long time."

Her eyebrows lifted with interest. "So, um..." She pretended to examine a broken nail to prove she didn't care too much. "How is Levi, anyway?"

"That boy needs to get his head out of his ass. He's reckless. He's gonna get himself killed out there."

Jessa doubted that. Levi Cortez was making a name for himself in the rodeo world.

"Lance, now, he's the only one of my boys who's got his head on straight," Luis went on. "He always was a smart kid."

From what she'd seen, the oldest Cortez brother had never been a kid, but she didn't say so. After their mom ditched the family, Lance took over a more parental role. Not that she had any right to analyze him. "He's handsome, too," she offered, because every time she did happen to run into him, his luscious eyes had completely tied up her tongue. Yes, indeedy, Lance happened to be a looker. Though it was in a much different way than his cocky brother. "He looks the most like you," she said with a wink.

Luis's lips puckered in that crotchety, don't-want-to-smile-but-can't-help-it grin she loved to see. Her dad used to have one like that, too.

"Anyway...," the man said, obviously trying to change the subject. "What're we gonna do with Cam gone? I assume he didn't leave any money behind for the shelter."

"Not that I know of." Apparently, he hadn't left anything. Not even the toothbrush she'd kept at his house, Cam it.

"You got any other donors yet?"

"Not yet." She'd been so preoccupied with the most recent love—infatuation—of her life that she hadn't exactly made time to go trolling for other interested parties. Her dad had a big heart, but he'd always hated to ask for money, so when she'd come to take over, the list of benefactors had been…well…nonexistent. In one year, she'd already used most of what little money he'd left her to purchase supplies and complete the critical repairs. She could live off her savings for a couple more months, and at least keep up with the payroll, but after that things didn't look too promising. She'd probably have to lay off her night shift guy.

With Cam's generosity, she hadn't been too worried. Until now, of course.

"Don't you worry, Jess. Somethin'll work out." Luis's confidence almost made her believe it. "You're doin' okay. You know that? Buzz would be proud."

She smiled a little. Yes, her father definitely would've been proud to see his old place cleaned up. When she'd finished veterinary school and started on her MBA, he'd been so excited. He'd owned the rescue for thirty years but had never taken one business class. Which meant the place never made any money. He'd barely had enough to live on.

She had planned to change all of that. They'd planned it together. While she worked her way through business school, they'd talked on the phone twice a week, discussing how they could expand the place. Then, a month before she finished school, her father had a heart attack. He'd been out on a hike with Luis. Maybe that was why the man felt the need to take care of her, check in on her, help her fix things up around the house.

Familiar tears burned. She'd never blame Luis, though. That was exactly the way her dad would've chosen to go. Out on the side of a mountain, doing something he loved.

"We'll find a way, Jess." Pure determination turned the man's face statuelike, making him look as pensive as his eldest son. "All we need is some inspiration." Which he always insisted you couldn't find while stuck indoors. "I'm headin' up the mountain tomorrow. You wanna come?"

She brushed a grateful pat across the man's gnarled hand. "I can't, Luis. Thank you."

As much as she'd like to spend the day on the mountain, drowning her sorrows about Cam and the rescue's current financial situation in the fresh mountain air, she had things to do. This breakup had to be the dawn of a new era for her. She was tired of being passed over like yesterday's pastries. To hell with relationships. With romance. She didn't have time for it anyway. She had walls to paint and supplies to purchase and animals to rescue. Which meant she also had generous donors to find.

She shot a quick glance down at her attire. Might be a good idea to invest in herself first. Typically, she used her Visa only for emergencies, but this could be considered disaster prevention, right? She needed a new wardrobe. Something more professional. How could she schmooze potential stakeholders looking like she'd just come from a half-price sale at the New Life Secondhand Store?

"You sure you don't want to come?" Luis prompted.

"I'd love to but I have to go shopping." Right after their book club meeting, she'd enlist her friends to help her reinvent herself so she could reinvent her nonprofit.

By the time she was done, the Helping Paws Animal Rescue and Shelter would be everything her father dreamed it would be.

It would keep the memory of his love alive.

Acknowledgments

This is the best job in the world. I love what I do, but I could not do it without the many people who continue to work so hard behind the scenes to support me. First, to my editor, Alex Logan—my comma guru—thank you for your patience and incredible eye for details. You make me want to learn grammar so I can someday be as smart as you.

Elizabeth Turner, thank you for beautiful covers that help bring my stories to life. Thank you to the sales, marketing, and publicity teams who work so hard to place my books and get the word out. I appreciate everything you do.

I'm so grateful for Suzie Townsend and the team at New Leaf. Thank you for helping me navigate the business side of writing.

To my friend Kristen Wade, thank you for answering my questions and giving me insight into the EMT world. You're amazing! Any inaccuracies or errors are all mine.

Writing can sometimes be a lonely endeavor, and I'm grateful for my friends and family who are so understanding and supportive (and who give me reasons to walk away from the computer). Melissa, Erica, Jenna, Gretchen, Kimberly, Elaine, Lori, Megan, Niki, Erin, Traci, Stacey—thank you for making sure I still have a life and for always celebrating with me.

Will, thank you for being a constant source of love, strength, and encouragement in the midst of all the ups and downs. AJ and Kaleb, you continue to amaze me every single day with your compassion and joy and energy. I love our life together.

Last, but definitely not least, thank you, dear readers, for the e-mails, comments, reviews, and shares. They mean everything to me.

About the Author

Sara Richardson grew up chasing adventure in Colorado's rugged mountains. She's climbed to the top of a fourteen-thousand-foot peak at midnight, swum through Class IV rapids, completed her wilderness first-aid certification, and spent seven days at a time tromping through the wilderness with a thirty-pound backpack strapped to her shoulders.

Eventually Sara did the responsible thing and got an education in writing and journalism. After a brief stint in the corporate writing world, she stopped ignoring the voices in her head and started writing fiction. Now she uses her experience as a mountain adventure guide to write stories that incorporate adventure with romance. Still indulging her adventurous spirit, Sara lives and plays in Colorado with her saint of a husband and two young sons.

Learn more at:

http://www.sararichardson.net/

@SaraR_Books

http://facebook.com/sararichardsonbooks

for. Fans of Robyn Carr will undoubtedly enjoy the Heart of the Rockies series."
—*RT Book Reviews*

SOMETHING LIKE LOVE

"The author's compassion shines through her beautifully flawed and earnest characters and takes readers on an emotionally wrenching journey to the elusive goal of love."
—*Publishers Weekly*

"Sizzles with sexual tension on every page. The ending was a perfect, lovely, and sigh-worthy happy-ever-after."
—*USA Today*'s **"Happily Ever After" blog**

NO BETTER MAN

"Charming, witty, and fun. There's no better read. I enjoyed every word!"
—**Debbie Macomber,**
#1 *New York Times* bestselling author

"Fresh, fun, well-written, a dazzling debut."
—**Lori Wilde,**
***New York Times* bestselling author**

"Richardson's debut packs a powerful emotional punch. [Her] deft characterization creates a hero and heroine who will elicit laughs in some places and tears in others."
—*Publishers Weekly*

Renegade
Cowboy

SARA
RICHARDSON

FOREVER

NEW YORK BOSTON

Copyright © 2017 by Sara Richardson
Excerpt from *Hometown Cowboy* © 2017 by Sara Richardson
Cover design by Elizabeth Turner
Cover photograph © Jake Olson/Trevillion Images

Forever
Hachette Book Group
1290 Avenue of the Americas
New York, NY 10104
forever-romance.com
twitter.com/foreverromance

First Edition: December 2017

Forever is an imprint of Grand Central Publishing. The Forever name and logo are
trademarks of Hachette Book Group, Inc.

The publisher is not responsible for websites (or their content) that are not owned by
the publisher.

The Hachette Speakers Bureau provides a wide range of authors for speaking events.
To find out more, go to www.hachettespeakersbureau.com or call (866) 376-6591.

ISBN 978-1-4555-4081-5 (mass market edition)
ISBN 978-1-4555-4080-8 (ebook edition)

Printed in the United States of America

OPM

10 9 8 7 6 5 4 3 2 1

To Melvin and Phyllis Richardson,
proof that love really can last a lifetime

Renegade Cowboy

Chapter One

Welcome to Topaz Falls, Colorado
Elevation 7,083 feet

Cassidy Greer blew past the green welcome sign, knowing full well she had another two miles before she'd pass Dev's patrol car. The deputy would likely be stashed off to the south side of the highway while he waited for unsuspecting drivers he could slap with a $300 fine. The town had to make money somehow, but since it was May, their modest ski hill wasn't open. So during the spring and summer, traffic tickets were the town's main revenue source.

Right at mile marker 316, she tapped the brakes, bringing her old Subaru's speed down. She knew pretty much everything there was to know about Topaz Falls. Living within the same eight square miles for her entire twenty-four years meant there were few surprises in her life.

She knew that every Tuesday and Thursday, Betty Osterman and her group of blue-haired matriarchs did their morning jog-walks down Main Street, arms swishing, hips swinging, while they gossiped about which names had shown up in the latest Police Calls column of the local paper.

She knew that when she drove past the fire station on Sunday mornings, all those hot volunteers would be in the third bay with the garage door rolled up while they pumped iron, shirtless and sweating. A girl had to satisfy her cravings somehow. It was fair to say she hadn't over the last six years. She'd been too busy putting herself through nursing school, working as an EMT, and trying to keep her mother alive. Which was why every Sunday morning, she, along with at least twelve other women ranging in age from sixteen to ninety-three, made sure to take the long way to the grocery store, passing by the fire station nice and slow to keep her lady parts activated. Because someday she might actually have time for a social life. A cautious wave of excitement rippled deep inside her chest.

Slowing the car, Cassidy took a quick right on Main Street. The town looked the same as it always did. Eclectic shops and small restaurants were all laid out along the cobblestone sidewalks. Nothing had changed, and yet today everything looked different. Topaz Falls had always been her home, but it might not be for much longer.

She applied more pressure to the accelerator. She hadn't seen Dev's patrol car, and she was in a hurry. She'd just come from Denver. From an interview with one of the most prestigious pediatric nurse residency programs in the country, and it had gone well. Really well. They told her they'd let her know within a month, but the director had given her a smile as she'd shaken her hand. Kind of a silent *don't worry*.

Don't. Worry.

All Cassidy had to do was catch a glimpse of her house down the street and pure, unadulterated worry crammed itself into her stomach so tight she couldn't find the space to take a breath. Now she knew why she hadn't seen Dev's patrol car out on the highway. He was at her little house on Amethyst Street, cruiser parked at an angle, lights flashing.

She floored it down the block and jerked the wheel, bouncing the car to a stop in the crumbling driveway. "What the hell happened?" she called as she threw open the driver's door.

Dev stood on the front stoop, his broad shoulders barely stuffed into the crisp navy blue uniform. She'd gone to school with Dev back in the day. He'd always been a man of few words, and true to form, he waited for her to hightail it up the steps to where he stood.

"Got a call from Turnasky," he said, eyeing the front door as if he half expected a serial killer to emerge.

"What did he say this time?" Turnasky was a tyrant who lived in the house behind hers. He always had something to complain about—the leaves from her aspen tree falling into his yard, "her" weeds growing through the fence...

"It's an indecent exposure call," Dev clarified awkwardly. "Seems your mom's runnin' around the backyard without any clothes on."

That inspired a contemplative pause. Well, shit. This was a new one.

"Turnasky claims he yelled at her to go inside, and she threw a handful of elk scat at him."

Now that sounded like her mother. "Why doesn't she have any clothes on?" Cassidy demanded, shoving past him. "How did this happen?"

The deputy stayed right where he was on the stoop, poking his head inside the doorway and squeezing his eyes shut like he wanted to make sure he wouldn't witness anything he couldn't unsee. "Hell, I don't know, Cass. Okay? All I know is Turnasky called me and said your mom was jogging around the backyard in her birthday suit and that the little kids next door were standing on the fence laughin'."

That last part put another kick in her step. She loved little Mellie and Theo. She'd hate to see them move away because of one of her mother's episodes.

Skirting the kitchen table—which was strewn with empty wine bottles—she bolted out the open back door. Sure enough, there was her mother, now crawling across the grass on her hands and knees, white butt in the air while she called to Loki, their cat, who was cowering behind the overgrown juniper bushes in the corner of the yard.

The kids were gone, thank the lord, but Turnasky was standing on a chair on the other side of the fence, getting quite an eyeful.

Cassidy gave him the look of death and hurried to her mom, snatching a cushion off the wicker loveseat on the way. "Mom?" She knelt down next to her, nearly knocked over by the same pain that pinged her heart whenever she smelled the woman's lilac scent. It was the fragrance Cassidy remembered from her childhood. The scent that used to mean comfort and security and assurance.

"Cass-a-frass!" Her mom turned, white hair frizzed and unwashed, her eyes glazed with the telltale gloss of a drunk. "You're home!" she sang, completely oblivious to the fact that Dev now stood behind them on the deck, his hand covering his eyes.

"Is she okay?" he asked, eye protection still firmly in place.

"Of course I'm okay!" Lulu Greer sang. She abruptly stood, dusting off her thighs the way she might've done with pants, had she been wearing any.

Cassidy quickly shielded her mother's skinny front half with the cushion. "Mom..." She wasn't oblivious to the fact that this was the same tone her mother used to use on her and Cash when they'd done something stupid. But that was before her brother had died. Before her mother broke and Cassidy was forced to become the adult in the relationship.

"What happened to your clothes?" Cassidy demanded. "Why are you out in the backyard naked?"

Her mother laughed. "It's *our* backyard, honey," she said as though that made a difference. "It's not like I'm running down the middle of the street giving the neighbors a show."

"Actually, you *are* giving the neighbors a show," Cassidy pointed out, nodding toward Turnasky. When they all looked at him, he quickly climbed down from the chair and dragged it away.

She turned back to her mother, a familiar sorrow leaking through the anger. Once again she wondered how they'd gotten here. How had her healthy, devoted, superhero of a mom collapsed? "You can't do this. You can't walk outside naked." Add that to the list of things she never thought she'd have to say to her mother. "The neighbors have little kids," she reminded her.

"Well, what was I supposed to do?" Her mother placed her hands onto her bony hips. "I was in the bath, and Loki climbed right out the window. I had to go after him! He knows he's not supposed to go outside."

Cassidy uttered a silent prayer of thanksgiving that her mother had gotten out of the bathtub. What would've happened if she'd passed out and drowned? That was all it took to diffuse the exasperation. "Come on," Cassidy murmured, nudging her mom toward the back door. "Let's go inside."

Lulu stomped through the door like a pouting two-year-old and headed straight for the hallway that led to their bedrooms. "Sheesh. A woman can't even step out into her own backyard without a public inquiry anymore," she muttered.

"Put some clothes on, Mom," Cassidy called after her. "We have to be at the ribbon-cutting ceremony in thirty minutes." Which would be about as much fun as finding her mother wandering around the backyard naked. She had no desire to see Levi Cortez receive a standing ovation for his work rebuilding the rodeo grounds over the last year, but she'd lost a bet with her friend Darla.

Before she forgot, she dashed back outside and crawled through the prickly bush until she reached Loki. "Come on, you turd." She grabbed him by the scruff of the neck before bringing him in close for a snuggle. "Look what happens when I leave you in charge," she muttered as she hauled the cat back inside and set him on the floor. He promptly swung his rear end in her direction and pranced to his favorite spot underneath the table.

Dev had already retreated into the living room and was hanging out by the front door pretending to be completely engrossed in the old pictures she'd hung on the wall—ones of her previous life, her perfect family. If she didn't have the proof in the pictures, she'd question whether it had been real.

"I'm sorry about this, Dev," she said, walking him outside. "I was gone overnight. She doesn't do so well on her own when I'm away." Which would really throw a wrench in her plans to go to a nurse residency program. She'd thought about it all the way home. Maybe Mom could come with her and they could get an apartment close to the hospital. But the truth was that she'd be working full time—twelve hours a day at least three days a week. She wouldn't be able to keep an eye on her mother. And who knew what kind of trouble Lulu would get into in a big city like Denver.

Sighing, Dev gave her that empathetic look she'd come to hate. The one that blended pity with embarrassment. "Yeah, I get it. No big deal. Just make sure it doesn't happen again. Got it? You don't want your neighbors to press charges."

"Nope. Definitely don't want that." She didn't have the money to bail out her mother or pay any fines. While Cassidy worked long hours as an EMT and Lulu received a modest retirement check from her years as a mail carrier, there wasn't exactly anything extra.

Dev hesitated before he got into his cruiser. "Hey, Cass...have you thought about getting her some help? Maybe you could take her to an AA meeting or something."

"Yeah, I'll look into it," she said, brushing him off. She'd tried a few times in the last couple of years, but her mother wasn't interested in AA. In all honesty, alcohol wasn't Lulu's biggest problem. It was depression. The heavy weight that seemed to cling to her, that told her to stay in bed, that's why she drank. She was trying to lighten her load.

"Let me know if I can help out. Okay?" Dev slid into the driver's seat. "I can give you some brochures. There're a lot of resources out there."

"Sounds great." She strained the muscles in her cheeks to keep her smile intact. "Thanks, Dev."

After a polite nod, he tore out of there, and she turned to face her little dilapidated house. She'd purchased the small two-bedroom for her and her mother after her dad decided he couldn't handle the grief and left for Texas. While the shutters might've been the wrong color blue, and the entire house the epitome of a bad 1970s remodel, Cassidy loved the house because it was hers.

She trudged back up the walkway. Facing the house was the easy part. Facing what was inside would hurt more, but she didn't have a choice. This had to stop. Bailing her mom out of trouble. Begging her to get up, to get dressed, to eat something.

Somewhere inside that shell of a woman, Lulu Greer was still there. She was still funny and compassionate and friendly and honest. She was still Cassidy's mother.

Rolling up the sleeves of her sweatshirt, Cassidy opened the door armed with a purpose and a deadline. If she got into that nurse residency program, she had less than two months to turn her mother into a functioning adult again so Cassidy could move on and have her own life.

Which meant she'd better start now.

* * *

Levi Cortez had spent his fair share of time in front of cameras.

As a bull rider, he'd competed in front of cameras, he'd done interviews in front of cameras, he'd posed with fans in front of cameras.

Hell, his main sponsor—Renegade Jeans Company—had even taken countless pictures of his ass filling out designer denim. So he was no stranger to cameras. No stranger to attention from large crowds. Even in an arena filled with thousands of spectators, he'd never once been nervous.

Until now.

As he made his way to the cheap, portable podium the town council had set up in front of their new rodeo facility, the hundred or so people gathered around whispered and elbowed one another. Some wore scowls while others narrowed their eyes with suspicion as though they were waiting for him to screw up. *Again*.

Admittedly, he'd made plenty of mistakes in his life. The worst one being letting his brother take the fall and go to prison for three years because of something Levi had done. When the truth had come out last year, everyone discovered he was the one responsible for burning down the rodeo grounds when he was a delinquent teen, and these same people had done their best to run him off.

Hank Green, the uncontested mayor of the town, had even started a Facebook page calling for Levi's voluntary banishment. But Levi couldn't do it. He couldn't leave. For once in his life, he'd stuck around, determined to make things right.

Levi placed one hand on either side of the podium and faced the crowd directly. Their faces blurred together. A dribble of sweat itched on his back. Speaking in front of cameras was a hell of a lot easier than speaking in front of a whole crowd of people you'd disappointed. Cameras didn't tend to see through a facade the way people did.

But this was it. This was him. A screwup who'd hurt the town, disgraced his family, and spent the last year doing penance to save his career and reputation.

He inhaled a deep, even breath. *Don't let them smell fear...*

"I wanted to thank you all for coming out today," he said, well aware that some of them had likely been bribed by his brother Lance and sister-in-law Jessa. Those two stood in the very front row, Jessa snapping pictures on her phone like a proud mom.

She waved at him, and he gave her a grateful smile.

"Over the last year, I've worked diligently to make up

for the hardships my actions caused..." That was an understatement. He'd spent every hour he wasn't competing raising funds and draining his own investments in order to rebuild an arena and stables, a place where the town could host rodeos again. "Which is why we're here." He glanced over his shoulder at the new facility.

It was ten times nicer than the old one—complete with a covered metal roof. The old arena had consisted of stands, a small call box, and lackluster stables. But during the rebuilding phase, he'd gone big. "My goal in leading this effort was to give our town a place to gather, a place to compete, and a place that will make Topaz Falls one of the most popular stops on the circuit again."

A murmur buzzed around the crowd. Someone actually applauded.

Levi eased out a breath, grateful for even the minimal show of support.

"There's still more work to do. But I'm thrilled to be here today to dedicate phase one of the project. And I will keep working until we expand the stables and add the educational spaces we've promised."

This time Jessa started to clap. She elbowed Lance, and he joined her, rolling his eyes. The rest of his family started in on the applause too—his father, Luis, and Evie...Levi still wasn't sure exactly what to label her. Girlfriend, probably, though neither one of them would admit it. And then there were his brother Lucas and sister-in-law Naomi, who stood off to the side. She had only a month until her due date and was fanning herself with the flyer they'd passed out earlier.

Levi scanned the crowd again. More people had started to clap. That was a good sign, right? The tension that had pulled at his neck dissolved. "I'm proud to officially welcome you all to the Cash Greer Memorial Arena." A tremor ran through his voice, but he didn't care. Cash had been his best friend, and everyone knew it.

As they'd rehearsed, Hank Green walked forward and handed him a pair of giant scissors. Levi cut the large red ribbon that Jessa had made. Then he gritted his teeth and shook Hank's hand. They both walked back to the podium, and Levi stood to the side while Hank launched into one of the monologues he was famous for. The man loved to hear himself talk.

"I would like to thank Mr. Cortez for his contributions to ensuring that our town will…"

Levi gazed out at the blur of faces. No one seemed to be listening. Most people were either staring at their phones or chatting. He squinted to see the back row. A punch of air hit him in the lungs.

Cassidy Greer stood next to her friend Darla. Shock rolled through him, rooting his boots to the ground. She'd come. And she looked good—like she was dressed to go out. The sleeveless sundress she wore showed off her tanned shoulders. Her mid-length blond hair was wavy, shining in the evening sun.

Daaammmnnn. His body heated. He shouldn't be looking. He knew that. She was Cash's little sister, and she'd always been off limits. That was how she seemed to want things anyway. Ever since he'd come back to Topaz Falls, she'd blown him off. If she wasn't glaring at him, she was ignoring him. And he got it. He knew she blamed him for what had happened to her brother. She seemed to blame all bull riders.

But she'd still come…

"We'd like to invite everyone far and wide to our first rodeo event in twelve years," Hank said dramatically into the crackling microphone. "Mr. Cortez has put together a benefit rodeo featuring some of his famous friends to raise money for the completion of the facility. You should have received a schedule of events when you arrived. We hope to see you all tomorrow."

Another round of applause rose, louder this time, actually bordering on enthusiastic. A newspaper reporter stepped forward and snapped a quick picture, but Levi wasn't looking.

He held his gaze on Cassidy as the crowd started to scatter. She'd already made it to the edge of the dirt parking lot when he finally caught up with her. "You came," he said behind her.

She stopped but didn't turn around. "I didn't have a choice. Darla made me." Her tone could've formed icicles in his eyebrows.

He moved in front of her so she'd have to look at him. Hadn't she punished him long enough? Everyone else in town had forgiven him for his past sins. Hell, they'd actually cheered him on up there. Everyone except for Cassidy Greer.

"I'm glad you're here," he said, wondering how things could be so awkward with this woman he'd once been so close to.

"I can't stay." She looked past him. "My mother's waiting in the car."

Lulu had come? Wow. He hadn't seen much of her since he'd been back either. "You should go get her. I'm sure she'd love to see the sign with Cash's name on it."

Cassidy's striking blue eyes dulled. "She's not feeling well."

She went to walk around him, but he reached out and

snagged her shoulder. He couldn't let her walk away again. Not this time. "I'm sorry," he murmured, emotion mucking up his throat. "I'm sorry I couldn't stop it from happening. I'm sorry I couldn't save him."

Her full lips parted in surprise as she stared up at him. "Seriously?" A lengthy sigh condemned his ignorance. "I don't blame you for Cash's death, Levi."

"Well, you obviously blame me for something," he shot back before she walked away. This was the closest thing they'd had to a real conversation in years. "You've been giving me shit ever since I came back, so I just assumed..."

"Cash's death was an accident." Her voice had softened. "It wasn't anyone's fault."

"That doesn't mean I don't wish I could go back." It had been only him and Cash out in the corral that day. Training, trying to one-up each other like always. They'd done it so many times. But his friend had lost his grip and slid off the back of the bull, getting trampled before Levi could save him.

"None of us can go back." Her gaze targeted his. "We all had to move on. It wasn't as easy for some of us as it was for others."

The insinuation jabbed him. Yeah. He'd walked away. He hadn't been able to face everything in Topaz Falls after Cash's death, so he'd left as soon as he could. Was that why she couldn't stand him?

"I need to get Mom home." Without a goodbye, she hurried across the parking lot and got into her car.

"Wow, you sure know what to say to a woman," Lance said as he walked over. Levi's eldest brother never missed an opportunity to give him a hard time. "I think she was actually jogging to get away from you."

"Not in the mood right now." He turned to walk away, but Lance followed on his heels.

"Why does it bother you so much? So she doesn't like you. Who cares?"

He paused. Why indeed. "Cass is..." Special. There. He said it. Okay, he thought it. She was special to him. They'd grown up together. He'd been a part of her family. And there was a time when she'd liked him a whole lot.

His brother's eyes narrowed. "Cass is what?" he asked suspiciously.

He and his brothers had come a long way in the last year and a half, but Lance didn't need to know what he thought of Cass. If Levi told him how he really felt, he'd never hear the end of it. "She's a friend. She *was* a friend," he clarified. Once. They'd been close. They shared a history and a deep grief. Instead of bringing them together, that's what stood between them.

But maybe it didn't have to.

Chapter Two

The gang was back together, but something told Levi they weren't thrilled about it.

He sauntered to the bar and ordered drinks for Ty Forrester, Mateo Torres, and Charity Stone. Beer for the two men and a straight-up scotch for the woman. She'd always been able to outdrink the lot of them.

"Drinks are on me," he called, carting over the booze on a tray like their own personal waiter. Usually he preferred to be waited on, but he owed it to these three. Without them, the rodeo wouldn't be sold out.

Years ago, the four of them had trained together under Gunner Raines, famed all-around cowboy champion, and each had become a champion in his or her own right. Ty as a bull rider, Mateo as a bronc rider, and Charity as a barrel racer. They'd lived on Gunner's ranch, training and competing and gaining notoriety, thanks to their mentor. He'd become a master at publicity, and in no time, he'd secured them a sponsorship with Renegade Jeans Company.

"When is this thing supposed to start, anyway?" Charity demanded. She might look like a sweet Midwestern farm girl with that long blond hair and dimpled smile, but the woman was a force.

"Fifteen minutes before our fans start showing up." He slid her scotch across the table, where he'd set up for the pre-rodeo party at the Tumble Inn, which was the town's only country western bar. "Which means you'd best use up the attitude now." This was supposed to be an autographing party for the kids, so she needed to be on her best behavior.

"No one I'd rather use it up on." She raised her glass in a mock toast and threw back a shot. She might've given him attitude, but underneath it all she loved him like a brother.

Ty and Mateo sauntered over to collect their free beers. "Gotta hand it to ya, Cortez. Looks like you pulled it off." Ty straddled a stool, resting his elbows and meaty forearms on the pub table. He was taller than most riders and built like an MLB star with a stocky upper body.

"Didn't think you had it in you," Mateo added, taking a seat on the other side of the table. He was shorter than both Ty and Levi, which was what made him such a good bronc rider. With his longer dark hair and light gray eyes, he was popular with the ladies. Gave Levi some serious competition. He'd emigrated from Mexico with Gunner's help, which apparently made him exotic too. "Raising the money, rebuilding the facility, and launching an all-star event." Mateo nodded at him and took a swig of beer. "Impressive."

"Yeah, well I couldn't have done it without you." Not that these three weren't taking full advantage of that fact. They were getting star treatment at the Hidden Gem Inn, which happened to belong to Lucas and Naomi.

The door crashed open across the room, and Cassidy Greer stormed into the bar so fast that her wavy blond hair sailed over her shoulders.

Levi bit back a smile. *Right on time.*

Sure enough, she marched straight to him. Even all fired up the way she was right now, everything about her seemed soft...from those curved hips to her plump lips to her smooth cheeks. Her eyes too, the same color blue as the early morning sky. Now though, they blazed with indignation. "We need to talk," she said as she reached him.

"I expect we do." He was actually surprised it'd taken her this long to track him down. Earlier that morning, he'd called her boss and specifically requested that she cover the rodeo this weekend. Not that he expected anything to go wrong but he figured, if it did, Cass was the best. The best-looking EMT in the county too. Besides all of that, this would give them a chance to spend a little time together.

He turned to his friends. "Guys, this is Cassidy Greer, EMT extraordinaire. She'll be stationed at the rodeo tomorrow in case anyone needs medical attention."

Mateo and Ty both stood so fast their stools knocked into the tables.

"Nice to meet you." Cassidy's smile was as stiff as the leather on her tall boots. Which went up to the knees of her tight jeans, he couldn't help but notice. Which led him to notice her shapely thighs...

"Levi?" She turned to him without giving any of them a chance to return the greeting. "A word."

Mateo whistled low and elbowed Ty.

"Let me know if you want me to kick his ass for you,"

Charity called as Cass hustled him to a corner. "It wouldn't be the first time."

Cass stopped and turned back to Charity, sporting the only real grin he'd seen on her face since she'd come with Jessa to pick him up at the police station last year. "Thanks. I'll keep that in mind."

"Charity caught me off guard once," he explained when they were out of earshot. "And it wasn't like I could hit back. I'd never hit a girl."

"That why you're whispering?" Cass had always been too perceptive for her own good.

And he'd always known when to change the subject. "So, I assume you heard the news."

"Yeah." She crossed her arms and stuck out that sexy hip. "I don't do rodeos."

She obviously didn't want to be anywhere near him, given the way she inched back every time he moved closer to her. But he wouldn't let her escape this time. "I need the best for this event," he said, locking his gaze with hers. "And you're the best. Which means I want you." The words hung between them with an awkward vulnerability.

She looked away. "And I need you to call up Walsh and tell him you're fine with Molly and Brady working the rodeo instead."

"But I'm not." He could be just as stubborn as she could.

Her low growl ended in a sigh. "Look, I can't be there all day."

"Why?" He leaned a shoulder against the wall, inching closer to her. She smelled good. Like lemon drops.

Cass hesitated and stepped back from him, her blue eyes flitting everywhere but toward his face. "I don't want to leave Mom alone that long. I've already worked overtime this week."

"Bring her," he suggested. "I'd love to see Lulu." It'd been too long. Far as he could tell, the woman didn't get out much. "It'd probably be good for her."

"I don't want to bring her." Cass's teeth had clenched, reminding him of the way she used to sass him when he would pull on her braid years ago. "*You* don't want me to bring her. Trust me."

Over her shoulder, he saw the doors open. People started to stream in. He took her shoulders in his hands and looked into her eyes again. The touch seemed to rattle her.

"I need you there, Cass. Okay? Bring your mom if you want. Hang out by the food trucks outside. You don't have to watch the events. Just make sure you're there."

* * *

Well, wasn't that typical? Cassidy gave Levi a serious stink eye as he swaggered over to his fans before she could argue with him. After five seconds of staring at his nice ass in those jeans though, she forced herself to look away. He was one damn fine-looking cowboy, and he knew it. The last thing she wanted was for him to catch her taking a peek. Lord knew the man didn't need *her* fueling his ego.

Keeping her head down, she marched to the main doors of the Tumble Inn, still fuming. He had no idea what she was dealing with. Her mom had gotten so much worse during the last couple of months. Didn't help that the anniversary of Cash's death was coming up. Cassidy already had her hands full dragging her mom out of bed every day and trying to find productive activities to keep her occupied. She didn't need extra hours at work.

"Whoa." A hand reached for her arm. Looking up, she

noticed Darla and Jessa waiting in the line to greet the illustrious Raines's Renegades.

"What are you two doing here?" she demanded, as though it was their fault Levi was such a jerk. "Isn't this a kids' event?" She swept a gaze over the line of people—mostly parents with their kids, but yes, there also seemed to be a few eligible bachelorettes there too.

"What are we doing here?" Darla repeated. "Are you kidding? The first rodeo back in Topaz Falls. Have you seen pictures of Mateo Torres, honey? There's a reason he was one of the poster boys for Renegade Jeans."

Cassidy glanced over to where the cowboys, and one cowgirl, all stood in a line behind the table, signing autographs and posing for pictures with their fans. Yes, Mateo was good looking—dark and exotic—but her eyes drifted to Levi again, to that all-American grin complete with a shallow dimple in his right cheek. He kept his brown, sun-tinged hair short and spiked, more clean-cut than he used to wear it, but the sexy stubble across his jaw still gave him a rugged appearance.

Ugh. She rolled her eyes. *Stop. Looking.*

"I'm just here because Darla promised me chocolate," Jessa informed her. "I have all the cowboy I need at home."

Yeah. Lucky her. Jessa's husband had been a renowned bull rider until his retirement last year.

"Not all of us have the luxury of staring at a hot cowboy every day," Darla said sharply, her eyes never breaking focus from Mateo.

"What are you doing here?" Jessa asked Cassidy. "This is the last place I ever thought we'd run into you. Given your distaste for a certain Cortez brother."

"I had to come down here because of said Cortez

brother." She shot Levi a glare. At that same moment, he happened to glance up and grin at her from across the room. She quickly turned back to Jessa and Darla. "Levi is demanding that I work the rodeo tomorrow."

"But you hate rodeos." Jessa's eyes crinkled with concern.

"Exactly." See? Everyone knew that. Everyone except for Levi, apparently. "Not to mention, Mom has been having a hard time lately. I hate to leave her alone."

"I'm not surprised, with the anniversary coming up." Darla finally looked away from Mateo. "Anything we can do to help?"

"Maybe swing by tomorrow and take her out to lunch?" If she knew someone was coming over, maybe Lulu wouldn't drink and start wandering around naked again.

"I'm on it," Jessa offered. "I wasn't planning to be at the rodeo all day anyway."

Even though that was likely a lie, Cassidy accepted. "Thanks," she said, squeezing her friend's hand. There was nothing she hated more than being needy, than asking for help, but whenever she had no choice, her friends had her back.

"So, is there a reason Levi keeps looking at you?" Darla's suggestive expression made Cassidy squirm.

"No." The word came out garbled. "No," she said again, stronger. "Why?"

"Maybe his summoning you to the rodeo has more to do with your sex appeal than your EMT skills," her friend suggested, nudging Jessa.

"Ohhhhh," Jessa crooned. "I could totally see that!"

Cassidy shut them down with a glare. "That's crazy."

"Not really," Jessa argued. "I mean we all know how smooth Levi is."

Cassidy snuck a glance toward the table again. The man in question was hugging a middle-aged woman who happened to be fawning over him. "That's an understatement."

"But he's totally awkward around you." Jessa tapped a finger against her lips as though drawing a conclusion.

"That's because he's afraid of me." Cassidy would be the first to admit she hadn't exactly been nice to him since he'd returned to Topaz Falls. But she'd figured what was the point? He'd be gone again soon anyway.

"Or because he thinks you're hot," Darla put in. "I'd appreciate it if you would use that to my advantage and introduce me." Before Cassidy could object, her friend linked their arms together and dragged her over to the table of cowboys, where she cut in front of the line.

"What're you doing?" Cassidy hissed, trying to squirm free. But Darla was a lot stronger than her petite frame would have you believe.

"Ask Levi to introduce me to Mateo. Please," she begged while the people behind them gave them dirty looks.

"Please," Jessa echoed. "Let's get it over with so I can go home. Lance and I like to go to bed early on Friday nights."

"Right," Darla muttered, rolling her eyes. "Maybe I wouldn't be so hard up if I didn't have to listen to you talk about the great sex you're always having."

Cassidy heaved out a long-suffering sigh. "Listen you two, I'm not cutting in line—"

"Hi, Cassidy!" Theo Mullins stepped out of the crowd right in front of them. Her seven-year-old neighbor, with his dark skin and round, somber eyes, was probably the most adorable little boy she'd ever seen. Of course, he hated when she told him how cute he was, especially in front of a crowd, so she kept it to herself.

"Hey, Theo," she said, ruffling his hair while she glanced around. "Is your mom here?"

"No. I rode my bike." A proud smile made him seem so much older. "And I brought my cowboy hat so I could get it signed by Raines's Renegades!"

"Wow," Cassidy said with an awed expression. At least coming here hadn't been a total waste of time. Now she could keep an eye on Theo and bring him home after the party. His mom worked as the building superintendent at the elementary school, but to make ends meet, she also cleaned houses and businesses around town whenever she could get extra work, which meant the kids were on their own a lot.

Darla leaned over. "I love the cowboy hat," she told Theo. "Did you know Cassidy is friends with Raines's Renegades?"

The little boy gawked up at her. "Really?"

The woman nodded emphatically. "She was just about to introduce us to all of them. I bet you could come with us."

Cassidy shot her a look. Leave it to Darla to use a seven-year-old to further her agenda.

"Can I come with you?" Theo asked, and then looked down like he was embarrassed.

"Of course you can." Cassidy tucked the sweetie under her arm. "Come on. I'm sure Levi will be happy to talk with you for a while." He owed her big-time anyway.

Leading Darla and Theo to the table, she skirted past the barrier that had been constructed with bar stools and snuck up behind Levi before tapping him on the shoulder.

He turned. "Hey, Cass." The sudden affection in his eyes brought a tingling warmth to her face. "Hey." She cleared her throat and focused on Theo. "I have a friend who'd like to meet you."

The boy had backed up to hide behind her, but Levi saw him. He turned back to the line. "We're gonna take a five-minute break," he called out. "Feel free to order some food and drinks while you wait."

"Wow," Darla muttered next to her. "He literally just dropped everything for you."

Cassidy shrugged her off. It didn't mean anything. He was only trying to charm her the way he charmed everyone else. Levi happened to hate it when someone didn't like him. He always had. Which meant he would be working extra hard to be nice.

Cassidy took a hold of the boy's hand. "Levi, this is Theo. He's my neighbor."

"Nice to meet you, Theo." Levi stooped to a knee. "What grade are you in?"

"Second." Shyness bowed the boy's head, once again tempting Cassidy to pinch his cheek.

"He's one of the smartest kids in his class too," she bragged. "He's in advanced reading *and* math."

Levi widened his eyes as though impressed. "That true?"

Theo shrugged.

"Well, if Cass says it, it has to be true." The man gazed up at her with an intimate smile, as though they shared some juicy secret.

Her face flushed almost immediately. Why did he keep looking at her like that? Like there was something between them?

Theo seemed incapable of words. He simply stared at one of his cowboy idols and nodded.

"So you like cowboys, huh?" Levi asked, standing to his full height again.

The boy nodded. "I wanna be a bull rider just like you."

"Yeah?" Cassidy had expected the admission to be met with Levi's typical arrogance, but instead he almost looked surprised. "Well, maybe I could show you a few tricks sometime."

"Really?" Theo asked in wonder.

"Like when?" Cassidy demanded. She wasn't about to let him make Theo some promise he didn't intend to keep. He had a knack for doing that, and the boy had experienced enough disappointment from his own absentee father.

"Uh. Well…" Levi's gaze darted around as though he was searching for an escape.

Yeah, that's what she thought.

"I've tossed around the idea of doing a clinic," he finally said. "A day where we teach kids all the important stuff they'd need to know to compete in a rodeo someday. Would you be interested in something like that?"

"Yeah!" Theo shouted, but then his face sobered. "Wait. How much would it cost?"

Levi glanced at Cassidy as though he didn't know what to say. She gave him nothing. Not a nod, not a quirk of her lips. He had to figure this one out on his own.

"Maybe it'd be free…"

Maybe?

The boy gasped. "Free? Then I could do it for sure!"

"Perfect." Relief seemed to loosen Levi's jaw. "Hey, you want to meet my friends? Mateo, Ty, and Charity," he called, "get over here."

While he introduced Theo to the others, Cassidy hung back and watched, intent on keeping a healthy distance from Levi. Sure, he might be sexy and charming and funny, but he was a bull rider, and she wanted nothing to do with the sport. She also wanted nothing to do with how the sight of him kneeling next to Theo made her heart all soft and gooey…

She glanced at her watch. In fact, she really should be going.

"Why's your face all flushed?" Jessa asked, coming up beside her. She was munching on a handmade truffle from Darla's chocolate shop.

"It's not flushed." Cassidy touched her fingers to her cheek. She may have been a little warm...

"Hmm. Must be the lighting." Her friend licked the chocolate off her fingers. "Levi's good with Theo, huh?"

"I guess." She wasn't about to let her friend in on the secret that the man suddenly had her heart beating a little faster. "But I swear, if he lets that kid down, I'll do much worse to him than a three-ton bull could do."

Jessa laughed. "I don't doubt that at all." Her friend looked around. "Darla sure seems busy." She'd managed to hook both Mateo and Ty, chatting with them in that flirty way Cassidy had always envied. She didn't have time to flirt.

"Wait until they find out she makes her own chocolate," she muttered. That always seemed to be a huge plus in scoring Darla a date.

"Speaking of chocolate, I need water." Her friend grimaced. "I may have overdone it."

"Been there." In fact, seeing as how she didn't drink much alcohol, Cassidy hit up Darla's confectionery, the Chocolate Therapist, at least once a week. Everyone had their coping mechanism...

"You want anything?" Jessa asked, stepping away.

"No thanks." She refocused on Theo. Ty Forrester was now teaching Theo how to lasso a rope.

"That kid's pretty awesome." Levi headed over to where she stood.

Cassidy tried to swallow but it was more like a gulp. Was her face still red? "Uh. Yeah. He's a great kid."

"Raised by a single mom, I take it." Being raised by a single parent obviously made a difference to Levi.

"Yeah. She's great too," she said quickly. "Just really busy trying to keep things afloat." Even though Cassidy didn't have kids, she could relate to the woman. Seemed it was all she could do some days just to hold everything together.

"Well, I hope I can do it then." Levi glanced over at Theo, his eyes narrowed with concern. "The rodeo camp, I mean."

She snapped her head to gape at him. "You *hope?*"

"Yeah. I hope it works out."

Anger flared, resurrecting her past bitterness. "You'd better do more than hope. You'd better make it happen. He's counting on it now. And you don't always keep your word."

The man flinched as though the comment had cut him. "What's that supposed to mean?"

She stared into his eyes, letting him see it. All of it. Her disappointment with him. It wasn't his fault Cash had died. She knew that. She'd never blamed Levi a day in her life. But Cash had been his best friend. And Levi had completely written off her family. Her mom had loved him like a son, and he never even came around to check on her.

Suddenly the weight of everything—all these years she'd been trying to carry so many heavy burdens on her own— threatened to crush her. "You know what?" she managed. "Forget it. Do whatever you want. If you can't make it happen, I'm sure he'll get over it. Just like I did."

* * *

Levi didn't know how he'd done it. After Cass had walked out on him, he'd somehow managed to go back to signing autographs and posing for pictures and slapping high fives with the little kids who came through the line. All he'd really wanted to do was go after her.

He might've too, if he'd had any clue what to say.

He sank into a chair at a nearby table. For the most part, the party had ended. A few stragglers still hung around chatting at the bar. Mateo, Charity, and Ty were over shooting pool and having another drink, which gave him the perfect opportunity to finally sit and wallow in guilt.

His earlier conversation with Cass replayed yet again. She'd told him she was over her disappointment with him, but that wasn't true. She wasn't over it. And she had every right to be mad as hell. That was the problem though. She wasn't mad. She was hurt. Still. After six years. And it killed him that he'd caused her pain. He'd rather have her scream in his face than get all bleary-eyed and walk out like that.

"You look like you could use a drink." His father sat down across from him. Luis moved a little slower these days, with the combination of arthritis and Parkinson's weakening his body. But all things considered, the man looked pretty good. His thick white hair and neatly trimmed mustache still made him look like a distinguished cowboy. Levi only hoped he'd age as gracefully.

He looked around, expecting to see the woman his father would refer to only as his "friend." "Where's Evie?" Lately, Levi would've called her Luis's constant companion. It had become a rare occasion to see his dad without her somewhere nearby. The other night, he'd caught them holding hands as they'd walked the pasture on the ranch.

"I took her home an hour ago," his father said, face coloring the way it always did when someone brought up Evie. "She had a project she wanted to finish tonight."

Evie happened to be a talented stained-glass artist. She sold many of her goods in the shops around Topaz Falls. She was also one of the kindest, most interesting people Levi had ever met. It was easy to see what his dad saw in her. "You know, if Evie wanted to spend the night at your house once in a while, I'm sure I could bunk up with Lance and Jessa. Or even take the other suite at the Hidden Gem." Though Levi wasn't sure he wanted to be that close to his friends. He could find a way to give his father space though. Luis had already mentioned that Evie had a roommate who complained about everything.

He expected his father to mumble a gruff response like he always did when he was embarrassed, but instead he looked thoughtful. "You wouldn't mind?"

"Oh. Uh, no. I mean, I've been thinking it's time for me to get my own place anyway." When he'd first come back to town after his dad started having health issues, he hadn't figured he'd stay long. But now things were definitely looking more permanent. "I mean, now that I'm planning to make this my home base, I guess I could always call a realtor and see what's out there."

"Or you could build a house on the ranch." An eagerness lit his father's eyes.

A smile pulled at Levi's lips. He knew how much it meant to Luis to have them all back together after being estranged from him and Lucas for so many years. "Yeah. I could look into that." In the meantime though, he'd better pack up his things, because his father was ready for a new roommate.

A pang of envy riffled through him. It seemed everyone else was moving on with their lives. His father was moving forward with Evie. Lance was moving forward with his booming business. Lucas and Naomi were about to have a baby. He'd never thought he wanted any of those things. So why did it feel like he was stuck?

Across from him, his father yawned, trying to hide it behind his gnarled, age-spotted hand.

"You didn't have to come back after you took Evie home." Usually, at this time of night, his father was settling in and getting ready to go to bed. On a normal night, the party would just be getting started for Levi, but tonight he might turn in early himself.

"I wanted to come back," his father insisted stubbornly. He probably took exception to the fact that Levi had suggested he was tired. "It sure was something watching all those people come here to see you. I'm proud of you, son. You've accomplished a lot this year."

"Thanks." The word sounded as hollow as he'd felt since he'd seen those tears in Cass's eyes. "But I'm not sure it matters much."

"'Course it matters," Luis insisted. "You righted your wrongs. That's more than a lot of men could say."

He'd righted *a* wrong. He'd worked his ass off to earn his way back into the town's good graces, while he'd gone on completely ignoring Cassidy. Why'd it take him so damn long to figure out she was the only one who really mattered?

"I haven't righted all of my wrongs." He searched his dad's face. His skin was lined from years of sun exposure, but his eyes still had a youthful spark. "Why didn't you ever tell me how much Cassidy and Lulu were struggling?" Not that it was his father's responsibility, but if he would've nagged him about it, maybe he wouldn't have stayed away so long.

Luis didn't seem to take offense at the question. He simply shrugged. "I didn't see much of 'em. They both kept to themselves after the funeral." He hesitated. "And I didn't hear from you much either. Didn't want to cause more issues between us by making you feel bad."

Levi accepted that with a nod. Sitting across from his father now, it was easy to imagine they hadn't had any issues between them back then, but that'd be a lie. In his late teen years, he hadn't appreciated his father, and after he left, he'd rarely talked to him. "It's not your fault." He sighed. "I should've checked in with her. I should've kept in better touch with you." The responsibility rested solely on his shoulders. Unfortunately, he'd been too young and selfish to take it on.

His father didn't disagree, but his lips folded in that proud dad expression again. The one Levi didn't deserve. "You were finding your way, son. Don't be so hard on yourself."

Yeah, and while he was out building a name for himself, Cassidy was stuck in Topaz Falls caring for her mother, putting herself through school, and working full time. "I don't think she'll forgive me." He hadn't thought about it, about how it must've felt like she'd lost a brother and a friend. At the funeral, he'd had to hold her up. She couldn't even walk down the aisle at the church. He'd held her while she cried, every tear adding another weight on his regrets. One week later, he'd gotten word of the opening at Gunner Raines's ranch, and he'd left without saying goodbye.

"Have you asked her to forgive you?" his dad asked pointedly.

"No. I guess I haven't." He'd almost been afraid to talk to her since he'd been back. He could hop on the back of a three-ton bull, grinning and showboating for the cameras, but he couldn't find the words to tell a woman how much he thought of her.

"I would start there." His father pulled himself out of the chair. "And don't wait, son. Take it from me, you want something bad enough, you gotta go after it." He clapped Levi's shoulder with surprising strength. "It might take time, but she'll never forgive you if you don't ask."

Chapter Three

Hey, girl. You okay?" Molly peered in the passenger's side window, frowning as if she already knew the answer.

Cassidy debated about telling a lie, but her coworker was a good head taller than her and had the stocky build of an ultimate fighter. She'd even competed in some competitions. Molly also happened to be strikingly gorgeous, with sleek black hair she wore in a twist and powerful hazel eyes. Her looks completely threw off her opponents in the ring, and almost everyone underestimated her. She hadn't lost a match in two years.

Yeah, Cassidy wouldn't have a chance against the woman. So instead of risking an interrogation, she went for the optimistic truth. "I'll be fine." She always had to be fine. She was the sane one, the strong one, the one who always kept it together.

It couldn't matter that she'd gotten sick to her stomach the second they'd backed the ambulance into Levi's new arena. It couldn't matter that sorrow had broken open in her chest when she'd seen the Cash Greer Memorial Arena sign hanging from the roof's wide steel beams. God knew she had plenty of practice pretending she was okay. Now if she could just force herself to climb out of the ambulance...

"You want me to beat Levi up for you?" Molly asked, flexing her forearms.

The woman always knew how to make her smile. "Maybe. I'll let you know."

"Seems like he could've asked for someone else today, considering what happened to your brother." Her coworker's scowl might've been enough to frighten one of Levi's bucking bulls. "That man must be ten cents short of a dime."

"Mmm-hmmm," she murmured, busying herself with re-organizing the contents of the glove compartment. She didn't want to talk about Levi. Didn't want to think about the emotions he'd triggered in her last night. God, she couldn't believe she'd almost *cried* in front of him. She didn't cry in front of anyone. Not since Cash's funeral. She always put on a smile and did what needed to be done. And that's what she'd do today too.

Letting go of a sigh, Cassidy closed the glove compartment and pushed open the door, slipping past Molly.

The stands were nearly full of spectators who were sipping their beers and placing bets on which riders would take the top titles. Excitement buzzed in their murmurs, but the whole scene weighed on her shoulders. Didn't they know this was the sport that had killed her brother?

She turned to find Molly standing beside her. "You want to take a walk outside? I can hold down the fort."

Before she could take Molly up on the offer, Theo came running over. "Cass!" He bounced around, dressed in a western button-down shirt and genuine leather chaps over his jeans.

Cassidy ruffled his hair and waved at his mom, who never seemed to be able to keep up with him. "Awesome outfit, buddy," she said, tipping up his cowboy hat.

"Thanks!" The boy's eyes lit up like sparklers. "Levi brought it to me this morning. With tickets for the rodeo!"

"Really?" She hadn't meant to sound so surprised, but Levi was doing that a lot lately. Surprising her. Catching her off guard. As far as she knew, he'd never been particularly fond of little kids.

"You know what else Levi said?" Theo asked, his eyes growing even wider. "He said he was gonna do a clinic this summer. When he's home between competitions."

"He did, huh?" Her voice had dried up. She didn't want to say anything to Theo, but she had serious concerns about Levi following through on that promise.

"I can't wait! It's gonna be awesome!" The kid hugged her waist. "Thanks for letting me meet him. I gotta go get in my seat so I can cheer real loud!" He bounded away before she could say goodbye.

"Wow. Levi's doing a clinic for kids?" Molly sounded impressed. "Maybe I won't beat him up after all."

Cassidy crossed her arms and watched Theo run back to his mom. "He's setting that kid up for disappointment. Levi doesn't follow through on anything."

Molly panned her gaze around the arena. "He sure went all-out with this facility. Bet that took some serious follow-through."

As much as she wanted to, Cassidy couldn't argue with that. Everything about the arena was state-of-the-art. And supposedly he'd raised every penny himself. The town had been waiting for this for a long time. After the old facility had burned, there'd never been enough money to rebuild. The vacant land had always sat there on the edge of town— a scarred reminder of what they'd lost. But today this place was sold out. Everyone seemed to be there. Most of the businesses on Main Street had closed so everyone could be part of this historic day.

The house lights dimmed, hushing the crowd. On the other side of the arena, the bulls were led into the chutes.

Even under the layers of her polyester-blend uniform, a chill prickled across Cassidy's skin.

The loudspeaker crackled. "Welcome to the first rodeo in the brand-new Cash Greer Memorial Arena." Hank Green stood in the judge's booth and waved at the crowd.

Cheers and hoots rang out. Molly even clapped and hollered beside her. But Cassidy couldn't move. Instead of clapping, her hands squeezed into fists.

Hank waited until the noise died down. "For our first event, one of our own homegrown cowboys—Levi Cortez— will be riding Ball Buster." The crowd went crazy again, people jumping to their feet, chanting "Le-vi, Le-vi!"

Cassidy crept closer to the action, stopping just outside the corral's steel fence.

It's time to party. That had been her brother's phrase before every ride. She could still hear his voice, the anticipation, the fire. Levi had it too—the same drive, the untamable spirit. He always had.

Over in the bucking chute, Levi slid onto Ball Buster's back.

Her heart competed with the crowd's noise, drumming its own erratic beat. She gripped one of the fence rails tightly as a restless energy rushed through her legs. She wanted to run over there and tell him not to do it. It wasn't worth a life. But the chute opened and Ball Buster charged into the ring, snorting and kicking and bucking. Dirt flew in clumps. The crowd's applause muted into an awed hush.

Fear barricaded itself in Cassidy's lungs as she watched Levi ride.

He looked so broad up there, so fully in control. Even underneath his helmet, she could see that wide, cocky grin, his eyes glistening with passion. He'd rolled up his shirtsleeves enough to show off his bulky forearms, which strained as he held on with one hand and whipped the other freely over his head.

Something caught in her chest. The same girlish flutter she used to get when she'd watch him out on the ranch training with her brother. He looked boyish and free. Unburdened. And something in her wanted that so badly...

The crowd praised his showy ride—his arm lifted over his head, waving as he passed the south side of the stands. The bull stampeded past, and Levi turned his head. He looked at her and flashed an even brighter smile.

She hated the way it warmed her through, the way it sent the sting of anticipation straight to her heart. *I don't want you!* she screamed in her head. She couldn't want him. She wouldn't. It didn't matter how much he flirted with her, how much time he forced her to spend with him, he was reckless, just like her brother.

Turning away, she headed for the ambulance. She didn't have to stand here and watch him. She should've refused to come. It's not like Walsh would've fired her. And who cared if he did anyhow? She was supposed to leave. Which meant she should be spending all her free time getting Lulu ready to live on her own again...

Behind her, a collective gasp left an eerie, deafening second of silence. Cassidy whirled back to the arena.

"Shit, that didn't look good," Molly muttered, staring into the corral.

Levi lay sprawled on the ground, flat on his back near the north fence. Tucker, the Cortez's stable manager and trained bullfighter, had already dashed out to lure Ball Buster back to the chute.

"Oh god…" The words eased out of Cassidy in a long breath. He wasn't moving. Wasn't bouncing back up like he usually did.

"Looks like we've got a live one." Molly ripped open the ambulance door and hauled out the backboard.

"He's okay," Cassidy whispered. This was Levi. He had to be okay. Her eyes strained as she waited for him to stand. Nausea swirled through her, sending a tingle up her throat.

"Medic!" Tucker waved frantically from the chutes, giving them their cue, but Cassidy couldn't move forward. Her brain had already gone backward.

She'd seen her brother sprawled out in the dirt like that. As still and lifeless as a stone. It still shocked her that a soul could be snuffed out so quickly. It took only one small mistake. A seemingly insignificant error. She hadn't been able to help him. Levi couldn't help him. No one could help him. He'd been crushed. In one second.

You're not helpless anymore. The whisper came in Cash's voice. She wasn't. She'd trained for every kind of emergency so she could make sure she'd never be helpless again. It was the lifeline that pulled her out of the past.

She found the courage to raise her head. Molly had knelt next to Levi on the ground and seemed to be assessing his injuries. It didn't matter how hard Cassidy's heart pounded or that her legs shook the same way they did after a long mountain-bike ride. She had to get out there.

In a quick maneuver, she threw herself over the rails and into the arena, sprinting hard to the scene. Fear pounded through her pulse points, blurring everything.

She hit her knees across from Molly. "Levi?"

His eyes were open, staring up at the ceiling. A shot of relief fortified her hands as she leaned over him. At least he was conscious. "What're we dealing with?" she asked as though this were some random patient instead of someone she didn't want to care about.

Was it his spine? She should've been watching…

"Head injury," her coworker reported.

"Not a head injury," Levi countered.

Molly huffed. "You lost consciousness."

"For maybe two seconds." He went to sit up. "I feel great."

The loudspeaker crackled again. "It looks like Mr. Cortez is conscious and moving," Hank Green intoned. "Please be patient as our medical staff evaluates him."

Grinning, Levi waved to the cheering crowd. "I'm ready to get back on my bull," he said to Cassidy.

"Like hell you are." She pressed her hand into his shoulder and laid him back down. "We're taking you in."

His eyes narrowed as he stared up at her. "To the hospital?"

"Yeah. The hospital." She motioned to Molly, and before he could protest, they'd tipped him on his side and backboarded him.

"I don't need a hospital," Levi grumbled. "My head doesn't even hurt."

He reached over and covered her hand with his as she

tightened the straps on the board. "Come on, Cass. I'm fine. Seriously."

She jerked her hand away and glared into his eyes. "You're the one who wanted me here." He'd forced her to come and face all the things she didn't want to remember. "So now I'm doing my job."

* * *

Once again, Cassidy drew the short end of the stick in having to ride in the ambulance with the patient. Molly obviously wanted to torture her. As soon as they loaded the backboard onto the gurney, her coworker hopped out of the box.

"Hang in there, dream boy," she said, closing up one of the doors. "I'll have you to the hospital in no time."

As soon as the other door slammed shut, Cassidy settled in and went to work taking his vitals. Fear had nearly submerged her, but now it hardened into anger. She worked briskly and silently, taking his blood pressure and then monotonously going through the routine of other tests.

Levi was the first one to speak. "This really isn't necessary." He didn't sound nearly as cranky as she felt.

"You're in no position to decide what's necessary." She finished charting his vitals and moved onto the health history portion of the show. "Any allergies to medications?" she asked, even though she already knew the answer.

"No," he said, looking at her too intently. "No allergies."

She avoided his eyes. "What about previous surgeries?"

"Sorry I made you do this, Cass." Levi lifted his head as much as he could, being strapped down and all. "Sorry I made you come today."

"It's fine." The stress of seeing him lying on the ground

hadn't shaved a good ten years off her life or anything. Nope. This was all just a normal day in her world. She was trained to deal with emergencies. Levi was just another patient. She didn't care that he had the most beautiful eyes she'd ever seen. Didn't care that his hair made her want to run her fingers through it...

"I miss you, Cass," he murmured, laying his head back down. "We were good friends once."

"Yeah. I guess we were." In another life. An easy, carefree life. She refocused on the questionnaire. "Do you have insurance?"

"I know you hate me. And I get it."

"I don't hate you." She'd never hated him. No matter how much she wanted to.

"I still miss Cash," Levi said, a tremor of emotion in his voice.

"I do too." But it had gotten easier to miss him. They had so many good memories. Her brother had been her favorite person in the world. After losing him, she couldn't imagine being close with anyone else. Especially not with the man lying in front of her.

"Your brother was a hell of a guy," Levi said. "Even though he almost killed me once."

The cryptic statement baited her, just like he obviously wanted it to. She lowered the clipboard. "He did?"

"Yeah. Took a few swings at my face." Levi laughed. "Gave me a pretty sweet shiner."

"Really?" How had she missed that? "Why?" She could see Cash hitting a lot of guys back then, but not Levi. He was like his brother...

"Because I was gonna ask you to homecoming. My junior year. And he found out."

Was it getting hot in there? Maybe Molly had turned on the heat. "Why...uh...would you have asked me to homecoming?" He could've asked any girl to homecoming. Hell, he could've taken five girls to homecoming. Actually, he might have one year...

"I thought you were beautiful."

"Oh." Something flickered in her heart. Probably lust. Because even though Levi had likely suffered a concussion and was strapped to a backboard, he still had that sexy, in control look about him.

"Cash knew I liked you," he said easily. "He always reminded me that you were off limits."

"He was overprotective." Cassidy busied herself with glancing over the paperwork she'd better finish filling out before this conversation went any further. Cash wasn't around to protect her heart, which meant she was on her own. And something told her it would be much harder now than it had been when she was fifteen.

"Did you ever like me?" the man had the balls to ask.

"Um. Yeah." She studied the clipboard as though all the words were written in Chinese. "Sure. I liked you okay."

Levi reached over and tipped the clipboard down as though he wanted to see her face. "*Okay?* Like a friend? A brother?" His eyes were on the hunt, intent on hers, determined to dig out all her secrets.

"Does it matter?" Would it have mattered? "It was a long time ago."

"It matters," he insisted, staring at her like he already knew the answer.

That was because her face had to be as red as the flashing lights on the ambulance. She was blushing so hard it actually hurt.

"Did you like me, Cassidy?" he asked again, teasing her.

That was it. Anger overpowered her embarrassment. "Of course I liked you," she snapped. "You were a damn bull rider. Hot as hell. Dangerous. And as smooth as Don Juan." She threw up her hands. "You made all the girls fall in love with you." He made them all love him, and then he played around with them. Obviously, some things never changed.

Instead of a triumphantly cocky grin, he simply gazed at her, his face more serious than she'd ever seen it. "I wish I would've known that," he finally said.

"Yeah, well, like I said, it was a long time ago." She held the clipboard firmly between them. "Now I have to complete your medical history before we get to the hospital." Stick to the facts. Things she could observe and record.

That was much safer than this sentimental walk down memory lane.

Chapter Four

Give it to me straight, Doc." Levi was only half kidding. Judging from the grim look on the doctor's face, he likely wasn't about to get the best news.

The man was your standard-issue ER doctor—dark hair, no sense of humor, and little emotion. His frown was so firm that Levi wondered if he'd ever cracked a smile.

"Based on the test results and CT scan, I'd say you have a minor concussion."

"That's it?" Well, hell, then why'd the man look so concerned? "So, what? I rest for a couple of weeks?" He'd miss only a few events and then be back on his bull in time for the rodeo in Tulsa.

The doctor sat on a rolling stool in front of a small desk. "How many concussions have you had, Mr. Cortez?"

"Not sure." That was the honest truth, seeing as how this was the only one he'd ever bothered to get diagnosed. And that was only because Cass had forced him to.

"I don't have to tell you that repetitive head injuries can cause lasting damage to your brain."

"So I've heard." These days, most rodeos were implementing concussion protocols. Not that any of the riders willingly participated.

"In order to give your head the time it needs to heal, I'm recommending you take four to six weeks off and watch carefully for more severe symptoms."

"Four to six weeks?" That was almost the whole summer.

"At least," the doctor said sternly. "And you really should be evaluated by a concussion treatment center in Denver before you go back to riding."

"Wow." Levi had to stand and let that sink in. He paced the room. "Okay. I guess if that's what you think…" See? This was why he didn't go to doctors after he hit the ground too hard. They loved to bench riders.

The doctor stood too. "In a job like yours, you have to take care of yourself now so you don't suffer later." The man handed him a slip of paper. "Here's the information on the treatment centers. Feel free to call me if you have any other questions."

"Thanks." He couldn't find the energy to make it sound heartfelt. He'd never been sidelined longer than two weeks, even when he'd broken his foot. What the hell was he supposed to do with himself?

The doctor ducked out of the room, and Cass peeked in. "How's it going?"

"Things are dandy," he muttered, milking it. "Doc says I have a concussion. I'm out for four to six weeks."

A sympathetic smile softened her face as she stepped into the room. She still wore a crisp white paramedic's shirt that fit her snugly. He'd never dreamed a uniform would do it for him, but somehow the polyester only made her curves more enticing.

"At least the rodeo was a hit," she said brightly. "Tucker and Lucas stepped up to help run the rest of the events, and everyone had a great time." Her smile turned shy. "So you can consider all of your hard work a success."

"Is that why you came back?" He worked an unspoken question into his tone. "To tell me how it went?" Or had she been worried about him?

Cassidy stared up at the ceiling, her lips creased as though she was thinking of something snarky to say.

He didn't give her a chance. "What I meant to say was thank you for coming back." He may be taking all kinds of liberties here, but . . . "It means a lot to know you're concerned about me."

She shot him a dark look. "Concerned about you?"

Damn. Too far. "Sure. Isn't that why you're here?"

"Not exactly." She held up a plastic grocery bag that had been dangling at her side. "Jessa put together some stuff for you. Clothes, I think. In case yours were ruined. She asked me to bring you this bag since I knew where to find you."

"Oh." He reached out a hand, and she tossed the bag over. *Great.* Leave it to his sister-in-law to dig through his underwear drawer and find the only pair of tighty whities. He let the bag dangle behind his back. Thankfully, they'd let him wear his own clothes for all the tests—minus his belt. But he'd put that back on the second he'd gotten out of the CT scan.

Cassidy looked like she was trying not to laugh. "So when can you get out of here?"

"Sounds like I'm free to go." Which meant she had perfect timing. "Any way I could trouble you to give me a lift home?"

"Oh." Her smile faded into that guarded expression she typically wore in his presence. "Sure. Yeah. Of course." She turned abruptly and led the way out of the hospital room, keeping a few steps of distance between them. "Theo was pretty worried about you." Cass glanced over her shoulder. "But I assured him you'd be fine."

"Yeah, doc says it's minor." Sort of. Not that she needed to know the extent of his diagnosis. Levi followed her down another corridor. "Wish I could've stayed to hang out with him." And her too.

Cassidy paused at the doors that led out to the parking lot. "Thanks for making sure he got to go, Levi." She faced him. "Seriously. That was pretty awesome of you."

Her steady gaze kicked up his pulse. Getting the kid a ticket wasn't a big deal. He could do more. He could do a lot more. "It looks like I'll have extra time on my hands this summer." As much as he hated sitting out, every cloud had a silver lining. "So that youth rodeo clinic might be a go." But there was no way he could pull it off alone. "Can I count on your help?"

"Oh. Um…" She deflected his stare with a shake of her head and walked through the doors, leaving him to follow behind again. "I can't. Sorry. I have a lot going on right now."

He fell in stride beside her. "Like what?"

At the edge of the parking lot she stopped, but this time she didn't turn to him. She gazed out at the mountains instead. "I applied to a pediatric nurse residency program. I'm hoping to move to Denver at the end of July."

"Denver?" Cass was leaving Topaz Falls? He stumbled off the curb and tailed her across the parking lot, a hollowness spreading through his chest. His whole life, Cass had been a fixture of this town. A fixture in his life, even when he'd been gone. She had a place in most of his memories, seeing as how he'd practically lived at the Greer house. He may have been gone for years, but when he'd thought of home during that time, he'd also thought of Cass, the bright-eyed wonder he'd never quite left behind. Now she was fixing to leave him behind.

"Aren't there nursing jobs around here?" He gestured back to the small county hospital. "This seems like a fine establishment. I bet they're always looking for nurses."

They reached the Subaru, and Cass unlocked the doors. "I've always wanted to specialize in pediatrics."

"Why pediatrics?"

They both climbed into the car, and he quickly shoved the bag with his tighty whities under the seat.

Cass didn't seem to notice. "My first call as an EMT was to the scene of an accident." Her voice quieted. "It was bad. A woman had rolled her car on Jewel Pass, and her four-year-old daughter was thrown."

He recognized the intensity in her eyes. It was the same passion that carried him when he rode a bull.

"We saved her," Cass said. "We found her and stabilized her, and I held her hand until the helicopter came." A tear slipped down her cheek, but her voice didn't waver. "I felt like I'd finally done what I couldn't do for Cash. And I decided then that I wanted to do everything I could to make sure a parent didn't have to lose a child."

She didn't have to say more. He knew. In her way, Cass was also still trying to save her mom. "You're so brave." She put him to shame.

"I feel like I'm always afraid."

"But you don't let your fears hold you back." They

seemed to motivate her, to make her stronger. She was the strongest woman he'd ever met. In six years of dating and traveling the circuit, he'd never met another woman like Cass. And now he was going to lose her.

Panic gripped him by the throat. "What if I did the clinic before you left? Then could you help?"

She finally shoved the key into the ignition and started the car. "I don't know. Rodeos aren't really my thing."

And yet she'd shown up for him earlier. "This is a junior clinic. We're talking mutton busting, barrel racing, roping. Easy stuff. And it'd be great to have you there to help with any scratches or booboos. It'd be the perfect start to a career in pediatrics."

She shot him a guarded smile as though she was onto his persuasive tactics. "I might not even get into the program." Her face sobered as if the thought depressed her.

"You'll get in." She was the hardest worker he'd ever seen. Determined. According to Jessa, she'd aced nursing school. Yeah, she'd definitely get in. Which meant this clinic would be his last chance to convince her to stay. He'd never had much to do with kids, but he could learn. How hard could it be? "If you don't do it for me, do it for Theo." Hopefully, that'd be the kill shot. She seemed to love that kid.

"Fine." She sighed. "I'll help with the damn clinic. But—"

Her phone rang and cut her off. She dug it out of her back pocket. When she glanced at the screen, a look of concern gripped her delicate features. "Hey, Darla." After a pause, Cassidy's face paled. "What do you mean she's gone?" With the phone tucked between her shoulder and ear, Cass threw the car into reverse. "I'm coming. I'll be right there." She let the phone drop into her lap and peeled out of the parking lot.

Levi put on his seat belt. "What's up?"

"I sent Darla over to check on Mom." Cass drove faster, passing an Oldsmobile on the right. "The Jeep's gone, and she can't find her anywhere."

And that was a reason to go twenty miles an hour above the speed limit? He turned to her so he didn't have to watch the car swerving in and around traffic. "Maybe she went to the store or something."

"I've asked her not to drive." Her jaw was clenched. "I even hid the keys in my dresser." She merged the car aggressively onto the highway. "She must've torn my room apart looking for them."

Levi eyed the speedometer. Hopefully Dev wasn't hiding in his favorite spot today. "Why don't you want her driving?" He got that Lulu had some issues, but it seemed a little harsh to take away the woman's keys.

"She's an alcoholic," Cass informed him. "I don't want her to kill herself or someone else."

"Oh." That explained a lot. Like the fact that Cass never seemed to want to leave her mom alone. "I'm sorry. I didn't know." He should've. He should've known a long time ago.

Cass shrugged. "Hardly anyone knows. I do my best to protect her reputation."

She meant she did her best to manage everything on her own—school and work and taking care of her mom. "How can I help?" How could he make up for all the years he should've been there for her?

She shot him a sideways glance. "I don't need help." The edge in her voice left him no room to argue.

After taking the last few turns quickly, she pulled up into the driveway of her house.

Darla ran down the front steps and peered in through

Levi's window. "I swear, I thought she was fine. I came to check on her a few hours ago, and we had a great time. Then I went to the shop, and when I came back, she was gone."

Cass let the car run. "It's not your fault."

"Cass…there's a bottle of vodka on the table." Darla looked like she was close to tears.

That wasn't good. Levi rubbed his forehead, finally noticing his headache.

"Of course there's vodka on the table," Cass muttered. "Doesn't matter how many times I talk to her, nothing ever changes."

"Maybe she's not drunk," he suggested. "Maybe she just wanted to get out for a while."

Cassidy and Darla both turned their heads and gave him a *seriously?* look. This obviously wasn't the first unapproved adventure Lulu had gone on.

"I already drove around town," Darla said. "Didn't see the Jeep anywhere."

Cass heaved a sigh, her shoulders slumping.

"Hey." Levi touched her arm. Surprisingly she didn't shrink away. "We'll find her." Hopefully before Dev did. "Where does she usually go?"

Cass raised her head wearily. "Places that remind her of Cash."

"Then it shouldn't be that hard to find her." He glanced at Darla. "Why don't you make a run by the cemetery?" He'd been a regular there himself since he'd come home. Whenever he went, it always seemed there were fresh flowers. Lulu likely spent a lot of time there.

"Good idea." Darla dug keys out of her purse.

"And we'll head to your old house," he said to Cass. "You want me to drive?"

"No. I'm fine."

She wasn't fine. Her shoulders drooped, and her eyes looked empty.

"I don't mind—" Before he could finish, she backed the car down the driveway.

Cass said nothing as they proceeded through town, headed to the outskirts where her parents had once owned ten acres. Levi didn't know what to say either. Actually, he hadn't earned the right to say anything. So even though it killed him, he let the silence stretch between them, doing his damnedest to give her the space she seemed to need.

He kept his eyes on the world outside, and when she drove in front of the Greer's old house, the sight of it hit him hard. Growing up, he'd spent most of his time at the log palace Mr. Greer had built on the edge of town. At least, it'd seemed like a palace to him. Cassidy's father was a contractor and had spared no expense in designing and building the refuge for his own family. Rustic hand-carved beams held up the high, arched ceilings, and the entire four thousand square feet were decked out with expensive accents. It was a grand house, but it hadn't been enough to keep things from falling apart.

"She's not here." Cass slowed the car.

The streets around the house were empty. No Jeep.

She pulled over on the side of the road and stared at the house with the same lost look on her face Levi must've had. "A new family lives here now," she murmured. "They bought it last year. They have a little boy and a little girl." There was a longing in her words, like she wished she could go back to being the little girl in that house.

God, he wanted to touch her. Take her hand or ease his arm around her shoulders and pull her close so he could take on some of her burden. Instead, he said, "It was the perfect place for us to grow up."

She smiled a little.

"I don't know what would've happened to me if I didn't have your family around." He'd gone to a dark place after his mom walked out on them. His dad was hardly home, and Lance did his best, but he was only a kid himself. Back then, Lulu had been the strength he'd needed. She'd been the one who showed him that not all moms left.

He turned to Cass. "When did she start drinking?" As a kid, he'd only ever seen Lulu drink half a glass of wine. She always said it made her tired.

"After Dad left. At first it was only at night. So she could sleep." For once, Cass's expression didn't seem so guarded. "But then she started hiding it from me. I'd get phone calls from people in town, telling me she was passed out in the park."

"Has she been to AA?" He didn't know what else to ask. What other options were there for this kind of situation?

"She's made it through a few meetings, but she always quits." She spoke the words with a resigned hopelessness.

"She's lucky to have you." A lot of people wouldn't have cared how much their parent needed them. A lot of people would've walked away regardless.

She shrugged, her face stony again, those eyes steeled. "Sometimes I hate her. But mostly I love her. That's the problem. Love doesn't let you walk away. No matter how bad things get."

And yet he had. He'd walked away from this family he'd loved. Which only proved one thing. Lance was right. He was too self-absorbed to love anyone. "Damn it, Cass. I'm sorry. I didn't know things were so bad."

"It's not your fault." Her tone pushed him away and dismissed the entire conversation. She didn't seem to want his sorry-ass apology. "I don't know where else to look for her. If Darla hasn't found her, I don't know where she'd be."

"Where did Cash hang out?" Besides right there in that meadow where the corral used to be? Levi squinted, studying the house again, looking out past the back garden to the rutted dirt road where they used to ride the ATVs. "The tree-house."

"What?" Cass looked out the window as though searching for what he was looking at. But you couldn't see it from the road. "That has to be a mile back in," Cass murmured. "And it's private property."

Which would explain why no one could find Lulu. "I don't see any cars in the driveway." Obviously the family wasn't home. "And I'm sure they won't mind us trespassing once we explain the situation."

Fear flickered across her face, but Cass put the car into *drive* and turned into the driveway. Bypassing the house, she drove across the meadow to the ruts in the grass. They disappeared into the trees and bumped along the uneven path, taking it slow.

Levi remembered these woods. They'd build forts and teepees and log cabins out of sticks, all under the shelter of an eclectic mix of pine and cottonwood trees. The deeper they drove in, the more the memories flooded him. Memories he'd held at bay to keep the pain of loss contained. "I'd forgotten how much we loved it back here." By shutting out the bad memories, he'd let time rob him of the good ones too.

"It was like a haven," Cass said quietly. "It still is."

They peered out the windshield in silence. The sun had

started to set, filtering through the trees, filling the forest with a peaceful glow.

Up ahead, the sunlight glinted off something metal. Levi sat straighter. "The Jeep."

It was pulled off the road, down in a ditch.

"Oh no." Cass parked behind it, and they both scrambled out. There was no sign of Lulu.

"Mom!" Cass took off into the trees with Levi following behind.

The treehouse had been built about fifteen feet off the ground in the biggest cottonwood Mr. Greer could find. Back then they'd had a nice wooden staircase to climb, but that had long since fallen apart. The whole top section was missing.

Levi reached the tree first. He gazed at the rotted wooden platform.

"There's no way she's up there." Cass was out of breath. "Maybe she—"

There was a shuffling sound above and then creaking boards. "Cass?" Lulu peered over the edge.

Levi's heart took a dive. The thing had gone to ruin. The boards were cracked and splintered, the walls collapsed in. How the hell had she gotten up there?

"Mom! What're you doing? You're going to kill yourself!" Cassidy went right for the old rope ladder, but Levi held her back.

"That thing is about to snap." He pointed up higher where the ropes were frayed and the wooden rungs had cracked.

Cassidy's mom peered over the side of a fallen wall. "Levi? *Levi Cortez?* Is that you?"

"Hey, Lulu." He gazed up at her, shocked by how much she'd changed. When he was a kid, the woman had been one of those refined, graceful moms. Blond hair like Cassidy's, always styled perfectly. She'd worn elegant clothes, and he'd never seen her without makeup. But now...Lulu Greer was a shell. So skinny her clothes sagged on her frail frame. Pale, sunken cheeks made her look sick. No wonder she'd been able to make it up the ladder. She hardly weighed anything.

"God almighty, Levi. It's been so long. You've grown into quite the handsome devil, haven't you?" The woman's feet shuffled closer to the edge of the platform.

"Get back," Cassidy shouted. "You're drunk! You'll fall!"

"I'm not drunk," Lulu insisted. As if intent on proving it, she walked a line along the edge of the platform. It would've been more convincing if she hadn't stumbled. "I'm fine, honey. I'll climb down there—"

"No! Get back!" Cass yelled again. "That ladder might not hold you." She turned and paced away a few steps. "I can't believe this. I have to call the fire department to get my mother out of a tree."

"Hold on." Levi assessed the height. This didn't have to be a whole scene. He knew from personal experience how humiliating it was to have your dirty laundry exposed in this town. If the fire department came, everyone would know about it by tomorrow morning.

"We have to get her down somehow." Cass pulled her phone out of her pocket. "Unless you have a better idea."

Actually, he did. Levi held out his hand. "Can I have your phone?"

She gave it to him.

"Lulu," he called up. "You remember that time Cash and I made you dinner in the treehouse?"

"Of course I do. You two were such good boys." Her voice turned weepy. "You were always doing sweet things like that. Oh, I miss him so much." She walked out of his view. Boards groaned and creaked. Wouldn't be long before one of them broke.

"I miss him too." He walked around the base of the tree until he could see her again. "You know what I do when I miss him? I think about all the good times we had." At least, that's what he'd started to do. "Lulu?" He waited until he had her attention. "Why don't you tell Cass all about that dinner we made you?"

"It was in the fall," Lulu said sadly. "A few weeks before Halloween."

"That's right." He kept his eyes trained on her. "Sit down. Okay? Sit down nice and easy. Right there."

She did as she was told, seeming completely obvious to the fifteen-foot drop mere feet away.

"What else, Mom?" Cass asked, the first hint of relief in her voice. "What did they make you for dinner?"

"The first course was salad from plants in the forest." Levi smiled, remembering how she'd oohhed and ahhed over their foraged greens. "It tasted awful, but I ate every bite." The sadness left her voice, and she actually laughed. "I think I even ate a dandelion!"

Satisfied she was safe for the moment, Levi snuck away and used Cassidy's phone to call Lance and Jessa.

Chapter Five

Cassidy had learned a long time ago to count her blessings. That was what had gotten her through the really terrible times. Way back when she was a little girl, her mom had called it playing the Pollyanna game. *No matter what happens, you can always find something to be glad about,* Lulu would say. Then they'd take turns listing every single thing that made them glad.

Something to be glad about...something to be glad about...

Well, at least her mother wasn't naked in the tree.

She kept her eyes focused on Lulu, who now sat on the rickety floor of the treehouse like a little kid, but Cassidy's heart still pounded. When she'd seen her mother up there, she finally understood how heart attack victims felt.

"What about that time Cash and I followed the bear prints and got lost?" Levi called to her mother. He'd kept her talking and giggling since he'd gotten off the phone. Somehow he'd managed to maintain a complete calm while Cassidy teetered on her own ledge—battling back the fear and the anger and the hopelessness that threatened to push her over the edge.

She inhaled deeply, trying to pull the serenity of the forest into her body. They just had to keep Lulu still until Lance and Jessa showed up, and then Levi would use their extension ladder to go up after her.

"I was so worried about you two that night," Lulu said, her tone chiding. "I gave Cash a good talking to."

"I think you gave me one too," Levi said with a laugh.

Behind them, the unmistakable hum of a diesel engine released the tension from Cassidy's shoulders. Lance's truck rumbled through the underbrush. He parked by a pine tree, and the doors opened. There were her friends—Jessa carrying an armload of blankets and a shopping bag filled with snacks and Lance hauling the massive ladder from the bed of his truck.

"Hey, Lulu," Levi called gently. "Lance is here with a ladder. I'm gonna come up there and get you, but for now I want you to stay put. Don't move. Got it?"

"You don't have to do that, honey." Her mother rose to her knees. "I can just climb down the ladder."

"No!" Cassidy rushed to the base of the tree. "Don't move, Mom! You understand? Sit back down!"

"All right, all right." Lulu plopped down in a pout.

"We've got this." Levi gave Cassidy's shoulder a squeeze as he and Lance passed. The two of them positioned the ladder against the thick, sturdy branch next to the treehouse platform.

What if it didn't hold? She had to turn away.

"I brought cookies." Jessa caught Cassidy in a one-armed hug.

"I don't think I can eat anything." Her stomach hurt worse than it did when she'd taken her nursing boards.

"Everything will be fine," Jessa assured her.

"All right, Lulu." Levi called. "I'm coming up."

Cassidy forced herself to turn around and watch.

Lance positioned himself at the base of the ladder and held on to it.

"Oh god." Cassidy wrapped an arm around her stomach as Levi ascended the ladder, climbing higher and higher until he'd reached the platform.

"Easy now." He stepped onto the boards, testing each one, and helped Lulu stand. "I'll go down first." He eased back onto the first rung of the ladder. It was painstaking work—taking a step down and then waiting for her mom to do the same.

Little by little, Levi urged Lulu down—guarding her—until she finally stood on the grass only a few feet away. But Cassidy couldn't move. She couldn't run over there and wrap her arms around her mom the way she wanted to. Too much weighed her down.

"Are you cold?" Jessa wrapped a blanket around Lulu's shoulders. "And I have some snacks too. Have you eaten lately?"

The alcohol still hazed her mother's eyes. "I'm not hungry. And I don't understand what all the fuss is about."

Cassidy's jaw dropped. "You don't?"

"No, honey," her mother sassed back. "I don't. I used to climb up there all the time when you were kids."

"Years ago, Mom. That was years ago."

Without a word, Lance folded up the ladder. Jessa hurried over to take the other side, and the two of them hauled it to the truck.

But Cassidy didn't care if they heard. She didn't care who heard. For so long she'd kept her emotions in check, but she couldn't hold them in forever. The pain was too overwhelming. "We don't own this property anymore." Raising her voice released the pressure that had built in her chest. "And the treehouse is falling apart. You could've fallen. You could've been seriously injured."

Levi stepped between them. "Hey…it's okay. Everything's okay now. No harm done."

She spun to face him. "It's not okay!" He didn't know. This was one time. He hadn't been there for all the other times.

He reached for her. "Cass—"

"I want you to go." She backed away. "Go home with Lance and Jessa." This was between her and her mother, and she couldn't stop herself from saying what needed to be said. Not anymore.

Levi didn't budge. "I can stay. You'll need someone to drive the Jeep back to your house anyway."

"No." Her eyes heated but she refused to cry in front of him. "I'll have Jessa bring me back for the Jeep tomorrow." She didn't want his help. She didn't want his sympathy. She could handle this on her own. She'd been handling it on her own for years. "I want you to go. Please."

"Fine. If that's what you want." Levi's broad shoulders caved as he turned and walked away.

She waited for the truck to start and drive out of sight before she approached her mom. "I can't do this anymore."

Lulu looked startled, like she'd fallen asleep somewhere else and woken up in the place she'd least expected. Cassidy could relate. Sometimes it seemed like she'd gone to sleep right after Cash's death, and every time she woke up she wondered how she'd gotten here.

Lulu's body wilted into a posture of regret. "I'm sorry, Cass-a-frass," she murmured. "I didn't mean to upset you."

Of course not. She never meant to upset her. But this time Cassidy didn't tell her it was okay. In the past, she'd always been able to let it go, to forgive her and move on, but it got harder every time. "We need to get home." Before it got too dark and she couldn't find her way out of there.

Lulu didn't move so she went to her side to support her. Her mother leaned heavily on her shoulder as they soldiered down the road to the Subaru—and that's exactly how Cassidy felt. Like a soldier. Like she'd been carrying her mom across the battlefield of life. She wasn't sure how much longer she could do it before she collapsed too.

After loading Lulu into the passenger's seat of the car, she took her time making her way to the driver's side, reciting the same script she'd used a hundred times. It wasn't Lulu's fault she was such a mess. She'd had a perfect life too. A perfect family. Her kids had always been her purpose, and then one of them was taken away.

She's just sad. Wounded. Traumatized.

The words didn't bring any relief this time. Closing her eyes, Cassidy leaned against the driver's side door instead of getting into the car. She'd never had the chance to be sad, to let the wounds keep her down. She'd never had anyone carry her.

She glanced over her shoulder at her mom, who was peering out the window fearfully. It had been years since Cash had died, and instead of making strides and taking her life back, her mother was becoming more of a shell every day.

And she was letting her. Instead of helping Lulu piece herself back together, Cassidy had taken over every responsibility, giving Lulu the power to stay broken.

It had to stop or her mother would stay broken forever.

"That's it." She opened the door and slid into the driver's seat. "I'm done."

Lulu's gaze fell away in a display of outright shame. But that wasn't what this was about. Shame. Whose fault it was. What she wasn't doing. It couldn't be about any of that. It had to be about the future. A future for both of them.

"Listen to me, Mom," Cassidy said, taking her mother's hands in her own. They were cold and wrinkled and bony. She held them tightly, as though she could restore them with a loving touch. "There's so much more than this." There were dreams and joy still waiting for them. "I love you. But there are things I want to do with my life. Things I've wanted for a long time."

Her mother simply stared at her, her bottom lip quivering. "What things, Cass?"

This was the opening she'd been waiting for. She hadn't told Lulu about the program, about her interview. She'd simply told her she'd visited some friends in Denver. Because what if her mother didn't improve and she couldn't go? She didn't want her to feel guilty. Guilt would never be a strong enough motivator to help her change. But maybe a vision of the future would.

"I applied to a nurse residency program in Denver," she blurted before she lost the courage.

Her mother finally raised her eyes to Cassidy's and lifted her chin as though trying to be strong. "Then you should go."

"I can't. Not until you're in a good place." She couldn't live in another city constantly worrying that her mom would drink herself into despair and climb a tree. Or even worse, that she'd kill herself or someone else on the road.

Lulu shook her head sadly. "You don't have to worry about me—"

"Yes I do." What more proof did she need than the scene tonight?

"I know I've made some mistakes..."

"It's not about the mistakes. It's not about the past. You can have a good life. You can have friends and you can laugh and you can go out to fancy dinners." She could get a job and find a new purpose. "I want this for you as much as I want it for myself." She had to believe they could both take this second chance. A chance to seek out a joy that was greater than their pain.

Her mother reached up and rested her palm against Cassidy's cheek the way she always used to when she'd tuck her into bed at night. "You've always been so strong."

"I got that from you." She placed her hand over her mother's, letting her tears fall. "You raised me that way." For so many years, she'd been the one who Cass had leaned on. The one who would hug away her hurts and help her face her fears. That woman was still inside there somewhere. "The same strength is in you, Mom. And I need you to find it again. I need you to hold on to it."

Lulu pulled her hand away and stared out the windshield. "I don't know if I can."

Cassidy didn't know if she could hold on to her strength either. How could she leave behind everything she'd known her whole life? "We have to try." Because what they had now was not a life. "It'll be hard. You'll have to stop drinking. And maybe talk to a doctor about the depression."

Inhaling deeply, Lulu turned to her. "I'll try. I'll do my very best," she said, and Cassidy thought she saw a flicker of resolve in her eyes.

A flicker was all they needed.

Chapter Six

Levi couldn't believe Cassidy lived here.

He climbed out of his truck and walked across the patchy front lawn. The small bungalow on Amethyst Street couldn't be more than eight hundred square feet. It looked like a box. The white siding was peeling off, dented and chipped in places. Faded blue shutters hung askew. Compared to her childhood home, this place was a shack.

A car turned onto the road behind him. He watched Cassidy's blue Subaru cruise down the street and turn into the driveway. Even from behind the cracked windshield, he could read the shock in her wide eyes.

She probably hadn't expected him to show up at her doorstep, but after the whole treehouse ordeal, he'd been worried about her. So right when Lance pulled into his father's driveway, he'd hopped out and gotten in his truck. Cass might be used to handling things on her own, but he'd prove that he could be there for her. Even when she didn't want to need him.

He waited patiently on the grass while Cass struggled to open the door and climbed out. "What are you doing here?" She crossed the driveway and stopped a few feet away, her glare firmly intact.

Lulu's door opened too, and Levi helped her out of the car. "I thought I'd come by to make sure you two got settled in okay." He did his best to summon the smile that had never once failed to charm a woman, but it waned.

"That's so sweet of you, sugar." Lulu threaded her arm in his and prodded him toward the front door.

Cass followed at a distance as they made their way up the porch steps. In his humble opinion, the scowl on her face only made her blue eyes prettier.

"Thank you for the brave rescue," Lulu murmured, leading him inside. "I'm so sorry I ruined everyone's night."

"You didn't ruin mine." Hell, if she hadn't gone missing, he wouldn't have been able to spend all that extra time with Cass. She would've likely driven him straight home from the hospital.

"That's nice of you to say." Lulu flicked on the lights. The front door opened into a small living room. It was spotlessly clean and simple. One couch, a recliner, and a small coffee table he recognized from their old house.

Behind him, a collage of pictures hung on the wall. They were scenes he remembered well—portraits of a happy family. Seeing Cash with his wry grin wrenched some of the pain loose. He hadn't seen a picture of him since the funeral . . .

"He loved you like a brother." Lulu touched her fingers to the image of her son's face.

"I loved him too." He'd loved all of them. Glancing up, he stole a look at Cassidy, but she quickly ducked into the kitchen.

"Did you hear my daughter's gonna be a nurse in the big city?" Pride lit Lulu's eyes as she sat on the couch and patted the cushion next to her.

Levi settled in. "She'll make a great nurse," he said, finding Cassidy's gaze and holding it firmly with his own. She obviously didn't want him here, intruding in her life, but she was fixing to leave. Start a whole new life, and he'd lose her. Crazy how he didn't want to lose something he'd never had in the first place.

Cassidy stared at him, a fight brimming in her expression.

Lulu looked back and forth between the two them, her lips hinting at a smile. "You know, I'm feeling awfully tired after all of the excitement." She rose slowly from the couch. "I think it's time for me to say good night."

He tried not to laugh at her obvious attempt to give them time alone. "Good night, Lulu."

Cassidy was the only one who didn't look amused when her mother disappeared down the hall. "Why are you here?" She marched into the living room and sat stiffly in the recliner across the room. As far away from Levi as she could get.

Why? Because he hadn't stopped thinking about her all day. Memories of her leaning over him in the ambulance, of her touching him, had flickered like sparks. "I thought you might need someone to talk to."

"I don't." She directed her gaze away from him. He couldn't read the emotion on her face. Was it anger? Or had pain just taught her to block out every emotion?

Maybe she'd gotten used to pretending, but he couldn't.

He couldn't pretend he felt nothing for her. "If you ever do need someone to talk to, I want you to know, I'm around."

Her jaw twitched as she gave him a good long look. "Why are you around now, Levi? All these years later..."

"I was too scared to come." She deserved the truth. And he'd thought about it all the way over here, about why he'd avoided the Greers, about why he hadn't come home for so long. "I thought Lulu blamed me. I thought *you* blamed me. Every single day, I still wonder what would've happened if I'd convinced Cash to go fishing or mountain biking instead of riding..."

"You couldn't have." Her lips curved into a fond smile. "Cash was obsessed. All he ever wanted to do was ride."

"I still wonder if I could've stopped it from happening." He'd always wonder. If only he'd done this or that differently. If only he'd been the one to ride first...

"I've never blamed you, Levi," Cass said softly. "He knew the risks." For once she didn't look away from him. "He always used to tell me, 'If anything happens, Cass, you take care of Mom. You help her through it.' And I have. I *am*. Maybe I'll always be helping her through it."

She wasn't though. They were both surviving, but from what he could tell, Lulu was only getting worse. "Can't you find a treatment center?" Maybe if she went away, she could focus on healing...

"She has to be the one to decide," Cass said, as if she'd resigned herself. "And she doesn't want to stop drinking. It's the only time she feels happy."

"Then you have to keep her away from alcohol."

Somehow she didn't look at him like he was an idiot, though she would have had every right. "I've tried. I find it hidden all over the house. And yes, I always throw it out. But she'll go dig in the trash can until she finds it." She leaned her head against the chair and stared up at the ceiling. "I can't watch her every second. I've got too much to do."

She was weary. He could see it in every movement. Which was why Cass needed someone to be there for her for once. No matter how much she tried to deny it, she needed support or she wasn't going to make it.

Levi pushed off the couch. "You need to do more than throw it out." He walked into the kitchen and started to open cabinet doors.

"What're you doing?" Cass wandered in behind him.

"Find it. All of it." He snagged a bottle of wine from behind a stack of bowls in a lower cabinet and set it on the kitchen table. "We'll find every bottle she's stashed in the house."

Cassidy watched warily while he went through the kitchen. She'd gotten so good at hiding her emotions, but they were there, they were weighing her down. He could see it, and he knew how to help her process them.

After searching the last cabinet, he found an empty box in the pantry and loaded up three bottles of wine, a brand-new bottle of vodka, and a half-empty bottle of gin. He carried the box out the front door with Cassidy following close behind.

"I'm telling you, she'll find it in the trash. She always finds it."

"It's not going in the trash." He carted the box to the sidewalk and set it at the edge of the street.

Cassidy watched him with a curious frown.

Levi selected the large bottle of vodka and held it out to her. "Smash it," he said. "Throw it in the street."

"What?" She stared at him, her jaw hinged open. "I can't throw it in the street. That'll make a huge mess."

"I'll clean it up. Every tiny piece," he promised. "So it's okay. You can smash it."

She looked at the bottle and then back at him.

"You know you want to."

A slow smile reached her eyes. She took the bottle out of his hands and raised it in the air and then hesitated. He slipped behind her, his chest to her back, and held his hand over hers against the bottle.

"One, two, three," he murmured, and jerked his arm down. They both let go, and the bottle shattered against the asphalt.

Cassidy stared down at the mess, her eyes wide.

Levi eased closer to her, unable to stay away. He'd been away from her for too long.

"I can't believe I did that." She turned her face to his.

He grinned. "It felt good, didn't it?"

She nodded slowly, as though it stunned her.

He picked up one of the wine bottles and pressed it into her hands. "Smash it. As hard as you can."

She looked at it for a second as though reading the label and then raised it into the air. With a scream, she let that thing fly into the street. "I hate it! I hate this stuff!" Cass frantically snatched another bottle from the box. "And I hate that I have to babysit my mother!" She slammed the gin down, the sound of shattering glass echoing around them. "I hate that Dad left me to deal with all of this!" She marched right through the broken glass on her way back to the box.

"Whoa. Careful." Levi reached to steer her around the glass, but she jerked away and grabbed another bottle. "And I hate that Cash died!" *Crash.* Another wave of glass scattered across the street. "He didn't have to die!" She turned to Levi then, her eyes wild with rage as she grabbed the last bottle. Violent breaths raised her shoulders. "You're just like him," she said, pointing the bottle in Levi's direction.

"What?" Oh shit, he was in her line of fire.

"You're just like him," she yelled, raising the bottle higher. She sounded mad as hell, but tears streamed down her cheeks. "You're just like Cash!" She took a step closer, as though she didn't want to miss when she chucked the bottle at his head. "You're reckless and you're selfish and you have no right to make me care about you!"

Her pain—pain he'd caused—drove straight into him. "I'm not like him, Cass." His boots crunched through the glass until he got close enough that she could see into his eyes. She couldn't scare him off with a bottle. She could hit him with it, knock him down, and he'd get right back up, ready to take another blow if that's what she needed from him. "Maybe I was once. Maybe I was reckless and stupid and too blind to see what was right in front of me, but I'm not that kid anymore." He'd grown up. And he knew what he wanted.

She cried harder, the bottle still raised above her head, shaking in her hand.

"You don't have to care about me." He closed the distance between them and carefully took the bottle away to toss it aside. Then he lifted her chin and stared deeply into her eyes so she'd know the truth. "But I will always care about you."

Cassidy collapsed against him with a sob, and he closed his arms around her. She felt warm in his embrace. Warm and soft and perfect.

"I'm so tired," she cried, resting her forehead against his shoulder.

"I know." He wrapped her as tightly as he could, wanting to be the one who held her together.

She moved to glance up at him, her forehead grazing his chin on the way. "Why are you here?" she whispered again.

The answer had become so simple. "Because I need to be." If he'd known how it felt to hold her in his arms, he would've been here his whole life. But she'd always been off-limits. Cash had warned him once that he would no longer be a part of their family if Levi ever touched his sister. But his friend was gone now and Levi had to believe he'd be glad someone wanted to take care of her.

"You needed me to be here a long time ago but I wasn't. I let you down." Seeing just how much he'd let her down dealt a crushing blow. "I'm here now though," he murmured, lowering his face to hers. "I'm not going anywhere."

Her eyes still glistened from the earlier tears. And hell, she was striking, those blue eyes and her flawless skin.

A breath eased out of him, leaving behind a stark emptiness only she could fill. He clasped his hands at the small of her back and pressed her into him.

She gasped when he covered her lips with his, and for a second, he thought she would pull back, but she didn't. Her arms reached up and wrapped around his neck, drawing him closer. Together, their lips found a rhythm he'd never experienced with anyone else, savoring and sensual.

Cass inched closer, fitting her curves tightly against him.

Red-hot lust curled through him, waking his body. He glided his hands up her back and held her head in place as his tongue swept through her mouth.

A faint whimper came from her throat.

"I can't believe I've never kissed you before," he uttered between tastes of her. Had he ever been this turned on by a kiss?

"Cash would've killed you," she panted, sliding her hands into his hair.

"Would've been worth the risk." He dragged his lips over to her neck and traced his tongue down her soft skin. He wanted to keep going, all the way down her chest, but there were so many clothes...

And they were standing in the street. "We should go inside," he murmured, finding her lips again. Straight to her bedroom so he could take her away from the stress and complications of her life.

"We can't go inside." She brushed soft kisses across his jaw. "My mom is in there."

"Right." He groaned. His lips grazed hers. They didn't need to go inside. They had his truck. The backseat was pretty big...

Closing his arms around her, he hoisted her against him, still kissing the hell out of her, and danced her toward the truck. With one hand, he groped the door until he found the handle and threw the thing open. As she climbed in, his hands wandered, caressing the sexy curves of her body.

"What about your head injury?" she gasped between staccato breaths.

"What injury?" There was nothing. No pain. Only a deepening ache to feel her against him.

As she lay down on the backseat, Levi climbed in and straddled her waist, catching her hands to pin them against the seat cushion just above her head. Before kissing her again, he stared down at her, at the shine of her blue eyes, at her wild blond hair. "You're a beautiful woman, Cass." But it was her heart and strength that made her perfect for him.

Why the hell had this just now occurred to him? He could've been kissing her—making love to her—for years.

"What are we doing?" she asked him, still breathless

from all the kissing. Or maybe breathless with the same anticipation that pounded through him.

"We're making out in my truck." He couldn't wait. Not when he'd already wasted so much time. He bent and lowered his lips to hers.

She sighed as she kissed him back, tugging on his shoulders until he was lying on top of her.

Easing to his side, he turned her body to his, sealing her lips in a long, hot kiss. Her mouth was so insistent.

Pulling back, he traced his finger along her jaw and then her neck, until he could unbutton her shirt. He kissed his way down, his chin grazing the edge of her bra.

"God, Levi," she murmured as he slipped his fingers beneath the lace.

"Just wait." He brought his lips back to her neck. Her soft skin smelled like some kind of succulent flower. He reached around her back to pop the clasp of her bra, but a clink against the window hijacked his focus. The beam of a high-powered flashlight cut into his vision.

"Hey," he growled, shielding his eyes.

"Sorry," Dev called from outside the window.

"Dev!" Cass scrambled to sit up, fumbling with the buttons on her shirt. "Oh great. Just great. What are the cops doing here?"

"Don't know, but I'll get rid of him." Levi cranked open the door. "Can I help you?"

The deputy cleared his throat like he was trying not to laugh. "Got reports of someone breaking glass in the street. There's quite a mess over there."

"Yeah. I was gonna clean that up." But he'd gotten distracted in the best way.

Cassidy poked her head over Levi's shoulder. "Sorry,

Dev. I was having a moment. Found a bunch of alcohol in the house and wanted to get rid of it."

"I could see how that would be romantic," he teased, eyeing Levi.

He had half a mind to slam the door shut on Dev's arm. "I'll clean it up. Promise." *Now get out of here...*

But Dev was obviously enjoying himself too much to leave. Humor glimmered in his dark eyes. "Usually when I bust a couple for making out in a car, they're sixteen."

"Yeah, well neither of us have our own place." He had to fix that. Soon.

"There's always the inn," Dev suggested. "I bet Lucas and Naomi would give you a sweet discount."

"That's okay." Cass patted her hair back into place. "It's getting late anyway. I need to get back inside." She scooted past Levi and hopped out of the truck. She didn't even glance over her shoulder on her way into the house.

Dev seemed to take that as his cue to leave. "Have a good night." He shot a stern look at Levi. "Make sure you clean up the glass."

"I'm on it," Levi muttered, his lips still burning. He headed toward the garage to look for a broom. Just his luck Dev would interrupt and give Cassidy an excuse to run away from him. He wouldn't let that happen again.

The next time he kissed her, he'd make sure he had plenty of time to prove how much he wanted her.

Chapter Seven

"Come on, Mom. Hurry!" Cassidy hustled Lulu past the corral fence toward the entrance to Jessa's Helping Paws Animal Shelter, keeping an eye out for a certain Cortez brother.

Her mother continued to mosey as though they were out for a stroll in a rose garden. "I don't see why I should have to run just because you won't return Levi's calls." Lulu sure had a lot of opinions now that she'd quit drinking.

Cassidy waited for her to catch up. "I haven't had time to return his calls." She'd been too busy babysitting her mother 24/7 to make sure she didn't restock her secret supply. Hence the reason she'd had to bring Lulu with her to the book club meeting at the shelter this evening. She still didn't trust her.

"A polite phone call takes five minutes," her mother reminded her. Back in the day, Lulu Greer had been a stickler for good manners.

"I'll get around to it. Promise." She took her mother's arm and urged her on. First, she had to figure out what she wanted to say to Levi about that kiss. Then she had to figure out how to make sure a kiss like that didn't happen again. It was just her luck that Jessa had moved their meeting from Darla's place to the shelter tonight.

Under normal circumstances, Cassidy loved visiting her friend here. A few years back, Lance had converted an old barn into an animal shelter to surprise Jessa. The structure still had that old charm—barn-red siding with crisp white trim—but inside it was stocked with all of the modern equipment and supplies Jessa needed to rehabilitate animals and find them homes. Over the years, Cassidy had helped out at the shelter as much as she could, so, in some ways, if felt like a second home to her. It didn't matter how stressed she was or how bad things were with Lulu, the animals never failed to cheer her up.

But that was before. Before Levi had been around the ranch so much. Before he'd turned all sweet on her. Before *The Kiss*—a story-changing chapter in her life. The knowledge that Levi lurked somewhere nearby right now made Cassidy want to put her Nikes to full use.

Finally, she got her mother to the door without any cowboy sightings. Before she could knock, it swung open. "I have puppies!" Jessa held up a basket of six teeny-tiny squirming fuzz balls.

"Puppies!" Cassidy nudged her mother inside and quickly shut the door behind them. When she looked up and saw Darla and Naomi already sitting on the leather loveseats in the waiting area, she locked the deadbolt for good measure.

"Aren't they darling?" Lulu peered into the basket.

Yes, they were. All of them were a beautiful chestnut color, so fluffy and new. It was almost enough to distract Cassidy from her worry about running into Levi.

"I'm estimating they're about four weeks old. Cocker spaniel mixes." Jessa set the basket on the coffee table. "Someone found them abandoned near the campground outside of town, along with the momma." She pointed to a dog bed that lay in the corner across the room. A matted, pathetic-looking dog barely raised her head, even with all the visitors.

Jessa sighed. "Haven't gotten her to perk up yet. Can't find anything wrong with her, but all she wants to do is lie around."

"Poor, sweet thing." Lulu wandered over and knelt, slowly reaching out her hand so the dog could sniff it.

The dog took her time nosing Lulu's hand before sitting up and licking her.

"She likes you," Jessa said with a wink at Cass.

Her mother smiled. "I like her too."

"Would you like to take her out?" Jessa walked over and took a leash off a hook on the wall. "She hasn't been out for a while. It would do her good."

Joy pinged around Cassidy's chest at the way Lulu's face lit up. It was such a rare sight.

"I'd love to."

"You can walk her down to the meadow." Jessa hurried over to the dog and clipped on the leash before handing it over.

"The meadow?" Cassidy sat straighter. "Like outside?" Where Levi might see her? The whole reason she'd parked her car down the hill was so he wouldn't see it if he happened to go out to the corral.

"Yes, outside." Confusion furrowed Jessa's forehead. "Where else would the dog go potty?"

Cassidy didn't have a good answer.

"Does she have a name?" Lulu asked, already leading the dog toward the door.

"No. I didn't find a collar or anything." Jessa unlocked the deadbolt and shot Cassidy a questioning glance.

She occupied herself with lifting a puppy out of the basket and cuddling it against her chest.

"I'll call her Sweetie then," Lulu said as though she'd made up her mind. "Come on, Sweetie. Let's go out for a walk."

"Don't go too far, Mom," Cassidy called as Lulu stepped out the door. *And don't go find Levi and drag him up here.*

Her mother waved and then disappeared.

Jessa closed the door before coming over to join Cassidy on the loveseat. "Is there a reason you locked the deadbolt?" she asked pointedly.

The three women looked at her as though they knew something was up, so what was the point in denying it? "Levi kissed me," she blurted. "Like *really* kissed me." If Dev hadn't interrupted, she was almost positive things would've happened in the backseat of Levi's truck. Big things. Things that couldn't be undone.

"Well, that sounds a hell of a lot more interesting than this." Darla slipped her paperback into her purse.

Naomi clasped her hands under her chin with a smirk. "I knew your cheeks were glowing."

All of her was glowing. Every neglected nook and cranny of her body. The longing he'd stirred up still burned through her pulse points. "I can't believe I let it happen." She was still trying to understand it. When she'd seen him standing on her lawn, emotions had clashed—anger and curiosity and fear. So much fear. She didn't like the way her body reacted to him. Didn't like the way every part of her seemed to come alive when she saw him.

And before that…he'd been so sweet to her mom, so careful with her as he helped her down from the tree. Cassidy wasn't sure how she would've made it through that whole horrible scene without him. And then shattering those bottles in the street had been the best therapy she'd ever experienced…

"Hell, I'd let it happen," Darla said with a smirk. "Levi is hotter than sin."

Jessa and Naomi shared grossed-out looks. Being married to his brothers obviously cast him in a different light.

"Why can't you believe it?" Jessa asked as though Cassidy's naïveté amused her. "You're single, he's single. You two have known each other for years…"

"I'm sure not surprised," Naomi chimed in, rubbing her baby bump. "I think it's fabulous."

"It's not." Cassidy nuzzled her nose into the puppy's soft fur, smelling that skunky, new puppy-breath scent. "This is Levi. He's a total Casanova." At least that's what she'd heard when he'd been out on the circuit. That was a problem because, when he'd taken her face in his hands and kissed her, her heart had opened, responding to him in a way she never had to anyone else.

She didn't want to love someone. She couldn't let herself. When she'd lost Cash, the grief had almost killed her. And there were plenty of other reasons it would be a bad idea. "He's not serious about anything except for getting a woman into bed." Or into the backseat of his truck, apparently. She cuddled the puppy into her lap. "Besides that, I interviewed for a residency program in Denver."

"Denver?" Naomi echoed.

"Say what?" Darla demanded.

This wasn't how she'd planned to tell them. She hadn't wanted word to get out until she'd heard from the director, but now she didn't have a choice. It gave her the perfect out with Levi. "There's a pediatric residency program at Children's in Denver. And my interview went really well. They should call any day."

Her friends traded around smiles, but she knew them well enough to recognize they weren't exactly happy.

"I'll come back and visit a lot," she promised. Out of everyone in Topaz Falls, she'd miss these women the most. They were the ones who'd been there for her, who'd made her laugh when all she wanted to do was cry, who'd forced her to put down her school books to go out for a girls' night when she needed it the most. "But if I get in, I'm moving to Denver in July."

"Of course you'll get in," Jessa murmured as though trying to keep a hold on her emotions.

Naomi didn't even try. Tears already brightened her eyes. "It sounds like a great opportunity."

"Which is why I can't start something with Levi right now. I want this new career so much." All through school, it had been her goal. To work with kids, to make a difference for families. "And I've already got my hands full trying to get my mother in good shape so I can go. Which means I don't have time for a relationship." Time or the capability.

"Now you listen to me, honey." Darla scooted to the edge of the couch, her expressive brown eyes somber. "You don't have to have a relationship, but you deserve a good fling. You've spent so much time taking care of your mom that you haven't taken care of yourself."

"She's right," Jessa agreed. "Why not have a little fun this summer? Especially if you're only here through July. Let Levi take you out and spoil you..."

Darla rolled her eyes. "I think what she means is, let him make all of your fantasies come true."

"I don't think so." A fling with Levi would be a dangerous prospect. There was too much history between them, a whole lifetime of memories woven together. Something told her getting involved with Levi would be a lot more complicated than hooking up.

"Maybe you could have more than a fling." Naomi's voice still wobbled. "Levi has changed a lot this past year. I could see him being ready for something more serious."

"He really has." Jessa nodded emphatically. "I mean, he seems more settled now. And he's worked so hard to make a difference in the town this last year."

"Yes, but—"

"And have you seen how attentive he is to Luis these days?" Naomi asked. It seemed neither of them were willing to let Cassidy get in a word.

"Who cares about that?" Darla dismissed them both with a wave of her hand. "He's as sexy as a Hemsworth brother and probably just as experienced in satisfying a woman, if you know what I mean."

Oh, she knew what Darla meant. She knew from personal experience. Levi's kiss had promised a whole hell of a lot. Why else would she have let him lead her to his truck in T minus two minutes?

* * *

"You ready for this, Cortez?" Ty zipped up his pro vest and walked the length of the bucking chute as though sizing up his competition.

Reckoning II tossed his head and snorted, already pissed off.

"Yeah, I'm ready." Levi adjusted his own safety gear, making sure to tighten the strap on his helmet. He was far more experienced in riding bulls than he was in luring them back to the chute, but being out of commission made him bored as hell, so he figured stepping in as a bullfighter while Ty trained would at least get him into the corral.

"Hell, I don't know if I'm ready." Mateo couldn't seem to stop staring at Reckoning II. Over the last year, the behemoth had become one of the most sought-after bulls for competitions across the country. Levi had ridden him only three times, and three times he'd been bucked in less than four seconds.

Yet this is what Ty wanted. When he'd asked them to make an appearance at the rodeo, the three other Renegades had agreed to hang out for a couple of weeks in between competitions, as long as they had plenty of training time. Free lodging and a chance to hone their skills had meant more to them than money.

Besides that, summer in the mountains could charm anyone. It'd sure charmed him back into thinking he might want to make Topaz Falls a more permanent home again. Stuck in Oklahoma all those years, he'd forgotten the power of the mountains, the hypnotizing pull of the pristine royal sky, the grayish-purple peaks that met its shimmering horizon, and the soft green mountainsides that rolled down into the valleys. It was pretty much paradise.

And Reckoning II was pretty much the best practice a rider could get.

"You can't bail on me now," Levi reminded Mateo. Neither one of them had any training for this. So once Reckoning bucked Ty—and the bull would buck Ty—they'd work together to lure it back to the chute before anyone got injured. At least that was the plan.

"This guy makes my bronc look like a kitten."

Levi grinned at Mateo. "Just run fast." That was his strategy. Once they got Reckoning's attention, Levi planned to beat his best time for the hundred-yard dash.

"Hi, fellas."

Levi turned. Cassidy's mom was walking a dog on the other side of the driveway. She didn't look much different than she had when he'd seen her last week during the treehouse debacle, but at least she seemed sober. "Hey, Lulu." As he walked over, he did a quick scan of the area for Cass, but there was no sign of her. "What're you up to?"

"I told Jessa I'd take this sweetie for a walk while the girls have their book club meeting."

"Book club, huh?" So that meant Cassidy had to be around somewhere. Likely still hiding from him. He'd left her three messages and stopped by the house twice since he'd kissed her, and so far she'd managed to elude him.

Lulu leaned in closer. "Well, they say they read books, but I think they mostly eat a lot of chocolate and gossip."

Levi laughed. He had a feeling he knew exactly what they were gossiping about this evening. Too bad he couldn't find a glass and listen through the wall like he used to when they were kids.

Lulu reached down to pet the dog. "What are you three up to?" she asked, glancing across the corral to Mateo and Ty, who were still evaluating the bull.

"Ty wanted to do some training, so Mateo and I will be

filling in as bullfighters since Tucker's visiting his mom." Yeah, the idea didn't sound much better out loud than it had in his head.

Judging from her frown, Lulu didn't think it was a good idea either. "You sure you're healed up enough after that bump on your head?"

"I hardly noticed it." No headaches, no dizziness, and yet he still had another three weeks of sitting around. At least. Damn concussion protocols.

"Well, I'd better get Sweetie back into the clinic." Lulu made smooching sounds in the dog's direction. "Come on, girl." She tugged gently on the leash and looked back over her shoulder. "You boys be careful now. Understand?"

The glimpse of the old Lulu made him smile. He'd heard that same phrase from her a hundred times in another life. "We'll be careful," he promised before heading back to his friends.

"We gotta do this now. Before I lose my nerve." Ty was already climbing up on the fence to slide onto the bull's broad back.

"All right." Levi got into position to open the gate. "Mateo, you head down to the south side of the corral and be ready."

"Don't think it's possible to be ready," he muttered, but he went anyway.

Levi looked up at Ty. "Count of three?"

His friend nodded gravely.

"One...two..." Ty slid onto the bull's back. "Three!" Levi threw open the gate, and Reckoning II charged through the dirt, jumping and kicking and jerking—throwing Ty around like an amateur instead of a decorated rider.

Levi followed at a jog and met Mateo in the center of the

corral. They didn't have to wait long. Three seconds into the ride, Reckoning II had had enough. The bull arched his back and put on the brakes, sending their friend flying head-over-ass into the dirt.

A shot of adrenaline burned down Levi's legs. *Here we go.* He waved his arms and flagged down the bull. "Hey, Reckoning," he taunted. "Over here, big guy!"

The bull turned and pawed the ground before launching into an all-out sprint right at them.

"Shit!" Both he and Mateo spun and hotfooted it toward the chute. At the last second, they dodged right and ducked the fence, but Reckoning ran straight through the open gate.

"Gotcha!" Levi swung it closed and clicked the latch into place. He leaned against the post to catch his breath.

"Whew!" Ty jumped up and shook off the dirt. "That was one hell of a ri—!"

"What do you think you're doing?"

At the sound of Cassidy's voice, Levi stood up straight. She stomped around the outside of the fence, her eyes narrowed and her movements branded with fury.

"Uh-oh," Ty muttered.

"Busted," Mateo added. The two of them hightailed it to the other side of the corral.

"What the hell were you doing?" she asked again as she approached. "Mom said you're standing in as a bullfighter. Please tell me she's wrong."

If she thought anger would drive him away from her, she was dead wrong. It was actually quite the turn-on. "I was luring the bull away from Ty," he said simply. And he'd done a damn good job of it too.

"Are you kidding me?" Her face flushed. "With a concussion?"

"It's not like I was riding the bull."

"It doesn't matter! He was running straight at you!"

"And we got him back into the chute."

"Unbelievable." Cassidy spun and started to walk away. Only then did he notice her hands were shaking. She wasn't angry. She was scared.

Damn. He trotted to catch up with her. "Hey, everything's fine. No one got hurt."

She paused. "You told me you're nothing like Cash anymore. You said you've grown up."

"I have." He was following the damn concussion protocols, wasn't he? There was no way he would've done that when he was nineteen.

Cassidy looked right through him. "A grown-up would take a concussion seriously."

"I'm sorry. I didn't mean to scare you." He swept his hand down her arm, but she shook him off and walked away.

"Do whatever you want, Levi. I don't care."

And yet obviously she did.

Chapter Eight

Whenever he needed solid advice, Levi always found himself heading to his father's breakfast table. He'd been trying to make himself scarce around Luis's place, making sure to give the two lovebirds some nights alone, but he actually missed spending the evenings with his old man. Not that Jessa wasn't going out of her way to make him feel welcome when he stayed. Last night, she'd even changed his sheets and left chocolate mints on his pillow.

But in the mornings, he'd gotten used to sitting across from his father, drinking a cup of bitter cowboy coffee while they discussed whatever happened to be on Levi's mind. Over the last year, he'd come to rely on his father as he went through the process of taking responsibility for his past mistakes. He never would've made it through without his dad on his side. The man had helped him rebuild his confidence and his courage, advising him gently but also calling him out when he needed it. And he needed it now.

He hadn't seen Cassidy at all lately. According to Jessa, she'd been working a lot. He'd tried calling. He'd tried stopping by. But after what had happened in the corral the other day, she seemed determined to keep him out of her life. So here he was, trucking down the driveway to his father's house, hoping the man had some stellar advice because he had no idea what to do.

He took the porch steps two at a time and went to open the screen door but stopped when he saw the small piece of paper taped to the wood. It was a note, scrawled in his father's writing.

Lance, Jessa, Lucas, Naomi, Gracie, and Levi,

Evie and I left to drive to the Gulf Coast. We're getting married. We talked last night and realized we don't want to wait. Life is too short, and this woman makes me happier than I've ever been. We didn't make plans. As Evie likes to say, we're living in the moment. I hope you'll understand. We would've told you but we didn't want anyone to make a fuss. We're planning to be back before the baby is born and will see you all soon.

Dad and Evie

Levi ripped the note off the door and stumbled backward. A smile came first and then a laugh. "Way to go, Dad." The last few years, nothing about Luis Cortez had been spontaneous. Or impulsive. It seemed Evie had influenced him in the best possible way. Or maybe it hadn't been impulsive. Maybe his father had taken him up on his offer to move out so he could bring home a wife.

He read the note again as he hiked up to Lance's house. If anyone deserved happiness, it was his father. There'd been a time Levi had thought the man would never remarry. After their mother left, he'd gotten himself into trouble messing around with different women in town—some of them married. At the time, Levi had hated him for it. Now though, he understood what loneliness could do to a person.

He busted through the door into Lance and Jessa's house. They were seated at the table finishing their breakfast.

Jessa stood quickly, looking concerned. "I'm so sorry. I didn't make you a plate. I thought you were having breakfast with Luis."

"I was going to." He held up the note. "But it seems Dad and Evie took a little road trip." He couldn't help but laugh again.

"What? Where'd they go?" His brother snatched the paper out of his hand.

Wait for it...

"Holy. Shit." Lance lowered the note and gaped at him. "Did you know about this?"

"I was as surprised as you." Their father didn't exactly open up about these kinds of things.

"Know about what?" Jessa didn't take kindly to being left out of any family business. She liked to *run* the family's personal business.

Lance suddenly looked panicked. He tried to hide the note behind his back. Levi didn't blame him. She wouldn't take too kindly to being left out of a wedding either.

His brother might've been strong, but his wife was quick. She stole that note out of his hand before he could dodge out of the way.

"What?" she gasped as her eyes scanned the paper. "Are

you kidding me?" She waved the note in Lance's face. "I could've thrown them a wedding. We could've done it right out there in the pasture..."

Levi took a seat at the kitchen table. They'd likely be here a while.

"We could've had the new reverend do the ceremony. Oh! And Gracie would've been adorable in that dress I made her." She paced in front of her husband. "I don't understand. Why wouldn't they want us there?"

Lance glanced at Levi, an understanding passing between them. "Because that's not how Dad is. You know how much he hates to be the center of attention."

"I know, but this is his *wedding*. There should be music and friends and flowers and cake. They're not even going to have a wedding cake!"

"Can't imagine why he was worried anyone would make a fuss," Levi mumbled, all in good fun, of course.

Lance seemed to be losing the battle against a smile that might very well get him in trouble with his wife.

"So I like celebrations," Jessa huffed. "And weddings. It's supposed to be the happiest day of your life. I can't imagine why anyone wouldn't want to be surrounded by their friends and family."

"Aw, come on, baby." His brother pulled his wife into his arms. "How about you plan a small party for them when they get back? A low-key reception where we can all celebrate together."

"I guess that'd be okay." She still had a scowl on her face, but she returned Lance's embrace.

When his brother started to kiss her, that was it. Levi was out. "I'll see you two later," he called on his way to the door.

They didn't seem to hear him.

Outside, he headed for the corral. Mateo, Ty, and Charity would be there soon. He'd promised them a stellar morning of training on some of the finest stock the Cortez Ranch had to offer. This time, he would only be supervising.

As soon as they left though, he'd track Cassidy down. He'd go to her house, to her work…hell, he'd even show up at her hair appointment if that's where she was. If her behavior lately had told him anything, it was that she wanted him too.

She was just too afraid to admit it.

* * *

Levi kicked back in the lawn chair he'd positioned between the Cortez Ranch's two outdoor corrals and sipped the health smoothie Jessa had brought him, insisting it would speed up his healing time.

On one side of him, Mateo and Ty were taking turns trying to break Ball Buster for fun, and as of yet, neither had succeeded. In the other corral, Charity raced across the mud on her trusty stead, Ace, her body crouched, long blond hair sailing behind her, doing her damnedest to beat her fastest barrel racing time.

As much as it pained him to not be out there with them, Levi was sitting in a chair acting like a grown-up and taking his concussion seriously. He was also making a to-do list. Far as he figured, the youth rodeo clinic would serve two purposes. One, it would give him an excuse to spend more time with Cass. Two, it would help her to see that the sport could actually be fun. She was obviously still traumatized from losing Cash that way, and he got it. But the rodeo wasn't about being immature and reckless; it was about competing and pushing yourself and learning the value of discipline and hard work. Those were the things that had made him grow up. Maybe being close to it would help her understand why he still rode, even after he'd lost his friend.

Okay. So. A to-do list...Well, he'd already booked the rodeo facility and had a friend at the print shop make up a flyer. So he supposed the next thing he should do was convince the other Renegades to stick around longer and help him out. He just had to decide the best way to ask for another favor.

"Did you finish the drink?" Jessa walked over, carrying a tray full of lemonades along with a bowl of fresh-cut fruit and cheese and crackers. She set the refreshments down on the small table she'd set up next to him. The woman was thoughtful like that. Always taking care of people, cooking for everyone, complimenting them. How Lance managed to snag her, he'd never know.

"I've chewed on grass that tastes better than that drink," he told her. He'd managed to choke down a few sips but one more would have had him gagging.

"It has nutrients and calcium," she informed him. "Exactly what you need so you can get back on your bull."

"I'm not in a hurry." He stood to help her arrange the food and drinks on the table. "I've got plans this summer. Goals I can't accomplish on the back of a bull."

"Oh, really?" She eyed him. "Like what?"

He swiped one of the lemonades. Man, the glass was even frosted. "Let's just say I need to win something other than a purse before the end of July." He needed to win over Cass, and he couldn't do it without help.

A knowing smile raised her eyebrows. "Ah, yes. Cassidy told us all about your little kiss."

"*Little* kiss?" There hadn't been anything little about that kiss. Over a week later, it was still simmering on his lips, but Cassidy wouldn't even return any of his phone calls. "What'd she say about it?" he prompted.

"What is shared at book club stays at book club," the woman said sternly, but her eyes glimmered. He happened to know that Jessa was a hopeless romantic. She'd do anything to help two people find true love.

"Just tell me how hard it'll be to convince her to give me a shot." That was all he needed. To know what he was up against.

"Well, hmmm." Her eyes rolled up to stare at the sky as though she had to think about that. "Let's just say I think you'd have an easier time convincing Reckoning II to roll over."

Ouch. "Seriously?"

"She's planning to leave Topaz Falls." The words were ten percent sympathetic and ninety percent berating. "You had years to pursue her. You didn't."

"I know." He'd been too busy taking his sweet time to grow up. "She sure didn't seem to mind when I kissed her though," he said, fishing for anything he could get.

"No. Judging from the way she blushed when she was talking about it, I'd say she didn't mind at all."

So he hadn't imagined the way Cass had sighed and clung to him. Or her fiery reaction to him when she'd caught him being a bullfighter. She cared about him too. "How can I change her mind?" There had to be a way.

"Spend time with her." Jessa might as well have added a *duh* at the end of the sentence. "Without trying to get her into bed," she added.

"I'd love to spend time with her but she won't return my

calls." It'd be mighty hard to spend time with her if she kept avoiding him.

His sister-in-law glanced around and then leaned in. "She and her mom are having lunch at the Farm today," she whispered. "But you didn't hear that from me."

"Right." He finished off his lemonade and set down the empty glass. Give him sugar over grass any day. "Then tell Lance we won't be needing burgers for lunch. I'll take these guys out to the Farm instead."

"What've we got here?" Ty asked, approaching the table. The other two followed.

"I'm starving," Charity said, ripping off her helmet and setting it on his chair.

"It's only a few snacks," Jessa said.

"Too bad you're married," Mateo said, looking her over. "You like to prepare snacks, and I like to eat."

She laughed. "Happily married," she confirmed. "But we can't thank you enough for what you've done for this town. That rodeo really brought people together. We wouldn't have had nearly the turnout if you all hadn't come."

Wasn't that the truth? Without Raines's Renegades, he never would've gotten a sellout. Without Raines's Renegades, he wouldn't be able to pull off the youth rodeo clinic either.

"I was going to have Lance whip up some burgers for lunch, but Levi wants to take you out instead." Jessa gave him a conspiratorial wink.

"Out?" A look of suspicion tightened Charity's jaw. "What's the occasion?"

"It's a business meeting," he said carefully. "I have a proposition for you three." Or more likely he'd end up begging them to help.

"What kind of proposition?" Charity asked warily. "This isn't gonna be like that photo shoot in Vegas, is it?"

He laughed. He'd gotten a tip on a casino that wanted some big names from the rodeo world to do a western-themed campaign, but when they'd shown up, it turned out they wanted Charity to wear a string bikini. "No. It's nothing like that. It's actually another event. A rodeo clinic. For kids."

"Oh boy," Ty muttered.

"Here we go," Mateo grumbled.

"Come on, guys. Hear me out." Levi dug his truck key out of his pocket. "We can discuss it over lunch." He'd order some of those grass-fed T-bone steaks to butter them up.

And he wouldn't take no for an answer.

Chapter Nine

Deep down, Cassidy knew you couldn't solve someone's issues by changing their appearance, but it hadn't stopped her from trying.

"You look so pretty, Mom." Sitting across the table from Lulu Greer, you'd never guess she had a problem. Before they'd come to the Farm for lunch, Cassidy had woken her at seven o'clock in the morning and made her a big, healthy breakfast. Then she'd dug in the back of her mom's closet until she'd found the clothes she used to wear, selecting white capri pants and a light blue silk blouse.

After breakfast, they'd gone to the beauty salon where her mom had gotten her hair cut into a stylish bob. Then they sat side-by-side in those obnoxious massage chairs for manicures and pedicures. It was the most put together Lulu had looked in a long time, and yet even though she was smiling and chatting while they ate their salads, her eyes were still dull. Almost fearful. As though she knew the passing moments of happiness were only temporary.

Cassidy couldn't stare into those eyes for too long or she'd fear it too—that the spell would be broken when they got back home—and Lulu would go back to being miserable and stuck. She couldn't go back. They couldn't go back. As far as she knew, her mom hadn't had a drink for over a week, but she still rarely smiled. She wasn't happy.

That was why, after Cassidy had gotten home from work last night, she'd come up with a schedule for their day. A way to keep her mom busy, to remind her of the life she used to live. She had to keep giving her glimpses until Lulu was strong enough to reach out and grasp it again.

"Noticed you were running low so I brought you more tea." Everly Brooks bustled over to their table just in time. She carefully removed two tall glasses of iced pomegranate tea from the tray and set them down.

"Thank you," Cassidy said, relieved by the interruption. She liked Everly, though she didn't know much about her. The woman was new in town. She'd shown up about a year ago and leased the land to start an organic farm. Within only a couple of months, her preserves and homemade baked goods were so popular that she'd turned the summer house on the property into a humble restaurant where she served up farm-to-table dishes you couldn't find anywhere else.

"How are the salads?" Everly clasped her hands in front of her waist nervously. The woman was maybe a few years older than Cassidy. She had a quirky cuteness about her with short, curly reddish-brown hair and sparkling green eyes, and even though she was quiet, she smiled a lot. Today she wore a polka-dotted apron with a pink paisley bandanna tied on her head.

"They're delicious," Lulu said, though Cassidy noticed she'd hardly eaten anything. "Such a charming place you have here."

Charming and quaint, which was why Cassidy loved it so much. The main dining area had been set up in the house's living room, with original oak wood floors and a redbrick hearth on the back wall. There were only about ten tables— all basic farmhouse style with bench seats. Through the leaded glass picture windows, glimpses of the farm made it feel like you'd stepped back in time. There were chickens and goats running around in generous pens and huge plots of vibrantly colored vegetables scattered around the large acreage.

"I'm so glad you're enjoying everything." Everly's face beamed. "Please let me know if you need anything else." She quickly moved to the next table and busied herself with filling Hank Green's water glass.

Which meant they had no more interruptions and Cassidy was forced to have the conversation she'd been waiting to have all morning. Trying to build courage, she sipped her pomegranate iced tea and smiled at her mother. "So, Mom…this afternoon, I thought we'd go out and find you a job." A good, steady, low-stress job would be key to maintaining stability in her life.

"A job?" Lulu set down her fork. "Oh, honey. I don't know if that's a good idea right now."

Cassidy didn't flinch. She'd anticipated that reaction so she'd prepared. "What was your favorite part about being a mail carrier?" she asked pointedly. Lulu had to know what she was after.

Sure enough, her mom's gaze dropped to the table. "The people. I loved having an excuse to talk to all those people."

"Exactly. People have always made you happy, but now you're so isolated. It would be good for you to get out there again. Interact with people on a daily basis. You're so good with people." When all else failed, flattery was the best motivator. "Maybe it would help give you a sense of purpose."

Lulu quietly pulled her hands into her lap. Her shoulders bent under an unseen weight again, as though the spell had already been broken and she was reverting back into the unsure woman who wanted to hide in her house. "I'm not the same person, Cass. I know what you want me to be. But I don't think I can."

"You don't have to be the same person." Cassidy pushed her plate away too. "Neither of us can be the same as we were before Cash died, but we can honor his memory in the way we live." Which meant giving back, contributing, standing for something. Which meant putting themselves out there. "I know the flower shop is hiring."

Lulu shook her head. "You know how my allergies are."

"Fine. What about—"

"Well, hello, ladies."

Damn. It. There was the voice from her hot, lustful dreams as of late. Right on time. How did Levi always seem to show up when she was at her most vulnerable? She looked right through him.

"Levi!" Her mom quickly scooted over, making room for him. "Won't you join us?"

"Only for a minute." Aiming that smart-ass grin at Cassidy, he slid onto the bench next to her mother. "I've got the Renegades over there. We're having a business meeting."

Cassidy glanced at the table near the door. Charity, Mateo, and Ty all waved at her. She waved back but didn't react to Levi. He had only a minute. She could stay silent for a minute.

"What kind of business meeting?" her mother asked politely.

"I'm glad you asked." His gaze wouldn't leave her alone.

Though she wanted to, she couldn't glance away. Did he have to look so damn good all the time? The sharp angle of his cheekbones and jaw made him look strong and determined. And she swore those hazel eyes had hypnotic powers.

"We're actually here to discuss the junior rodeo clinic I'm sponsoring in July." He leaned forward as though wanting to capture her attention, but he already had it. He'd had it the second she'd heard his voice.

"I'm still counting on your help, by the way," he said to Cassidy, his gaze lowering to her lips. "I'll need all kinds of assistance."

She slid her hands under her thighs to keep them steady. "I don't have a lot of time."

"I think it sounds like a wonderful idea." Her mother gave him a nod of approval. "Cassidy was just saying how much she wanted to find a way to honor Cash's memory."

"Um, that's not exactly what I was saying." She'd been talking about *living* to honor Cash's memory. Not spending a bunch of alone time with Levi, which was obviously what he wanted.

"I'll count on your help then."

Before she could tell him not to, he turned to Lulu. "So, what are you two up to today? Love the new hairdo, by the way."

"Thank you." Her mother smiled shyly, yet another victim of his magnetism. "Cassidy is trying to find me a job," her mother informed him. "Can you imagine? An old woman like me getting a new job?"

"You're not old." Levi bewitched her mother with a wink. "Any of these fine establishments in town would be lucky to have you."

"Oh, you little charmer." Her mother swatted at him.

Funny. When Levi talked about it, Lulu actually seemed open to the possibility of finding a job. Annoying as it was, Cassidy could use that to her advantage. "If you don't want to work at the flower shop, what about the Farm? Everly would be a great person to work for." She seemed kind and compassionate, but also strong...

"I can't work with money," her mother said without even considering it. "Cash registers scare me. And I'm too much of a klutz to carry food around like these pretty waitresses." She gestured to the young girl taking orders across the room.

"Huh." A thoughtful frown pulled at Levi's lips.

They were nice lips, skilled and scorching and provocative...

"I might have a possibility for you."

That broke Cassidy's concentration on his mouth. "Really? Where? What kind of job?"

"Don't want to say too much until I know for sure," he said mysteriously. "I'd better get back to the Renegades." He slid out of the booth but hovered near her. "When can we get together to talk more about the rodeo clinic?"

"I don't know." *How about never? Would never work?* She'd sat across from him for all of five minutes before she'd started to fantasize about kissing him again. There was no way she'd be able to spend any time alone with him. "I'm pretty busy this week."

"You are?" Lulu asked. "Really?"

She kicked her mother lightly under the table. "Yes. Remember? I have all those things..."

Amusement flickered in her mom's smile, but at least she remained silent.

"Lucky for us, I'm wide open." Levi rested his hand on the back of the booth just behind her, grazing her neck on the way. He leaned down in an alluring cloud of some spiced aftershave. "So you name the time and the place, and I'll be there."

"Don't have my calendar with me," she managed. As though she actually had a calendar. Or a social life. "I'll have to let you know." Maybe after a few weeks of radio silence, he'd take the hint.

"I'll be waiting for your call." He glanced at Lulu. "Wonderful to see you, as always."

Her mother's face lit up. "Don't make yourself scarce."

"I'm not planning to," he said with a purposeful look at Cassidy.

After one last *I'd be the best sex you've ever had* grin, he turned and walked away.

* * *

Family dinners had taken on a new meaning since Levi had come back to Topaz Falls. Naomi and Jessa both loved to cook so, at least once a week, they found an excuse to get together for a gathering—someone's half-birthday or Naomi's daughter, Gracie, got an A on a test, or it was some obscure holiday like National Pie Day and those two just had to celebrate.

Not that he was complaining. He happened to like their rhubarb pies. And it was nice, having people around. People who actually cared about what was happening in your life. Not that his brothers showed it. They mostly gave one another a hard time, but still, he knew they'd have his back when he needed it.

Levi sat and watched the chaos ensue in Naomi's kitchen at the inn, and he couldn't help but wonder what dinner looked like for Cass and Lulu. It was probably quiet and depressing compared to this. Gracie skipped through the kitchen singing at the top of her lungs while their German shepherd, Bogart, trotted behind, howling along. Lance stood next to Jessa, stealing strawberries out of the salad she was making along with kisses every chance he got, the sap.

Lucas had been tasked with setting the table, and Naomi had obviously trained him well. The napkins were folded neatly, and he'd even put all the forks on the same side of the plates. Last time Levi had been assigned to set the table, he'd tossed the silverware and napkins onto the plates, and Naomi and Jessa had spent ten minutes reorganizing everything, shaking their heads and *tsk*ing the whole time. After that, he'd lost the privilege to set the table.

Naomi skirted past Levi carrying a huge pan of lasagna. He quickly stood and stole it out of her hands. "You shouldn't be carrying heavy stuff around, should you?" He wasn't an expert, but the woman looked like she was about to pop out that baby right there on the kitchen floor. "You sure you're not having twins?" he asked, eyeing her belly. Carefully, he set the lasagna on the table.

"Twins!" Jessa snapped him with a dishtowel. "You're not supposed to say that to a pregnant woman!"

"Why not?" It wasn't like he was calling her fat. He knew she had a baby in there.

"Just don't," Lucas advised. "Don't mention anything about the belly," he whispered in passing.

"Or any other body parts," Lance added as he came to the table. "Even I know that."

"Seriously, Levi," Jessa grumbled.

"Sorry." He raised his hands. "I wasn't aware." When it came to pregnancy, babies, and birthing, he was blissfully ignorant and happy to stay that way.

"It's okay." Naomi let him off the hook with a shrug. "I'm not offended. I know how clueless you are."

"Thanks," he said drily.

"It's not his fault." Lance winked at him. "He inherited it from Dad."

"Papa Luis isn't clueless." Gracie gave her uncle a dirty look. "He's super smart."

"Hey," Levi ruffled the girl's curly red hair, "you don't think I'm smart?"

"Not if you think my mom's having twins," she sassed with a smile that poked a dimple into her cheek. That kid was too darn cute for her own good.

"Well, you'd better wise up quick if you want to pursue Cassidy," Jessa said. "It's not like you have all day."

The room got so quiet he could hear the distant buzz of a fly outside.

Oh yeah. That was the other thing Jessa and Naomi did during family dinners. They minded everyone else's business.

"Cassidy?" Lance repeated. "As in Cassidy Greer?"

"That'd be her," he replied with a scowl at Jessa.

She smiled sweetly. "Levi has a crush on her."

"A crush?" Gracie squealed. "Levi has a cru-ush, Levi has a cru-ush!"

"I take it the feeling's not mutual," Lucas said above the girl's song.

"Why would you say that?" he demanded. Was it so hard to believe Cass might be interested in him too?

His brother shrugged. "Cassidy seems so serious about everything."

"And I'm not?"

"You really want me to answer that?" Lucas asked as though he'd be glad to.

Levi ignored him. Sure, there'd been a time when he'd been irresponsible and self-centered. But people could change. And Cass was worth changing for.

"That girl is one hell of a hard worker," Lance said with admiration. "All she's been through and taking care of her mom like that? She deserves the best."

"I agree." Maybe Levi hadn't been the best in the past, but he could step it up.

"She doesn't exactly seem like the type to go for a fling," Lucas commented, serving out huge portions of Naomi's authentic Italian lasagna as everyone gathered around the table.

"What's a fling?" Gracie asked.

"A very quick romantic relationship," her mom answered with a disapproving look at her husband. Sometimes they all forgot there was a curious eleven-year-old in the room.

"Which is all Uncle Levi here has ever known," Lance added.

"Which was all you ever knew until you met the right person," he reminded his brother. Yeah, that shut him up. Lance had little room to talk when it came to previous romantic relationships.

"So how are you planning to win her over?" Jessa asked, drizzling oil over the salad. She handed him the bowl, and he took a modest portion. Lettuce wasn't really his thing.

"Seems to me what she needs right now is someone to be

there for her for a change." He helped himself to a hunk of garlic bread from the basket in the center of the table.

"Wow, Levi." Naomi looked him over. "That's actually very wise."

Jessa rolled her eyes. "I wonder how you figured that out."

"I had help." He wasn't above admitting he needed help with this whole relationship thing. Obviously. When he'd ambushed Cass at the Farm, she'd been as cold as ever. But he didn't need some big elaborate plan to win her over. He needed to do what he hadn't done for the past six years. Show up. Listen to her. Offer whatever support he could. Which reminded him... "You still looking for someone to help out at the shelter?" he asked Jessa.

Her fork froze midair. "Why?"

He sawed off a bite of lasagna and shoveled it in. "Thought Lulu might be the perfect candidate," he said when he'd finished chewing. "She's looking for a job. And she looked really happy when I saw her out walking that dog."

"*Lulu's* looking for a job?" Jessa and Naomi said the words in unison. Those two spent too much time together.

"Well... Cass is looking for a job for her. She thinks it'll help her find purpose again." At least that was what he'd overheard at the restaurant the other day. "And the shelter would be perfect." Low stress, working with animals instead of people. It'd be a great place for her to get her mind off everything else.

"But I already work at the shelter," Gracie said, her lips pouting.

"And you're a great helper," he assured her. "But you can't be there all the time. Especially with school."

"I don't know if that's a good idea." Jessa shared a look with Naomi.

"Why not? You need help, and she needs a job. Seems perfect to me."

The woman sighed as though there were so many things he didn't understand. "Lulu has a drinking problem."

"She's working on that." They could all help her work on that. "But she needs a reason to quit. She needs something stable in her life."

"It won't be that easy," Naomi cautioned. "From what I've seen, she needs professional help."

"I know. Cass is already thinking about that." And he could help her. He could look up the resources available in the area. He could drive Lulu to meetings. He'd do whatever it took.

"That's your plan?" Jessa pointed her fork at him as though she had him all figured out. "You're gonna try to save Cassidy's mom so she'll fall in love with you?"

"This is me trying to be there for her. For both of them." The way he should've been after Cash's death. "If we do this for Lulu, maybe Cass can move to Denver without worrying about her mom." Much as he wanted her to stick around Topaz Falls, he wanted her to be able to chase her dreams even more.

"I think it's a good idea." Naomi nodded encouragingly at Jessa. "You could do it on a trial basis. With conditions."

She looked at her husband uncertainly. "It wouldn't hurt to give it a shot," Lance said.

"Okay." Jessa gave him a nod. "We can try it out. I just don't want to jeopardize my friendship with Cassidy if anything goes wrong."

"Nothing will go wrong," Levi assured her. "We'll all

keep tabs on her. With the right support, I think she can do this."

"I hope so." Jessa actually smiled. "It'll be nice having someone else there. I'll call her tomorrow—"

"Actually, I'd like to tell them, if that's okay with you." This news would best be delivered to Cass in person. During an impromptu visit.

"Sure." Jessa went back to eating her salad, no trace of the earlier uncertainty in her tone. "Tell them to stop by the shelter sometime this weekend so Lulu and I can chat."

"Perfect." He pushed away his plate. Right after this next discussion, he would head over to the Greer's house. "I need one more favor from all of you."

His brothers groaned. "I think you're out of favors," Lucas muttered.

"Think of it as a win-win proposition."

"I'm listening," Lance said with about as much enthusiasm as a slug.

He didn't let his brother's lack of excitement derail him. In all of two minutes, Levi quickly and efficiently went through the pitch he'd prepared last night detailing his plan to do the youth clinic at the rodeo grounds. "The way I see it, I need your equipment and animals, and you need good publicity." That was a stretch, but Lance and Lucas were trying to get the word out about their new stock contracting operation, and this could earn them a few write-ups.

"That sounds so fun!" Gracie had enough enthusiasm for all of them. "I want to come!"

"I'm guessing you're not planning to pay to rent the equipment." Lance was the miser in the family. Always thinking about money, which Levi supposed was a good thing.

"Not when I own a share of the ranch." There should be some perks to being a silent investor, after all.

"Well, I think it's a great idea," Naomi said before his brothers could come up with any more complaints. "I'd love to do whatever I can to help."

"Actually, seeing as how you're the queen of numbers and details, I could use your help with logistics." He didn't plan to burden Cassidy with those jobs. He had other things in mind for her...

"Oh, I'd love to." Naomi didn't even hesitate. "That'll be the perfect distraction from my swollen ankles and huge belly."

"It's not huge, hon." Lucas leaned over to give his wife a kiss.

"Come on, guys. Not at the dinner table," Gracie scolded.

Lucas grinned and slipped his arm around his wife.

"We're happy to help too," Jessa said, speaking for Lance. "Whatever you need—the space, the animals. Right, honey?" she asked, patting her husband's leg persuasively.

"Right." Lance—always the skeptic—narrowed his eyes and glanced at Levi. "July doesn't give you much time to plan this thing."

"I know, but I have to make it happen before school starts up again." And before Cassidy left to pursue her new life. "I figure if we all work together, we can get it done."

"Then let us know what you need," Lance said. "We'll do everything we can to help."

"Thanks." Every once in a while, his brothers' generosity surprised him. "I was hoping you'd say that."

Now he just had to convince Cassidy.

Chapter Ten

Levi had never walked out on a plate of lasagna. Not once in his life.

But tonight he couldn't wait to get over to Cassidy's house. Naomi and Jessa had been all too eager to push him out the door. Once they'd agreed to help with the clinic, he'd told them he needed to talk with Cassidy. Next thing he knew, Jessa was handing him his car keys and Naomi was stashing food into leftover containers, and then they'd sent him on his way, each offering her own advice.

Touch her a lot, Naomi had advised.

But don't come on too strong, Jessa had cautioned.

Unfortunately, *too strong* happened to be his default setting. What was wrong with that? When he saw something he wanted, he went after it. And Cass sure hadn't minded him coming on strong the night he'd kissed her. In fact, he seemed to recall that she'd enjoyed it. A lot.

With that memory simmering, he climbed out of his

truck, carrying the food Naomi had stowed in some fancy dish-warmer thing. He could've called first, but that wouldn't have done him any good. Cass had become an expert at avoiding his calls. Lucky for him, her Subaru was parked in the driveway, which meant she wouldn't be able to avoid him now.

He knocked on the door, hardly having to wait before it swung open.

"Levi!" Lulu staggered, leaning into the wall.

At first he tried to force a smile but quickly gave up. She'd been drinking. "Hey, Lulu." He stepped inside. "Is Cass around?" Stupid question. If she'd been around, her mom likely wouldn't be tipsy.

"No," Lulu said with a pout. "She's on one of her marathon bike rides." She wobbled over to the couch and plopped down. "I hate that she rides in those mountains alone."

"Yeah." He walked past her and eyed the bottle of vodka on the kitchen table as he set down the food. Jessa and Naomi were right. Lulu needed some serious help.

He left the food on the table and went to sit next to her on the couch. "How much have you had to drink?" he asked bluntly.

She let out a twinkling laugh. "Hardly anything. Just a nightcap. It helps me sleep."

He didn't pretend to be amused by her playful tone.

The silence seemed to make her uncomfortable. She leaned forward and organized the scattered magazines on the coffee table into a neat pile. "I'm sure Cass-a-frass will be back in no time, if you want to wait."

Oh yeah. He would wait. But he wouldn't keep quiet. If he wanted to help Cass, that meant helping her mom too. Which also meant he couldn't ignore this. "Actually, I wanted to talk to you."

She continued to mess with the magazines, avoiding his eyes. "Sure, hon. Talk away."

It was crazy how much she seemed like the old Lulu when she drank. Happy and unburdened. Except it wasn't real.

He turned to her, employing the same stern expression his own father had used on him a time or two. "I found you a job."

"A job," she repeated, finally looking at him directly.

"Working with Jessa at the shelter." Hopefully this wouldn't be a mistake. "There's no cash register, no carrying food trays around. All you'll have to do is work with the animals and keep things clean and organized."

The sparkling humor drained from her eyes. She sat back, her shoulders slumping against the couch.

"It'll be flexible hours," he went on before she could say no. "Not full time to start, but it could turn into more if you want it to." That was the key to this whole thing—working, getting sober, functioning again.

"I don't know what to say." Lulu stared at her hands.

He lowered his head to look into her eyes. What he saw was not apathy or detachment. It was fear.

"You can do this." She had to do it. "And you'll have help. Here's the thing though. You have to quit drinking."

"I know." She nodded slowly, as though her head was almost too heavy to hold up. "I was going to have only one drink tonight. Cass has been gone a while, and I got nervous—"

"You can't have any drinks." He cut off the excuses. "You have to be the one to decide. You have to want this."

Her head lifted, and her faded blue eyes raised to his. "I do want it. I want it for Cass."

Eventually, he hoped she'd want it for herself too. "All right, then." He stood and strode into the kitchen, going right for that bottle of vodka and uncapping it so he could dump the rest down the sink. Lulu followed behind him, moving like a shadow.

"This is the start of a new day." Levi tossed the bottle into the recycling bin and riffled through the sparse contents of the cabinets until he found some coffee grounds. "Now we need to sober you up." He measured out the coffee and poured water into the pot on the counter before flicking it on.

"I hate coffee." Lulu crept to the kitchen table.

"If you don't have coffee, Cass will know you've been drinking," he reminded her.

The woman looked up at him with a small smile. "You're not going to tell on me?"

"I don't have to." He narrowed his eyes at her. "Right? Because you're done. You're done hiding alcohol in the house. You're done drinking."

"Right," she mumbled.

He wished she'd put more energy into the words, but that would come in time. And with the right support group.

"Here." He filled up a tall glass from the tap and set it in front of her. "Drink all of that before you drink the coffee."

Lulu gazed at the glass and made a face before lifting it to her lips.

While the coffee pot steamed, he went to sit across from Cassidy's mom and gave her a pestering nod whenever she tried to set the glass down. Finally, she finished the last gulp of water and shoved the glass away.

"It's a good thing I got here before you'd finished that

bottle or I'd make you drink three more of those," he told her.

A smile snuck out, though it didn't light her eyes. "You can be very persistent."

"Yes. I can be." He liked to think it was one of his better qualities.

"I wonder how long it'll take Cass to give in." Already the woman's eyes were looking clearer.

"I have no idea what you're talking about." He grinned at her and hopped up to fill a mug of coffee and then set it in front of her with a grand presentation.

"No sugar?" she whined, peering into the cup.

"Straight-up black motor oil." The one time he'd been stupid enough to get drunk on Gunner Raines's watch, the man had woken him up at 5:30 a.m. and forced him to drink the blackest, most bitter coffee he'd ever tasted. Then he'd told him he'd be off the team if he ever drank like that again.

"Come on now," Levi coaxed. "Like you said, Cass could be back anytime." And he'd rather spring the good news about the job on her than tell her he'd caught her mother drinking again. This day could be the dawn of a new era for Cass too. For them.

"She likes you more than she lets on, you know." Lulu lifted the mug to her lips and took a feeble sip. She coughed, a grimace crumpling her face.

"I'm glad to hear that." After everything that had happened between them as of late, he'd figured she liked him, but it was nice to hear someone say it. "I like her too. A whole lot."

"She's guarded though, you know?" Cassidy's mom choked down a few more sips of coffee. "She won't make it easy for you."

"I noticed." But he could be as stubborn as Cass. "Do you think she'll come around?"

This time Lulu's smile sparked with some of that old spunk in her eyes. "How any young woman can resist your charm is beyond me, Levi Cortez."

He laughed. "There have been a few—"

The front door banged open. Cassidy maneuvered in, wheeling her mountain bike along with her. She stopped cold when she looked up and saw him sitting at her kitchen table.

"Nice bike," he managed to say, even with his jaw hanging open. It wasn't the bike his eyes had fixated on. It was the spandex shorts and hot pink tank top that hugged every perfect curve. She'd pulled her hair back, but most of it had escaped from the loose ponytail and now haloed her face in a carefree, unbelievably sexy way. It was a picture of how she might look after a long, rowdy night in his bed...

"What're you doing here?" she demanded, breaking his concentration on her body.

Not *hi,* or *how's it going?* or *nice to see you, Levi.* Yeah, he had his work cut out for him.

Lulu shot him a fearful glance, but he simply shrugged. "I came by to see you." He said it as though it shouldn't surprise her. Judging from the color in her cheeks, she already knew why he'd come. "But I've enjoyed chatting with your mom while we waited for you to come back."

Cassidy leaned her bike against the living room wall and marched into the kitchen, her eyes narrowed with suspicion. "You're drinking coffee?" She wore the same expression a detective might wear during an interrogation.

Surprisingly, Lulu didn't cower. "I was tired, so Levi of-fered to make some coffee." Good to see that she was at least sober enough to come up with a solid cover story. "But then I took a sip and remembered why I hate it."

"I'm not very good at making it," he admitted. She'd probably be better off going out in the backyard and filling her mug with dirt and water. But it seemed to be serving its purpose.

Cassidy leaned a hip against the countertop, crossing her arms while she glared at them both.

He knew he should say something, but damn that spandex...

"Oh, and he brought the most wonderful news too." Lulu prompted him with a nod.

Right. The news. The job. He tried to banish thoughts of peeling those shorts off Cassidy's body with his teeth. So many games they could play with spandex...

Cass looked at him expectantly.

Damn, she made it hard for him to think. "Jessa wants to hire your mom to work at the shelter."

"What?" The word came out breathless, but it was impossible to tell if that was good or bad.

"We were at dinner tonight, and Jessa was talking about how much she needed help at the shelter," he explained, still trying to gauge her reaction. "I suggested Lulu, and Jess thought it was a great idea." That might've been a stretch, but it would all work out great and everyone would be glad he'd butted in.

Cassidy turned her attention to her mother. "You want to work at the shelter?"

"It seems like a good place to start."

He had to give the woman credit. She may have been afraid of starting a new job, but she spoke with more confidence than he'd heard in her voice since he was a kid.

"Jessa said you two could stop by sometime this weekend to discuss the details," he added, drawing her attention back to him.

"Sounds like the perfect plan to me. We can go on Saturday morning." Lulu pushed out the chair next to her. "Now why don't you sit down, sweetie? I wouldn't recommend the coffee, but there's iced tea in the fridge."

"Actually, I need to take a shower. I was out longer than I planned, and I need to get cleaned up." She headed for the small hallway that led to the bedrooms. "That's great about the job though," she said awkwardly on her way past him. "Thanks for thinking of her." Without a goodbye, she disappeared.

Damn. Levi kneaded his forehead. She'd perfected her disappearing act whenever he got within ten feet of her. He'd gladly follow her down that hall, but Jessa had warned him about coming on too strong. "I guess that's my cue to leave."

Lulu stood. "You should stay. You still have all that wonderful food Naomi sent. You could warm it up in the oven for the two of you." She hurried to the kitchen counter and dug her phone out of her purse. "I'll get in touch with Darla and see if she'd like to go shopping. A few of the boutiques are open until nine, and I'll need some new clothes for my job."

Levi tried not to look shocked, but he hadn't seen Lulu wear anything except for sweatpants since he'd been back. "You want to go shopping? With Darla?"

"Out of all of Cass's friends, she comes over to visit the most." She tapped her fingers on her phone. "I'll send her a text. That woman has quite the sense of style. I'm sure she'd be happy to walk around with me and give me some advice." She finished typing and gave him a mischievous look. "Then you can surprise Cass with a nice, quiet dinner. Alone."

Surprise her or send her running for the hills? He had no idea what Cass would do when she saw him in her kitchen, but he couldn't wait to find out.

Chapter Eleven

Cassidy took her sweet time showering and getting dressed. As a general rule, she could be ready for anything in twenty minutes. Working and going to school full time hadn't given her the luxury of fussing over her appearance, but in the last half hour, she'd done everything she could think of to drag out the process, even exfoliating and using some special lotion Jessa had given her for Christmas last year.

When she was sure enough time had passed for Levi to take the hint and leave, she threw on a T-shirt along with a pair of yoga pants and paused by her bedroom door, holding her breath and straining her ears.

No murmur of voices, which meant the coast should be clear.

Her twelve-mile mountain-bike ride had been exactly what she'd needed to clear her head and refocus on her future plans. Riding was the only time she felt free—moving weightlessly forward with nothing dragging her down. But when she'd cruised into the driveway and seen Levi's truck parked in front of her house, all the peacefulness she'd felt on her bike had fallen away, leaving room for the tension to crawl back in.

Levi affected her. He charmed her and teased her and touched her in a way that made her want him. And that drove her crazy. She didn't need competing desires right now. She had a singular focus—get her mother healthy so both of them could actually have a life.

Sure, she appreciated that he'd found Lulu a job, but she didn't need him showing up all the time. Especially when he insisted on wearing those rugged, form-fitting jeans. The man had quite a lot to show off. Seriously. She hadn't thought about sex this much since their book club had read *Fifty Shades of Grey*.

And there she went again.

Cursing Renegade Jeans Co., she charged out of her room, ready to have a long talk with her mother about going back to work. That's what she needed to think about—not how Levi's jeans accentuated certain parts of his body.

"Let's get takeout and cel—" The words drowned in a gasp as she came around the corner and got a full view of the kitchen. Her mother wasn't sitting at the table where she'd left her. In fact, she didn't seem to be around. Levi, though, was standing at the counter tossing a green salad. And the table was set. Two plates, silverware, glasses. Lit candles flickered between them.

She blinked, wondering if she'd stepped into some alternate universe. Or maybe she'd had some sort of fall in the bathroom and hit her head...

"Hungry?" He carted the salad over to the table as casually as if this was something they did every evening. "I kept the lasagna in the oven. Didn't want it to get cold." He hurried back to the oven.

"Lasagna?" She smelled it now—that delicious garlicky scent of meat and melted cheese. Hunger rolled through her stomach, ending in a grumble that he hopefully didn't hear. "Where's my mother?" She stood her ground in the living room. Lulu was supposed to be sitting at the kitchen table so they could discuss the new job. Levi was supposed to be long gone...

"She texted Darla and asked her to go shopping." Levi slipped on two oven mitts and slid a casserole dish out of the oven, bending over just enough to display that perfect ass of his.

Damn jeans. "Shopping?" She really had stepped into an alternate universe. Her mother hadn't been shopping in years.

"Yeah. She wanted to look for some new clothes to wear to work." He set the steaming dish on a hot pad next to the salad. "Naomi sent me home with all this food so I figured we could have dinner together."

She opened her mouth to tell him she didn't want dinner, but her gaze shifted to that rich casserole, still bubbling and sizzling. She loved Naomi's lasagna, and the woman knew it. "Did she know you were coming over here?" Cassidy asked in a clipped tone. This little dinner had conspiracy written all over it. First, Naomi—and likely Jessa—packing up food for him to bring along and then her mom calling Darla out of the blue to go shopping.

"Does it matter?" He worked his lips into that sly, sexy grin. "I'm here. It's dinnertime. And we have all this amazing food. What's wrong with sharing it?"

"Nothing." At least there shouldn't have been anything wrong with it. She'd shared a meal with plenty of men. Even men she didn't particularly like. Maybe that was the problem. After years of completely disregarding Levi as a selfish, conceited jackass, maybe she was starting to like him a little too much.

The thought trapped her where she stood. He would know it. If she spent any time alone with him, he would see it. Then they'd end up right where they had the other night—in the backseat of his truck halfway to making love. Except now they had a bedroom accessible. And a couch...and a kitchen table...

"You okay?" Levi approached her. "You look a little warm." His eyes seemed to see past her calm facade. "Aren't you hungry?"

Starving. Nerves fluttered up and down her chest, softening her knees in that amorous way. God, she was in trouble. "I'm definitely hungry," she mumbled, slipping past him.

Before she could sit, he stood behind her. "Good. I am too." He pulled out her chair, and she settled into it, glancing once again at the lasagna. Inhaling the garlicky scent, she forced her heart into submission. She'd make this quick— wolf down her lasagna and salad, thank Levi for dinner, and send him on his way. No big deal. She'd spent all her high school years pretending she didn't have a crush on him; she could easily continue the charade.

"So why didn't you eat with your family?" she asked when he sat across from her.

"I wanted to tell you and your mom the good news about the job." He unwrapped his silverware from the cloth napkin and set it on his lap.

Where the hell had he found the cloth napkins anyway?

She hadn't used them in years. As she unwrapped her silverware, a memory struck her. Christmas morning her junior year. Levi had spent the night and joined them for breakfast. While they'd eaten her mother's traditional egg casserole and blueberry pancakes, he and Cash had turned these same cloth napkins into lassos, trying to snatch the bottle of syrup from the middle of the table...

"Besides, it's nice to eat with someone other than my family once in a while." He served her a generous piece of lasagna and a helping of salad. "Sometimes I feel like a third wheel when I hang out with the newlyweds."

She could relate to that. At least Darla was still single though. "What about your dad? Don't you two stick together?"

"Haven't you heard? Dad and Evie eloped. We think they're coming back soon, but I have no idea when."

If her mouth hadn't been full, her jaw would've dropped. "Seriously?" She almost laughed. Luis Cortez had gotten hitched? "You didn't know they were planning to get married?"

"Had no idea." Levi's head tilted as he stared at her across the table. "He just went for it. Knew what he wanted and made it happen. I find that very inspirational."

The deliberate hint in his tone dropped her gaze back to her food. She took a few bites to derail that line of conversation. "So...um...how's Naomi feeling?" She simply had to control the topics of discussion. As long as she stuck to the safe ones, like his family, she could sail right through this.

"She seems fine," he said as though he saw right through her tactic. But he must've decided to let it go. "I made the mistake of asking if she was having twins..."

"Twins?" Cassidy couldn't help but crack a smile. "You

asked a nearly full-term pregnant woman if she was having *twins*?"

"I know, I know." He shook his head. "I already got the lecture. Trust me."

She could picture Jessa jumping all over him. Smiling bigger, she ate more, letting the sauce and cheese and pasta all melt together in her mouth. *Wow*. Naomi must have a magic spatula. "I wish I could cook like this." All she had time to make was grilled cheese.

"It's my mom's recipe," Levi said, his eyes downcast, focused on the food.

"Your mom's?" She studied him. He never mentioned his mom. After she'd left their family, it was like she'd ceased to exist in his world. Cassidy had always wondered if he ever tried to contact her. Every time she brought it up when they were in high school, his face would get all dark and angry, and he'd tell her he didn't care about his mom. "She used to make lasagna?"

"When we were little." He stirred the salad on his plate with a fork. "She left most of her stuff behind. There was a book with some recipes. Naomi and Jessa have perfected them." There was no hint of his charming grin now. His jaw had clenched with tension. He took another bite, but Cassidy couldn't. She couldn't look away from him.

After his mom had left, Levi changed overnight. All the Cortez brothers had, but for him, it seemed to be more of a dangerous turn. He'd stopped caring about school, took more risks, drank a lot, and experimented with drugs. Then he'd started that fire at the rodeo grounds one night after discovering his father was having an affair with the rodeo commissioner's wife.

Lucas had taken the blame and had gone off to prison for

three years. That had seemed to turn Levi around. Not long after Lucas was arrested, Levi started hanging around her family's house more. He'd never talked about any of the issues with his family, and she'd almost forgotten he'd been through all that pain. He'd hid it well.

"Did you ever hear from her?" She'd always wondered. With all of Levi's notoriety, surely his mother had followed his career.

"Nah." He shoved his plate away, though he hadn't finished eating. "I looked. We all looked, but she must've changed her name or something."

It was a rare thing to see his expression so still, so subdued. Levi almost always grinned, always had that glimmer of humor in his eyes, but not now. Instead of the flirtatious glances he usually gave her, a look of pain haunted his eyes.

She'd rarely caught a glimpse of him so unguarded. Almost vulnerable. Sympathy spilled through her. For all of Lulu's problems, she'd never abandoned her kids. She'd never rejected them. That was a wound Cassidy couldn't even begin to fathom. "It must be awful not to know. Where she went or what happened to her." Though it had nearly broken her when Cash died, she couldn't imagine how hard it would be to have someone missing from your life and not know where she was or if she was even still alive. There'd be no closure...

"It's hard." Levi's jaw tightened. That devastated expression struck her. Ever since Levi had come back to Topaz Falls, she'd looked at him like the same cocky high school kid who'd always found a way to lighten the mood with a joke. But now she could see that boy was long gone. Levi was a man. A man with much deeper feelings than she'd realized.

He raised his gaze to hers. "I've never been good at dealing with hard."

It was maybe the first time ever he'd let her see something besides overflowing confidence in himself.

"Most of us aren't good at dealing with hard." Her voice lost power.

"You seem pretty good at it. You don't run away from it. Not like I have."

She couldn't hold his gaze. It was too intense, said too much. "I guess I didn't have a choice. Mom needed me. She still needs me." There'd been times when she'd been tempted to run away from it—from the constant pressure of work and school and worrying about the woman she loved most in the world. But in the end, she'd always forced herself to remember how often Lulu had taken care of her. How often she'd come to her rescue. How often her mother had sacrificed her own happiness and needs and dreams to give her a good life. Lulu had taught her that you make sacrifices for the people you love. Levi hadn't learned that. His mother had taught him to run.

"People needed me too," Levi said hoarsely. "*You* needed me."

Emotion charged the air between them. For the first time, she saw something deeper in him. An unrelenting desire to undo the past. "It's fine," she murmured, fisting her napkin in her hand. "We managed. And you did really good for yourself, Levi." She was desperate to let him off the hook. Maybe then he'd leave her alone.

"It's not fine. I was selfish. And immature. And stupid." He groaned with frustration. "After we lost Cash, I could've stepped up. I could've been there for you."

"Stop." She reached for his hand across the table, squeezing it lightly. "It's okay. I forgive you. You don't have to do this. Show up at my door with food and make me dinner. Find my mom a job. I don't expect you to do penance."

The sudden longing in his eyes dried up her throat. She quickly pulled back her hand and reached for the glass in front of her, lifting it to her lips for the first time. A familiar but forgotten sweetness flooded her mouth. She sipped again, savoring the taste, smiling at the memories it brought. "You made me a Shirley Temple."

Levi's hard frown relaxed. "It was always your favorite."

She peered into the glass, marveling at the thick reddish color. "But...where'd you get the syrup?" It wasn't like she kept grenadine in the refrigerator.

"I made it." Levi lifted his own glass and sipped, wincing slightly as he swallowed.

"You made it?" She laughed. She couldn't help it. The man really was trying to do penance.

"I had plenty of time," he said with a pointed raise of his eyebrows, as though he knew exactly why she'd taken so long getting ready. "Found a recipe online. Is it any good? Is it supposed to be that sweet?"

She took another sip, drinking in the flavor of her early teens. "It's amazing." Even better than she remembered.

"Glad *you* like it." Without taking another drink, he stacked their plates. "But if you think that's amazing, wait until you taste dessert." Just like that, the flirtatious Levi with the million-dollar smile was back.

That was fine with her because that other version was getting harder to resist. "I like dessert. What did Naomi make?"

"Nothing. I made it while you were taking a shower." His eyes lingered on her as though he liked the thought of her in the shower.

"Oh." That long, heated look was enough to make her hand fumble with her napkin as she tried to lay it on the table. She stood, her legs as unstable as her resolve to keep him from reaching her heart. "I'll go ahead and do the dishes." She stood, desperate for something to keep her busy...

"Nope." Levi blocked her path to the sink. "I've got it." He put his hands on her shoulders, all rough and manly, and directed her to the couch. "You sit. Relax. I'll do the dishes and bring out dessert."

Relax? She wobbled the rest of the way to the couch and sank to the cushions. There would definitely be no relaxing. His touch seemed to have the opposite effect on her. At the moment, her heart beat faster than it had when she'd ridden her mountain bike up Topaz Mountain. Unable to sit still, she rearranged the magazines on the coffee table. Old copies of *Self*, *Real Simple*, *Cosmo*...

"Five Positions to Enhance Your Orgasm," a hot-pink headline blared.

Whoa! She'd missed that article. She quickly turned it over just as Levi came into the room.

"Hope you like chocolate." He set down a tray of chocolate-covered strawberries right next to the issue of *Cosmo*.

"Yep. Chocolate is good," she said quickly, shoving the magazine farther aside. Something told her he'd be happy to try all five of those positions in that article tonight. She cleared her throat. "So, you just happened to have a dozen chocolate-covered strawberries lying around in your truck?"

He grinned and sat next to her. "I found the strawberries in your fridge. And there were some dark chocolate chips in the pantry."

Yes, she always kept plenty of those in stock. "Wow. Very resourceful of you." She picked up a strawberry and bit into it, the sweetness and sourness mingling on her tongue. "So good," she said when she'd finished chewing. "Thank you. It was a great dinner." And it was almost over. A trace of disappointment snuck past her better judgment.

"You're welcome." Levi bit into a strawberry too. "I wanted to do something special for you," he added, turning to face her.

She knew she should look away from him, from that passion brewing in his eyes again, but anticipation held her there. "Why is that?" she half-whispered.

"Because you're always doing things for other people." He studied her face, like he was trying to see more than she wanted to let him. "It's about time someone took care of you."

"Maybe I don't need anyone to take care of me." Especially since she was getting ready to move, to start a whole new life somewhere else. She shifted closer to the edge of the couch, putting more distance between them.

"Everyone needs to be taken care of sometimes," Levi insisted, appearing unfazed that she had moved away from him.

She shot him a skeptical glare. "Even you?" Seemed to her he'd spent most of his life doing his best to not need anyone. Hadn't he just alluded to that in the kitchen?

"Even me," he murmured, gazing determinedly into her eyes.

She turned to the coffee table and popped another strawberry into her mouth. She didn't know what to do with this Levi. The one who had feelings, the one who kept apologizing. She'd always known how to handle the old Levi. The cocky, joking around, shallow cowboy who'd thrived in front of the cameras. Sitting here with him tonight—sharing dinner with him—made her wonder if she'd ever truly known him at all.

"You seem tense." He moved closer, his thigh brushing against hers.

"Do I?" she squeaked. Tense wasn't exactly the right word. Conflicted. Aroused...

"Whenever I'm tense, I go to the trainers and get a massage." His gaze moved down her body. "I've learned a few techniques over the years. Want me to show you?"

"Um." She cleared her throat, every protest melting in the heat that coiled through her.

Seeming to take her silence as a yes, Levi turned to her and eased his hands onto her shoulders. His fingertips kneaded all the knots and strained muscles brought on by worry and work, caressing them with a firm tenderness. God, he really did know what he was doing.

"Wow. You're tight." His hands slipped lower, following the contour of her spine, applying pressure and stroking through her thin T-shirt in a way that made her flesh prickle with pleasure.

A moan slipped out as her head tipped forward.

"See?" His lips drew close to her ear. "Everyone needs to be taken care of sometimes."

She agreed with a mumbled "Mmmm-hmmmm." She would've agreed with anything he said. She'd never been taken care of quite like this before.

His hands glided over her back with skilled motions, relaxing her muscles.

"Feeling better?" Levi's deep voice vibrated against her neck, so close she could feel his breath on her skin.

Air pounded in and out of her lungs, building the craving he'd already kindled inside her. Somehow she lifted her head enough to peer at him over her shoulder. "You've definitely picked up some solid skills." But something told her this massage was a lot more sensual than the ones he got from his trainers.

She expected him to bring up another certain skill set he could offer her, but he stayed quiet and continued caressing the sore, tender muscles up and down her back. The more he touched her, the more she ached for him. She couldn't help it. Couldn't keep resisting that pull between them. She leaned her head against his chest, feeling his sharp intake of breath near her ear.

"You smell good," he murmured.

She hardly heard him over the whoosh of blood that ignited her body. "So do you." Like chocolate, dark and seductive.

"I can't stop thinking about that kiss." A husky desperation edged into his voice.

"I've thought it about it too." Longed for it... ached for it...

"Maybe we should stop thinking." He traced his warm lips down her neck, giving her a delicious shiver.

"Maybe we should." She closed her eyes to let the feel of him drown out the faint warning sounding in a dark corner of her mind. She hadn't properly made out with anyone in years. She was always too busy. Too stressed. Too worried. "Screw it," she muttered, turning fully to Levi.

"What?" He half-laughed.

"Nothing." She pushed to her knees and straddled his lap. Screw being so careful. Being so closed off. For once, she wanted to feel something that resembled passion.

Levi's grin had returned. He eased his lips over hers with more tenderness than she had expected. His fingers rose to her face, stroking her cheeks lightly. "Why have you been avoiding me?" he asked, pulling away.

"I don't know," she answered breathlessly. For the life of her, she couldn't remember. All she knew right now, in this moment, was that she wanted to kiss him. She wanted to abandon herself to him without analyzing what might happen tomorrow.

She inched her knees forward and kissed his lips greedily, seeking out his tongue.

Levi groaned against her mouth as he pulled her in tighter. His body was so strong, a shelter in her lonely world. His powerful arms wrapped around her, and for once, she gave up the fight. For right now, he had her, he was holding her, and she could give herself over to the desires she'd hidden too long.

Levi's lips seared her skin with a blinding heat, leaving his mark all down her neck. "I want you, Cass," he rasped. His hands lowered and caught the hem of her T-shirt, slowly raising it up before he pulled it over her head. Greed pooled in his eyes as he brushed his fingers along the edge of her red, lacy bra.

Desire poured into her heart, encroaching on her lungs. "I need this." All of it—the dinner magically prepared for her, and the Shirley Temple, the chocolate-covered strawberries, his hands on her body. It had been too long. Too lonely...

His lips worked their way back to hers while he reached around and undid her bra clasp with one hand. "Nothing would make me happier than fulfilling all your needs," he growled, taking the straps down her shoulders and then tossing the bra away. He ran his fingers over her breasts as though taking in the details, his eyes growing hungrier with each stroke.

Cassidy struggled to breathe. No one had ever touched her this way, so skillfully, as if he knew exactly what she wanted.

"I used to think about this," Levi said, his eyes searching hers. "A lot."

"Really?" She clasped her hands behind his neck and tried to decide if he was feeding her a line. Back in high school, he hadn't shown much interest in her. Besides being a protective, irritating older-brother type of influence in her life.

"Really." He lowered his lips to her neck, kissing his way down until his teeth grazed her nipple.

"Ohhhh..." A long moan flowed out of her. She dug her fingertips into his shoulders. "You never said anything," she gasped, trying to hold on to coherence.

"I couldn't." His hands held her hips, urging her closer. The hard bulge at his crotch pressed between her legs, grinding against her. She moved her hips until he panted harder.

"Don't worry," he uttered. "I'll prove how much I thought about it." He wrapped his arms around her, shifting and lifting until he lowered her back to the couch. Kissing her lips, he eased onto his side next to her. "When I'm done, there won't be any doubts."

He'd already taken care of her doubts, scattering them like brittle fallen leaves caught in a fierce wind. "I'm not worried." About anything. Cassidy turned her body to his. He was so strong and solid. Hot as hell with those wild hazel eyes and quick, sure smile. "This might be the first time I haven't been worried in six years." That's how long she'd been holding everything together.

"You deserve to feel good." He kissed her again, slow and sensual, prying open her lips and grazing his tongue against hers. "I'm gonna make you feel real good, Cass." His large, calloused hand slid down her body, fingers catching the elastic waist of her yoga pants and taking it down to her thighs. He propped himself up on his elbow, hovering over her, eyes examining her body, flashing with desire.

Even just that intoxicated look on his face was enough to turn her on.

"It's a good thing I never saw you naked," he murmured, lowering his lips to her chest again. "Because I wouldn't have been able to keep my hands off you. And your brother might've killed me."

"You don't have to keep your hands off me now." She tugged his face to hers and kissed his lips thoroughly, feeling him grin against her mouth.

"There's no way I could. Not now. You're too sexy. I have to touch you." His finger traced a line from her collarbone to her waist and then traveled down over her thigh.

Cassidy tugged at his shirt, trying to get it off, but he took her hands in his. "Nope. Tonight is all about you."

Before she could protest, his hand slid up her inner thigh and parted her legs.

Her head fell back to the cushions as Levi slid his fingers inside her, stroking her in a rhythmic caress.

"Oh god." The soft touches made her whole body quake. "Levi…"

"I like it when you say my name that way," he whispered, kissing her lips. His fingers pressed deeper into her, and she arched her back, raising her hips to meet his movements.

Sounds came out of her mouth, but she had no control over them, no control over anything. Her hands fisted his shirt. "What about you?" she asked between ragged breaths.

"Oh, I'm enjoying myself," he assured her, dragging his tongue over her breast again. His fingers pulsed inside her while his thumb stroked the outside of her swollen flesh. Breathing hot and heavy against her chest, he lightly bit her nipple and swirled his tongue over her skin.

That was all she felt—his tongue and his fingers dominating her, controlling every sensation, raising her higher and higher. "It's so good." How could it be so good?

"Tell me how good." Levi's fingers worked faster, firm and insistent.

She couldn't. Her breaths came too fast, and her hips trembled. She tried to fight it but the convulsion overtook all sense, shattering her control, wrenching a cry from her lips.

When the room finally came back into focus, she let her head roll to the side, staring up at Levi in disbelief.

He gathered her in tighter, kissing her cheek, her ear, her lips. "That was fun."

"Mmm-hmmm," she murmured, unable to form more complicated sounds. It had been the most fun she'd had in a long time, but it had also been...intimate. The way he touched her, the way he held her, the way he kissed her—it had been tender, selfless.

It had been loving.

The realization overpowered the lazy contentment that hazed her body. How would she protect her heart from him now?

Chapter Twelve

Cass lay on the couch next to him, her cheeks flushed, her breath ragged. It was the most erotic thing he'd ever witnessed, her sexy, curvy body moving next to him, arching her back and bucking around while he'd made her come with one hand...

"It should be your turn," she said dutifully, reaching for his belt buckle. He'd be lying if he said he wasn't aching to be inside of her, but Lulu would be home soon, and like he'd mentioned...tonight was all about her.

"Man, this thing is complicated." Her fingers still fiddled with his silver belt buckle half-heartedly, like she didn't quite have the strength to unclasp it.

"I'm good," he lied, easing his arm underneath her back and pulling her tightly against him. The feel of her soft body deepened the throbbing ache, but he fought it back.

"That's not fair." She propped her cheek on her hand and gave him a seductive smile. "We should...make it good for you too. We could do more..."

Hell, yes. "You want more?" He slid his hand along the contour of her hip, savoring the feel of her.

"Well, yeah." Her gaze wandered down his body, lingering at the crotch of his jeans.

It was gonna take one hell of a cold shower to remedy that.

"You're pretty good at that stuff," she murmured, feeling her way up his chest.

He almost whimpered. "You haven't seen anything yet." They had years to make up for, and he planned to offer her the performance of his life. But... "Not tonight, darlin'." The words actually hurt. "Your mom'll be home soon. And it probably wouldn't go over well if we were holed up in your bedroom too busy to greet her."

Judging from the construction of the house, she'd hear everything through the walls, and he didn't want Cass to be quiet. Nothing turned him on quite like those sounds she made...

"Right." She sighed and shimmied her pants back to her waist before sitting up. "I guess now's maybe not the best time."

He forced himself to sit up too. "Which means we'll have to get together again soon." So he could continue proving how much he wanted her. "Speaking of... let's go out."

"Out?" Not looking at him, she snatched her bra off the floor and slipped it back on.

"Yeah. You know, dinner or a movie or some country line dancing at the Tumble Inn?" He leaned forward to take care of the clasp for her... and couldn't resist brushing a kiss over her sexy bare shoulder.

"Um..." She scooted away from him and collected her shirt, pulling it back on in one panicked motion.

Here we go again. He braced himself for another swift escape. Every time he got closer to her, she backtracked.

Sure enough, Cass turned to him, still disheveled and lovely, but her eyes, which had been soft and open only a few minutes before, shot him a familiar glare. The one that built an invisible force field between them. "I'm hoping to leave in July," she said, as if he wasn't well aware.

"So am I." He glared back and set his jaw. *Not this time, honey.* Not after what just happened between them. "By the end of summer, I'll be all healed up, and I'll have to hit the circuit again." In return for his friends' helping him out with the clinic, he'd agreed to join up with them for a tour of sorts—appearances at some of the bigger rodeo events around the country.

"So there's really no point in doing this." Cass calmly smoothed her hair back into place, as though it would be that easy to move on. "There's no point in spending time together."

"No point?" He pretended to be offended. "I think I just proved my point about five minutes ago." He hadn't seen her bailing out on him when he was kissing her, touching her.

Her lips strained as though she didn't want to smile but couldn't help it. "You know what I mean. Making out with you is really . . . well . . . you know . . ."

"Really good," he finished for her. "You mentioned that. A few times." He'd be hearing that in his dreams tonight.

"Yeah. It was good."

Damn, he loved making her blush. It brought her face alive.

She scooted down to the next couch cushion like she didn't trust herself to be too close to him. "But you don't have to do this, Levi."

"Do what? Make you feel good? Make you a priority?" He wanted to do that. He could live to do that…

"Make up for the past," she said stiffly. "I know you feel guilty about not being around, but it's okay. You've won me over." She faced him directly, though the few feet between them may as well have been an ocean. "I forgive you. I even like you again. So you don't have to keep trying so hard."

He shouldn't be surprised. After years of silence, she had no reason to trust him, but her doubts about the depth of his feelings still lit a fuse on his frustration. "That's not what this is about." He moved closer to her so she could read the intention in his eyes. Maybe it had started out that way. He couldn't stand that she didn't like him. Everyone liked him. So maybe initially he'd wanted to simply win her over.

But now he knew what it was like to kiss her. What it was like to hold her against him. What it was like to make her feel good. It was addictive. And he couldn't give it up.

"This isn't about guilt," he told her, turning her face to his. "I like you. I like being with you. I like being here for you." It meant more than anything he'd done in his life. It reached deeper.

"I like you too." It would've been more convincing if she hadn't moved her gaze to the floor. "But that doesn't do either of us any good right now. We're going our separate ways. We'll be living two completely different lives."

He shook his head. Didn't she understand? They couldn't go their separate ways. They were a part of each other. Their past and present were woven together—linking their futures too.

He stared at her for a long, silent moment, taking in the fear reflected in her eyes. If he pushed her too hard, he would lose her. She wasn't ready yet. Wasn't convinced he had any staying power. Which meant he'd have to spend the rest of her time in Topaz Falls convincing her that they belonged together.

He put on the grin she'd recognize—the one he used to flirt. "When's the last time you had a summer fling?"

A humorless laugh slipped out of her mouth. "I've never had a summer fling. I haven't had the time."

"Then this is it." He pinned her gaze to his. "Once you move away, you'll be even busier. So this is your last chance to let loose and have a little fun. Believe me, Cass, I'm good at fun." He accentuated the word with a suggestive lift of his eyebrows.

She seemed to consider the proposal. "So that's it then?" she finally said, giving him a skeptical frown. "We have a summer fling, no strings attached, then go our separate ways in July?"

"Exactly." He said it as though they'd completed a negotiation, though he had no intention of sticking to it. To close the deal, he snaked his hand up her thigh and turned up the wattage on his grin. "I promise I'll be the best fling you'll ever have."

"You'll be the only fling I've ever had," she corrected boldly, but she didn't brush his hand away.

That was a good sign. "So when can I take you out?"

Cass hesitated. "I work the next few days. Maybe next week?"

"Perfect." That'd give him plenty of time to plan the most epic date she'd ever been on. Something that would help his cause. "Since that's settled, our agreement starts now." He pulled her against him on the couch, unable to force himself to get up and go home. He wanted to hold her. Maybe kiss her some more. He'd love to do more than kiss her, but Lulu would be home soon.

"Since we can't head to your bedroom to start this fling off properly, maybe we should watch a movie." He grabbed the remote and turned on the small television. "What're you in the mood for?"

"I don't have time for movies." Cass rested her head against his shoulder.

He closed his eyes, only for a second to lose himself in her warmth against his body.

"But I have about twenty chick flicks saved on the DVR."

"I love chick flicks." He clicked through the vast selection of romance and comedies. "Ohhh, *How to Lose a Guy in Ten Days*. Classic."

She wrinkled her nose with distaste. "I'm in the mood for something more historical. How about *Pride and Prejudice*?"

"I was hoping you'd say that."

She rolled her eyes at him and laughed. "I'll bet you were."

"Seriously. Mr. Darcy is a smooth operator. Maybe I'll pick up some new moves."

"You don't need new moves." Turning to him, Cass rose to her knees and kissed his lips.

He breathed her in—the lemony sweet scent that was uniquely hers—and slowed the kiss into something more sensual.

When she pulled away, her wide eyes were dilated with arousal. "Nope. Definitely don't need any new moves." Shifting, she nestled against him. "We should probably just watch the movie."

"Probably." He forced his finger to click the play button. He was pretty sure he could have her gasping his name again in less than a minute, but then he wouldn't want to stop. So he settled for holding her in his arms while they watched the idyllic scenes of the English countryside flash in front of them.

With Cass cuddled against his side, every part of him felt warm and full. As though he were holding everything he'd ever wanted in his arms. This feeling of contentment had eluded him his whole life. It hadn't mattered what he'd accomplished, how much he'd been paid, how many women invited him to spend a night in their beds.

This was real.

Against his shoulder, her breathing grew rhythmic. She'd fallen asleep. He shifted slightly, doing his best not to wake her but wanting to bring her in closer, to study the details of her face. There were still echoes of the precocious girl from his childhood—the sassy curve of her lips, those full, blushing cheeks. But she'd become a woman. Beautiful. Wise. Dedicated.

"I love you, Cass," he murmured, careful that she didn't hear. "And I'm gonna make you love me too."

* * *

This was exactly what she'd wanted.

For so long, she'd dreamed about it, thought about it, obsessed over it. Cassidy stuffed her cell phone back into her purse. The director of the pediatric residency program in Denver had called with the good news. She'd been officially accepted into the program. Which meant she'd leave Topaz Falls in just over a month.

Instead of elation, a sense of grief crowded her heart. Damn Levi. Damn him for staying away for all those years and then suddenly coming back and tempting her to forget her future plans and get swept up by him instead.

She gritted her teeth against the threat of tears. Luckily, there weren't many patrons at the Farm, which meant she didn't have to put on a happy facade. The rushes at the café tended to come right at the breakfast and lunch hours—eight o'clock and noon. The retirees in this town had a very strict schedule. That was why she liked coming mid-morning. That and Everly made the best organic green tea blends. Today Cassidy had ordered a plate of her homemade applesauce doughnuts too. Some days just called for pastries.

"Here you go." Everly strolled over to the table in her animated, cheerful way, carrying a small tray piled with the petite, frosted doughnuts that smelled of warm cinnamon and sugar.

"Thank you." Cassidy did her best to smile, even with the confusion clouding her heart. "I love these things." She pulled one off the plate right when her friend set it down.

"I'm so glad." Everly's smile brightened at the compliment, which made Cassidy smile too. Spreading kindness always had a way of improving her mood.

"I'm glad you moved here," Cassidy said. "It's about time we had some good organic food in town." She'd heard Everly had left some high-powered job in California, but despite the local gossip queens' best efforts, no one really knew what it was. "Have you always been interested in food?"

"Um, yeah. Can I bring you anything else?" The offer was clearly meant to deflect the question, so Cassidy let it go. She knew all about not wanting to discuss the past. Sometimes clinging to the future was the only thing that got you through.

"How about three more teas? My friends are meeting me here soon."

A look of relief engulfed Everly's face. "Of course." She scurried away and called over her shoulder, "I'll have them right out."

Cassidy watched her go, unable to hold off her curiosity. It was none of her business, but the woman sure seemed to keep to herself. Maybe she and Darla should invite her to hit the Tumble Inn for a girls' night before she left town.

"Doughnuts!" Darla and Jessa traipsed into the cozy room, bringing with them the cheerful chatter she needed to distract her from thoughts of Levi. Naomi waddled along behind them, looking even more uncomfortable than she had the last time Cassidy had seen her.

"Finally." She stood to hug them all and then took her time fawning over Naomi's adorable belly. "Hey, sweet little peanut," she sang, patting her friend's tummy. Naomi happened to be one of those moms who invited everyone to touch her belly. It had been eleven years since her last baby, and she glowed with excitement. "You have to make your appearance soon," Cassidy murmured. "So I can babysit you..." Before she moved away.

"I get first dibs." Jessa slid onto the bench and claimed her seat on the other side of the table. "We are related, after all."

"Which is exactly why she's going to leave the baby with me." Darla sat next to Jessa. They'd both thoughtfully left the end seat for Naomi, seeing as how she'd likely get up to pee twice while they sat there.

"Good luck getting Lucas to leave this baby with anyone," Naomi muttered with an affectionate roll of her eyes. "You should see him. Already so overprotective. I don't know if he'll let anyone else touch the baby."

"He'll relax." Jessa picked a doughnut off the platter.

"And if he doesn't, you'd better believe Lance'll have a talk with him."

At that moment, Everly came out with another tray and passed around their drinks.

"Thanks," Darla said with a warm smile. She could win the award for the friendliest person in town. She had a gift for gently drawing people out of their shells. The more they resisted, the more determined she got. "How are things around here?" she asked Everly.

"Good. So busy." A proud smile made the woman seem less guarded. "Some company recently contacted me about selling my preserves in their stores."

"That's amazing!" Jessa stirred a splash of milk into her tea. "I'm not surprised. Are you going to do it?"

"I'm hoping to. I might need to hire more help around here though." Everly glanced around, as though the prospect overwhelmed her. As far as Cassidy knew, she employed only four high school kids to help her out waiting on and busing tables. "If you hear of anyone looking for a job, let me know."

"We definitely will." If only her mother were open to a restaurant job. While it might be hard work and a bit more stressful than the shelter, the Farm was a local hub. It could be the best place for her mother to connect with people.

"You should try posting a job opening on the town's Facebook page," Darla suggested. As one of the chamber of commerce members, she was always advocating for people to interact on the town's page.

"Great idea. I've been meaning to join anyway." Everly glanced over her shoulder, stress lining her features again. "I should get back to the kitchen. I have a ton of cleaning up to do before the lunch rush. Let me know if you need anything else."

"Thanks! Good to see you," Naomi called.

"Don't worry about us," Darla added. "We're pretty low maintenance."

Everly gave them a grateful smile before she disappeared into the kitchen.

Cassidy sighed. She used to be low maintenance. When she was working and going to school and didn't have time for a social life or flings—or lusty make-out sessions on her couch. Life had sure gotten a lot more complicated since Levi had forced her to attend his rodeo.

As though sensing her thoughts, Darla leaned halfway over the table and got in Cassidy's face. "So what's with the SOS text? Does this have anything to do with your hot dinner with Levi last night?"

"You didn't tell me things got hot with Levi last night," Jessa said. Cassidy had called her to discuss details about her mom's new job after Levi had gone home. But no, she hadn't mentioned the extracurricular activities on the couch.

"It wasn't supposed to be a date." She shot accusatory looks at both Jessa and Naomi. "You guys totally set me up. Sending him there with lasagna. You know I can't resist your lasagna."

"Apparently, you can't resist Levi either," Darla mused.

No. She sure hadn't resisted him. And the way her body heated every time she thought about last night, she wouldn't be able to resist him when she saw him again either.

"So what happened?" Naomi asked. "Did you two..." She let the lift of her eyebrows fill in the blank.

"No." Cassidy shut them down before the chorus of squeals started. "But he did stay late, and we did make out on the couch." The heat swirled low in her belly and flowed to her face. "And then he said he wanted to have a fling. Until I leave in July."

"Hold on," Jessa said.

"Back up," Naomi added.

"You're really leaving?" Darla finished.

Cassidy grinned at their tag-team conversation. They'd obviously spent too much time together. Or just the right amount of time, depending on how you looked at it. "The director of the pediatric nurse residency program in Denver called. I've been officially accepted." Excitement swirled with apprehension, making her want to laugh and cry.

Before she could do either, a small celebration broke out.

"That's so…great." Naomi's voice wobbled. She dabbed at the corners of her eyes. "Sorry. It's just…I'll miss you."

"But Denver's not that far away," Jessa put in quickly.

"Yeah." Darla patted Naomi's shoulder. "We'll totally come down for girls' weekends." Out of all of them, Darla would likely visit the most. She traveled to Denver at least once a month to go dancing. "You'll love the city."

"I know. It's just…" How could she tell them her hesitations without sounding pathetic? Or without letting it slip how far things had gone with Levi? She couldn't go there or they'd totally encourage her. So she decided to lead with the less dramatic issue. "I'm worried about my mom." Lulu hadn't had a drink since the night of the tree incident, and Cassidy had found a solid AA program only an hour away, but she still hated to leave her. "I guess she's made some progress. And working at the shelter will help, I think. But I'm worried about her being lonely."

Darla set another doughnut on her plate. "You've taken care of her for a long time, honey. But she'll be okay. We'll all be here. We'll check in on her."

"Of course we will," Naomi assured her. "We can invite her to our family dinners. And we'll make sure to stop by the house regularly too."

"I'll see her most days at the shelter," Jessa added. "So I can keep you posted if there's anything you need to know about."

"Thank you." She'd been holding off the tears as best she could, but they finally overpowered her. "You guys are amazing."

"You deserve this." Darla gave her hand a good squeeze. "Now about the thing you mentioned with Levi..."

"Fling," Cassidy corrected. "It's not a *thing*. It's only a fling."

The whole table erupted into laughter.

"A fling?" Darla repeated. "*You're* going to have a fling?"

"Yes." The word came out a little too defensively. "We agreed. No strings attached. Friends with benefits. Until I move."

Naomi and Jessa shared an undecipherable look. "That's what Levi said he wanted?" Jessa asked with a doubting smirk.

"That's what we both want." Cassidy lifted her mug and sipped her tea in an evasive maneuver. Truthfully, she was with her friends. She had no faith in her ability to carry on a fling while keeping her heart detached. Maybe it would be possible with someone other than Levi. But they were already so connected...

"Levi is a damn idiot," Jessa mumbled. She bit off a big hunk of a doughnut and scowled while she chewed.

"What she means to say," Naomi corrected in her soft, sweet way, "is that we were under the impression he was interested in a committed relationship with you. Long term. That's the only reason I sent the lasagna last night. I never would've encouraged a fling."

"What's wrong with a fling?" Cassidy demanded.

"Absolutely nothing," Darla, aka the Queen of Flings,

said. "You deserve this. You deserve to have some fun after all the stress you've been under. And Levi Cortez is a special brand of fun."

Jessa shushed their friend with a disapproving look and studied Cassidy. "Are you sure this is what you want?"

No. Yes. Maybe what she wanted and needed were different things. She had to be practical. Levi made her feel good. More alive. But he wasn't ready for a commitment any more than she was. "I don't want anything tying me down when I move to Denver. I've never lived anywhere else. I didn't get to go away to college and have all of those experiences." That was easier than telling them the truth. That her heart was still broken. That she'd never healed. That she couldn't give someone all of herself.

"Sure. We get it." Naomi wasn't smiling.

"Just be careful," Jessa warned. "A fling might not be a big deal with someone you just met, but you and Levi grew up together—"

"Which means I know him," Cassidy interrupted. "Don't worry. I know how he is with women." Ever since high school, women were like a challenge to Levi. A game. "But I do need to have more fun in my life." Even just those few hours with him last night had made her feel lighter, not so burdened. "As long as I keep my expectations in line, everything will be fine. It's not like we're going to spend every minute together." They'd simply hang out once in a while, make out, maybe spend a night together here and there.

The thought revived those sensuous longings she'd experienced last night. Hopefully they'd spend a night together...

"As long as you know what you're doing," Jessa muttered.

She didn't. She had no idea what she was getting herself into.

Chapter Thirteen

When Levi walked into Jessa's kitchen, he was mighty tempted to do an about-face and walk right back out.

His sisters-in-law both sat at the table glaring at him. He'd agreed to meet Naomi at the ranch so she could show him the website and registration process she'd set up for the clinic. Basically, the woman had happily taken charge of all the administrative details, telling him not to worry about a thing, but he'd seen that look on their faces before.

His mind jogged backward over the last week, trying to figure out what he could've done to piss them off. Nothing came to him.

"Where are Lance and Lucas?" He held his ground a good twenty feet away from the women. Something told him he might need reinforcements for this conversation.

"They left early to head up to Casper." Naomi's stern tone held no mercy. "They're looking over a possible new purchase."

Likely another champion bull. When Lance had started

their stock contracting operation after retiring as a bull rider, things had floundered until Lucas came on full time. Man, he should've tagged along with them instead of walking into some kind of ambush.

Levi ambled into the kitchen and focused on Naomi. "Ready to start talking logistics?" Maybe they could skate right past whatever had riled them up.

"What the hell did you do?" Jessa demanded before Naomi could answer. "Seriously, Levi." She popped out of the chair and marched over to him. "You told Cassidy you wanted a fling?"

Why did women always feel the need to tell one another everything? You didn't see him detailing his plans to his brothers, and they were connected by blood. "Wow. You sure didn't waste time meddling, did you?"

"What are we supposed to do?" Naomi stood with some difficulty. She braced her hand against the table. "It's not like we had to drag it out of her. She came to us."

Which meant they were coming to him. The beginnings of a headache pulsed in his temples. "She doesn't want more than a fling right now." Not with him at least. "I only made the proposition so I could spend time with her. Convince her to give me a shot."

"So you're not planning to sleep with her and move on?" One of Jessa's eyebrows raised sharply. The woman had the best prying expression he'd ever seen. No wonder his brother never lied to her.

"Of course I'm not planning to move on." He did plan to sleep with her though. If that's what she wanted.

"Okay, then." Jessa kept her eyes on him, like she wanted him to know she'd be watching him.

Yeah, he had no doubt.

"Then I'll let you two get your work done." She finally broke the death stare and walked over to the coat rack near the front door to collect her purse. "I'll see you later."

Naomi followed behind her. She seemed to be moving pretty slow this morning. Hopefully it wasn't the stress of everything she'd taken on lately.

"Where are you headed?" he asked Jessa, helping himself to a cup of coffee.

"To Denver."

When he'd first come in, she'd practically incinerated him with all the glaring, but now she refused to look at him. He didn't get women. "What's in Denver?"

"I have some appointments." Her tone was clipped.

Naomi gave her a hug. "Keep me posted," she murmured, likely not wanting him to hear, but those two were louder than they thought.

"Posted on what?" Levi joined them by the door.

"Nothing." Jessa shot a desperate look at Naomi.

"None of your business," Naomi said in the nicest possible way.

"Oh, well pardon me. Since you two make everyone else's business yours, I thought I had the right too."

Surprisingly, Jessa didn't shoot back a smart-ass comment. She simply turned and walked out the door.

"What's going on?" Jessa never missed the chance to spar with him, never let him have the last word.

"Nothing you need to worry about." Naomi plodded back to the kitchen table, rubbing her belly with a grimace. "We should get started. We have a lot to talk about." She was suddenly all business, and while he recognized an effort to distract when he saw it, he also knew she'd never give up Jessa's secret so he let it go.

Naomi opened her laptop. "I thought we'd start by going over some options for insurance coverage. I've been doing a lot of research."

Thank god someone had. He'd been a little preoccupied with Cass lately. Levi sat next to Naomi, and she pulled up a massive spreadsheet. "Wow." He'd known she'd be the perfect person to help him with the details. He sucked at details. Sucked even worse at spreadsheets. "Damn. I owe you big for this." Maybe he'd offer to babysit Gracie and the new rug rat overnight so she and Lucas could get away. Or maybe flowers. Flowers would be easier...

"I loved it," she said, scrolling through endless rows of numbers. "It's been the perfect distraction."

Over the next hour, they went over supply and insurance costs, coming up with a budget that seemed relatively doable given the short amount of time they had to work with.

"So by my estimations, we can serve about fifty kids, breaking them up into groups of ten and running them through the different stations," Naomi said.

Was it just him or did she sound winded?

"Fifty's pretty good." He'd initially hoped they could include more. He didn't want to turn anyone away, but maybe they could grow it over time. "So how many additional volunteers do I need to recruit?"

"Based on state regulations for—" A sharp intake of breath cut her off. Naomi sat straighter and poked her stomach.

Uh... "You okay?" She definitely seemed to be breathing harder than a normal person.

"I think so." She shifted as though trying to get more comfortable. "Anyway, like I was saying, the state requires a ratio of one adult for every fifteen children over the age of five."

Levi quit listening and assessed her face. He didn't like how pale she'd gotten. "You don't look so good." Worry churned in his gut. He was starting to not feel so good.

"It's nothing. Just muscle cramps, I think." Naomi exhaled slowly and held a hand at her abdomen, poking and prodding. "I've had them off and on all morning."

All morning? "Are you sure they're cramps? Maybe we should call your doctor." He wasn't qualified to take care of her. Hell, he'd never even been able to watch an animal give birth on the ranch. When he was eight, their dog had puppies, and he'd passed out cold.

"No. There's no reason to call." She waved him off. "I still have three weeks. I mean, we're not ready yet. We haven't finished sorting through all the clothes. I haven't even bought diapers…"

"I don't think the baby cares if you're ready." *Hello!* Had she lost her mind? People had babies early all the time, and he did not want to be the one delivering it. *Okay.* He blew out a breath. *Stay calm.* He had to stay calm.

A gasp punched out of her mouth and turned into a groan. "Oh my god." She doubled over.

"Holy shit, Naomi." He lurched to get to her and knelt by her chair. "Don't tell me you're in labor." His knees threatened to buckle. "Please. You can't be in labor." Lucas was in Wyoming for chrissake. And Jessa was gone. It was just the two of them. He didn't know anything about labor. He couldn't deliver a baby…

He shot to his feet. "We need an ambulance."

"No! I don't think it's labor." She pushed out of the chair with a staggering effort and started to pace away from him. "I mean, I don't know. It's been so long. I had Gracie eleven years ago. And I was eighteen! I don't remember much…"

"I'm calling nine-one-one." Levi felt around his pockets for his phone. *Shit*. He'd left it in the truck.

"Don't be ridiculous," Naomi snapped. "You're not calling anyone. Geez, Levi. Get ahold of yourself. Even if I *am* in labor, it'll probably take hours."

He blew out a breath, then inhaled deeply. "Really?"

"With Gracie, I was in labor for eighteen hours."

"Oh." That took the edge off his panic. "Okay. Eighteen hours. Good. That's good." That would give him plenty of time to get her settled with a qualified professional and get the hell out of there before he had to see any blood. "Get your shoes on. I'll drive you to the hospital."

Naomi didn't budge. "I'm not having the baby at the hospital."

"Why the hell not?"

"I'm going to a midwifery center in Vail," she said as though he were an idiot. As though he should know it wasn't trendy to have a baby in a hospital anymore.

How was it possible she didn't already realize that he knew jack shit?

"It's a brand-new facility," she babbled. "Just opened a couple of months ago, and I've heard great things about it. Tons of celebrities have had babies there."

He didn't care who'd had a baby there. "We're not going to Vail. That's almost a two-hour drive."

"It's all planned out." Naomi sat on the couch stubbornly. "When I start having contractions, Lucas and I will grab my suitcase and drive over to Vail. We'll have plenty of time to get there."

"Well, Lucas isn't here." And this wasn't fairy-tale land. "Which means I'm driving and we're going to the hospital."

"You're not even supposed to go in until the contractions

are every five minutes and lasting for—" The sentence ended in a grunt. Naomi wrapped an arm around her midsection and heaved out ragged breaths. "Ohmygod, ohmygod, ohmygod," she moaned.

"Ohmygod," Levi echoed. He stumbled to where she sat hunched over, her body seized in pain. "Come on." He slipped an arm around her, prodding her to get up and urging her to the door. "Let's get you into the truck." At this point, he could get her to the hospital much faster than an ambulance could get all the way out to the ranch.

"Oh. *Ohhhh.*" Naomi shuffled along beside him, holding on to him. "Holy fucking shit," she wheezed. "Why does it hurt so bad?"

"I don't know." His breathing wasn't any better than hers. "We just have to make it to the truck. Okay?" He urged her on. "Then you can relax." And he'd try to steady his hands so he could drive.

Naomi stopped suddenly, a look of horror widening her eyes. Slowly, her gaze moved down to the floor.

He looked too. A large puddle spread around her feet.

A hard swallow knotted his throat. "Your water just broke. Didn't it?"

"I can't believe this is happening." She fisted his shirt. "It was supposed to be this beautiful birth. Calm and serene. Lucas was going to be with me, holding my hand. I was going to play Adele!"

"It'll still be beautiful." He choked out the words. From what he'd seen in health class, there was nothing beautiful about it. In fact, it was messy. And there was blood. Lots of blood.

His stomach roiled. *Fuck it.* He swept her up into his arms and hauled ass out the front door. Adrenaline carried him down the steps and across the driveway to his truck. He set her feet on the ground right next to the passenger's side, fumbling to get the keys out of his pocket.

"Oh no," she whimpered. "Oh god, another one's coming." She leaned against the truck, her body folding in on itself.

No way had it been five minutes since the last contraction. Levi held her up with one arm while he ripped open the passenger's side door with the other. He lifted her into the truck and sprinted to throw himself into the driver's seat. "Hold on, honey." He tried to sound soothing, but panic broke through.

While Naomi curled up on the seat and panted heavily, he gunned the engine and tore down the driveway. Swerving out onto the highway, he dug out his cell phone and called Cass. "Pick up, pick up, pick up," he yelled into the phone.

Finally, there was a click. "Hey, Levi. Now's not a good—"

"Naomi's in labor," he growled. "I'm trying to get her to the hospital, but I don't know if we're gonna make it." They were still twenty minutes away, even though he was driving like a NASCAR racer. "We're on the highway at mile marker eighty-six..."

"Wow. Okay."

Why the hell did she sound so calm?

"How far apart are her contractions?"

He glanced over at Naomi. Once again, she was gasping and swearing. "Not far enough." He put the phone on speaker.

"Like a minute? Two minutes?" Cass asked.

"I don't know." He couldn't even think straight, much less count out the seconds between each contraction.

"I don't think they're a minute apart," Naomi said, crying. "Oh my god, Cassidy. I'm having this baby. I already feel like I have to push…"

"No!" Levi's body broke out into a cold sweat. "No pushing." This couldn't be happening…

"Levi," Cass said sternly. "Take me off speaker."

He did as he was told, trying to focus on the road, his vision threatening to double.

"You listen to me," Cass said. "You have to be strong for her. You can do this."

"I can't." He was pretty much the worst person in the world to do this.

"You're all she has." Cass's voice soothed. "Now, I need you to pull over. Do you have any blankets in your truck?"

"Um…ye…yeah…I think so," he stammered, swerving the truck onto a wide dirt shoulder. "But she can't have the baby in my truck. I can't help her with that." Panic and fear sent the world into a spin. What if something went wrong? What if something happened to the baby? "Shit, Cass, I think I'm gonna pass out."

"You can't. Do you hear me?" Her voice had raised. "I'm coming right now. I can be there in a few minutes. But I need you to find blankets. And water bottles. I need you to help her get comfortable in the backseat."

"Okay," he breathed. "Okay. Blankets. Water bottles."

"I'm only a few minutes away," she assured him. "I'll call dispatch and be there as soon as I can."

The line went dead.

He cut the engine and dropped the phone on the seat before clawing his way out of the truck. Blankets. Water bottles. He kept both in the locked toolbox in the back of the pickup.

Somehow he threw himself over the side and into the bed and popped open the box. Quickly, he selected two of the softer blankets and grabbed as many water bottles as he could carry. He jumped back to the ground and then opened the backdoor and threw everything on the floor. Hands shaking, he smoothed one of the blankets onto the seat.

"Cass'll be here any second." He opened the passenger's side door and leaned in to lift Naomi.

She clung to him, sobbing. "I can't do this, Levi," she cried. "Oh god, it hurts. Why didn't I want the drugs? Can she bring me some drugs?"

"I don't know, honey," he murmured, settling her on the backseat. Whimpering, she lay down. "We're gonna do our best for you. Got that?" he said stronger than he felt. "You're gonna be fine." She had to be fine.

Chapter Fourteen

Gas pedal is on the right, genius," Cassidy muttered to the clueless semi-truck driver in front of her. Even though it was a double yellow line, she swerved around him and floored it— sneaking back into the right lane just as an oncoming SUV honked at her.

"Yeah, yeah, yeah." She pushed the speedometer as high as it would go. Up on the right, she caught sight of Levi's truck pulled off on a dirt shoulder, the hazards blinking. She skidded to a stop behind it and somehow managed to kill the engine as she flew out the driver's side door.

Levi ran to meet her. "Thank god you're here." His tanned skin had paled. Sweat caked his forehead. "I think something's wrong. She's in so much pain..."

"She'll be fine." Refusing to consider the alternative, Cassidy jogged alongside him, toting the medical bag she kept in her car for emergencies. "The ambulance should be here in less than ten minutes." At least it'd better be. She'd told Molly to haul ass.

Loud cries and gasps came from the backseat of Levi's extended cab. Cassidy turned to him. "You need to calm her down. I want you to stay right next to her head. That's your job. Stay next to her and keep her calm."

From the sound of things, they were going to deliver this baby, and they had to keep Naomi stable in the process.

"I'll try," Levi's face turned a ghostly shade of white. He jogged away and opened the door on the other side of the truck.

Cassidy bolted to Naomi and climbed up on the running board. "I'm here, honey."

Her friend lay on the backseat, curled up on her side. "Cass?" she panted. She was pale too. Pale and breathing too fast.

"Yep. I'm here, and we're going deliver that baby." As soon as possible.

"I don't want to," her friend moaned. "Not in a truck. Not on the highway."

"The ambulance will be here any minute," she assured her, pulling on a pair of rubber gloves from her kit. "But I need to check you and see where we're at." Another blanket lay near Naomi's feet. She carefully smoothed it over her friend's lower half. "While I get you undressed, Levi's gonna help you breathe." She shot him a glare. "Deep, even breaths. Try to make sure each one lasts at least three seconds." Judging from the purplish tint to her lips, Naomi was already on the verge of hyperventilating, and she didn't have any oxygen to give her.

"Deep, even breaths," Levi repeated hoarsely. He eased onto his knees next to Naomi and took her hand. "Ready?" He breathed in, lowering his face over hers.

Naomi nodded, inhaling as though trying to stay with him.

While Levi coached, Cassidy slipped off her friend's shoes, pants, and underwear, careful to keep her covered. "I'm just gonna check to see how many centimeters you are," she said. Not that either of them heard her. Levi was completely focused on Naomi, speaking gently to her while he brushed his hand over her hair.

"That's it, honey," he murmured. "Good job. Keep breathing just like that. You're doing great."

Cassidy shot him an encouraging smile. He was doing great too, considering ten minutes ago he thought he was going to pass out.

"You might feel some pressure." She performed a quick check of Naomi's cervix. Oh. Yeah. Wow. "Ten centimeters." She shared a look with Levi.

He seemed to have stopped breathing. Dread flared in his eyes, but Cassidy nodded toward Naomi. He had to help her focus.

She scanned the highway. No sign of the ambulance. *Damn.* If only she knew when they'd be there…

"Ohhhh," Naomi moaned, writhing in pain. "I have to push, Cass. I have to…"

"Okay. Then let's do this." They couldn't wait. Not even for five more minutes. She had no way to monitor the baby, to make sure she wasn't in distress.

"Will she be okay?" Naomi gasped, raising her head as though looking for the truth in Cassidy's eyes.

"She'll be fine." This was just another delivery. She'd done several, and only one had gone badly. "But I'd like to deliver her as quickly as possible so the ambulance can take care of her as soon as they get here."

"Okay," her friend whimpered. "Okay, let's try."

Cassidy pushed the blanket up over Naomi's hips and placed her hand low on her friend's belly to feel for the next contraction. "I'll count to ten, then I want you to start pushing. As hard as you can until I tell you to stop."

Naomi nodded, panting violently, holding tightly to Levi's hand.

He'd crouched over her, as though refusing to look at what was happening near where Cassidy stood.

She did the countdown, and Naomi's body seized. A strangled cry stuttered through her lips.

"You're okay, you're okay," Levi whispered over and over while he smoothed her hair away from her face.

Cassidy watched the baby's head crown. "Good. That was good. I need you to do that again when I tell you."

"I can't." Her friend writhed. "I can't do this. Please don't make me do this."

Levi sent a stricken look to Cassidy, but she simply glared at him. They had to get her through this. They had to deliver this baby.

Seeming to get the message, he hovered over his sister-in-law. "You *can* do this. You're so strong. It'll be over soon," he murmured. "Just a few more pushes."

"Another contraction is coming." Cassidy moved in closer. "Give me a really big push, sweetie. As much as you've got."

Naomi dug her heels into the seat and pushed, screaming.

Levi's eyes squeezed shut as though he couldn't take it.

"Come on, come on. A little more," Cassidy urged. The baby's head emerged. "Good!" Supporting the baby's head, she quickly cleaned her sweet little mouth. "Her head is out. But I need another strong push."

While Naomi grunted and pushed again, Cassidy positioned the blanket, guiding the infant's shoulders, and there she was...a beautiful little baby girl.

In the distance, sirens whirred.

"She's here," Cassidy called, tears pricking her eyes. "And she's so beautiful."

Leaving the cord intact, she maneuvered to snuggle the baby onto Naomi's chest.

"Oh..." Naomi sobbed. "Oh, hi. Hi, sweet girl."

"Dry off the baby's nose and mouth," Cassidy instructed Levi, who had frozen in place. "You need to rub at her chest and face to stimulate breathing. Now!"

He seemed to wake and got to work right away while Naomi cradled her against her chest and cried. Within seconds, the baby's strong wail put Cassidy at ease.

"We have to get the placenta delivered," she said, eyeing the amount of blood covering the blankets. It was a lot. Too much. Quickly, she went to work massaging the uterus.

The ambulance pulled up next to the truck, and Molly was out before it'd even stopped. She sprinted over.

Cassidy stepped aside. "Healthy baby girl," she said. "Born about two minutes ago." She lowered her voice. "Mom's losing a lot of blood."

Molly nodded grimly. "We've got this." She crowded the truck, followed by Brady, who was pushing the gurney. The medic wasn't Cassidy's favorite, but he'd have to do.

"You're in good hands," she called to Naomi, backing away to give them space to work.

Levi stumbled up from behind her. "Wow," he mumbled weakly. "That was...wow."

She turned to him. His color looked even worse than before. "You okay?"

"I'm…" He eased in a breath. "You were amazing," he uttered.

"Naomi was amazing." She peered over to make sure they were taking good care of her. They'd already loaded her up on the gurney. As they passed by, Cassidy quickly squeezed her hand, stealing another look at the beautiful baby girl. "She's so perfect!"

"She is, isn't she," Naomi murmured, cuddling the little bundle to her chest. "Can you call Lucas?" she asked as they loaded the gurney into the ambulance. "He'll be so devastated he missed everything…"

"We'll take care of it," Cassidy promised, looking to Levi for confirmation.

His gaze seemed to have locked onto the obscene amount of the blood that covered the blankets.

"Whoa." He swayed. Then, sure enough, down he went.

* * *

Bright light. Bright, painful light…

Levi squinted. His eyelids were so heavy…

"There we go," Cass murmured over him. "Rise and shine, cowboy."

Cass. The delicate notes of her voice were enough to wake every part of his body. He forced his eyes to open. "Shit." Wasn't he a badass, lying on his back, next to his truck, staring up at the sky?

Not far away, the ambulance peeled out onto the highway, sirens blaring.

"They wanted to put you in there too, but I told them to go on ahead." Cass knelt next to him, her blond hair haloed by the sun's glow.

Levi swallowed the sand in his throat so he could talk. "Couldn't ask for a hotter nurse," he said, earning himself a sexy little quirk of her lips.

"You just passed out, Romeo. You might want to wait five minutes before hitting on your nurse."

"I never waste an opportunity." Especially seeing as how he had limited time to convince said nurse he was worth the long-distance effort. Masking pain with a grin, he pushed himself to a sitting position. "Besides, I feel great." Minus a skull-crushing headache.

"You sure?" Cass looked into his eyes as though assessing his medical status. "No headache or nausea?" Concern pulled at her lips.

"Nope. Nothing hurts." The last thing he needed right now was for her to admit him to the hospital so they could diagnose him with yet another concussion.

"Luckily, you slowly slumped to the ground. Better than keeling straight over and hitting your head again." She stood up and brushed herself off, and he took the opportunity to study her legs. Mountain biking had sculpted every lean muscle, from her calves to her quads. Hell, he loved those biking shorts...

"That was quite a spectacle." Her smart-ass gaze teased him. "Watching a big, tough cowboy faint at the sight of blood."

Even the mention of the word was enough to bring on that woozy sensation again. "That was *a lot* of blood."

Cass's teasing expression dimmed. "Which was why I wanted them to get her out of here."

Another hit of adrenaline ripped through him, and he sprang to his feet. "Will she be okay?" He couldn't face his brother if she wasn't...

"She's in good hands. They'll get her stabilized. Molly's the best. She'll keep me posted." Cass smiled softly at him, the way she had that night when he'd made her dinner. "You did really good, Levi."

He laughed. "That's generous. I completely panicked." He had no problem keeping it real in front of her. She'd just seen him at his worst. If she could get past that, then maybe they could have a future.

"It's understandable," Cass said quietly. "A lot can go wrong in those situations. Trust me."

"You're so brave." She did this kind of stuff all the time—handling emergencies, delivering babies. He didn't want to know what could go wrong, couldn't stand to think about it. It was awful enough seeing Naomi in so much pain.

He eased out a breath, the remnants of adrenaline still pounding through him. "So you're sure nothing went wrong this time?"

"As far as I could tell, the baby is healthy. And Naomi is almost to the hospital by now. They'll take care of her." Cass leaned against his truck as though she needed a reprieve too. With the emergency now further behind them, he let himself admire her. He loved her hair that way—pulled back loosely to expose her graceful neck. He loved the petite frame of her body, delicate but also curved, somehow both soft and strong.

"Are you sure you're okay?" She eyed him as though doing a quick medical assessment.

"I'm good." In fact, he hadn't been this good in a long time. "We just delivered a baby together. I know you did most of the work, but it was so incredible." It was still sinking in, but he knew he'd never forget it. Never forget Cass working so methodically and focused but also somehow compassionate too. He'd never forget her handing the baby to Naomi so lovingly. He'd never forget that first glimpse of his new niece...

Cass's full lips curved again, drawing him closer to her. He couldn't stay away. Everything they'd just gone through had deepened the bond between them, whether she wanted it to or not.

It seemed she preferred the *not*. Cass stepped away from him and peered into the backseat of his truck, clearly avoiding any close contact. "So it looks like you did a good job protecting the upholstery. Molly took all the blankets with them, but I'm sure I can get them back for you."

"No. That's okay." He wouldn't be needing those back. Ever. He stepped close to her again, trapping her against the truck, unwilling to let her search for any more diversions to hold him off. Every time things got intense between them, she pulled away.

"You need to call your brother." Her eyes refused to meet his, but her voice had that same breathless quality she'd had when he'd kissed her neck.

He'd like to do that to her again, kiss his way down her neck until she was gasping, but she had a point. The phone call probably shouldn't wait.

Making his hesitation obvious, Levi backed off and dug out his cell. "What the hell am I supposed to say?"

"Tell him his wife had their baby and he'd better get his ass back here as soon as possible." The distance between them seemed to relax her. She looked boldly into his eyes again. Yet another reminder that he couldn't push her too hard. Even if it killed him, he'd have to give her space, keep things light. For now, anyway.

"I hope he's sitting down," Levi said as he dialed his brother. After a few rings, Lucas answered.

"What's up, Levi?"

"What's up?" he repeated, glancing at Cassidy for assistance. He'd never been good at things like this. Real conversations with his brothers. He'd rather be giving Lucas shit than telling him he missed the birth of his daughter.

Nurse Cassidy prompted him with a nod. "There's really no way to put it delicately," she said, letting him off the hook.

So he went for it. "Your wife just had a baby in my truck," he said. "That's what's up."

Lucas laughed. "Nice."

"I'm serious," Levi shot back.

Cass snatched the phone out of his hand. "I delivered the baby. According to a text I just got from Molly, your sweet little angel and your wife arrived at the hospital."

Even though the phone was a good two feet away, Levi heard the swearing.

"She's doing okay. Lost some blood, but the doctors are on top of it," Cass said patiently. "The baby is perfect. It all happened really fast. No one had time to call you. We were a little busy with the delivery." After a silent pause, she handed the phone back to Levi with a grin. "I think he may have passed out too."

"None of us are good at shock." And his brother had to be reeling right about now. He held the phone up to his ear. "How far away are you?"

"About two hours." His brother's voice wavered. "I can't believe I missed it. Did she look okay? Did Naomi do okay?"

"She did great." He decided not to mention the screaming. Or the fact that she'd nearly broken his hand. "She made it look easy."

"You're going to the hospital, right?" Lucas asked. Couldn't remember the last time he'd heard that kind of desperation in his voice. "Please. You and Cassidy have to stay with her until I can get there. Make sure she's getting the best care."

"Yep. We're on our way." Levi dug the truck key out of his pocket.

"Okay." His brother exhaled. "Let me know when you're with her. I need to talk to her. I need to hear her voice."

"I'll call you as soon as we get there." He hung up the phone and shoved it in his back pocket.

Before he could step foot near the truck, Cass snatched the keys out of his hand. "You just passed out. I'm driving."

"Yes, ma'am." He dutifully climbed into the passenger's seat while she went around the front. At least this way, he'd have some extra time with her. If he could keep it light and teasing, maybe she'd even let him kiss her again.

Cass climbed into the truck and buckled in, starting the engine without hesitation. She looked so dainty behind the wheel of his F-450 . . .

"Lucas sounded pretty devastated, huh?" she asked, handling his truck like it was a BMW as she peeled out onto the highway.

"Uh, yeah." He grabbed the *oh shit* handle above his head and held on for the ride. "Maybe I should've called him sooner." Like the first time Naomi had doubled over. That would've been good.

"It wouldn't have mattered. It happened too fast." Cass cruised around the car in front of them, going at least fifteen over the speed limit. Levi tried not to watch the speedometer.

"If they have another baby, they'd better camp out in the hospital parking lot," she said with a laugh.

"I'll recommend that to Lucas." He wasn't doing this again. He was not going to have any part in childbirth unless it was with his own wife. Even then… "I'm not sure I could ever do that to a woman I loved."

"Do what?" Cass kept her eyes on the road, thank god. Because now she was doing twenty-five over. At this rate, they'd cut the twenty-minute drive to the hospital in half.

"Get her pregnant," Levi said, bracing himself as they went around a curve. "Make her go through that."

"She doesn't remember the pain right now." Cass slowed the truck as though she knew exactly where Dev's patrol car would be parked. Sure enough, the deputy waved at them, seeming to do a double take when he saw Cass driving.

Her eyes softened. "She's holding her beautiful, healthy new daughter. Everything she went through is worth it."

Levi would have to take her word for it. She'd likely seen enough deliveries to know. "Do you want kids?" he asked, peering over at her. He'd thought he did, but that was before he knew how much trauma was involved.

"Someday." Cass glanced in the rearview mirror. With Dev's patrol car far behind them, she hit the gas again. "Down the road," she added quickly. "Why? Don't you?"

"Sure. Yeah." For the first time in his life, he could see it. He could understand the desire to create a little miracle that would be part him and part of the woman he loved. He could see it with Cass.

He gazed at her again, struck by that unrelenting ache to reach across the distance she kept between them. But then he'd lose her again. *Keep it light.* He had to keep it light. "I'm just wondering if maybe adoption is a better option. Something that doesn't involve so much blood."

She laughed. She seemed to do that much more in his presence now. He loved it, hearing her laugh. It was the happiest sound he'd ever heard.

"It won't be so bad when it's your own baby." She grinned at him. "And it probably won't happen in a car either."

"God, I hope not." He hated feeling helpless. He'd had nothing to offer Naomi, no skills, no knowledge, and definitely no composure. "That's what I get for asking her to help me finalize everything for the clinic." Speaking of… "With her out of commission, I might need help with the logistics." Late-night help. Endless hours of help…

"What kind of help?" Cass slowed the truck and turned into the hospital parking lot.

"Registration stuff, finalizing the insurance and budget." He could do all of it himself, but it wouldn't be nearly as much fun. "And it'd be great to have you help with the kids too. It doesn't pay, but I can promise you plenty of free massages."

Her face flushed. That was another thing he loved to see. The blush that told him he had an effect on her.

"You don't have to bribe me," she said, still looking mighty warm. "As long as there's no bull riding involved, I'm happy to help."

"No bull riding," he confirmed. The events she'd be helping with would be a perfect introduction to a different side of the rodeo world. Maybe she'd start to understand why he loved it so much.

Levi slipped his hand onto her thigh as she pulled into a parking space. "It'll mean spending a lot of time together."

Her seductive smile tortured him. "I'd be okay with that." She started to open the door, but he stopped her.

"You're okay with our arrangement. Right?"

"Yeah. Of course."

Levi didn't miss the slight hesitation that flashed in her eyes. "Why do you ask?"

"Naomi and Jessa mentioned something this morning. Before everything else happened." And he was hoping they were right. That maybe she wanted more...

"You know how those two are," she said, waving it off. "They want everyone to join the newlywed club."

She said it flippantly, but it didn't sound like such a bad club to him. "And you don't want that. You don't want a serious relationship."

"No." The word came out strong. "I already have enough complications in my life with the move. I can't handle one more big thing right now."

He fought back the disappointment with a naughty grin. "Seems like someone already needs another massage."

She shook her head with exasperation, but a smile broke through. "Not here. Lucas asked us to go in and hang out with Naomi."

"Riiiiighhhhtttt," he droned, pulling her into his arms. She might not want to define the terms of their relationship, but as far as he knew, kissing happened to be one of the best perks of a fling. And he intended to take full advantage.

He took his time lowering his face to hers. Then he brushed a kiss over her lips, tasting sweet lemons and spice. Her body sank into him, and she laced her arms around his neck.

Desire clawed at his chest as he deepened the kiss, tangling their tongues together. Flashes of heat burst inside him, demanding more, but he fought them back.

When he forced himself to pull away, Cass sighed. "Flings are good..." she murmured, her blue eyes bright.

"They are," he agreed, leaning in to kiss her again.

But a fling wouldn't be enough for him.

Chapter Fifteen

Cassidy clung to the outskirts of Naomi's hospital room. Not because she didn't want to be close to her friend, but because the space had gotten so crowded. Lucas and Gracie sat on the bed with Naomi, taking turns holding baby Charlotte. Lance hung out by the window with Levi, the two of them taking good-natured digs at each other. Jessa was around somewhere—probably looking for a cup of coffee.

It was crazy how time had switched everything around. Back in high school, her family had provided Levi with a place to belong, but now his family had become hers. Her heart ached. She would miss them when she left.

Hours had passed since that morning's drama, but that was still all anyone could talk about. When Lucas had finally made it to the hospital, they'd relayed the whole birth story for him in enough detail that Levi had to leave the room. And when Lance and Jessa arrived with Gracie an hour later, they'd gone through it all again.

Each time, the details had grown, along with the laughter and jokes at Levi's expense. Multiple times, Cassidy had offered to leave Lucas and Naomi and Gracie alone as a family so they could focus on their new daughter, but they'd wanted everyone to stay to keep the celebration going.

"Tell everyone again how Levi fainted," Naomi begged Cassidy, passing Charlotte off to Lucas.

"Come on, Cass." Gracie bounded over and dragged her to the bed. "You tell it the best."

"I probably shouldn't." She eyed Levi to tease him again, but that backfired. Looking at him this afternoon had only ended up teasing her. Tempting her. The fire he'd kindled inside her when he'd kissed her in the parking lot still burned hot. "We've been making fun of him for a good hour now. It's not very nice."

"Yeah, let's move on to other topics." Levi rose from his chair, a playful scowl in place. Leaning over near the bed, he stole the bundled baby from his brother, cradling her like he'd been doing it for years. "Don't listen to them, little darlin'," he cooed to his niece. "Your uncle Levi is the *best*. Handsome and wise and—"

"So humble," Cassidy interrupted.

Everyone laughed.

"He's always had a weak stomach," Lance muttered with a shake of his head. "But confidence? That's never been a weakness for Levi."

"It's because I'm the best looking one," he whispered to the baby. "That's why they make fun of me. They're jealous."

"Lucas is the most handsomest." Loyal little Gracie took ahold of her stepfather's hand protectively.

Cassidy had to disagree. Levi was looking especially

sexy right now wearing those fitted Renegade jeans and a tattered gray T-shirt that hugged his biceps. His dark hair had been tousled by the morning's events, and his eyes...they were full of a sweet tenderness whenever he stared down at his new niece.

She inhaled deeply, a sense of longing filling her heart. She knew she shouldn't, but she liked when he flirted with her, when he kissed her all hot and desperate like he had in the truck before. It left her suspended in a glittering anticipation that she hadn't felt for so long.

Levi glanced up and caught her staring at him. A knowing smile played on his lips.

"Okay. That's enough. Quit being a bad influence on my daughter." Lucas swooped in and took the baby back. He was cute with her too, careful and slow-moving and completely enamored. Amazing how such a tiny person could break even the toughest cowboys.

Lucas settled in next to Naomi again, holding the baby against his chest. Despite the sting of envy, Cassidy's heart couldn't contain her happiness for them. It flowed through her, brimming over in a fresh round of tears.

Lucas and Naomi had been high school sweethearts before he'd gone to prison to take the punishment for the fire Levi had set. For years after, Lucas had stayed away from Topaz Falls, worried he would ruin Naomi's life if he came back. Though they'd been apart for more than a decade, Naomi and Lucas had always loved each other, and when they'd finally admitted it, they'd somehow managed to overcome the wounds of their pasts. Now, after everything they'd been through, their life together was very sweet.

Cassidy glanced at Levi again. He seemed to be watching her. Quickly, she dried her tears and looked away. Her wounds were much different from Naomi's, and over the last few years, independence and hard work had been her savior.

"Can I hold the baby again?" Gracie begged.

"You can hold her anytime you want," Lucas promised his stepdaughter. Holding the baby like a football, he settled the little peanut into her arms.

The four of them huddled together, the picture of the perfect family. That was Cassidy's cue. "I should get going." Truthfully, she should've gotten going a long time ago. Spending time with Levi and his family like this went way beyond their agreement. He'd already told her Jessa and Naomi were pushing for more of a commitment between them. Acting like a member of the family wouldn't help. Avoiding eye contact with everyone in the room, she gave Naomi and Gracie quick hugs. "I need to get ready for work."

"Thank you for everything." Lucas leaned in to hug her too.

"Oh. Wow." She awkwardly returned the embrace. He'd never hugged her before.

"Thanks for taking such good care of my wife," he murmured.

"I'm glad I got to be there." It was a privilege to take part in such a special moment for her friend. Giving Naomi's hand a squeeze, Cassidy turned to Gracie. "Maybe you can come over and have a sleepover with me soon." That might give her parents a little rest after a week or two of being up with the baby at night.

"Yes!" Gracie squealed. "And we can paint our nails and put on makeup and have a princess movie marathon!"

Actually, nothing in the world sounded better than that. After babysitting the girl since she was a toddler, she'd miss

Gracie as much as she would miss her mom. "I'll call your mom in a few days and set it up." She had to fit it in soon, before things got too crazy with preparing to pack and move...

"Okay," the girl sang, returning her focus to her new baby sister.

Sadness clouded Cassidy's heart as she ducked out of the room. Soon she'd be gone. She wouldn't be around to have sleepover parties with Gracie, to see baby Charlotte grow up...

"When do I get to have a sleepover?" Levi had followed her into the hall.

Somehow he made a pout look so damn sexy.

Amusement overtook her gloom. "Hmmm. I don't know. Somehow we'd have to fit it in between work and planning for the clinic and nosy relatives." If she spent the night with him at the ranch, everyone would know it—Jessa and Naomi and Lucas and Lance. She didn't want to give them the wrong idea. Or maybe it was herself she wanted to protect.

"Guess we'll have to get creative," he said, eyeing her mouth.

"I like creative." Her heartbeat had already gotten out of control.

"Me too." He edged her up against the wall and nudged his lips into hers, teasing her with a quick, light peck. She threaded her hands into his hair and held him in place so she could kiss him properly and then teased him with a nibble on his lower lip.

When she pulled back, he groaned. "I'd be willing to bet there's an empty bed somewhere nearby."

"And I'd be willing to bet we'd get caught by Dev again. Or a doctor. Or Nurse Ratched." That seemed to be their luck.

"So when am I going to see you?" His hands fit to her hips and tugged her body closer to his. "Alone?"

"You're taking me out next week," she reminded him.

His shoulders fell. "That's a long time to wait."

"Think of it this way...it'll build anticipation." She kissed him once more on the lips, finding it even harder to pull away this time.

His darkened gaze lowered down her body. "I've already got enough anticipation to last us all night. Trust me."

"Then I'll look forward to our date." Every part of her burned red-hot, but she slipped under his arm and hurried away before he sweet-talked her into finding a vacant room. It wouldn't have been that difficult for him to convince her.

Fighting the temptation to glance over her shoulder, she hurried out the hospital's main entrance, dragging along the weight of a conflicted frustration. Part of her knew it wasn't wise to drag out this fling and make it any harder to leave Topaz Falls. And the other part of her needed this fling.

Outside, the sun still radiated its bright heat, bearing down on the mountains with that ethereal glow. From here, the royal sky seemed endless, stretching over the horizon as though it's beauty continued on forever. There was nothing to obstruct the view—no apartment buildings or skyscrapers or a haze of smog. Pausing, she appreciated it in a way she hadn't in a long time. She'd kept herself too busy, which had only made her stressed and harried. And lonely.

She hadn't realized how lonely she'd been until Levi had showed up that night at her house weeks ago, until she'd sat across from him at the dinner table. Until he'd made her feel a long-forgotten passion. But it was shadowed by the knowledge that they had no future. Eventually, he'd go back to his career, he'd get back on a bull, and she'd have to walk away. She couldn't live like that—waiting for the next injury, wondering every time he left for an event if he'd come back home. The fear would consume her.

She started to walk again, trying to outrun the heartache, but when she turned the corner, a blur of blond hair flashed, and she collided with someone.

The woman turned away, gasping on a sob.

"Jessa?" Cassidy reached for her friend's shoulder. "Are you crying?"

Dumb question. The woman's eyes were swollen and red. Which meant she'd been crying for a long time.

Cassidy hugged her. "What's wrong?"

"Nothing." Jessa turned her back, frantically wiping her eyes. "Nothing. I didn't realize anyone else was out here."

"I'm on my way home to get ready for work." Cassidy slipped in front of her. "What happened?" Why wasn't she in Naomi's room celebrating with everyone else?

"I needed some air." Jessa waved her away. "It's nothing. You should get going. Can't be late for a shift."

"I have plenty of time." Not exactly true, but she'd already put in her notice. What were they going to do? Fire her? She took her friend's elbow and guided her to a bench that sat near a small rose garden bordering the south side of the hospital. They sat side by side.

"Talk to me," Cass said, the same way Jessa had said to her many times. The woman was always the one listening, the one offering help. She never asked for anything. She hadn't seen Jessa cry in ages—not since they'd first met and her friend was still grieving the loss of her father.

Jessa stared at her hands as though she was embarrassed. "I just thought—*we* thought—we'd be pregnant by now. That's all." Her voice barely rose above a whisper. "We've both been hoping—and trying—since the wedding, and nothing's happened."

"Oh, honey..." Cassidy squeezed her friend's hands tightly. How had she missed that? She'd been so preoccupied with her own life that she hadn't even thought about how Naomi's pregnancy had impacted Jessa. "I didn't know..."

"We don't want to make a big deal out of it. Especially not now. I'm so happy for Naomi and Lucas." Her eyes teared up again. "But it hit me in there. Holding her. Watching Lucas snuggle with her. I hope we can have that someday too."

Cassidy nodded, her eyes stinging. She knew how it felt to sit and stare at something you wanted so badly but couldn't have. "You will. I'm sure you will." Lance and Jessa would be the most devoted parents. "Have you talked to your doctor?"

"That's why I was in Denver this morning. I had a bunch of tests done." She dabbed at her tears with a wadded Kleenex. "We don't know the results yet, but I'm so afraid something is wrong."

Cassidy pulled her into a hug. "I'm sorry." What else could she say? "That's so hard. But I know you'll have a baby someday." There were so many options now.

"It's okay. I'm okay." Her friend straightened, inhaled a breath, and put on her dazzling smile. "I need to get back in there. I'm sure Lance is wondering where I went."

Cassidy dug in her purse and found some fresh Kleenex. "It'll all work out." Those two deserved a baby. "It might take time, but I know it'll work out."

"I hope so. I've never been good at waiting."

Cassidy heard that. "None of us are good at waiting. Especially for the things we want most in life."

Jessa's brilliant blue eyes perked up. "What do you want most?" she asked. So much for a hidden agenda...her friend made it pretty clear that she was asking about Levi.

Cassidy pretended not to notice. "I want to be a pediatric nurse." That was her future. It was safe. It was clear. She didn't need anyone else to help her accomplish it.

"You'll be the best pediatric nurse in Colorado." Jessa leaned closer. "Just remember...there's room for more than a career in your life."

Sure. Maybe in her life. But in her heart? That was a different story. "You're going to make a great mom," she said with a teasing look.

Her friend simply smiled. "I'm happy to practice giving lectures and advice anytime."

"I appreciate it." She hugged her again. She loved and appreciated this family more than she could ever say.

* * *

"What the hell is that?" Levi stared at the mess in Charlotte's diaper. It looked like something out of an alien movie.

Lucas fastened the diaper back into place and darted a gaze around the room as though assessing what he'd need for this mission. "Apparently it's called meconium, aka newborn poop." His brother held the diaper firmly in place. He didn't seem to know what to do next.

Levi sure as hell didn't.

Charlotte, however, seemed content to snooze through the ordeal.

"Hard to believe all of that came out of such a tiny, two-day-old package," Lance commented. They were all crowded around the changing table in Charlotte's ladybug-themed nursery. Naomi was still recovering, which meant Lucas was trying to let her rest as much as possible. When Levi and Lance had stopped by to bring them breakfast, he'd suckered them into helping him change his first seriously messy diaper.

"You probably should've called someone more qualified." Levi backed up a step. "Where's Jessa this morning?"

"She's busy." There was an edge to Lance's voice. In fact, there'd been a harsh edge in everything his oldest brother said lately.

"We can do this." Lucas inhaled deeply. "It's just a diaper."

"A diaper full of tar." At least that's what it looked like to Levi.

Charlotte squirmed and started to fuss.

"Uh-oh. Okay. We've got to do this now." Lucas unfastened the diaper again. "Can't let her wake up Naomi." He glanced at Levi. "You get the wipes ready."

"Roger that." Levi opened the package and armed himself with enough wet wipes to make a blanket.

Lucas gave Lance a pacifier. "If she starts crying, try this."

"Got it." Their older brother held the pacifier near Charlotte's mouth.

"Here we go." Lucas slipped off the diaper. "Wipes! Hurry!"

Levi handed them over, and his brother went to work cleaning her off.

Charlotte seemed to take exception to the disruption. Her face scrunched, and she let out an ear-splitting wail.

"Whoa." Lance leaned over. "Here you go." He brushed the pacifier against her lips, but she only cried louder.

"Oh shit! She's pooping again!" Lucas furiously swiped more wipes from the package.

"How can there be more?" Levi snatched another handful of wipes to help, but the stuff was everywhere—on the changing table, on her clothes, on the soft pink blanket he'd given to her as a gift. Wiping it up only seemed to smear it worse.

"She doesn't want the pacifier," Lance announced.

"Keep trying." Lucas ripped the package of wipes in two, taking them by the handful and trying to mop up the mess.

Charlotte continued to howl.

"Man, this stuff won't come off." Levi tossed some of the dirty wipes into a nearby trashcan. "It's like glue..."

"You boys need some assistance?" Naomi walked into the room and peered over Levi's shoulder.

"Thank god." He stepped aside, but Lucas dragged him back. "We got this, hon. You can go rest."

Levi shot his brother a look. They clearly didn't have this.

Naomi winked and crept in between them. "It's okay. I feel great this morning." She lifted Charlotte, mess and all, into her arms and gave her daughter kisses.

Instantly, the baby quieted.

"She needs a bath anyway." Holding the baby in one arm, Naomi wadded up the soiled blankets and tossed them effortlessly into a hamper. "You guys should go enjoy some coffee on the porch." She paused next to her husband and brushed a kiss on his lips. "You're amazing by the way. Best daddy in the world."

"Love you, babe." Lucas's hard frown disappeared, and it was one of the best sights Levi had ever seen. His brother had a painful past. He'd always been hard on himself, but Naomi seemed to soften all his rough edges.

"Did you see that, sweet girl?" Naomi murmured to Charlotte as she left the room. "Your daddy and uncles love you so much, they're willing to get their hands dirty."

Hands and clothes. Levi eyed a dark spot on his shirt as he followed his brothers into the kitchen, where they washed up in the sink. He scrubbed a good three times before drying his hands on a towel.

"Whew, that was intense." Lance pulled out a stool at the island and hunched, resting his elbows on the counter.

Lucas sat next to him. "Yeah."

Levi faced them across the counter and looked his brother over. He'd never seen Lucas look so tired. "Seems like hard work bringing a baby home."

"It is. I haven't slept more than two hours in a row since she was born." He chugged coffee from a mug. "I'm constantly worried. Hearing her cry tears me up. And I suck at changing diapers. Obviously." A grin somehow erased the bags under his eyes. "But I've never been happier. It's the best feeling in the world."

"You deserve it." On a normal day, Levi didn't do sentimental, but seeing his brother finally get everything he'd ever wanted really got to him. It gave him hope too. Which reminded him. "Since we're all here, I wanted to run something by you two."

His brothers shared a look he'd seen countless times. *Here we go again.* But he'd like to bet this wasn't exactly what they were expecting.

"I want to build a house. Up in the west meadow. Right on the creek."

Lance straightened. Yeah, he'd caught him off guard. "A house? At the ranch?"

"I can't stay in your house forever." Soon Lance and Jessa

would have their own rug rats running around. "I want some-place permanent. Something'll that fit the future."

"The future." Lucas raised his eyebrows with a knowing look. "This have anything to do with Cassidy?"

"Yeah." No use denying it anymore. It had everything to do with Cassidy. After watching her deliver the baby, after spending the whole day with her at the hospital watching her interact with his family, he was convinced. Cassidy was his future. He wanted it all—everything his brothers had, a solid marriage, a comfortable home, even babies who pooped on everything.

"Wow." Levi had seen that proud big brother smile on Lance's face only one other time—at the rodeo grounds dedication. "Welcome to the club."

Always the skeptic, Lucas frowned. "Isn't Cassidy moving to Denver?"

"Yeah, but our families are both here, and I want a place for us to come." A home base, even if they couldn't be there full time. "Besides, from what I've heard, nurses have to work only three twelve hour shifts a week. So maybe we could split time between Denver and Topaz Falls." Never thought he'd admit it, but now that he was back home with his brothers, he appreciated them and wanted to be part of their lives. He wanted their kids to grow up together, their families to be close.

"You've really thought this through," Lance said as though impressed.

All he'd been doing lately was thinking. Especially about Cass. "So you're fine if I use the land?"

"Sure." Lance shrugged as he said it but the grin gave him away. "It'll be great having you around more."

Lucas nodded his approval too. "Have you talked it over with her?"

"Not yet." He was still working on that.

* * *

Undercover detective work happened to be a lot more complicated than it looked on television.

Cassidy slowed the Subaru, letting another car merge onto the highway in front of her. Three cars between her and her mother's old Jeep should be enough to keep her cover intact.

When Lulu had told her she was going to an AA meeting in the next town over, Cassidy had gotten suspicious. This was supposedly her mother's third visit, but the woman couldn't seem to tell her anything about the group—specific names, how many people attended. When she'd ask, her mother would say, "Oh, I didn't really count how many people. Some men, some women, you know..." Then she'd quickly change the subject to something having to do with Levi as though she knew that was the one way to make Cassidy bow out of the conversation. It had worked, of course. She didn't want to talk about Levi any more than her mom wanted to talk about AA.

So, in the absence of talking, she'd decided to tail her own mother twenty miles to see what Lulu was really up to. It'd be an all-out miracle if her mother didn't catch on too. Everything Cassidy knew about tailing someone she'd learned from watching reruns of *Murder, She Wrote* with Lulu, but it was more difficult to keep distance than she'd thought it would be.

Three cars had already honked at her for going too slow as the line of traffic passed through spots of shade and sun within the red canyon's walls.

Finally, a sign welcoming her to Glenwood Springs glinted in the sunlight.

Up ahead, her mom's Jeep exited the highway and headed into town.

Reducing her speed even more, Cassidy followed, taking the off ramp at a crawl. So far so good. At least her mom had gone to the right town. Now, if she'd go straight to the Episcopal church where the meeting was supposed to be held, Cassidy could turn around and drive on home, her suspicions proven wrong.

Glenwood Springs was much bigger than Topaz Falls, and she had a hard time keeping up with her mother between all the stoplights and traffic. Near the edge of downtown, she thought she'd lost her, but then saw the Jeep make a quick right at the last second. Cassidy gunned it down the block and made it through the yellow light, still drawing the finger from some pedestrians who were waiting to cross.

"Sorry!" she yelled through the open windows as she sailed past. The tires squealed when she took a right. Her mom's Jeep was parked a few blocks ahead of her along the curb in front of the library.

Despite the fact that she'd been right, her shoulders slumped. Her mother had already gotten out of the car and was hurrying to the library's entrance.

For a few minutes, Cassidy sat and let the car idle, waiting to see if her mother simply had a book to return, but after a while, she knew. Lulu wasn't attending AA meetings. She was obviously hanging out at the library for an hour before driving back home.

The familiar struggle between anger and sadness warred once again. The battle that had raged for the last six years. Since her father had left and she'd taken on the burden of worrying about her mother, she'd think Lulu was making progress—she'd see glimpses of hope in a smile or a cheerful morning—but then she'd find another bottle stashed behind the microwave, another secret, another thing her mother had hidden from her, and the anger would rise. Most days she struggled to hold on to that anger, because sadness admitted defeat. Sadness meant accepting this is how it would always be. Sadness meant grieving the other Lulu, the one she still wanted back.

Letting the anger seal off her heart, she threw open the car door and scrambled out, slamming it again before she stalked into the library.

The building was modern for a town that prided itself on its western heritage, all uniform brick and sleek glass windows. Judging from the stark emptiness, it definitely wasn't the town hangout. Cassidy marched down row after row of shelves, her irritation gaining momentum with each step. Her mother was actually hiding. Unbelievable.

Down the very last row, she spotted Lulu, sitting on a cozy couch in a reading nook off in a secluded corner. Her mother was all settled in, flipping through an issue of *Woman's Day*.

"Anything good in there?" Cassidy asked as she approached.

Her mother's head snapped up, eyes wide with the same panicked look Cash used to get when the school would call about another unexcused absence.

"Cass…honey." Her mom quickly tossed the magazine aside and sat up straighter. "What are you doing here?"

This was always the tricky part. Clinging to the anger but also doing her best to manage her temper so she didn't make a scene. "I had a feeling you weren't going to the meetings." Her voice was cold and hard. It had to be or she'd cry.

Lulu's sigh erased her panicked expression. "So you followed me all the way to Glenwood Springs."

"Yeah, Mom." She fought the rise in her voice. "I had to. Because you've been lying to me." She'd always heard that about alcoholics. That they lied a lot. But Lulu hadn't. She'd hidden things, but she hadn't lied right to Cassidy's face. Not until now. She sat down, caving under the crushing weight of defeat.

"I didn't want to disappoint you anymore," her mother murmured, shame flushing her face. "I've been disappointing you for too many years."

Cassidy didn't disagree. "So why not just go to the meeting?" If she knew how much it meant, why not do it for her?

"I'd planned to. But then I drove up to the church, and they were all going in." Her mother snuck a fearful glance at her face. "They were all young. And they were chatting like they already knew one another. I panicked. I drove away and passed the library and decided to stay here instead."

That was the other thing she'd learned about alcoholics. They hid. Not only from people but from their problems. "You can't do this alone, Mom." The power of that truth weakened her anger. "And I won't be here to help you. I'm leaving. You're going to need support."

"I know. I know." Lulu patted her hand as though trying to reassure her. "But I haven't been drinking. Not at all. Even when I've gotten shaky. Even when the anxiety hits."

The withdrawal symptoms. She'd noticed them a couple of times, but her mother always insisted she was fine.

But was she? How could she trust anything Lulu said anymore? "When is the last time you had a drink?"

Her mom gazed steadily into her eyes. "That night you came to the treehouse. That was the last time."

So it had been quite a while...

"I felt horrible that day. Shaky and sick. Thinking about

Cash." Her voice wavered on his name. "But I haven't had anything since. Just like I promised you."

"That's great." It was the longest she'd gone without a drink in the last year or so. But still…"I'm worried about leaving. You'll be lonely, and I want you to have people you can call…" For those moments when her mother felt weak. When Lulu needed someone to remind her why she couldn't drink.

"Darla said I can call her. And Jessa and Naomi. They've all been so sweet." Her mother looked into Cassidy's eyes, and there it was—a glimpse of the old Lulu.

"I want you to go," she said firmly. "You deserve this, honey. It's time for you to think about yourself for a change. Trust me. Things are different now. You don't have to worry about me anymore."

If that was true, then why had she lied?

Chapter Sixteen

Holy, sappy, love explosion. Did you have to use so many glittery hearts?" Levi glanced around his father's living room and kitchen. It looked like Cupid had thrown up everywhere.

Lucas and Lance had been tasked with hanging a heart-shaped garland across the hearth. Naomi and Gracie were scattering glittery heart-shaped confetti across the table. And Jessa was tying heart-shaped balloons to everything that could anchor them—chairs, lamps, doorknobs...

"What else would I use for a last-minute *surprise happy-wedding, welcome-home-from-your-honeymoon party*?" Jessa demanded.

He had nothing.

When they'd gotten a hold of his father and told him Naomi had had the baby, Luis and Evie had headed for home right away. Levi mentioned their impending arrival to Lance, and the next thing he knew, Jessa had planned a small surprise party to welcome the newlyweds home.

Well, kind of a surprise party. Levi had called back to warn the old man. His father wasn't fond of surprises or parties, though he tolerated them when Jessa was in charge. The hearts though? Something told Levi his dad wouldn't be impressed.

"I think it looks beautiful," Gracie said, tossing another handful of confetti into the air.

"Careful, sweetie. Let's try not to get any on the floor." Naomi followed along behind her with a broom, trying to sweep up the stray pieces. Baby Charlotte was tucked neatly into some wrap contraption that seemed to keep her contentedly asleep almost all the time.

"Oh, by the way." Jessa eyed Levi intently. "I invited Cassidy and her mom."

"Great." He played down the eagerness that bucked his heart. He hadn't seen Cass in a couple of days. She'd been busy packing and working, and he'd been inundated with stuff for the clinic. So, yeah, he couldn't wait to see her. Maybe pull her outside onto the porch and steal a quiet moment so he could kiss her, trace his lips down her neck again. He kept his expression neutral. Jessa didn't need to see his desperation. Next thing he knew, his sister-in-law would be trying to plan *their* wedding. That'd scare Cass away for good.

"There she is!" Gracie squealed, pointing out the large picture window. "Auntie Cass is here!"

"I'll go meet her—" Levi started to say, but Gracie had already bolted out the front door.

Damn. So much for catching a minute alone with her.

The door banged open, and Gracie towed Cassidy into the living room. "Wait till you see all of the sparkles!" the little girl sang.

While Cass oohhed and ahhed over the decorations, Levi checked her out. Was it really possible that she looked sexier every time he saw her? Tonight she'd pulled her blond hair back loosely, and she was wearing one of those bra-optional sundresses that just about brought him to his knees. Yeah, he needed a minute alone with her.

He was about to walk over to greet Cass when Jessa blocked him. "I need your help hanging this." She unrolled a large banner.

Congratulations Papa Luis and Grammy Evie!

Levi winced at the sight of more sparkly hearts.

"Gracie helped design it," his sister-in-law explained as they hung it on the wall behind the dining table.

"Then Dad will love it." His father had the softest heart when it came to his granddaughter. He glanced at Naomi, who was gently shushing a whimpering Charlotte. Now his father would have another granddaughter to spoil. Levi was actually shocked he didn't have more by now.

He secured the corner of the banner with a piece of tape Jessa handed him. "Man, you and Lance had better get caught up," he said to his sister-in-law. "Can't let Lucas and Naomi have all the kids."

The roll of tape fell from Jessa's hand. A pained expression gripped her mouth, almost like she wanted to cry.

Before he could ask if she was okay, Cassidy rushed over. "Hey, Levi, could you help me get something out of the car?" She grabbed his hand and dragged him past Lulu and Gracie, who were chatting near the window.

"What's wrong?" he asked as soon as the front door closed behind them. He'd obviously missed something.

Cassidy let go of his arm. "You shouldn't say things like that," she whispered, as though afraid someone would hear.

"Like what?" He didn't remember insulting anyone...

"You shouldn't say anything about having kids." She took his arm again, leading him down the steps and closer to her Subaru. "Not to a woman who's newly married and wants a baby as much as Jessa does."

"Oh." He closed his eyes. "Shit." Of course she wanted a baby. She mothered everyone. But she wasn't pregnant yet. And she'd gone to Denver that day for some mysterious appointment. Opening his eyes, he turned to Cass, desperate for her understanding. "I didn't know. I swear. I feel like such an ass."

"Of course you didn't know." She opened the back door of her car and leaned in, hoisting a huge, beautifully wrapped present off the backseat. "Jessa doesn't want it to be a big deal. Especially now when Lucas and Naomi are so happy."

Levi took the present out of her hands. "She'd never want to take away from that." Jessa was too selfless to let anyone focus on her problems. Levi set the present on the hood of Cassidy's car and turned to her. "So what do I do? Should I apologize?"

"No." She walked closer to him, and his knees nearly gave at the way her hips swayed.

"Try to be sensitive." Cass stopped too far away. He wanted her up against him, in his arms.

"I'll do my best," he managed, unable to hold his gaze still. It wandered all over her.

She smiled up at him. "I know you will. You can actually be very sensitive. You've managed to surprise me a few times." The words were almost shy.

He definitely wasn't feeling shy. "I love to surprise you." Unable to resist, he pulled her close and kissed her. One light touch of her lips was enough to loosen his control. "It's too bad my father's coming home," he said, breathless at the feel of her hands rising up his chest. "I would've invited you to sleep over tonight."

"That *is* a bit disappointing," she agreed, her lips quirked. "Maybe we can find a place to stay after our date."

"I'll work on that." Damn, he couldn't wait to get that house built. If he hadn't been so consumed with rebuilding the rodeo grounds over the last year, he might've been working on his own house. Which meant she could've spent the night whenever the hell she wanted.

"You look very serious all of a sudden." She pulled back and studied his face.

He couldn't tell her how serious he was. Not yet. But he could show her. "Want to see something incredible?" Of course to him, nothing could top the sight of her standing there in that dress with the wild and utterly pristine mountain backdrop behind her.

"Sure..." She drew out the word into a question.

Without an explanation, he left the present on the Subaru's hood and took her hand, leading her up the small hill behind his father's house, across the creek that carried the snowmelt into the valley and all the way over to the flat meadow nestled near the base of Topaz Mountain. A semicircle of full aspen trees sheltered the space, their brilliant green leaves dangling from tattered white branches.

"It's gorgeous over here." Cass was out of breath. Either from the trek over or from his hand pressed into the small of her back. He couldn't tell.

"I think so too. Which is why I'm going to build a house here."

"A house?" She stepped away from him.

"Yeah. It's the perfect spot." As long as his father approved, which Levi guessed he would.

Cassidy turned in a slow circle, looking out over the meadow again, but he couldn't read her expression. She kept it so guarded all the time . . .

"So you're staying in Topaz Falls then." Her flat tone held no clues as to how she felt about it.

"Yes." He gazed at her, but her eyes had gone blank. "At least, when I'm not traveling." For competitions or to visit her place in Denver. "I figure I can train here. Maybe run a few mentoring clinics each year. It'll be a good home base for me."

"Your dad will be thrilled."

He knew her well enough to recognize a forced smile. "But you're not?"

"I'm . . . surprised." Judging from the way her voice tightened, it wasn't a welcome surprise. "I didn't think you wanted to settle down. I thought you felt stuck here."

"That was before." Before he'd kissed her. Before he'd spent time with her. "I'm ready for something different now." Something more. "I'll likely have to retire in a few years. Maybe I'll get more involved in the stock operation." Before last year, the future wasn't something he'd cared much about. He'd preferred to live in the present, but everything he'd faced had taught him that he wanted his life to matter. That would happen only if he had people to share it with.

"I'm thinking four bedrooms." He'd already started to look at plans. "Nice open concept. A huge back porch up against the mountain with a hot tub."

"It sounds . . . great . . ." The words stumbled as though she didn't know what else to say.

He got that she was scared, that she didn't want to let herself love anyone and suffer another loss. But he was running out of time. *They* were running out of time. "Great enough that you'd want to come and visit?"

"Um...maybe. I don't know. I mean, I'll probably stay with Mom when I visit."

She must've known what he was asking, but she obviously didn't want to acknowledge it. Eventually, they'd have to, though. He already knew he wouldn't want to let her go after she moved away. "Look, Cass..." His back pocket vibrated. Damn phone. He snatched it out and nearly tossed it into the grass, but according to the screen, it was Jessa. With a disgruntled sigh, he answered. "Hey."

"Where are you?" she asked in a full-blown panic. "Luis called Lance. They're only ten minutes away! You need to get in here so you don't ruin the surprise."

He didn't have the balls to tell her he'd already ruined the surprise. Besides, he owed her one for the comment he'd made earlier. "We're coming. Be there in a few." When it came to Jessa, he'd do whatever he was told.

* * *

It was supposed to be a fling. Some kissing, a couple of fun dates. Maybe a hot night together here and there.

Levi had promised her uncomplicated entertainment. Now he was talking about building a four-bedroom house? And her coming to visit him? She had no idea what her life would look like in two months. Didn't he get that?

Cassidy marched down the hill, the sound of Levi's footsteps chasing behind her. Unfortunately, his legs were longer, and she couldn't outrun him. At least not without sprinting, which wouldn't be the best idea given the fact that she wasn't wearing a bra.

"We have plenty of time to get back," Levi said stiffly. He walked alongside her, matching her frantic pace. "No need to run."

"I'm not running." She was walk-jogging. Like Betty Osterman. "I don't want to ruin the surprise." She didn't want to be the one to ruin Levi's excitement about his new house either. But what could she say? What did he want from her?

They approached the creek, and Levi effortlessly hurdled it before reaching for her hand.

"I think I can hop over a creek," she said, taking a leap. Her back foot slid on the other side of the riverbank, and she tumbled right into the icy water.

"Oh god, it's freezing!" She flailed, trying to get out. Her flip-flops came off, and her feet skidded on the slippery rocks in the creek bed, tripping her up again.

Holding a straight face, Levi stepped into the creek—boots, jeans, and all—and hoisted her up. Standing thigh-deep in the water, he crushed her body against his and gazed into her eyes. "Quit trying to run away from me." He hauled her to the creek bank, setting her feet on the soft grass, but he didn't let go. "And quit worrying about what will happen. Let yourself enjoy the minutes as they pass."

"I don't know how," she whispered, clinging to him. All she'd ever thought about was the future. Someday she'd be a nurse. Someday she'd have a life again. Someday Cash's death wouldn't hurt so much. Someday she wouldn't miss him anymore. Someday Lulu wouldn't drink.

Someday she could lose Levi in an accident the same way she'd lost her brother.

That was the one possibility that wouldn't leave her

alone. She couldn't shake it off, ignore it, pretend like it didn't stand between them. "*You're* thinking about the future," she said, finding the strength to push him away. "You're building a house. With four bedrooms." Don't tell her that was all for him.

"I have to build a house," Levi said patiently. "I can't keep mooching off my family." He took her hand again, tugging her in the direction of his father's house. "I used to be afraid of the future. That's why I avoided it. Just like you're afraid of the present."

She couldn't deny the truth. The present terrified her. Because the more time she spent with him, the less she wanted to leave, the less she wanted to have her own dreams. Every time he kissed her it would make it that much harder for her to say goodbye to him. "I don't know how it would ever work. A relationship between us. We're too different. We want different things."

"We're not that different." Levi took her hands in his, rubbing his thumbs over her knuckles. "Let's take it one step at a time, okay? Today...right now, we're going to the party together. You're my date," he added, as though he didn't want her to mistake his intentions.

She hadn't. His eyes were heated and possessive, wanting. The look he gave her was enough to make her want too.

"Tomorrow, I'm taking you on another date," he murmured, captivating her with a slow kiss, but he pulled away too soon. "That's all you need to think about right now, Cass. Forget everything else and lose yourself in the moment."

When his lips came for hers again, she did as she was told.

* * *

"Hide by me, Auntie Cass!" The second she and Levi walked through the door, Gracie yanked on her arm until Cassidy followed her across the room. On the way, Cassidy reached up to touch her cheeks. They had to be as red as the sparkly hearts that were dangling from the ceiling. Levi definitely knew how to make a girl blush. He'd nearly kissed her into a stupor before she'd finally convinced him they'd better chase her flip-flops down the creek and then get inside so they didn't miss the festivities. Though she wouldn't have minded missing them...

As she passed by her friends, Naomi and Jessa both teased her with their sly smiles.

"What the hell happened to you two?" Lucas asked. "Did you go for a swim?"

"Cass fell into the creek, and I saved her," Levi said, tagging along behind her and Gracie.

Even with the damp clothes clinging to her, Cassidy's face got hotter. That wasn't all he'd done...

Across the room, Jessa and Naomi elbowed each other. They knew exactly what she and Levi had been up to outside. They'd probably been spying.

"Can I hide with you and Cass?" Levi asked Gracie hopefully.

Gracie considered the request with a lopsided frown. "No," she finally said. "You're too big. And loud."

Cassidy laughed as Gracie spun on her heel and headed for the curtains.

"I'll give you M&M'S," he called.

The girl halted. She peered over her shoulder, somehow having already perfected that womanly suspicion, even though she was only eleven. "What kind of M&M'S?"

Levi's gaze darted to Cassidy, but she shrugged. He was

on his own. As far as she knew, Gracie liked all kinds of M&M'S.

"Peanut," he tried.

Gracie's spry green eyes narrowed.

"No, I meant peanut butter," he said quickly. "One of those big bags. Jumbo size."

"That's more like it." The girl held out the curtain and waved him over.

Cassidy shook her head. Gracie sure had all of the Cortez men right where she wanted them.

"They're coming," Jessa called from her post by the window. Everyone scattered. Somehow, Cassidy scrunched behind the curtain with Gracie and Levi. Her body ended up pinned against his. He snuck his hands onto her hips and pulled her even closer.

"Are you two in love?" the girl asked as if the word disgusted her.

"No," Cassidy said at the same time Levi said, "Yes."

Yes? Love? Levi loved her? She didn't have time to question him before the click of the door sounded and footsteps thudded into the room.

"Surprise!" Gracie threw the curtain aside and leapt out, waving her arms in the air.

"Whoa!" Luis jumped back as though she'd really shocked him.

"Oh my!" Evie added with an expression of perfect surprise.

"We're throwing you a wedding party!" Gracie ran to them and took both of their hands, leading them around the room to show off all the decorations she'd helped with.

Even though they weren't hiding anymore, Levi still held

Cassidy close, moving her to stand in front of him so that her back leaned against his chest.

She closed her eyes and let herself enjoy it. The feel of his strength, of his body against hers. Her heart hummed. It sure felt like he loved her.

"They look happy," he murmured, close to her ear.

"Very happy," she agreed, watching Luis and Evie follow Gracie around to admire every sparkly heart.

He leaned in, glancing at her face, then her lips. "Are you happy?"

"Yes." Right now, she was happy. She didn't know what would happen tomorrow, but she couldn't pretend Levi didn't make her happy.

He held her tighter and rested his chin on her shoulder. Only when Luis and Evie made their way over did Levi let Cassidy go.

"Welcome home you two." He hugged them, and it seemed to her that Luis held on to his youngest son a little longer than he'd held on to anyone else.

"Glad to see you here," Luis said, pulling Cassidy in for a quick hug too. For some reason, the gesture heated her eyes. She missed her dad. It'd been months since she'd seen him, and even then she'd had to go to Texas. He never visited Topaz Falls anymore. An intense craving to belong here with all of them overpowered everything else.

"Papa Luis, Grammy Evie, this is Charlotte! My little sister!" Gracie carried the baby over, as slowly and as carefully as if she were cradling a glass vase in her arms.

Levi's dad knelt to Gracie's level. "Would you look at that? She's as beautiful as you are."

Despite her best efforts to keep her emotions in check, Cassidy sniffled. There was nothing quite like seeing a weathered old cowboy cry as he held his brand-new grand-daughter.

"Okay everyone." Jessa clapped her hands, always the hostess with the mostest. "The food is out. We've got appetizers and drinks. In a little while, we'll cut the cake."

"But right now..." Gracie interrupted. "It's time to dance!" She skipped over to an iPod station set up on the table and pushed the button.

"Country Girl (Shake It for Me)" blared through the speakers.

"Yeessss." Levi clasped Cassidy's hand in his and pulled her to him, leading her into a perfect two-step. He spun her around the room, holding her close, singing along with the song the whole time.

Everyone else danced around them—Gracie with Luis, Lucas with his wife and baby girl, Lance and Jessa, even Lulu and Evie, but the room blurred and the others faded as Cassidy followed Levi's lead. When he dipped her low, she laughed away every worry over what would happen tomorrow.

There was no sense in trying to protect her heart anymore. It was already too late.

Chapter Seventeen

This had been the slowest damn day of his entire life. After driving to Denver and going through a full concussion assessment that morning, Levi was ready to move on to the fun part of his evening. He cruised into the dining room of the Hidden Gem Inn, where Charity, Ty, and Mateo were just sitting down to a dinner that Levi had special ordered from the Farm. The restaurant technically wasn't open for dinner, but he'd hired Everly to cook for the inn's special guests this week to give Naomi and Lucas some time off.

The food looked good. Barbequed ribs, baked beans, homemade coleslaw...exactly what they needed after traveling back from their previous event in Nevada.

Ty whistled low as Levi passed him. "Wow. You look slicker than a greased pig," he said, helping himself to a healthy portion of ribs.

Levi took a seat across the table next to Mateo. "Um, thanks. I think..."

"Oh yeah..." Charity's amused expression mocked him. "Tonight's your big date with Cassidy." She gave his attire a critical eye. "You went all out. Somebody wants to get some tonight." As though it were a competition, she piled enough food on her plate to rival the men.

Levi didn't deny it. He wanted Cass, and he didn't care who knew it. "It's our first date." The first of many, if it was up to him. "Which means I needed to go all out." Especially considering there was more at stake than there would be on the average date.

"What've you got planned?" Mateo asked. He'd already burned through half the pile of coleslaw on his plate.

Levi helped himself to a glass and filled it with iced tea. "It'll be epic." If he did say so himself. Far as he could tell, this was his best chance to convince Cass that a long-term relationship with him would be worth it. Even if they got to see each other only occasionally. "For starters, I rented a limo." He'd had to call three nearby towns to find one, but he figured that'd give them plenty of space if one thing led to another like he hoped it would. "We're headed up to the Diamond for dinner." That happened to be the only five-star restaurant within a fifty-mile radius. It was part of the ski resort, perched on the side of a mountain, overlooking the entire valley. "After that, we're taking a hot-air balloon ride."

"Geez." Charity looked at him like he was crazy, but she was the one who had a smear of barbeque sauce on her chin. "You're throwing everything at her. Coming on a little strong, don't you think?"

"I want it to be perfect." He'd make it as romantic as possible. Then he'd tell her the truth. He wanted more. A commitment. Maybe a future with her. "Who wouldn't love that kind of date?" he asked the two men. Charity didn't seem to love any kind of date. As long as he'd known her, she hadn't dated anyone. Her mom had been a rodeo queen, married and divorced at least four times, so he could see why she'd be a little gun-shy.

"Sounds like a hell of a way to spend an evening to me," Mateo said with a shrug.

"Yeah," Ty agreed. "Let me know if she stands you up. I'll go." His friend grinned at him. "But don't expect me to put out."

"Cass won't stand me up." Not after yesterday. They'd had a breakthrough at his father's party. He'd told her to let go, and she had. All evening while they'd hung out with his family, they'd been all over each other—holding hands, sitting close on the couch. He'd pulled her into his arms as often as he'd felt like it, and she hadn't flinched once. Then, when he'd walked her out to her car, he'd kissed her in a persuasive preview of tonight.

He glanced around the table. "I have to head out, but I wanted to stop in to make sure you have everything you need." Truthfully, he wasn't supposed to pick Cass up for another hour, but the anticipation had made him antsy. The minutes had crawled by all day.

"I could use a date," Ty said, dropping a clean rib bone onto his plate.

"Can't help you with that." Levi tossed him an extra napkin. Ty really had been raised in a barn—all the way up in Montana. He wouldn't even know where to start with finding him a date.

"I think we're set." Mateo looked around at the others. "But we wanted to make sure you're still on for the Cody Stampede. We'll have to head out a week after the clinic."

"Right..." Levi stalled with a long drink of iced tea. He'd

forgotten about that little commitment. He'd been too focused on Cass. But it was one of the biggest events of the summer, and he had promised to do some publicity with the Renegades.

"Your head is all healed up, right?" Charity asked.

"Actually, it is. Got the all-clear today." Along with a lecture about the risks associated with recurrent concussions. But when he'd asked the specialist point blank if he saw any damage on his MRIs, the guy had admitted he didn't. "So I'm in. Let's do it. We can load up the trailers and head for Cody a few days early." By then, Cass would've moved to Denver anyway. He could easily swing down to her place for a visit after he got back.

"Damn right you're in." Mateo tipped his glass in a toast. "The gang is back together."

"Hope I don't let you down. I'd best get back on Reckoning and get some training in." It'd been too long since he'd ridden. Though he'd tried to keep himself in decent shape, he needed a few practice rides before he could compete.

"Doesn't matter how much you warm up." Ty finished off another rib. "I'll still kick your ass in the competition."

"We'll see." Unwilling to be late for Cass because of yet another pissing match with Ty, Levi stood. "Everly will be catering your breakfast at the Farm tomorrow," he informed them. "But don't wait on me." He had a feeling he and Cass would be sleeping in.

* * *

It'd been a while since Cassidy had put on sparkly eye shadow. Gazing at herself in the mirror, she couldn't believe what a difference a little eye makeup made. She didn't wear much makeup. It didn't go with her EMT uniform, and when she wasn't at work, she was studying or fussing over her mother or riding her mountain bike, none of which demanded that her blue eyes stand out.

But she had a date tonight.

Excitement fluttered through her, the same way it had when she was sixteen. Once she'd taken Levi's advice to live in the moment, being with him seemed to take years off her life.

In the few short hours they'd spent at his father and Evie's house last night, Levi had made her feel everything—desired and protected and happy. He'd made her laugh, he'd wrapped his arms around her, he'd kissed her. And in the midst of it all, she'd managed to banish the nagging hesitations. Who knew if he would even go back to riding anyway? Maybe the specialist he'd seen earlier that day had convinced him it wasn't worth the risk. It wouldn't be such a bad thing for him to retire early. Surely there was plenty he could do to help out with the Cortez's stock contracting operation.

After a few more sweeps of the mascara wand, she went to her bedroom and unearthed her favorite cowgirl boots—light brown and broken in enough that she could dance, if the situation demanded. She had no idea what Levi had planned, but she kind of couldn't wait to find out.

Humming to herself, she left her room in search of the small leather purse she'd packed with all of the date essentials—extra lip gloss, mints, condoms...

The front door swung open, and her mom charged into the living room, eyes shining in a way they hadn't for years.

"You're back!" Cassidy ran to hug Lulu. "How was your first day?" She'd spent most of it at the shelter with Jessa doing an orientation for her new job, and Cassidy had been dying to hear how everything went.

"You know…" Her mother plopped down on the couch with an exhausted smile. "It was wonderful. I spent a lot of time with Sweetie, and she really seemed to perk up. Jessa said it was the most life she'd seen in her since she'd brought the poor dog in."

Cassidy sat next to her, hope beating through her heart. "That's amazing." It was exactly what her mother needed.

"I think I'm going to love it there," Lulu said, a genuine smile lighting her eyes. "I have a lot to learn, but Jessa is such a sweetheart. So patient and easygoing."

"Yes. She is." A sweetheart and a saint. A wave of her friend's sadness passed over her, but she had to believe that Jessa would eventually get her chance to be a mom. Someday it would happen. No one deserved it more…

"You look gorgeous, honey." Lulu smoothed the skirt of Cassidy's simple, white sundress. "My beautiful girl," she murmured. "Levi'd better treat you like a princess tonight."

A swell of emotion pressed tears into Cassidy's eyes. This was how the two of them had been all those years ago…Lulu the protective mom, Cassidy the girl going on a date.

"He sure seems enamored with you," her mother commented innocently.

"We're having fun." Actually, they may have taken one step beyond fun last night, but she wasn't ready to admit that to her mom.

"I'm so glad." Her mother smoothed her hand over Cassidy's hair the way she used to when she'd tuck her into bed at night. "I know these last few years haven't been easy."

"It hasn't been easy for either of us." But maybe that was changing now. Finally…

"I'm so sorry, Cass-a-frass." Her mother gave her hand a tight squeeze. "It'll never be enough, but I'm really trying this time. You deserve all of this. To go off and have the best life."

"So do you, Mom. It's a new start for both—"

A heavy knock rattled the front door and started Cassidy's heart fluttering again.

Lulu practically hopped off the couch. "Let me get it," she said, not waiting for permission. "This reminds me of when you were going to prom your junior year. Who did you go with again?"

"Sam Ellis." Cassidy groaned. He was the most pretentious, arrogant honor student to ever grace high school.

"That's right. I didn't like that boy." Pausing by the door, Lulu straightened her tunic and fluffed her hair, which made Cassidy smile again. It'd been so long since her mother had cared how she looked, but now she stood tall and proud and opened the door gracefully. "Levi! Wow, don't you look handsome."

Sinfully hot was more like it. Cassidy stood but couldn't seem to find the strength to walk. Every time she saw him, that hypnotic pull between them intensified. Tonight it was downright explosive. He wore dark jeans and a black button-down shirt tucked in. He'd left his cowboy hat at home, and his hair had been styled in a sexy, carefree way.

He stepped into the room. "You're lookin' pretty nice yourself, Lulu," he said, charming her mother into a blush. "How was the first day on the job?"

"I loved every minute of it." She leaned in to give him a hug. "I can't thank you enough for making it happen."

"No thanks necessary." Cassidy had never seen him look so humble.

"Wow." His gaze traveled down her body, those bright hazel eyes heating the way they always did before he kissed her. "You look...incredible."

"Thanks." She tried to say it casually, but her voice faltered.

"Is that a limo?" her mother suddenly asked, peering out the window.

A limo? Cassidy rushed over. Sure enough, a large white Hummer limo sat in front of their house, looking completely out of place. The driver leaned against the door, dressed in a crisp black uniform. Already, a small crowd of kids had gathered around, Theo among them.

"What's that for?" she asked, unable to take her eyes off the monstrosity that looked almost as big as her house.

Levi shrugged, as though he hadn't probably dropped a grand on a car for the evening. "Figured it'd be nice if someone else did the driving tonight."

"How thoughtful," her mother cooed, but Cassidy didn't say anything. She'd never ridden in a limo before. They didn't even have limos in Topaz Falls, except for when the occasional celebrity came up for a ski vacation. "Where'd you find it?"

"Don't worry about it." He tucked her under his arm.

How could she not worry about it? She looked down at her clothes again, which a few minutes ago had seemed nice enough. "I'm not dressed for a limo." Seeing as how a group of her neighbors had already found an excuse to walk down the block for a good look, people would be staring at them all night.

"You look perfect," he assured her. He leaned in and gave Lulu a kiss on the cheek. "Glad you had a good first day. We'll see you later."

"Bye now," her mom sang. "You two kids have fun." She squeezed Cassidy's shoulder lightly. "I won't wait up," she whispered.

Cassidy forced a smile and nodded. The whole limo thing had thrown her off. It seemed so...unnecessary. Hadn't he mentioned something about hanging out at the Tumble Inn for some country line dancing? Surely he wouldn't take her there in a limo.

"You look better than incredible," Levi said, leaning close as he led her out the front door and down her crumbling concrete steps. "Damn, you're sexy, Cass. But I didn't want to say so in front of your mom."

"Probably best," she agreed. "And thank you." For the first time in a long time, she actually felt sexy. And nervous. But she hadn't been. Not until he showed up in a limo.

The group of kids around the car parted as Levi walked her over.

"Are you getting married?" Mellie, Theo's little sister, asked.

Oh god. "No," Cassidy said quickly. "We're not getting married."

"On TV, that's what people ride in when they get married," the girl insisted, seeming put out that Cassidy wasn't following the rules.

"We're just going on a date." Levi gave the girl a wink.

Cassidy's face burned. Well, that was it. By tomorrow morning, the whole town would know she and Levi had gone on a date. Since Cash's death, she'd managed to keep herself out of the local gossip spotlight. Until now. She'd always hated being the center of attention...

"You must be going somewhere real fancy," Theo said, looking up at Levi in awe.

"We are." Levi stooped to the boy's level. "We're going to a restaurant on the side of a mountain."

"The Diamond?" Cassidy asked, horrified. Locals didn't go to the Diamond. It was ridiculously overpriced and dished out the smallest portions she'd ever seen.

"Surprise." He stood back to his full height and glanced down at Theo again. "Only the best for the best girl," he said.

Wow. He was really putting on a show. Why did it seem so different than it had last night when they were with his family? What the hell was he doing?

"You getting excited for the clinic?" Levi asked Theo as the driver opened the back door for them.

"Heck yeah!" the boy shouted. "I've been practicing lassoing my dog."

Levi laughed. "Maybe practice on a stuffed animal instead."

"I will," the boy promised. He bounded away like he couldn't wait to get started.

Awkwardly, Cassidy slid into the backseat of the limo. The inside was five times more obnoxious than the outside with sleek, white leather seats, a mini bar, and flashy neon lighting.

Levi scooted in next to her. "So this is nice."

It was . . . ridiculous. But she didn't want to seem ungrateful. "Yeah," she murmured, wishing she could muster more enthusiasm. "Have you ridden in a limo before?" Was this a normal thing for him?

The engine started, and they slowly pulled away from the curb. All of the kids waved and chased them down the block.

"I've ridden in a limo a few times." Levi poured them each a glass of white wine. "Mostly when we're doing sponsorship events." He handed her the glass. "So it seems like everything went well with your mom today."

"Uh, yeah." She took a sip of wine before setting it off to the side in a cup holder that was custom made for the glass. "Sounds like it. She actually seems excited."

"I know the feeling," he said, eyeing her. "I couldn't wait to see you tonight."

A familiar heat snaked through her. This was all she'd wanted. Just him and her, the chemistry sizzling between them. "I was looking forward to it too." As far as she was concerned, they didn't need a limo or a fancy dinner.

He set his wine next to hers and tilted her face to his. "I wanted to give you a night you'd never forget."

"Oh, I don't think I'll forget this." It was already proving to be very memorable. Mostly because this wasn't at all what she'd pictured when she'd thought about going on a date with Levi. Last night at his dad's house, he'd been so down to earth and humble that she'd forgotten he even rode bulls, that there were a whole slew of shirtless pictures of him online. She'd forgotten that he was borderline famous in the rodeo world. But tonight that part of him seemed to be on full display. And this wasn't the Levi she'd fallen for.

Staring into her eyes, he slowly slid his hand up her thigh. Despite the confusion muddling her heart, her breath hitched. One simple touch and he'd made her knees weak. She moved closer to him, hoping he could make her forget all of her hesitations.

"Since we're both leaving after the clinic, I wanted everything to be perfect." He started to lower his face to hers.

Wait. "What?" Her throat ached in anticipation of his kiss, but she pushed him back. "*Both* leaving? I thought you were building a house here."

"I am." He kept his face close and eyed her lips. "But I still have to travel. I'm headed to Wyoming with the Renegades a few days after you leave." He moved to kiss her again, but she held him off.

"A competition?" What the hell was he thinking? "You're injured," she reminded him. "You can't compete."

Levi sat back with a sigh as if he'd given up on the kiss. "I did a full evaluation today and aced every assessment they threw at me."

"But it hasn't even been four weeks." The desperation beating in her heart edged into her voice. "And there's no way this is your first concussion." How could he even think about getting back on a bull right now?

Levi's shoulders raised in a defensive stance. "My MRIs are clear. I have no symptoms. The Renegades are counting on me, and I'm ready to get back. I have to."

"Of course you do." The words garbled in her throat. Suddenly freezing, she turned to the window, watching the mountains roll past, but only seeing the scenes of her brother's accident. They were still there, still so vivid. The hot sun beating down, the smell of dust and manure. The sight of Levi's hands trying to shield her eyes so she wouldn't see her brother's broken body. Those images would always be there.

"Cass..." He gently turned her face back to his. "This is who I am. You know that. You know I have to ride." The pleading look in his eyes emptied her. Her body went numb. She'd been naïve to think he'd give it up. He couldn't. Riding was too much a part of him, just like it had been a part of her brother.

"What are you thinking?" He slipped his hand into hers. "What's wrong?"

She couldn't force herself to look at him.

"I've known you for twenty years." He caressed her cheek

in an intimate gesture that filled her eyes with tears. "Yesterday you danced with me. You kissed me back. I know you care about me as much as I care about you."

"I do," she murmured, shrinking away from his touch. "But I've already told you I don't want a relationship."

"With me," he clarified, anger flashing in his eyes. "You don't want a relationship with me. But you might meet some pediatrician at the hospital or a stockbroker in the city, and I'd be willing to bet you'd be open to a relationship with one of them."

The words stung with their truth. Yes, she might be open to a relationship with someone who never took the kind of risks he did every time he got on a bull. But she wouldn't ask him to give it up for her. "There's still this gaping hole in my life. Ever since Cash died, I haven't felt fully alive." Fear shadowed everything. Fear that something else would be taken away from her, and she refused to let her fear rob him of what he could achieve in the arena.

"I can make you feel alive, Cass." Taking her cheeks in his hands, he guided her lips to his. They'd become so familiar, that firm insistence, the pulsing heat against her mouth. Passion took over, moving through her body, pounding into her heart, torturing her with a growing hunger for him. She pulled back before she gave in.

"I love you." Levi rested his forehead against hers, his eyes as steely and determined as they were when he rode. "And I know you love me."

"It's too hard." Tears spilled down her cheeks. "You deserve someone who can give back to you. Someone who can support you in the things you love. I can't. Not with the grief I still carry."

His jaw tightened. "Maybe I don't need anything in return."

"I won't do that to you." She loved him too much. "You've grown up. You've become the man I always knew you would be. I do care about you, Levi. I always will." She swallowed past the painful kink in her throat. "But I want you to take me home."

Chapter Eighteen

In theory, getting back on a bull should be like riding a bike. At least he hoped so. Levi made his way to the bucking chute, weighted down by a protective vest and helmet. This was the longest he'd been off in five years, but he was ready. After the shitty date with Cass last week, he had a hell of a lot of frustration to take out on something. Reckoning could handle it.

"You sure you want Reckoning?" Tucker stood outside the bucking chute, doing a preflight check. "It's been a while. Maybe you should start with Ball Buster."

"Nah." He hadn't had this much pissed-off energy to burn in years. Maybe that'd give him a leg up with the big beast.

As he walked past, Reckoning eyed him. It was almost eerie how still the bull got before a ride. Then the second that gate opened, he'd turn wild, and all that would matter was holding on. Levi wouldn't have to think about anything else—not about how Cass had run into her house before he could say good night, not about how she'd ignored his phone messages. For the last week, he'd been pulling together details for the youth clinic, but even that hadn't been enough to get his mind off the whole mess. So this was it. His remedy.

"I'm ready." He pulled on his worn leather gloves and climbed the fence. At all of the rattling, Reckoning started to sway.

"Hang tight." Tucker held the ropes in place while Levi got ready to slide over.

Across the corral, his dad waved. "Don't let him get the best of you, son," he called.

He almost laughed. Reckoning got the best of every rider who was dumb enough to slide onto his back.

"Ready when you are, hot shot." Tucker positioned himself by the gate.

"Let's do it." Levi slid his leg over and eased on, anticipating the bull's stomps and lurches. He wrapped his hand around the bull rope, gripping until the familiar ache tightened his knuckles. "On three."

After a fast countdown, Tucker threw open the gate, and Levi was in the air. His thighs burned as he cinched his legs down in an attempt to anchor his body in the midst of Reckoning's acrobatics. The bull leapt and kicked, sending dirt flying into Levi's face. The jerks and violent jackknifes thrashed his joints, but the warm flow of adrenaline staved off pain. He lived for that feeling—that blind rush. Like when he'd kissed Cass...

Reckoning arched and took a hard right. Shit! His form was off. The bull spun and threw him sideways.

Levi hit the dirt hard and rolled, finally coming to a stop next to the fence. Tucker ran out, luring Reckoning away, so he stayed put, staring up at the sky while he got his breath back.

"You almost had it." His dad walked over and reached out a hand to pull him up. "But you've got to keep your arm square over the bull rope."

Levi dusted himself off. "Yeah. I remember." All it had taken was one thought of Cass to derail him.

They ducked outside the corral, and Luis faced him. "You've got a lot on your mind."

He had only one thing on his mind. That was the problem. "Things didn't go so well with Cass the other night."

"I wondered why I haven't seen her around." His old man leaned against the fence as if he figured they'd be there a while.

"I told her I had to get back to riding, and that was it. She completely shut down." He'd seen fear drain the color from her face and leave her cheeks as pale as the haze hovering over the mountains. Levi gazed at Reckoning, now penned back in the chute, and finally found the courage to voice the question he'd been asking himself. "Maybe I should give it up. Walk away." Then they could be together. Riding was the only thing that stood between them. And he wouldn't be able to ride forever anyway...

Instead of agreeing like he'd assumed his father would, the man stared him down. "Why do you ride, son?"

Something told him Luis already knew. "I ride for Cash. Because he can't anymore. When I'm out there, I feel like he's still with me." The very thing that made him feel closer to his late best friend was also the thing that kept Cass away.

"Then you can't give it up," his father said in his quiet, wise way. "It's helping you heal. Cassidy wouldn't want you to quit anyway. Unless I miss my guess, she wouldn't let you."

"She won't let me quit, but she won't let me get close, either." She'd all but admitted she'd rather be with someone she couldn't really love.

"Don't give up on her." Luis gripped his shoulder and squeezed—the same affectionate gesture he'd always used when Levi was a boy. "That girl has been through hell. She's still in the middle of it. Sometimes it's hard to remember the good memories when the ugly ones are still so much a part of your life."

"That makes sense." Cass still saw the evidence of her brother's death every day when she looked at her mom. She felt it in the constant stress she lived under. In all the time Levi had spent with her over these last weeks, they hadn't reminisced much about the good times with Cash. There had been so many. That's what he had to remind her. Even though they'd lost him, the good years were what made loving someone worth the risk.

* * *

Cassidy would've been content to never step foot on the Cortez Ranch again, but obviously her mother had other plans. When Lulu had called and said there was a problem with the Jeep and she needed a ride home from the shelter, Cassidy had been tempted to get her an Uber, but that likely would've taken hours and it probably would've cost as much as her first month's rent in Denver.

So here she was, driving down the familiar gravel road, doing her best not to look up at the meadow where Levi had told her about his plans to build a house or at the creek where he'd pulled her out and held her against his solid body...

The memories burned through her, leaving her heart raw,

but she'd gotten good at flushing out sadness with rational-izations. Once she moved, she wouldn't have time to miss him. Everything she saw wouldn't remind her of him. She'd get a clean start, and maybe she'd finally be able to leave the past behind.

Instead of staying on the main driveway, she veered onto the ruts in the grass that led up to the backside of the shelter, where she wouldn't even see the corral, and parked next to the outdoor kennels. She climbed out of the car and quietly closed the driver's door before slipping in the shelter's side entrance.

"Cass-a-frass!" Her mom sat on the floor with Sweetie, cradling the animal's head in her lap while Jessa changed a dressing on the dog's hind leg.

"Well, look who it is." Her friend eyed her as she finished taping the bandage in place. "My long-lost bestie sneaking in the side door."

"Not lost." Cassidy forced a smile. "Just busy." And yes, avoiding Levi's sisters-in-law. They would no doubt have a lot of opinions about the whole situation, and she wasn't in a place where she wanted to hear them. "So what's wrong with the Jeep?"

Lulu and Jessa shared a conspiratorial glance. "It wouldn't start," her mother said in the same fake voice she used when she talked to someone she didn't like. "Strangest thing."

"Mmm-hmmm. Okay." Cassidy headed for the front door. "Should I go take a look?" Without waiting for an answer, she marched out the door and over to the Jeep.

There was action in the corral—she could hear it, shouts and the sound of stampeding hooves—but she refused to look. Instead, she climbed into the Jeep's driver's seat and tried the key. It wouldn't even turn over. She rolled her eyes. "The battery is dead." Obviously. The overhead light hadn't turned on when she'd opened the door. "You must've left the lights on," she called to her mom, who was walking Sweetie through the door on a leash. Jessa wasn't far behind.

"Did I?" The surprise in Lulu's voice was a little too obvious to be believable. "Oopsy."

Cassidy scrambled out of the car. "You two are unbelievable." Seriously! She should've known.

"I don't know what you're so upset about," her mother said sweetly. "It was an honest mistake."

"Could've happened to anyone," Jessa added, batting her eyelashes. "But don't worry. I'm sure Levi would be happy to give you a jump. I'll just send him a text." She pulled out her phone and started typing.

Lulu pressed her fingers against her mouth as though she was trying not to laugh, and she looked so healthy and happy that Cassidy couldn't get mad. At least her mother was engaging in something—even if it meant she was meddling in Cassidy's life.

She walked over to them. "Listen...I appreciate what you guys are trying to do, but things aren't going to work out with Levi."

"Why not?" Jessa slapped her hands on her hips. "You two looked so in love at Luis and Evie's party."

"You really did," Lulu agreed with a sigh. "It was adorable."

Oh, the party. That word was enough to reinstate the hot flashes Levi had ignited in her body. Of course, it had all gone cold the minute he'd told her he was riding again. "Like I've said all along, we were only having a fling—"

"Everything okay over here?"

Cassidy froze, her shoulders straight, squared, and suddenly very, very tense. Instead of turning around, she shot her mother a stern frown. They could've told her Levi was walking over. A little warning would've been nice.

"Oh hi, Levi!" Lulu purred. "Everything's fine. We're just having a little car trouble is all." She gently tugged on Sweetie's leash as though she wanted to walk away. "Maybe you could help Cass figure it out?"

"There isn't much to figure out," Cassidy reminded her mother tightly. She'd been set up.

"We'll let you two handle this." Jessa rushed to the shelter's main door and jerked it open. "We really should get Sweetie back inside so we can feed her."

With a guilty smile and a little wave, her mother followed Jessa inside, leaving Cassidy with no choice but to turn around and face Levi.

If the memories of Levi's kiss had burned her, the sight of him standing there consumed her. Dust covered his body—the ripped, worn jeans and leather chaps, the heavy-looking vest he wore, the tanned skin on his face. His hair was tousled and sexy—exactly the way it had looked when he was lying next to her on the couch touching her and making her moan.

"So what's up?" His stance widened, and god, he was manly and hot and so in control that she had to look away. Because the sight of him broke her control.

"The Jeep," she croaked out. "The battery's dead." She decided not to mention that it was premeditated murder at the hands of her mother and Jessa.

"That's it?" His head tilted as he looked at her. "Jessa sent me an SOS text and said you needed me right away."

Shocking. "That's it." It took way too much effort to work her shoulders into a casual shrug. That so wasn't it. There were other things she should say to him, words he deserved to hear—that she wished things were different. That she wished she could be braver. That she would always remember how special he made her feel. But she was too damn scared to say any of it.

"I'll send Tucker over in my truck. He can jump it for you."

"Right. Great. Thanks." Levi didn't walk away. He simply stood there and stared at her as though he could see right through her polite pretenses. She dropped her gaze, focusing on his protective vest. "So you're training today?" There was an edge to her voice, a subtle reminder why she had to keep her distance.

"Yeah. I've gotten in some good rides." He said the words quickly, as though dismissing them. "You're still planning to help with the rodeo clinic, right?"

"Oh." *No.* Why did she find it so hard to say no to the man? "I'm not sure that's a good idea." It was a terrible idea. If she had to be this close to him for a whole day, her heart would likely give out.

He stepped closer, and her lungs drew in a sharp breath in anticipation of his touch, but his hands stayed at his sides. "I could really use the help, Cass. If you're up for it. We've got a full roster, and it'd be great to have a nurse around."

Those eyes. Those magic, sad, hazel eyes. She was caught in them. "Sure. Okay," she heard herself say. "I'll help out."

A hint of a smile moved like a shadow across his lips. "Guess I'll see you then."

Chapter Nineteen

You're driving awfully slow." Lulu pursed her lips into a knowing frown.

Cassidy glanced at the speedometer, which had barely inched up to fifteen miles per hour. "I'm being careful." She nodded toward Theo, who sat in the backseat. "We have precious cargo today." So there. Her caution had nothing to do with the fact that they were on their way to the rodeo grounds to help with the clinic. Where she would be forced to work with Levi for an entire day.

"The speed limit sign back there said thirty miles per hour," Theo mentioned helpfully, while he bounced as much as the seat belt would let him. His mom had to work early, so Cassidy had offered to drive him to the clinic, and he obviously couldn't wait to get there.

Unfortunately for him, *she* could. She should've told Levi she couldn't help. By now, she thought the sting of his dejected expression would've worn off, but she couldn't stop thinking about how sad his eyes had been when she'd seen him at the ranch.

"I heard Wilma Mackle got a ticket for driving too slow last week," her mother warned. "You know how Dev gets when he's low on his quota."

"Fine." She made sure both Theo and Lulu heard her sigh. "I'll go a little faster."

"Is there a reason you're taking your time?" A phony innocence brightened her mother's voice. "Are you nervous about something?"

"No." That was the biggest lie she'd told since she'd informed Jessa and Naomi she couldn't meet them at the Farm yesterday.

"When I'm nervous, my mom tells me to take deep breaths." Theo strained against his seat belt and reached up to give her shoulder a hearty pat.

Even with the anxiety knotting her stomach, Cassidy had to smile. That boy had the biggest heart.

"That's a good idea, Theo." Lulu's eyes were full of humor as she looked at her daughter. "Maybe you should take a couple of deep breaths."

Something told her deep breaths would not soothe the painful ache that gripped her heart when she thought about seeing Levi again.

"Are you okay, honey?" her mom asked quietly.

"Sure." Even to her it sounded hollow. She wasn't okay. She'd tried to be, but truthfully, it scared her how much she missed Levi. She'd seen him only a few days ago at the ranch, but she missed his cocky smile. The way he teased her. The way he seemed to sense exactly what she needed before she had to say it. Not that she wanted to discuss that in front of Theo.

Instead of meeting her mother's questioning gaze, she glanced in the rearview mirror. "What about you, Theo? Are you nervous about camp?"

"No way!" He scooted forward, both of his legs kicking the seat. "I can't wait to be a cowboy! I've been practicing real hard."

"I could tell." She'd seen him outside in front of his house every evening, swinging his rope above his head while he attempted to lasso the deer statue his mom had finally bought at a garage sale.

"You're a natural." That was the main reason she hadn't bailed on Levi. She wanted to be there for Theo.

Cassidy pulled the car into the rodeo grounds' parking lot. Already, a short line had formed outside of the arena's main entrance, where a crowd of kids impatiently waited to get checked in.

Uncertainty settled again, weighing heavy against her shoulders. "Hmmm…where to park?" She cruised down row after row of empty parking spots, pretending to take her sweet time weighing the pros and cons of each one.

"What about there?" Theo suggested, pointing. "Or that one! That one's perfect!" Panic flared in his dark eyes as the car rolled farther from the main entrance.

"I don't like to park right next to other cars." Turning down another row, she kept a lookout for Levi. She hadn't even seen the man yet and already her heart beat somewhere between anticipation and panic.

"How 'bout this spot?" Theo tapped her shoulder repeatedly.

The poor kid was obviously trying his best to be polite, but judging from the pained grimace on his face, he'd all but lost his patience.

"You know, buddy...that one looks perfect." She swung the car into the spot a good football field away from the entrance. Before she'd even cut the engine, Theo had set himself free from the seat belt and bolted outside.

"You guys comin' or what?" He danced around the car.

"We'll be right there, honey," her mother called through the window. Her smile fell away when she looked at Cassidy. "Now, I've done my best to stay quiet, to stay out of this whole thing between you and Levi..."

"Out of it?" She widened her eyes at her mother. "Really?"

"Okay, fine. I haven't exactly stayed out of it. But it's only because I love you, hon. And you seemed so happy. I don't understand what happened."

Lulu wouldn't understand because Cassidy hadn't told her much. During the last few years, her mother hadn't exactly been her confidant, but that was starting to change.

Outside the car, Theo had impatiently started his lassoing practice, ensnaring a small wooden pole that marked off the parking spots.

Her mother waited quietly, obviously content to sit there until Cassidy answered.

It still amazed her how much Lulu's face had changed in a few short weeks. Energy brightened her eyes again, and she'd gone back to wearing a touch of makeup. She almost looked youthful. Youthful and determined. Hope swelled in Cassidy's heart.

"Levi wants more than I can give him," Cassidy finally said. More than she could give anyone. She'd been giving for so long. She didn't regret it, but she was tired. "And..." This part was much harder. "I can't do it, Mom. I can't send him off to competitions every weekend wondering if he'll come back."

She expected sympathy, a pat on the hand, but instead, Lulu turned to her almost looking angry. "Don't do this, Cass. Don't push him out of your life because of fear." Her eyes flashed a strong warning. "There will always be risks. It doesn't matter who you love."

It did matter. She knew the statistics, the injuries bull riders dealt with, the high potential for something to go wrong, no matter how safe they were, no matter how much protective gear they wore...

"Hey guys! Are you ready?" Theo swung his rope in their direction as though he wanted to lasso them.

"Be there in a minute, buddy," Cassidy called. The forced cheerfulness stung her throat. She withdrew the keys from the ignition, but Lulu grabbed her hand.

"Your father added so much to my life," she murmured, her eyes misting. "Loving him made every experience more significant."

That was it? Her best argument? "But it fell apart. Dad left." Love hadn't been enough to save either one of them. Her mom had lost a son *and* her husband...

"I let it fall apart." Her mother squeezed her hand harder—another show of the strength that had eluded her for so long. "After your brother died, I couldn't let your father in anymore. I couldn't let anyone in. He tried, Cass. Instead of grieving with him, I shut him out. That's why he left. He couldn't handle the pain of losing both Cash and me."

That was what scared Cassidy. The pain of losing someone else she loved. So much could go wrong. Or the physical distance between them could be too much, too difficult to overcome. "I don't want to risk it," she admitted. The feelings she had for Levi already went so deep...if she let herself fall, she'd never recover.

"I understand." Her mother let her hand go. "Trust me. But I don't want you to make the same mistakes I made. It's so empty, sweetie. A life without loving anyone. A life without letting anyone love you."

Empty. That's exactly what the last six years had been. Empty and long. A wasteland.

"I would do it all again," Lulu said. "Even knowing the pain that was waiting for us. I'd still marry him." Passion echoed in her words. "Love can make the pain bearable, if you let it. I didn't know how. I wasn't brave enough." Her mother turned Cassidy's face to hers. "But you are. And so is Levi. You don't have to settle your entire future right now. You only have to find enough courage for each moment."

The tears Cassidy had been trying to swallow back spilled over. "I miss it," she whispered. "Our family. How it was before." She missed the security, the surety it had given her in this unstable world.

"I do too." Her mom hugged her tight. "But you can build that for yourself, Cass. You can build it and hold on to it. You don't have to make the same mistakes I—"

There was a knock on Cassidy's window.

She pulled away from her mother and peered up at Levi. His mouth curved slightly when her eyes met his, like he couldn't help but smile.

She couldn't help but melt, caught up in the warmth that flowed through her at the sight of him. Longing trembled in her hands, but somehow she managed to open the car door. "Hey."

"Hey."

"Come on, Levi," Theo urged, tugging on the man's arm. "We'd better get in there, right? We don't want to miss anything. You're in charge. You can take me in . . ."

"I'll take you." Lulu scrambled to get out of the car and hurried over to Theo. "We'll see you in there," she called, already leading the boy away.

Swiping at the lingering tears, Cassidy slipped out of the car and faced Levi, not dreading it nearly as much as she had ten minutes ago.

Concern tugged at the corners of his eyes. "You okay?"

"I'm…" There was so much she wanted to say to him, but she didn't even know where to start. "I'll be fine." She had a lot to think about. A lot to process. But her mom had said exactly what she needed to hear. *Find courage in the moment.*

"Thanks for coming today." Levi hesitantly eased closer, almost like he feared she'd turn her back on him.

Maybe it was time to be done turning her back. She smiled up at him, everything inside her going soft. "I wouldn't have missed it."

Interest lit his eyes as he looked her over. "I was hoping we could talk later. After things wrap up for the day. I have something I want to show you."

At the deep, mellow sound of his voice, her fears melted into a simmering anticipation. "Yes, of course we can talk."

"It's a plan then. Guess we should get over there." Levi placed his hand on the small of her back and guided her in front of him. Her legs stuttered at the intimate touch, and she let herself enjoy it, the rush of heat he brought, the weakening in her knees.

They approached the line, where around thirty kids squealed and laughed and chased one another around.

Slipping his arm around her, Levi leaned close. "You ready for this?"

"No." But maybe she didn't need to be ready. Maybe she simply needed to jump in.

* * *

This was exactly why she'd avoided him.

Kneeling next to Theo, Levi pretty much embodied every quality she could ever want in a man.

"All right, buddy. You're up." Levi helped Theo climb onto the sheep, those strong hands holding him in place.

Just when she thought he couldn't get any sexier...

"I got this." Theo leaned over and held on to the sheep while Levi kept the animal steady. "He's not gonna buck me off for nothin'." Obvious admiration for his mentor gleamed in the boy's eyes. He nodded definitely once, as though silently promising Levi he would do his best.

He had all morning. All the kids had done their best, thanks to that cowboy right there. She should've known Levi would assign her to volunteer at his station. Not that she was complaining. All morning, he'd made her laugh. He'd made all of them laugh actually. Together, the two of them had been in charge of the Mutton Busting clinic, teaching a bunch of four- through seven-year-olds how to ride a sheep without falling off. Which was interesting, because she was pretty sure she couldn't do it.

"I'll start the timer as soon as Cass opens the chute," Levi said, standing to his full height again. "Remember what we talked about. Keep your form."

"Ease up, and keep a low center of gravity," Theo said, reciting the words that had been indoctrinated into him earlier.

"That's right." Levi gave him a proud pat on the shoulder. "You're the man, Theo." He turned to the other kids, who were all lined up outside of the corral fence waiting for their turn. "Who's ready to cheer?" he called.

A dozen shouts rang out.

"Me!"

"I can cheer loudest!"

"Go Theo!"

The boy's face scrunched in determination, and Cassidy suddenly remembered she was supposed to open the chute. It was the hundredth time she'd gotten distracted from her job that morning.

Levi grinned at her—also for the hundredth time. He looked amused every time he caught her staring at him, and yet she couldn't stop. It wasn't only the snug jeans and that plaid shirt he'd rolled up over his defined forearms. It was the way he doted on the kids, the way he'd found the perfect balance between authority and friend. The way they'd all started looking up to him—wanting both his attention and approval.

She was right there with them.

"You ready, Miss Greer?" he asked with a teasing wink.

"Of course." She lurched over to the gate, stumbling in the process. Her face burned at being caught yet again. "I'm good," she sputtered, regaining her balance. Positioning herself by the gate, she waited for his signal.

"All right, partner..." Levi still held on to the sheep, but he backed away. "We're gonna do a countdown. Five...four..."

The rest of the kids joined in. "Three...two...one!"

Cassidy pulled open the gate, and the sheep tore out in the arena dodging and jumping.

Theo gritted his teeth and stayed in position, his arms around the sheep's neck and his legs cinched over its middle.

"Woo-hoo! Lookin' good, Theo!" Levi shouted, jogging along behind them with a stopwatch.

She followed too. He was doing it! Holding on so tight there was no way he'd fall off. "Go, Theo!" she called, snapping a picture on her phone for his mom.

Soft dirt flew up on all sides as the sheep abruptly skidded and switched directions, heading straight for her.

"Ahhh!" She tried to move out of the way but her boots stumbled on the uneven ground. Levi plowed into her, knocking her out of the way just before the sheep ran her over. They both tumbled to the ground and rolled. Somehow, she ended up on top of him.

The kids howled with laughter.

Theo's giggles rose higher and higher, his grip loosening until he was sideways on the sheep's body, barely holding on.

Looking down into Levi's eyes, Cassidy started to laugh too.

"You don't know how much I want to kiss you right now." His gaze moved to her lips.

"We don't want to gross out the kids." She pushed away from him so she could stand. That and the fact she was pretty sure, once the kissing started up, she wouldn't want to stop.

He stood too, brushing himself off. "Maybe later?"

"Maybe." Her voice was so husky she might as well have just said yes.

On the other side of the corral, the sheep took a sharp left, and Theo finally rolled off. "That was so fun!" His laugh was bigger than she'd ever heard it.

Levi jogged over to him. "Twelve seconds!" He helped the kid stand and took off his helmet. "Man, that's longer than I've ever held on."

"Really?" Theo gasped. "I held on longer than a famous bull rider?"

The rest of the kids cheered, jumping up and down. Theo sprang from the ground and sprinted over to join them, slapping high fives and dancing around like he'd just won the world title.

Levi joined Cassidy where she stood, and she had to say, this was a whole different side of him. There were obviously many facets of Levi Cortez she'd had yet to explore. "You made him feel like a million bucks. I didn't know you were so good with kids."

His smirk promised plenty of mystery. "There're a lot of things you don't know about me."

"I look forward to learning them," she murmured, glancing at him seductively over her shoulder as she turned to face the kids.

"Did you hear Levi?" Theo asked, swaggering around the group. "He said I held on longer than he ever has. That means I beat him!"

Levi strode to her side. "Wow, he's really running with that, huh?"

Cassidy laughed. "I would imagine holding on to a bull is a little different than holding on to a sheep." Judging from Levi's notable upper body strength.

"I don't know..." he mused. "Bulls are a lot slower."

She watched Theo beam as the other kids praised his ride. He seemed to be standing two feet taller than he had yesterday. "This is amazing. It'll be the highlight of Theo's year." He had a happy life, and his mom took great care of him, but they didn't exactly get to do anything extra—go on vacations or go to any of those fancy mountain camps other kids attended. They couldn't afford much.

"I might be having more fun than the kids." Levi said it as though that came as a surprise.

"Thank you for making it happen." She had to admit that she hadn't thought he would follow through. But the man had obviously changed. Or maybe he'd always been this wonderful and she had simply refused to acknowledge it. "I think this one day will change Theo's life."

"I'm actually hoping we can do it again." Levi turned to her, gazing down into her eyes. "Maybe more often. If I can convince the other Renegades to hang out in Topaz Falls more."

"Do you think that's a possibility?"

The kids had started to get antsy. Levi rested his hand on her back, directing her toward the group.

"My friends are as nomadic as I've been with their competition and training schedules. So I think I could convince them to travel out here a few times a year." Before they reached the kids, he paused. "What about you? Would you come back to visit and help once in a while?" There was a deeper question in his tone. Would she come back to see him?

Fear still churned with the uncertainty inside her, but her mother's earlier words held her steady. *You can build that for yourself and hold on to it.* A love. A family. Maybe she was strong enough. Or maybe they could be strong enough together. She slipped her hands into his, the steady humming of her heart drowning out the raucous noise behind her. "Yes, Levi," she said bravely. "I will most definitely come back to visit you."

Chapter Twenty

'

Hey, Cortez. You might want to mop up that puddle of drool at your feet before someone slips in it." Mateo gave Levi's shoulder a good nudge.

"What? Huh?" He didn't bother glancing at his friend. Nope. He was too busy watching Cass. After the morning clinics had wrapped up, all of the groups had met together to walk to the Farm for lunch. Everly Brooks had insisted on serving free food as a way to contribute to the camp, which made her the most generous chef in town.

And Cassidy was the finest woman in the room. Jesus, that smile. It was torture being so close to her all morning and not being able to touch her or kiss her. Especially now that she seemed a hell of a lot more open to both.

"Seriously, man." Mateo's hearty headshake mocked him. "Somebody's whipped."

"I'm keeping an eye on things. Making sure everyone has

what they need." He finally pulled his gaze from Cass and glanced around the restaurant.

Next to him, Mateo chomped on a sandwich. "If it makes you feel any better, she's checking you out as much as you're checking her out."

"You think?" Throughout the morning, Cass had definitely opened up to him, but after the last few weeks, things still seemed so tentative.

"Trust me," Mateo said around a mouthful of food. "I tried to catch her eye earlier. It was a no go."

"We have a history." At least he had that going for him. He looked over at her again. She sat next to Theo in a booth, and the two of them had been laughing nonstop.

"That's obvious." Mateo finished off his sandwich and tossed his napkin onto a plate. "Damn, that was a good sandwich. So who's the chef lady?"

Levi gave him his full attention. "Everly Brooks."

"Everly," Mateo repeated with a steady gaze at the woman who was refilling drinks on the other side of the room. "She's hot. Can you put in a good word for me?"

"I don't know her that well." And she didn't seem to be the type to go for a fling. Which was typically all Mateo wanted.

"I'll get to know her," his friend said with a grin.

Everly chose that moment to glance in their direction. She hurried over to Levi, flustered and nervous. "How's everything?" she asked, looking back and forth between them.

"It's amazing," Levi assured her. "The kids can't get enough of your mac and cheese."

"I couldn't either," Mateo broke in.

Levi had to blink so he wouldn't roll his eyes. "Everly,

I'm not sure if you've officially met my friend Mateo Torres." The least subtle cowboy in the West.

"I haven't," she said with a warm smile. "But it's nice to meet you."

"The pleasure's all mine." He leaned close to her, displaying the same smile Levi had seen him use at bars. "So I was wondering...what's the secret ingredient in your mac and cheese?"

While he would've loved to stay and hear that answer, Levi stepped away. "Excuse me a minute." Now that everyone was finishing up lunch and he was done dealing with swapping out food for allergies and cleaning up spills, he planned to spend the rest of the hour-long break with Cass.

As he slipped past the door, it opened, and Gunner Raines sauntered through.

Levi took a detour to greet his old mentor. "You made it." He'd invited him a couple of weeks ago, but he hadn't been sure Gunner would be able to take the time. "I'm glad you're here." He embraced the man who'd once been like a second father to him.

"It's good to see you, kid." Gunner took off his hat and set it on a nearby table. "Sorry I'm so late. Flight got canceled last night, so I had to catch one this morning."

"I'm just glad you made it. The kids'll be ecstatic." He'd been telling them stories about the living legend all morning, about how Gunner had set records and beat out champions in every rodeo event from steer wrestling to bronc riding. Though he'd aged, Gunner still looked the part, with his sundrenched face and bushy white mustache.

"Well, cowboy, you made it happen." The man surveyed the room with a look of approval.

Most of the kids still sat at tables, stuffing Everly's homemade chocolate chip cookies into their mouths as fast as they could.

A hint of pride lifted the old man's chin. "I always knew you'd do something important someday." That's what Gunner had tried to teach him. That being a champion had more to do with conducting yourself with honor and integrity and giving back than it had to do with winning titles. It wasn't something Levi had paid much attention to until recently.

"I figure I can help these kids the same way you helped me." When he'd shown up at Gunner's ranch, he'd been a broken, arrogant kid. And maybe it'd taken a while, but he'd come a long way. He'd come a lot closer to being the good person Gunner had believed him to be all along. Levi figured the best way to thank him for his confidence in him would be to show him who he was now. "Come on." He snagged the man's shoulder. "There're some people I'd like you to meet."

Cassidy and Lulu stood as they approached their table.

"Gunner, this is Cassidy Greer, an old friend of mine." He gazed at her a beat too long and made her blush. "And this is her mother, LuEllen Greer."

"Call me Lulu," she said, with a scolding glance at Levi.

"A pleasure to meet you both." Gunner turned on the charm, just like he always did in the presence of beautiful women. It was a cowboy thing.

"Nice to meet you too." Lulu smiled shyly, and if Levi wasn't mistaken, her cheeks turned a little pinker. He hadn't seen that expression on her face in a long time.

"We've heard a lot about you." Cassidy smiled at Levi and then at Gunner.

"All good things I hope," the man said with a stern look at Levi.

"Great things," he confirmed. In fact...Gunner happened to be the noblest gentleman he knew. Single too. Just like Lulu. Not that either of them seemed to be looking for anything romantic, but what was the harm in having a little fun? "Hey, Cass and I have plans after the clinic tonight. Maybe you could show Gunner around town, Lulu."

"Oh...I don't know..." The woman immediately looked down at the floor.

"That's a great idea." Cass put her arm around her mother. "Main Street is so charming. There's the Chocolate Therapist, that ice cream shop..."

"It sounds better than eating dinner alone," Gunner said. "If you're willing, that is."

Lulu tucked a lock of white hair behind her ear and glanced at her daughter nervously. "I guess so. I mean, sure. I can show you around."

"It'll be fun, Mom," Cass insisted. "You deserve to have some fun."

So did she, Levi thought. Which reminded him...he needed to get everything ready for their evening together. While he and Cass had played with the kids all morning, he'd thought about their years together. The fun things he'd done with her family. He needed to bring her back to that place. Where she was carefree and happy. He needed to remind her of that girl tonight.

While Gunner asked Lulu some questions about Topaz Falls, he slipped away, leaving Cassidy staring after him with a quizzical look. He simply shot her a mysterious grin and wandered to the kitchen, where Everly was wiping down the large stainless countertop.

"Hey," he said quietly, watching over his shoulder to make sure Cass hadn't followed him.

"Oh. Hi." Everly tossed the rag in the sink and wiped her hands on her apron. "Did you guys need something else?"

"No." He kept an eye on the door. "Well, at least not for the clinic." Unwilling to risk Cass overhearing, he directed Everly to a quiet corner of the kitchen. "I'm taking Cass out tonight, and I wanted to make her dinner."

The woman's face softened. "Wow, Levi. That's so sweet. How can I help?"

"Do you have any hot dogs? I need hot dogs."

"Hot dogs?" Everly repeated, like he'd just said a dirty phrase. "You're making Cassidy hot dogs?"

"It's a long story." And it would require going way back into their history, which he didn't have time for. "I mean, I could swing by the store, but I'm not sure if I'll have time this afternoon, and—"

"No." Everly's lips curled with a look of disgust. "I can't let you make Cassidy something like that for dinner," she said with conviction. "God, Levi. Hot dogs? For a romantic date?"

"She used to love hot dogs." And tonight he planned to take her on a little trip down memory lane.

Sighing heavily, Everly hurried to her industrial-sized refrigerator. She opened the doors and rummaged around. "Aha. I thought I had some of these." She pulled out a package wrapped in white paper and handed it to him. "This is organic chicken sausage. I use it in some of the pasta dishes."

"Never tried it." He held up the package but couldn't see much through the wrapping.

"Well, it looks like a hot dog," she said with a grin. "But it tastes a thousand times better, and it won't eventually kill you."

Sounded good to him. It'd be a plus if Cass actually liked the food. "Can you cook it over a fire?"

The question seemed to stump her. "I've never tried it, but I don't see why not."

"Perfect. I'll take it." He grabbed a brown paper bag branded with the Farm's logo and hid the package inside.

Everly walked him back to the dining room. "This sounds like some date you're taking her on."

"Yeah. I'm hoping she'll think so too." This time there would be no limo, no fancy restaurant. Nothing showy. Just the two of them and a bunch of memories he hoped to rekindle.

"If I had to guess, I'd say she'll be quite enchanted," Everly said.

That's what he was counting on. "Don't say anything about the hot dogs."

"Organic chicken sausage," she corrected. "And don't worry. Your secret's safe with me."

* * *

Levi stood outside the corral with Ty and Mateo, watching as Charity closed down the day's events by racing through the barrels on Ace. The sleek, black horse dodged barrel after barrel, guided by Charity's expert hands. She crouched low and had that killer look about her, the one that said she wouldn't stop for anything.

In the stands behind them, the kids cheered and whooped, giving her more praise than they'd given to either Ty on the bull or Mateo on the bronc. Somehow, she'd turned out to be the favorite performer by far.

"It's because she's blond," Mateo grumbled. "Everyone loves blondes."

"It's because they don't know her," Ty muttered with a grin. "All day she's been friendly and sweet. Hell, I feel like I don't know her anymore."

Levi laughed. "There's something about barrel racing. The speed. It's impressive to watch." He turned to his friends. "But I'd say you both impressed them too."

"*They* impressed *me*," Mateo said. "That's a bunch of great kids you found."

"Yeah," Ty agreed. "I didn't think this would be my thing, but I actually didn't mind it so much."

"I'm glad you both feel that way." This was the opening Levi had been waiting for. "What if we made it a more permanent thing?"

"Permanent?" Mateo had never seemed to enjoy that word. There'd been a time when Levi hadn't either. But he was ready for some stability in his life.

"What if we offered more programs? Mentoring young riders throughout the year and training them to compete?"

Ty frowned. "Kind of like what we did at Gunner's place?"

"Sure. Except the kids would be younger. And we'd prep them for the junior circuit." And they wouldn't live on the ranch. He may have come a long way, but he still couldn't imagine having kids around 24/7.

Mateo draped his arms over the fence. "And we'd do that here? In Topaz Falls?"

"It's as good a place as any." Better, seeing as how he had so many connections and they could use the facilities for free...

The kids' praise rose higher as Charity finished her ride.

She guided Ace into the chute and dismounted before ducking under the corral fence to join them.

Gunner headed up to the small podium in front of the stands. He'd agreed to round out the day with a motivational speech before they sent the kids on their way.

"Gun-ner! Gun-ner!" The crowd chanted his name as he stepped behind the mic. All afternoon, he'd rotated through the different clinics, chatting with the kids and signing autographs, earning their approval and respect.

The noise died down, and the man started in with a story about his first bull ride. It was one of Levi's favorite Gunner stories.

"What have you three been up to?" Charity asked suspiciously, glancing from him to Ty to Mateo.

"Levi wants us to move to Topaz Falls," Ty informed her. "To make these camp things a more regular deal."

Her mouth dropped open. "Seriously?"

"You three don't have solid roots anywhere." Levi aimed a glare at Ty. "You want to live with your parents forever?"

"Hey," his friend shot back, "my parents need help on the ranch."

"And you'd still be able travel home. I'm thinking maybe eight clinics a year. Some a week long. Some a few days." It's not like they'd have to relocate. Unless they wanted to.

"I don't know if I could make that work with my training schedule," Mateo said.

"You could train here," Levi reminded him. He could do the clinics alone, but his experience was limited to bull riding. "We have everything we need for training, between the rodeo grounds and my family's ranch."

Charity stared past them, seeming to watch Gunner as he spoke. "Or we could build our own training facility."

"Pardon?" Out of all of them, Levi had expected her to respond with a hell no. "You'd actually consider it?"

"I like it here," she said simply. "The mountains. The town. It's not like I have anything to go home to." She didn't talk much about her family, though her mother had quite the reputation. But Charity didn't seem to have any close ties with anyone.

He hadn't either. Not before the start of this summer…

Once again, Levi looked up into the stands to where Cassidy sat next to Theo.

"Does this whole clinic thing have anything to do with you wanting to stick around for a certain EMT?" Ty asked. "Because I don't want to agree to it and then have everything fall apart if things don't work out in that department."

"It has to do with wanting to give back, and this seems like the best place to do it." He was all in. Committed to staying in Topaz Falls as much as possible. Yes, because it would be closer to Cass than, say, his old training facilities in Oklahoma, but also because this place was part of him. Over the last year, he'd helped to build it, and he wanted a life here.

"Well, I'm in," Charity said definitively. She gave Mateo and Ty the same look she used to intimidate her opponents.

"I'll try it out." Mateo shrugged. "Give it a year and see how it goes."

They all looked at Ty. He heaved a sigh. "Fine. If we can schedule the camps around competitions and visits home, I'm in too."

"Perfect." Now all he had to do was create a nonprofit. And raise a shit ton of money. Speaking of…

"I think we should consider signing another sponsorship deal with Renegade."

"No." Charity shook her head. "Absolutely not."

Levi ignored her and focused on Ty and Mateo. "It could help fund the camps."

Ty gave Charity a look. "You'd say yes to spending most of the year in Topaz Falls, but no to some simple pictures?"

"They make me wear jeans so tight I practically have to use Vaseline to get into them," she complained.

"So we'll write that into your contract," Levi promised. "The jeans have to be in your size."

"And no more tight, low-cut shirts," she added. "I get to decide what to wear."

"Shouldn't be a problem," he lied. "I'll have my agent work on it." Which pretty much meant Renegade would dictate the terms. But he'd deal with Charity later. Right now he had bigger things to do. "You think you could close things down and supervise pick up?" he asked his friends. "I have to get a few things ready for tonight."

Mateo rolled his eyes. "Man, you're asking for all kinds of favors today."

"I'm happy to return them. Anytime." Yes, he was being particularly needy today. "I wouldn't ask if it wasn't life or death." He had one more shot to convince Cass they belonged together. And it'd better work because, after being with her today, he'd decided he pretty much couldn't live without her.

"Don't worry, Romeo." Charity intoned. "We've got it. Just make sure tonight doesn't bomb like your last date did."

"It won't." He never made the same mistake twice. This time, it would be all about Cass.

Chapter Twenty-One

That was the best day ever!" Theo bounded out of the arena behind the rest of the kids, who were being reunited with their parents.

"Whoa there." Cassidy caught his shoulder before he tore out into the parking lot. "Slow down, trigger. There're a lot of cars right now."

"Here." Lulu quickly collected his hand. "Why don't you help me to the car? After all that work, I'm tuckered."

"Yes, ma'am." Theo dutifully took the lead, guiding Lulu in the direction of the Subaru.

Cassidy followed behind them, smiling to herself. It warmed her heart to see her mom treating Theo like one of her own children. Working the roping station with Mateo had been good for her mother. Cassidy hadn't seen her that active in years.

Partway to the car, her mom turned to her. "Where do you think you're going?"

She stopped. "I'm coming with you."

"Aren't you supposed to spend some time with Levi?"

"Hey, where is Levi anyway?" Theo demanded. "I didn't get to see him after the show."

The evening sun beat hot on Cassidy's face. "I don't know." She hadn't seen him either. She'd figured something must have come up, and they could get together to talk another time. That wouldn't be a problem for her. She'd be just fine going home to hide from the obvious chemistry between them.

Theo turned in a slow circle, his eyes searching. "Oh! There he is!" He pointed across the parking lot. "I see him!" Without hesitation he took off in the opposite direction and headed straight for Levi's truck. The man was perched on the tailgate and seemed to be packing a cooler or something.

Butterflies swarmed Cassidy's stomach, threatening to lift her right off the ground. "Are you sure you'll be okay?" she asked her mom. "Maybe I should go home with you..."

"Honey," Lulu's voice was firm, "I'll be fine. Are you going to be okay?"

Her gaze drifted over to Levi again. She had to take her mom's advice. *Find enough courage for each moment.* "I don't know." Why did she find it so hard to gather her courage when she was with Levi?

Lulu looked straight at her. Her mother's eyes were beautiful, a watery green color that Cassidy used to wish she'd inherited. "Can I give you some advice?" Lulu never used to ask permission, but it had been a few years since Cassidy had sought her mother's advice.

"Of course." She was pretty sure she knew what was coming.

"Don't think so hard," Lulu said. "I know you've had to

worry about a lot. More than a young woman should have to worry. But it would mean the world to me if you'd stop fretting and enjoy your night."

She couldn't stop fretting. Her biggest worry was that she'd enjoy the night too much and then they could never go back.

Her mom pressed her palm against Cassidy's cheek, something she hadn't done since Cassidy was very young. "Sometimes it's okay to let your heart guide you, sweetie."

The warmth from her mom's hand seeped into her. "I'm not sure I know how." She'd managed to shut off that part after Cash's death. There were so many details to take care of. She willingly buried herself in them, letting the distraction soothe away the ache that nothing else could seem to touch.

"Maybe you should do whatever you did that night when Dev caught you making out in Levi's truck," her mom proposed with a wry smile.

Cassidy gaped at her. "You knew about that?"

"Neighbors talk, honey."

"Right." She thought back to that night. How it'd felt when he'd kissed her for the first time. How quickly she'd lost herself.

"I see how you look at him," Lulu said quietly. "I see how he looks at you. You both get a light in your eyes." She peered at something past Cassidy's shoulder. "See? He can't take his eyes off you."

Cassidy turned. Levi was on his way across the parking lot with Theo, and Lulu was right. He didn't take his eyes off her. Not to look for cars, not to watch where he was going. He simply gripped Theo's hand in his and stormed across the distance between them.

She couldn't look away from him either. Not when he

was ten feet away and not when he stood right across from her.

"Levi said I can come over and meet one of his bulls next week!" Theo seemed to want the whole world to hear.

"If it's okay with your mom." Levi didn't break his concentration on Cassidy.

"That sounds so fun!" Lulu opened the Subaru's back door for Theo. "But right now, we'd best get you on home. Your mama's going to want to hear all about your day."

"Okay," the boy grumbled. He threw himself at Levi in a super-sized hug. "Thank you. This was my favorite day in the world."

Levi did look away from Cassidy then. He knelt in front of Theo. "You're a great kid," he said, tapping the rim of the boy's hat. "We'll definitely keep in touch. I'll give your mom a call and ask when you can come and hang out."

"Sounds great!" Theo climbed into the car. "See you later, Cassidy." He waved from the backseat.

She waved too.

Her mom opened the driver's door. "You two have a good time tonight." Cassidy didn't miss the glimmer of amusement in her voice.

Levi didn't seem to either, judging by the sly way he grinned at her. "You too, Lulu. Are you and Gunner all set?"

"Um. Yes, I think so." Her mother's face colored in a way it hadn't since her father used to tease her. "We decided we'd meet up in town a little later on."

"I can't believe you're going on a date." Cassidy couldn't resist the urge to poke fun at her mother too.

"He's a quality guy," Levi said, as though he sensed how nervous she was. "Real laid back and easy to talk to."

"He'd better be." Lulu gave them both a stern look. "Or I won't agree to any more blind dates set up by you two."

"You'll have a great time." Cassidy leaned in to give her mom a hug.

"I'm sure we will," Lulu murmured, ducking to get into the car. Before she closed the door, she gave Cassidy an encouraging smile. "Make sure you have a good time too."

* * *

Funny how good she was at small talk when there were big things weighing on her heart.

Cassidy forced her mouth shut and pulled on the shoulder strap of her seat belt to give herself more space to breathe. She'd been babbling for five minutes straight about the camp—reliving every funny comment the kids had made, every success they'd experienced.

Levi had indulged her with the occasional "mmm-hmm" or a laugh, but otherwise he'd been abnormally quiet.

Which meant she should be quiet too. He was the one who'd asked if they could talk, after all. Ever since they'd gotten in his truck, she'd filled the silence. She couldn't help it. Her nerves kept jarring her into saying something.

She forced herself to look out the window. The sun hung low in the western sky, still bright and warm. She loved the way it backlit the mountains, fringing the horizon with a vivid glow.

Still quiet, Levi turned the truck out onto the highway.

She had no idea where he was taking her, other than the fact that they were headed in the general direction of his family's ranch.

"Want to know what my favorite part of today was?" Levi asked, drawing her gaze back to him.

She simply waited.

"It was watching you with the kids. You're gonna make one hell of a pediatric nurse."

"Thanks." The compliment warmed her through. "But you were the popular one." He'd entertained those kids all day, with jokes and stories and his fun, good-natured attitude.

"We made a great team." He slowed the truck and turned off on a jeep road a few miles from the entrance to the ranch. "Thanks for being there, Cass. It meant a lot to me."

"I'm glad I could help." Why did her voice sound so awkward? Thick and sultry. It was the emotions churning through her—anticipation simmering above them all. "So where are we going?" she asked, trying to get her bearings. She'd always been directionally challenged in the mountains. Once you were this deep in the forest, it was hard to tell one direction from another.

"You'll see." Levi guided the truck up a rocky slope. "How's the packing going?"

Oh, the packing. For the last eight hours, she'd forgotten the pain of trying to fit her life in boxes so she could move away. "It's good, I guess. I don't have much to bring to Denver, honestly. I'm leaving a lot for Mom. My apartment will be pretty bare for a while."

The uncertainty she'd been fighting off gained ground. Lulu seemed to have made a lot of progress in the last month, but how would she do once she was on her own?

"Naomi still has some of her old furniture in storage somewhere," Levi said. "I bet she'd be relieved to get rid of it."

"I hadn't even thought about that." She'd been so busy she'd hardly seen her friends at all, but she loved Naomi's style. When her friend moved into the Hidden Gem Inn, she'd bought all new furniture. "I'll have to check in with her." The truth was that she'd been avoiding everyone. Now that the move date was so close, she found herself getting choked up constantly. She'd miss them all so much.

The truck bounced along the dirt road, climbing higher until the trees started to thin. "Wait a minute…" She looked around, taking in the rock face off to her left, the way the trees opened into a view of the valley. She sat taller and tried to see what was ahead. "Are you taking me to the hot spring?"

A slow smile spread across his face.

"I haven't been up here in years." She'd almost forgotten about it. But as soon as Levi drove around the corner, it came into view—the thermal spring-fed pond they'd all used to visit frequently in high school. The place where she'd had the most daring night of her life. Not that Levi knew about it. Her junior year, not long before Cash's death, she and her friends had snuck up here to go skinny-dipping. Seeing as how they were all straight-A, rule-following goody-goodies, it had given them quite the thrill to think they were trespassing naked in the Cortez brothers' backyard

"We all had some good times here." Levi parked the truck a ways off the shore.

"I remember." Completely enchanted by the reflection off the turquoise water, Cassidy pushed out of the truck and wandered down to the water's edge. "This is where I tried my first beer."

"And if I recall, you spit it out." Levi came to stand next to her.

"You and Cash teased me about that all night." She meant to sound offended, but she couldn't hold off a smile. Around town, her memories of Cash were mixed—some happy and some painful. But here…there were only good memories. She walked along the shore a few feet. They used to come up here and build campfires, cooking hot dogs on sticks and then roasting marshmallows. The boys always brought beer, and eventually she'd developed a taste for it.

A rummaging sound rattled behind her. Levi had climbed into the bed of his truck and was unpacking a couple of boxes and a cooler.

She trotted over to see what he had. "What are we doing?"

"Re-creating the magic." He hopped down, his legs solid and firm.

Cassidy peeked into one of the boxes. Firewood and newspaper. She reached over to open the cooler, but he swatted her hand away. "Why don't you grab the chairs and blankets?" He nodded toward the two low camping chairs leaning against the truck.

"Fine." She grabbed the chairs and followed him down a small path to a rock fire ring surrounded by soft green grass.

He set down his armload of stuff and crouched to position the logs and newspaper in the center of the rocks.

She took the opportunity to sneak a look at his ass. Yep. She could understand Renegade Jeans Company's interest in him.

"Want to get the chairs set up?" he asked, glancing over his shoulder.

"Oh. Sure. Yeah." That damn blush wasn't going to go away all night. Clumsily, she fumbled around with the chairs until she figured out how to unfold them and set them out near the fire pit. When she turned around, Levi was watching her, the fire already glowing behind him, amusement glinting in his eyes.

"What?" she demanded.

"Are you nervous, Cass?" he taunted.

"Why would I be nervous?" She ducked away so he couldn't see her face and parked herself in one of the chairs.

Levi knelt next to the cooler and opened the lid. "Maybe because we're finally alone." His eyes rose to hers as he handed her a roasting stick. The same ones they'd used in high school, if she wasn't mistaken. "Out here there's no way for you to avoid me."

She harrumphed. "I haven't been avoiding you. I've been busy."

"Well, I'm glad you're not busy tonight." He handed her a hot dog. Actually, it wasn't a hot dog. It wasn't the right color. She inspected it.

"It's organic chicken sausage," he explained. "Everly gave it to me. Something about how deadly processed meat can be."

"Everly's so great." She skewered the meat onto her stick and held it over the flames. "I noticed she and Mateo seemed to be chatting a lot at lunch." See? Even in the wilderness, she could find something to distract her from any meaningful conversation with him.

Levi called her out with a look of exasperation. "Don't you want to know what I wanted to talk to you about? Why I brought you out here?"

"Sure." She focused on holding her sausage exactly the right distance from the highest-reaching flame. She already had a pretty good idea that it had something to do with him and her and feelings. Lots of feelings . . .

He looked at her over the crackling fire. "Do you ever feel like you're standing still?"

Oh yes. She'd become an expert on standing still. "That's how I've felt for the last six years."

"And now you are moving on," Levi said, watching her face carefully.

"Yes." Finally.

"And you don't want to take anything from your past with you."

Her heart softened as she gazed at his face. Would it be possible for her leave him behind after everything they'd shared? "I wouldn't say that."

Levi handed her a plate and took one for himself. "Then what would you say?"

The question pushed her to the edge. That's obviously where he wanted her. She could tell him everything—how she felt about him, how she longed for him—and let herself fall. Or she could continue holding on to the ledge, protecting herself from potential pain.

She bought time eating the nostalgic dinner he'd planned. The sausage was salty and seasoned. Even though it was fancier than the hot dogs they used to roast, it brought her back to those simple, carefree days.

Cassidy finished eating and set the plate on the ground. The truth was that reliving the past with Levi made her never want to leave it behind. "I guess I would say that some things are worth taking with you. Some things you can't leave behind. Like memories." Like the people you've always loved.

Levi set his plate aside too. "There are a lot of memories," he agreed, giving her a meaningful smile. "What are some of your best memories, Cass?"

She gazed over at the water's glassy surface. It caught the sunset in a shimmering reflection. "We went skinny-dipping here once."

"Riiiiggghhht." Levi laughed.

"We did!" She wasn't about to let him disregard her one

naughty memory from high school. "Homecoming night junior year. Me and Jessie and Heather and Michelle."

"You mean you and the *Math Club* girls?" he mocked.

"Hey," she warned. "They were fun. And we did. We drove Heather's dad's Jeep up here after the dance, stripped off our dresses, and ran into the water." It had been one of the highlights of her high school career. Of course, they'd run right back out of the water and quickly redressed, so the whole thing lasted only about three minutes, but he didn't need to know that. "I swear. We did. You were probably making out with the flavor of the month at the time."

His jaw dropped. "You trespassed naked on our land? But you were such a good girl..." He said it like it turned him on.

"I know." The memory sparkled inside of her again, all those feelings, the thrill. "That's what made it so exciting. We never did stuff like that."

"How come you didn't invite me?" he asked, the fire making his eyes glow dangerously.

"Cash would never have approved," she said with a teasing glance.

Levi didn't tease back. His eyes had locked on hers with the same intensity that seemed to grip him right before he'd kissed her those few times. "I love you, Cass," he said abruptly, as though he was tired of keeping it a secret. "That's why I brought you here. That's the only thing I wanted to tell you. I love you, and I think that means this thing between us would be worth the risk."

She gazed at him, unable to speak. Unable to draw in a breath.

His expression was grim. "I had to grow up. It took longer than it should've, but now I know. I know that you make me want to be a better person. I know that I can't imagine not seeing you again after you move to Denver."

Her eyes closed. She couldn't deny it. The truth beat in her heart. "I love you too," she whispered. "And it scares me so much."

He slipped out of his chair and knelt in front of her. His skin was rough and calloused with scars, but he held her hands tenderly. "You don't have to be afraid of me."

"It's not you I'm afraid of." She could hardly whisper. "I'm afraid I won't be able to do this. To be who you need me to be. To give you everything you need. I'm afraid something horrible will happen to you. Just like it happened to Cash." Tears brightened the world, stinging her eyes with a lovely kind of pain. She was safe with him. She was safe to admit the worst. "Sometimes, I feel so empty. Like I've been living on autopilot." And you couldn't do that in a relationship. You couldn't turn the feelings off and on...sometimes opening yourself fully to that love and sometimes closing yourself off. "You deserve more."

"I want *you.*" Levi stood and pulled her up. "Whatever that looks like. Whatever you can give." He leaned down and pressed his lips to hers, capturing them in a sensual rhythm while his hand came up to rest over her heart. "You're not on autopilot now," he murmured against her lips.

No. She wasn't. Her heart had quickened, drumming a solid pulse throughout her body.

His arms encircled her, pulling her in. "How did you feel when you went skinny dipping that night?"

She leaned into him. "I felt free. Alive." That night, it seemed anything was possible. They'd been so brave. It was how she'd pictured herself being in the future—unafraid of venturing outside of her comfort zone. But that was the last time she'd felt that way. A month later, her brother died, and responsibilities weighed her down.

"Don't you want to do it again?" Gazing into her eyes, he stepped back and pulled his T-shirt up and over his head and then dropped it on the ground.

She did her best not to react, but her eyes widened and her lips parted. He was exquisite. Lean muscle, chiseled detail, broad chest and pecs. The sight was even better than the pictures that were plastered everywhere online. "I thought they'd airbrushed you."

His head tilted. "Say what?"

"Those pictures they're always posting on the Internet. Of you without...um...your...um...shirt," she stammered, suddenly embarrassed to admit she'd been gawking at him for the past six years. Though with that body of his, it was kind of hard not to.

"You thought they Photoshopped me?" he repeated in mock disbelief.

"Well, yeah." She thought they did that to everyone. She eyed his chest again. Apparently they didn't have to with Levi Cortez.

He inched closer, the look on his face almost predatory. "You looked at pictures of me online?"

"Darla forced me to." Staring at hot men online was one of her friend's favorite pastimes. Of course, she'd looked him up on her own a few times too. Only to see his stats on the circuit, of course. Not that he should be privy to that information.

"Did you like what you saw?" he asked in a husky voice.

One of her shoulders lifted in a pathetically weak shrug. "Kind of."

He inched closer. "Do you like what you see now?"

Her gaze trailed down his body. Before she knew what she was doing, her hand brushed his chest and worked its way down his abs. "Mmm-hmmm."

"Want to see more?" He kicked off his boots, and his hands went to his silver belt buckle.

Whoa. She blinked hard. Wait a minute. Was he stripping? She shook herself awake. "We can't go skinny-dipping!" She backed away from him, nearly tripping over the chair in the process.

He unclasped his belt. "Why not?"

"Well…" Staring at his chest, she struggled to come up with one logical reason. *Rational thought, rational thought*…there had to be one in there somewhere. "What if someone else shows up?" Like Dev? "It's indecent exposure."

Levi laughed. "It's private property. No one will show up. Lucas and Naomi hardly ever leave the house anymore, and Lance and Jessa are in Denver for the night." He pulled her into his arms. "So it's just you and me, baby."

"And maybe bears." She glanced around nervously.

"They're not gonna bother us. Trust me. We'll make too much noise." He took another step back, undoing the button fly and shoving his jeans down his hips slowly, like he wanted to torture her.

He was. Torturing her. *Oh my stars.* She was in trouble. The man wore black boxer briefs. Tight black boxer briefs that hugged his hips…that hugged every impressive inch of him. Her knees faltered.

He stepped out of his jeans, kicking them aside before backing down to the water's edge. He waded in up to his ankles. "Water's pretty warm. Wanna feel?"

"Yes." The word sighed out of her. She wanted to feel

more than the water. She wanted to feel the thrill of his touch. She wanted to feel *him*.

She wandered to the shoreline, her legs already weak. Levi met her halfway. He knelt and slipped off her boots and socks. Then he stood and brushed her hair off her shoulders before sliding her shirt over her head. He lowered his lips to hers, warm and consuming, kissing her deeply as he unclasped her bra and slipped it off her shoulders. With his eyes focused on hers, he unbuttoned her jeans, sliding them down her hips, taking her underwear with them.

Holding on to his shoulders, she stepped out of her pants and kissed her way down his chest, catching the waist of his boxers with her fingers before pulling them to the ground.

She touched him, grazing her hands along his hips. His body was hard and alert. Beautiful and strong.

When her eyes found his again, she realized he was watching her. "You are the sexiest woman alive," he uttered, tracing his finger from her collarbone to her belly button.

"No one's ever accused me of that before." Usually she was either tromping around in her EMT uniform or at home studying in her yoga pants.

"I've thought so for a long time," he insisted, examining her closely. "A really long time."

She smiled, going for that seductive blend of sly and sweet. "It's no secret that I've been admiring your body for a while too."

"Come on." He held her hand and led her into the water, moving slowly until they'd waded in all the way up to their waists. It was warm and calming, just like she remembered.

"We were so scared that night..." She laughed, reliving the squeals and the splashing as she and her friends sprinted out of the water and hurried to put their clothes back on before they got caught.

"And what about tonight?" Levi drew her closer, holding her body against his, and she took it all in, the feel of his skin, the orange reflection of the sky dancing on the water's surface.

"Tonight is the most beautiful, perfect night," she murmured, reaching up to touch her lips to his. The fears and hesitations that had held her back burned up in the desire that blazed inside her. She wanted this. Wanted him.

"It's about to get better." He whispered the words against her neck as he lifted her into his arms. She wrapped her legs around his waist and let him carry her deeper into the pool.

Holding on, she kissed his neck, licking and biting his skin, earning a low growl. "Not sure I'll be able to hold out this time," he rasped.

"I won't let you." She brought her face level with his and shot him a meaningful smirk. Tonight wasn't about her. It was about them, about their past and their future, about living this present moment as fully as they could. And she intended to make it very, very good for him.

He kissed her again, hard and possessively, his tongue seeking hers.

Without breaking away from his mouth, she groped her hand down his body until she found what she was looking for.

"Fuck," he uttered, nearly breathless as she teased him with a firm caress.

"Say that again," she panted into his ear, lowering her other hand too.

"Fuck, Cass," he moaned helplessly. Lowering his head, he kissed his way down to her breast and toyed with her nipple, until all she could do was gasp. One of his hands supported her backside while the other moved between her legs. "Uh, uh, uh," she taunted, pushing away from him. "I thought we were only going for a swim." If there was too much touching, he'd have her crying out his name in a matter of minutes, and she wanted to drag this out as long as possible. Kicking her feet, she pushed into a back float and drifted away from him.

He stood and watched her as though completely mesmerized. "Normally I'd love to sit and watch you swim naked." Greed flashed in his eyes. "But tonight that won't be enough." He dove under the water's surface.

Cassidy bolted upright, her feet sinking slightly in the soft sand. She turned in a slow circle. "Where'd you go?" She scanned the water but couldn't see anything with the dusky shadows.

A splash sounded behind her, and Levi broke above the surface, wrapping his arms around her waist. "I like it when you tease me," he murmured in between kissing her neck. "Damn, Cass. I can't get enough of kissing you...of touching you." His hands wandered higher, cupping her breasts.

"I hope you never get enough." She turned to him so she could look into his eyes, so he could see all of her, everything she'd hidden from him before. This was what had been missing from her life. Levi. He made her want to feel again.

"I need you inside me," she murmured, her body strengthening in a surge of passion. Levi made her feel invincible. She couldn't wait, couldn't spend one more minute without that bond between them, without giving him everything she had.

"Yes." As he urged her back to the shoreline, he kissed her, taking tastes of her lips, her neck, her breasts. "Wait here," he uttered when they'd reached the shallow water. He broke away from her and jogged over to the box he'd set on the ground earlier.

Laughing, she watched him tear things out—more newspaper, a lighter, and finally a large, soft blanket.

He rushed back to the water, and she met him at the edge.

"We could go back to Lance and Jessa's place if you want." He pulled her against him and wrapped the blanket around them both.

"No." She slid her hands down his body. "Now. Here." In this place where they'd shared so many good memories. "No more waiting," she whispered, drawing his lips back to hers.

In case he had any lingering hesitations, she kissed her way over to his ear. "Make love to me, Levi," she whispered. "Right. Now."

"I'm on it." Still holding her body firmly against his, he moved her away from the water. When they reached a soft, grassy spot near the fire, he eased her to the ground, the thick blanket cushioning her back.

Levi hovered over her, the early twilight and faint stars stretching as far as she could see behind him. "I want to give you everything, Cass. I want to make all of your dreams come true." He kissed her lips, then her chin, then her collarbone.

"I can't believe I shut you out." She smoothed her hands over his broad shoulders. "I'm so sorry."

"It's okay. But I want you to be sure this time." He gazed into her eyes as though searching.

"I'm sure." She'd never been more sure about anything. "I'm really sure." Grinning, she shifted to a sitting position and pushed his shoulders to the ground. "Let me show you how sure I am." Starting at his mouth, she kissed her way down his body, flicking her tongue over his skin. His head fell back as she went lower, slowly working her way down his hips until she took him in her mouth. She wanted to make him feel good, to bring him outside of himself like he'd done to her all of those weeks ago. She wanted him to belong to her—completely captivated and defenseless.

"Your mouth," he uttered between rough breaths. "Damn, Cass, your mouth."

The utter ecstasy in his voice made certain parts of her tingle. She licked and sucked until he roughly pulled her up, bringing her body over his. "I'm gonna make you feel so good."

"I'm already feeling pretty good," she teased. "You're one fine cowboy, Levi Cortez." She settled next to him on the blanket, her body turned to his, her hands admiring his sculpted abs.

"And you, Cassidy Greer, are sexy and brilliant and tenderhearted and strong and so fucking hot." Levi slid his hand down the back of her thigh and brought her knee up to his hip. He brushed his erection between her legs as though he wanted to tease her. Every touch zipped an electrical current through her body, and she couldn't take it anymore. She held his hips in place and wriggled against him until he pushed into her.

"This is so right," she breathed. She belonged to him. Why had she fought him for so long?

Levi captivated her with a slow kiss, his eyes closed as he ground his hips into hers, bringing their connection deeper. "You're more than I deserve," he said, easing his hands to her backside. "But I'll do my best to earn you." Kissing her lips, he thrust into her, guiding her hips up to meet his.

She moaned as their bodies moved together in a powerful

rhythm. He obviously knew what he was doing, how he was positioning her to feel him everywhere, grazing the most sensitive spots, teasing her with long deep thrusts and then going shallow.

"More, Levi. Please," she begged. "Harder." Cassidy arched her back, digging her fingertips into his muscular shoulders until that was all she felt—his wet skin moving against hers, the heat and energy they generated together.

"Oh, Cass. My god, I love you," he panted, holding her tight.

Her body clenched around him, pulling him deeper, tightening everything until she broke apart in a surge of blinding ecstasy.

Levi's body tensed, his release pulsing inside her, which took her over again, electrifying her body with explosive aftershocks.

Their heavy breaths interrupted the stillness of the evening. Levi was draped over her, his body dead weight, and she'd never felt more content. "Thank you for bringing me here," she whispered, brushing a kiss on his cheek. "Thank you for reminding me to let myself feel something."

Chapter Twenty-Two

There was nothing sexier than a beautiful woman eating a gooey roasted marshmallow, her full lips moving slowly as she chewed and savored the sugary sweetness.

Levi fed Cassidy another one and then cleaned a smear of white off her chin with his tongue.

"Mmmmmm," she purred. That little seductive noise was enough to rekindle his arousal, but unfortunately, they'd finally gotten dressed. As soon as the sun had gone down, the temperature dropped about twenty degrees, which might have been chilly if they weren't huddled together under the blanket. They sat on the ground next to the fire, which had dwindled to a red-hot glow.

"I wish we could stay out here all night," Cass murmured, snuggling up against him and laying her head on his chest.

"Me too." Hell, he'd stay right here in this spot with her forever if he could. "But I'm thinking we should head back and check on your mom." Lulu had seemed nervous about the prospect of going out with Gunner, and he didn't want her to come home to an empty house. "After we check on your mom, maybe we should head over to Lance and Jessa's." They'd asked him to keep an eye on things while they went to Denver for more tests. "The guest room has a king-sized bed."

"I've slept in that bed before." Cass teased him with those soft lips of hers. "It's very comfortable."

"It is," he agreed. "But I'm not sure how much sleep we'll get…"

Cassidy turned and straddled his lap. "Over the next week, I'll have to finish packing." Sadness glistened in her blue eyes. "And then I'll have to leave…"

Yeah, that wasn't his favorite thought right now either. "This is what you've always wanted," he reminded her. "It's everything you've worked for, and you're gonna kick ass in that program." He wouldn't stand in the way. He'd never hold her back from doing what she loved the most.

Cass wrapped her arms around his neck. "You'll come and stay with me in Denver sometimes?"

He snuck a shameless peek down the V-neck of her shirt, making sure she noticed. "As often as you'll let me."

"After your performance this evening, you're welcome to stay every night." She worked her lips down his neck.

"Now see, that's just going to get us into trouble again." Red-hot lust prickled down his body, sending a rush of blood south. "You keep doing that, we'll never leave this blanket."

"I know." She sighed, scooting off his lap. "It's just… you're a very tempting man."

"And you're downright mouthwatering." He forced himself to stand and then pulled her up to meet him. "Which I will enjoy proving to you again and again later tonight. But for now…" He wrapped the blanket around her shoulders and gave her ass a pat. "Why don't you go keep warm in the truck while I load everything up?"

"Fine." Her playful pout tempted him to storm after her and kiss her until he had her moaning again. Instead, he dumped a bucket of water on the fire, stacked up the box of unused firewood with the cooler, and hauled everything to the truck in record time. He slid into the driver's seat next to Cass, who had belted herself into the middle of the bench seat.

"I can't believe you made me hot dogs." Her girlish laugh made him grin.

"Organic chicken sausage," he corrected. "And it worked, didn't it?"

"Oh, it worked." She slipped her delicate hand onto his thigh, caressing dangerously close to his hip. Automatically, his foot pressed into the gas pedal.

"You're going awfully fast," she teased.

"Yeah, well, I just remembered that Lance and Jessa also happen to have a bearskin rug right next to the fireplace…" Which would be much hotter than the bed.

"That sounds interesting," she mused, inching her hand closer to the crotch of his jeans.

Aw hell, he was already busting to be free. "Maybe we should talk about something else," he suggested. "Why don't you tell me more about the residency program?"

She smiled as though the request amused her, but she did give him a rundown of the program as they drove to her house. "So I'll basically have a chance to experience all the different floors at Children's," she said, just as he turned onto her street.

"Which area are you most interested—"

A dark shape in Cassidy's driveway snagged his attention. A car. Dev's patrol car. That couldn't be good.

Cass hadn't noticed. She was focused on him, waiting for him to finish the question.

He couldn't. Tapping the brake, he slowed the truck.

"What were you saying?" she asked, still looking at his face.

He turned to her, wishing he could drive right by her house to protect her, to pretend something wasn't wrong. "Dev's here," he said instead.

"What?" The word whooshed out of her. She turned her head to the driveway. "Oh no." He pulled up to the curb, and her hands fumbled with the seat belt. Levi released it for her and then undid his own.

Dev got out of car at the same time they climbed out of the truck.

Cassidy raced over to him. "What's wrong? What happened?"

The deputy glanced at Levi first, as if to warn him she might need his support. He slipped his arm around Cassidy's waist, bracing himself for the worst.

"Your mom was in an accident," Dev said gently.

Jesus. Levi tightened his hold on her.

"She sustained serious injuries," the deputy went on. "But she's stable. They transported her by ambulance to Vail Valley Medical Center."

"What are the injuries?" Fear ran wild in her eyes.

Levi squeezed her hand, helplessness weighting him down. How the hell had this happened? Was she with Gunner?

"I don't know specifics," Dev said before Levi could ask. "I'm sorry, Cass. They got her out of there pretty quick, and

I came right over here so I could tell you before you heard it from someone else."

"When?" she wheezed. "Where did it happen?"

"About an hour ago on the highway. She was headed into town. Said she was supposed to meet someone."

So she'd been alone. Regret slammed into Levi. They should've been here for Lulu...

"She lost control of the car and rolled it into a ditch just before Main Street." Dev glanced at Levi again, but he couldn't say one damn thing. A few hours ago, Cass told him this was the most beautiful, perfect night. Now it was turning into a nightmare...

"The thing is..." The deputy shifted as though he was uncomfortable. "Her blood alcohol was over the legal limit."

"No." Cass shook her head and pushed away from Levi. He let her go. "She hasn't been drinking. She hasn't had a drink for so long. Not since we had to get her out of that treehouse..."

Wait...

He'd caught Lulu drinking after that. *Shit.* "She has, actually." He should've told Cassidy. He should've known Lulu wouldn't stop after he'd told her about the job. "The night I came here to tell her about the job. When I got here, I could tell she'd been drinking."

"What?" Cass backed away, tears spilling down her cheeks. "That night you made me dinner? That night you kissed me?"

"Yes." He couldn't stand to look in her eyes. "I thought the job would make a difference. I thought it would help. We agreed that she wouldn't drink anymore."

"You agreed?" Cass raised her voice. "What the hell, Levi? You thought a job would fix an alcoholic?"

"I'm sorry." He went to her and held her shoulders in his hands, forcing her to stay, to hear him out. "I should've told you. But I didn't want you to worry. You already had so much to worry about…"

Cassidy wrenched herself away from him and turned to Dev. "Can you take me to the hospital?"

"I'll take you." Levi reached for her hand, but she bolted away from him.

"Please, Dev. I don't think I can drive myself."

"Uh…" Dev eyed Levi as though he didn't know what to say. "Sure. I can drive you over there, if you want…"

"I'd appreciate it." Cassidy started in the direction of the cruiser, but Levi wasn't about to let her escape that easily. She'd just opened herself up to him, and they couldn't go back now. He should be the one to help her through this.

"Talk to me." He blocked her path to the car.

"I can't. I can't even look at you right now." She shoved past him and climbed into the passenger seat before slamming the door.

"You want me to tell her I won't drive her?" Dev asked, still standing awkwardly in the middle of the driveway.

"No. That's okay." He studied her through the window. She stared straight ahead, her jaw set as though the fear and pain had given way to anger. But it wouldn't last. It couldn't. Not after what had happened between them tonight.

"I'll meet her at the hospital," he said, already heading to his truck. They would talk this out, and she would understand. He'd sit with her at the hospital, and he'd do everything he could to help her and Lulu get past this.

But first, he had to go find Gunner.

* * *

Cassidy had spent her fair share of time walking through hospitals, dealing with nurses and doctors. But it had been years since she'd walked in as a member of a victim's family.

After his accident, Cash had been airlifted to Denver, and by the time they'd made it there, he was already gone. That hospital had been much larger than this one—cold and fancy—almost like a museum. At least her mother's injuries must not have been severe enough for a Flight for Life, she thought as she hurried through the doors and into the emergency room.

Over the past couple of years, she'd watched so many people rush into the ER to search for their loved one, and it felt surreal to be one of them. A cloud of confusion hemmed her in, refusing to let her eyes focus on anything. Her legs churned in a clumsy jog that left Dev lagging far behind. The room became a blur of faces, white floors, fluorescent lights, chairs. She charged to the large check-in desk, where a woman sat typing on a computer.

"LuEllen Greer?" she choked out. "I'm her daughter."

The woman glanced at a chart. "She's in Room Three, honey. Right back through those double doors."

Cassidy headed in that direction, the heavy emotions weighing her down, making her feel like she couldn't move fast enough.

"I'll wait out here," Dev called behind her. She didn't turn. Didn't acknowledge him.

Everything she'd feared was chasing her through those doors, and she couldn't stop moving or the nightmare would claim her.

She pushed through, her breaths echoing back in her ears. Frantically she searched for a 3, finally finding it on a door around the corner.

"Mom?" she half-whispered, peering into the room. Her heart buckled. Lulu was lying on the bed, her head bandaged, her face badly bruised. "Oh my god." Cassidy slogged over to her, touching the bandage lightly.

Her mom's eyes fluttered open. "Cass?" Tears spilled over, carving a jagged path over the purplish marks that mottled her skin. "Oh, honey," she rasped. "I'm so sorry. I'm so sorry, Cass..."

"It's okay." It wasn't. Nothing about this was okay, but she didn't want her to worry right now. "What did the doctor say?" A quick visual assessment didn't tell her much—other than Lulu had multiple lacerations and contusions on her face.

"Please don't worry." Her mother shifted and tried to push herself up on the pillows. She winced, easing out a long, slow breath. "It looks worse than it is."

Judging from her guarded movements, Cassidy didn't believe her.

"I have a concussion. A few broken ribs." Lulu's eyes—the eyes that had been so energetic and full of life earlier that day—refused to meet Cassidy's. "They said I was lucky."

The first hint of relief she'd had in an hour and a half settled her erratic heartbeat. "You *were* lucky." She pulled a chair over to the bed. "You were *very* lucky." And so was she. How would she have ever lived with herself if her mother had been killed in a car accident while she was messing around with Levi? She couldn't even think about it.

"What happened, Mom?" Dev had told Cassidy what he could, but she wanted to hear it from her.

Lulu closed her eyes. A few more tears slipped out. "I had a couple of drinks before I left the house." She opened her eyes and looked at her daughter. "I was so nervous. But I wasn't drunk, Cass. I promise."

Cassidy didn't say anything. They would have to deal with that issue later. "How did you roll the car?"

"It was so stupid. I was running late, so I tried to put my earrings in as I drove. I dropped one and looked down." Her hands shook, and Cassidy grabbed them, holding them tightly, willing the fear to subside. She would fix this. She would do whatever it took to be the person her mother needed her to be so nothing like this would ever happen again.

Lulu eased out another pained breath. "The next thing I knew, Dev was there telling me an ambulance was on its way."

Now that she'd seen her, that she knew she'd be okay, anger started to filter past the relief. "Your blood alcohol was over the legal limit, Mom." She'd conveniently left out that important detail.

"But I didn't feel anything. I didn't feel like I'd had too much." Her mother scooted herself higher on the pillows, her breaths likely shallow from the rib pain. "I'm sorry. I never would've gotten in the car if I'd known..."

Of course she hadn't known. She was an alcoholic. Alcoholics didn't have limits. They didn't have one drink and call it good. She'd said "a couple of drinks." That could mean five...

"I'm sorry you were worried," her mother whimpered, and Cassidy couldn't stay mad. She couldn't stay mad when her mother's face was broken and bruised. When her spirit was crushed.

"Don't cry," she murmured, reaching for a Kleenex. Carefully, she blotted Lulu's tears the same way she had for Cassidy all those years. "Everything will be okay. I promise." She would take care of this. She would take care of her mother. "Are you in a lot of pain?"

"They gave me something to manage it." Her mother sighed and closed her eyes. "Now I'm just so tired."

"Then you should rest. Okay? I want to talk to the doctor anyway." So she could confirm that they weren't facing something more serious.

"Okay," Lulu murmured as though she'd already started to drift away. "I'm so glad you're here, honey."

Leaning over, she brushed a kiss on her mother's cheek. "I'm not going anywhere." She stood straighter and gazed down at Lulu. Makeup had smudged at the corners of her eyes. Blood had crusted along her hairline. Cassidy couldn't go anywhere. She couldn't move to Denver. Not after this. Grief rose up like a massive thunderhead, darkening everything, but she stuffed it deeper and ducked into the hallway.

A doctor cruised toward her, wearing the typical impassive expression. Luckily she'd been dealing with ER docs for a long time. Before he sailed right past her without a glance, she stepped in front of him.

"Hi, I'm Cassidy Greer. LuEllen's daughter. I got here as soon as I could."

"Oh." The man stopped. He looked to be in his early fifties, with dark graying hair and studious eyes. "Right. She said you'd probably be coming." He tucked a clipboard under his arm and held out his hand. "Dr. Wolfe."

"Nice to meet you," she said blandly. Nothing about this was nice. "So Mom said she has a concussion and a few broken ribs?"

The doctor's polite expression turned grim. "Yes. Based on her tests, I'd classify the concussion as moderate. And the ribs should heal up fine."

A nurse scurried past them. He waited until she was out of earshot. "Like I've already told your mother, she's very lucky, given what I was told about the accident. I've seen a lot worse when it's a DUI situation."

"I have too." She didn't mean for it to sound so harsh, but humiliation pulsed in her throat. "I'm an EMT."

"Then I don't have to tell you." His serious doctor expression softened into something more sympathetic. "We'll keep her overnight for observation, but you should be able to take her home tomorrow."

"Okay." She leaned against the wall, welcoming the stability in the midst of her warring emotions—anger and embarrassment and sadness. So much sadness. "Thank you, Dr. Wolfe." Once again, she extended her hand.

He shook it quickly, already moving away from her. "I've asked the nurse to put together some information on alcohol treatment centers," he said, as if it would be that simple. "Feel free to contact me if you have questions."

"I appreciate it," she managed. Still bracing herself against the wall, Cassidy watched him walk away. As soon as he turned the corner, she finally let herself cry.

Chapter Twenty-Three

Levi parked next to Dev's cruiser and sprinted across the empty parking lot. Just as he approached the doors, Dev appeared. Alone.

"Where's Cass?" Levi paused to catch his breath.

"She's inside. I just talked to her. Sounds like her mom'll be okay. But she's gonna stay with her tonight so she told me to go home."

The news gave him some space to breathe. "Lulu's okay?"

"She's got a few cracked ribs and a concussion. But if you would've seen the car, man..." The deputy shook his head. "It could've been a hell of a lot worse."

"I wish I could've gotten here sooner." He'd gone to look for Gunner, and just like he'd suspected, the man was still waiting for Lulu to show up at the ice cream shop. After he explained what had happened, Gunner insisted on going to the flower shop to buy her a get-well-soon arrangement. Which Levi had left in the truck for now. "How's Cass?"

"She seems to be doing okay," Dev said. "You know her. From what I can tell, she's taking charge, ordering the nurses around, and making sure Lulu is getting the best care."

"Of course she is." That's what she'd done for the last six years. That's what he'd wanted to save her from having to do anymore.

"Anyway, I gotta head out." Dev gave him a nod. "Good luck with everything. I'm sure you guys'll work it out."

"Yeah. Thanks." Uncertainty needled him as he made his way through the waiting room and checked in with the receptionist. Telling her he was Lulu's son wasn't really a lie. She'd always been his second mom.

When he turned the corner to head to Room 3, he stopped. Cass stood just outside the door, her face buried in her hands, her shoulders shaking with sobs.

"Hey." He ran to her and wrapped her up in his arms. "It's okay. Everything'll be okay."

Her shoulders tensed in his embrace. "It's not okay, Levi." Instead of clinging to him like she'd done earlier, her arms hung limply at her sides.

He refused to let her go. "I'm sorry I didn't tell you that I caught her drinking. I should've. I didn't want you to worry."

"I know." Her red puffy eyes looked exactly the same as they had the night she'd broken all those bottles in the street—lost and unsure. "But I have to worry. She's my mom. I have to take care of her." Something in her tone steeled, emphasizing the word *I*. As in *independently. Individually.*

He refused to acknowledge it. "I'll help you. We can get her through this." They'd do all the research; they'd fight to get her the help she needed...

"I have to do this myself." She closed her eyes and inhaled a long breath before opening them again. There were no more tears, but he recognized that distance in her gaze. "I don't have the energy for anything else. Getting her healthy is going to take everything I have."

She said it as though she'd resigned herself to giving up. He wanted to shake her. "You don't have to do this alone." Hadn't he proven that to her by now? "We'll get you moved into your apartment like we planned, and you can come back when you have some time off. I'll schedule people to check in with her..."

She gaped at him. "I'm not moving. I can't go to Denver."

She'd already decided. In the midst of shock and fear, she'd decided to bail on what she'd been working toward for years. "You can't give up on your dream because of one small setback."

"*Small* setback?" Disbelief rang in her tone. "This is my mom's life. I know you want me to be free and to feel good all the time, but that's not my reality. That's never been my reality. It's different for you. There're other people to take care of your father. My mom has no one else."

"She has me." He wandered a step closer to her. Raised his hand to her hair and brushed it off her cheek so she could feel his touch. "And so do you."

"I was wrong before. In your truck. I'm not sure about anything." Tears brightened the deep hue of her eyes again. "This isn't something you can fix, Levi." Her voice trembled. "Not with a dinner or a job or a back massage or a picnic at the lake. So please don't try."

* * *

"I need a favor." Levi waited for the rolling eyes, dirty looks, and grumbles his friends were famous for.

Sure enough, they didn't disappoint. "I think we've done you enough favors," Mateo said, helping himself to another hefty piece of the spinach and mushroom quiche they were enjoying at the Hidden Gem Inn. Since it was their last morning in Topaz Falls—for now anyway—Levi had joined his friends for breakfast. And for another negotiation meeting, though they didn't know it yet.

"I need a favor too," Charity said with a glare. "Stop asking for favors."

Ty simply ignored him and dumped more hot sauce on his roasted potatoes.

"I wouldn't ask if I wasn't desperate." They already knew that. It had been three days since Lulu's accident. She was home and resting comfortably. He'd dropped by the house twice—once to bring her the flowers Gunner had insisted on buying and another time to see if he could catch Cass. She hadn't been home, of course. Somehow she always seemed to know when he was on his way over there. He swore she was tracking his movements somehow.

Charity heaved a dramatic sigh and tilted her head, her eyes demanding that he just come out with it already.

Yeah, it wasn't like him to beat around the bush. "I need cash. A big chunk of cash." He had investments, but he'd used up a good portion of his cash flow rebuilding the rodeo grounds. "And I got a lead on another sponsorship opportunity that could happen fast." But once again, he needed the other Renegades to make it a go.

A practiced ensemble of groans met his ears.

"I'm happy to do more clinics," Charity said. "But there's no way in hell I'm doing more embarrassing photo shoots for you, Levi."

"It won't be embarrassing." He grinned at her. "You have

nothing to be embarrassed about, Char. If you've got it, flaunt it." Flattery never hurt. He looked at the others to back him up.

"Nothing could be as bad as that casino gig," Ty said. "Even though, I have to say, you looked pretty hot, Char."

She threw her wadded-up napkin at his face.

"It's not a casino this time." He'd learned his lesson after that. Charity hadn't spoken to him for a good month. "It's a beef jerky company."

Mateo perked up. "I love jerky."

"Me too," Ty agreed. "Can we negotiate a year's supply into the deal?"

"You guys are total lunkheads." Charity belittled them in obvious exasperation. "All he has to do is offer you meat and you roll over. Once again, you're willing to jump right into something without thinking through the potential risks. Without weighing the pros and cons..."

Levi had heard that tone before. Lecture time. *Here we go.* He settled in.

"Do you even care how much it pays?" Charity demanded. "Or what will be required of us? Or what the schedule would look like? Need I remind you that we're all booked up for the next three months with events? Don't you care about any of those things?"

Mateo and Ty looked at each other. They both shrugged.

"No," Ty said, snatching another piece of bacon off the platter.

"Not even a little," Mateo put in.

Charity growled out a frustrated sigh. "I swear, hanging out with you guys is like hanging out with barnyard animals."

No one disputed that point. And yet for some reason, she

stuck it out with them. Levi suspected it had to do with the fact that she couldn't stand her own family, so she'd kind of adopted them as brothers. They watched out for her on the circuit too, and even though they irritated her nonstop, she seemed to appreciate it. Much as she complained about them, she was grateful, which he could use to his advantage.

Levi put on a smile to butter her up. "The pay is excellent, trust me," he said. "And it's very minimal effort on our parts. A quick photo shoot and a commercial." He garbled the last word so hopefully they'd miss it.

"I'm sorry. What was that?" Charity didn't miss anything.

Levi sighed. "They want us to do a commercial."

"Sweet." Mateo and Ty slapped high fives over the table.

"Commercials go over big with the ladies," Ty informed Charity.

She was too busy glaring at Levi to pay him any attention. "What kind of commercial?"

"We don't have all the details worked out yet." That wasn't exactly true, but there was no way he could tell her the commercial would be themed as a spoof of an old western. Then he'd lose her for good. They'd already demanded Charity wear a saloon girl costume, complete with a corset and fishnet stockings.

"Why do we have to do the beef jerky?" she whined. "We're already negotiating another contract with Renegade."

"But we likely won't start anything until early next year. And I need the money now." He'd asked for plenty of favors over the years, but begging for money was new. He wouldn't have to if there were any other way to help Lulu and Cass, but he'd been over his finances and he simply couldn't cough up the money unless he signed this deal now. Which meant he might as well level with Charity. "Cassidy's mom is in rough shape. She's been struggling with alcoholism for years." Among other things like depression...

"Oh..." A look of understanding widened her eyes. "That's why she crashed her car..."

Levi let the silence speak for him. He didn't want to make Lulu look bad, but he also wanted this money.

"Wow," Ty muttered. "That sucks."

"Yeah." It still got to him to think that he'd enabled the accident. That he hadn't taken the drinking more seriously. This time, he didn't want to leave any room for Lulu to relapse. She had to be isolated in a place where she could deal with the underlying issues. "There's no way Cass can afford to send her to an inpatient treatment program on her own."

"So you're going to." The hard edge had disappeared from Charity's tone.

"I'm hoping to." But the best one he could find nearby—in Utah—was one of those luxury deals complete with yoga, counseling, and holistic health education. Which would cost about thirty grand by the time it was all said and done.

"That's one way to win Cassidy back," Ty commented, looking impressed.

"I'm not doing it to win her back." She'd seemed pretty adamant that she didn't want him anymore. "I'm not even going to tell her about it." This would be between him and Lulu.

"Are you crazy?" Mateo gaped at him. "Man, seriously. You're not gonna tell her? She'd forgive you for everything."

"I don't need her to forgive me." That's not what this was about. He still loved her. He'd always loved her, but he couldn't force her to love him back. "I just want to make sure she can do the program in Denver without worrying about her mom." He was only doing what he should've done years ago—what Cash would've wanted him to do.

"You *want* her to move to Denver?" Charity's scowl made it no secret what she thought of that plan. "Wouldn't you rather have her stay in Topaz Falls? I mean, maybe it's better this way. If she goes to Denver, she might meet someone else. A children's hospital will be crawling with hot, benevolent doctors. Nothing sexier than a man who devotes his life to helping kids," she said sweetly.

"Yeah, thanks for that." The thought had crossed his mind. It was tempting to stay out of it and simply let her continue living in Topaz Falls. At least then she'd be connected to him and his family. Over time, he'd probably have a better chance at earning her forgiveness. But... "She's always wanted to be a pediatric nurse. She's put her life on hold for everyone else all these years. She deserves this."

"Damn it, Levi," Charity grumbled, "why can't you be an asshole? Then I wouldn't feel like I had to help you with anything."

He grinned at her. "If I was an asshole, you wouldn't love me so much."

She flipped him off.

"We're in." Mateo nodded at the others. "Right, Char?"

"Fine," she griped. "But I'm telling you right now, Levi. If they make me wear any stupid costumes in that commercial, I'll rip off your head and shit down your neck."

Well then. That would give him something to look forward to.

Chapter Twenty-Four

Levi pulled up in front of Cassidy's house, and once again, her car wasn't in the driveway. Which was just as well today. Since she'd made it clear she didn't want his help, he'd come to offer it to Lulu instead. Something told him Cass's mother would be more open to what he had to offer.

"Come on, girl." He lifted the dog from the passenger's seat and climbed out of the truck. "Something tells me Miss Lulu's gonna be mighty happy to see you." Carefully, he set Sweetie down and took a hold of the leash.

The dog cowered slightly, but Levi gently urged her across the lawn. "We're gonna get Miss Lulu all fixed up," he said. "While we're at it, maybe we should fix up this whole place." The house needed a paint job. New shutters. A whole new concrete walkway complete with steps up to the front door. The old ones had crumbled and cracked as though they were about five footfalls away from caving in completely. Another thing he could add to his to-do list for when he got back from Wyoming.

Carefully maneuvering around the cracks, he climbed the stairs and peered through the screen door. Lulu was lying on the couch. "Levi!" She waved but didn't move to get up. "Oh my! Is that Sweetie, too?"

"Sure is." He opened the door and unclipped the leash. Wagging her tail with delight, the dog made a beeline for the couch and put her paws on Lulu's legs.

Levi walked in too. The living room was dim, but cheerful. There had to be twenty flower arrangements decorating the space. Somehow, Lulu looked more cheerful too. The bruising had faded since he'd seen her last. She was propped up on at least three pillows and had a variety of snacks and drinks within an easy arm's reach on the coffee table.

"You're looking good," he said, scooting himself into the chair on the other side of the couch. Maybe not good but at least better.

"You're sweet. I'm *not* looking good. But I will soon." She stroked the dog's head affectionately. "Seeing this sweet girl makes me feel a hundred times better. Thanks for bringing her for a visit."

"Actually, it could be more than a visit, if you want."

Hope gleamed in Lulu's wide eyes. "Really?"

"Jessa said to tell you she's available for adoption now." Though Lulu might have to wait a while if things went as he planned. Which brought him to the reason he'd come. He'd thought about the best way to do this, but now he felt as skittish as a newborn calf. She might be offended by his offer. She might hate him for thinking she needed to go away. How did you come out and tell someone you thought they should check themselves in to an inpatient treatment program? He wasn't good at conversations like this.

"Of course I'll adopt her!" Lulu leaned over, wincing, and hugged the dog. "Oh, Sweetie, we'll have such a fun time together." She suddenly looked up at Levi. "I'll have to run it by Cass first though." Her smile faded. "I'm sure you've heard that she's staying in Topaz Falls. I can't believe I let her down. My baby. She's giving up on her dream because of me."

This was the opening he needed. "I heard, but we can't let her stay."

"She's adamant." Tears filled the woman's eyes. "After what happened, she won't leave."

"Maybe we can convince her." He eased in a slow breath and pulled the program brochure out of his back pocket. Hopefully Lulu wouldn't hate him. "I found this treatment center. In Utah. It's in the mountains. Looks like the facilities are really nice." The words rushed out, not giving her a chance to speak. "They focus on healing for the whole person." Man, he practically knew the brochure by heart. "In addition to the rehab therapies, they do counseling and yoga. Nutritional guidance. Art classes..."

Lulu didn't look up. She flipped through the brochure, her hands unsteady. "If I do this, you think Cass would move to Denver?"

"I do. But even more important, I think this is the only way for you to heal." If she stayed, she wouldn't have space from the memories, and she wouldn't get away from the habits she'd developed to deal with them. "That's what helped me after Cash passed away." Even though he regretted it and it'd been wrong to leave Cassidy and Lulu behind without keeping in touch, he'd been able to deal with that pain out on his own. When he went away, all of his crutches were gone. "Gunner made a big difference for me." Emotion clotted his throat. "Taught me to face up to things, that I couldn't run away like my mom did. It still took a while, but I made peace with the past." Sometimes the guilt still haunted him, but trauma could never be fully erased. He just didn't let it take over the way it used to.

"It seems like a lovely place..." Though she wouldn't look at him, he noticed the tears in her eyes.

"I've already talked to them," he said before he lost the nerve. "They have an opening, and it's yours if you want it. Everything's covered financially." But the decision had to be hers. She had to be ready to take this step.

Cassidy's mom set the brochure on the coffee table and sat up, easing her feet to the floor slowly. Sweetie laid her head in Lulu's lap. "Does Cassidy know?" the woman asked, resting her hand on the dog's head as though it brought comfort.

"No. I haven't talked to her." Much as he'd tried, he couldn't keep the dejection out of his tone. But this wasn't about him and Cass. "I think it should be your decision. And I won't be offended if you decide not to go. I don't want you to feel like you were forced into it." Then it wouldn't matter how good the program was, it still wouldn't make a difference. "It seems like a good place to figure out how to live again." Like Gunner's ranch had been for him.

"I want to go," she said, her voice catching. "I need to go. I never dreamed I'd be able to." When she looked up at him, tears brimmed over. "It must be so expensive."

"It's worth it." If it gave her a chance to have a healthy life full of the joy she used to know, it would be worth far more. He patted the dog's head. "I'll even take care of Sweetie while you're away."

Lulu squeezed his hand and held on. "I'll pay you back someday."

"I won't let you." Hell, he might as well join in the blubbering. "I should've been around, Lulu. I should've helped you and Cass get through it. You always treated me like your son, and I abandoned you." But he could do this. He could give her the chance to pick up the pieces of her broken life and create the picture she wanted.

"You were hurting too." She sniffled. "And it didn't matter to me. I still love you like a son. I always have."

"I know. I never doubted that." Though he'd definitely doubted that he deserved it.

"Cash would be so proud of you." Lulu patted his cheek like he was a boy again. "And he'd be thrilled to know you were taking care of his sister."

He was glad she thought so. "Cass is definitely not thrilled with me at the moment. But I don't want you to tell her that I'm the one who paid for the program." He wasn't trying to force her to come back to him. "Please. I don't want her to feel like she owes me something. I just want her to be able to chase her dreams."

"What am I supposed to say?"

"Tell her it was a scholarship." That wouldn't be a lie. He would be paying the place directly. It wasn't like he was giving Lulu the money as a gift.

"Fine. I won't tell her. But she'll come around eventually," Lulu said with a firm nod. "Her fears are my fault, I'm afraid. She's done everything herself for so long. Now she doesn't know how to let someone else do things for her."

"This time she doesn't have a choice."

* * *

"It's...nice." Cassidy walked around the empty living room, still unable to believe she was here. In Denver. Looking at a townhome to rent near the hospital. When her mother told her she'd gotten into a thirty-day program at a treatment center, Cassidy had sobbed with relief. She'd gone from feeling helpless to feeling like things would work out, like her mother would truly get better this time. Even though she'd offered to accompany Lulu to Utah, her mother insisted that she go ahead with her plans to move, so here she was, on a whirlwind trip to Denver, trying to get everything settled.

"Sure. It's a nice place." Darla lingered by the large bay window that looked out onto a quaint neighborhood street.

"You don't sound convinced." She tried to keep her tone light, but they'd already looked at four places, and this was definitely the best option. Maybe she should've brought Jessa instead. Darla could be so picky, and they didn't exactly have much time. Sure, the place was small and basic— no frills except for the old brick hearth and the bench seat in the window—but the price was right.

"It feels a little lonely, that's all." Darla turned to face her. "But maybe that fits you best right now."

Here we go. Cassidy inwardly groaned. It was hard to believe they'd made the whole trip to Denver without Darla mentioning Levi once. She should've known it was too good to be true.

"How long are you planning to avoid him?" Beating around the bush was not one of her friend's strengths. Yep, Cassidy definitely should've invited Jessa.

"I'm not avoiding anyone. I'm moving." There were a million details to take care of, and she'd willingly buried herself under them, not coming up once to think about what had happened between her and Levi.

Darla crossed the room and stood directly in front of her. "Jessa told me you ordered her to text you every time she thought Levi might be headed to your house." The woman's sculpted eyebrows rose into accusatory peaks, a silent *don't bother denying it*.

Busted. "I'm not ready to see him."

"So you don't want to see him because you're mad at him?" her friend asked as though she was taking a blind shot in the dark.

"I'm not mad." She had no reason to be angry with Levi, as her dear mother kept pointing out.

"Okay. You don't want to see him because he was an ass to you?" Darla knew that hadn't been the case, so she was obviously trying to make a point.

"No," Cassidy snapped. "He definitely wasn't an ass." Yes, he'd neglected to tell her about Lulu's drinking, but she could forgive that.

"I'm sorry. Then why aren't you with him instead of me? Why isn't he here helping you look for a place where you guys can have rowdy cowboy sex every time he comes home from a road trip?"

"He wants this big commitment." And what if she did it? What if she built this wonderful relationship with him and then she lost him? God, when Dev had told her Lulu had been in an accident, fear had knocked her down. Familiar. Overpowering. Debilitating. It had brought back all of that trauma, remembering how fast you could lose someone. "I need to focus on Mom. And Levi is going on the road again anyway." He'd move on.

"You're grasping," Darla informed her as though bored by her excuses.

"I'm being careful." She had the right to protect her heart.

"I know how hard it is to lose someone you love," her friend said. "Trust me. But you can't let that stop you from loving someone else. From what I could tell, Levi made you happy."

Cassidy wouldn't deny it, but that didn't mean she would acknowledge it either. "*You* don't love anyone, and you're fine."

"You're using me as an example?" Darla made a show out of rolling her eyes. "Don't. I'm having fun playing the field. I might want to play the field forever. I love a lot of men."

"Maybe I want to play the field."

"Mmm-hmmm." Somehow her friend could infuse sarcasm even into wordless syllables. "All right. That's it. I've had enough." She walked to the window and sat down on the bench seat, patting the space next to her.

"The property manager is waiting outside," Cassidy reminded her. "We really should go sign the papers."

The woman crossed her arms. "Sit."

Cassidy did as she was told but rebelled with a disgruntled sigh.

"How'd your mom get into that place again?" Darla asked with a sideways glance.

"Some scholarship." She'd explained that already. "Mom applied, and they offered it to her."

Darla sighed extra loud. "Where do you think that money came from, Cass?"

"Uh...well...I guess...I don't know," she stammered. She hadn't thought much about it, but the look in her friend's sharp, dark eyes made her heart drop. "It's Levi's money, isn't it?" She should've realized that, should've known he would do something, even when she'd asked him to stay out of it.

For once, Darla's smile was more sad than sassy. "That boy loves you. So much that he wanted to make sure you could live your dream, even though it didn't include him."

Cassidy closed her eyes against the sting of tears. If she'd let herself dream—really dream—it *would* include him. "Why didn't he tell me? Why didn't Mom tell me?"

"He didn't want you to know," Darla said. "He didn't do it to manipulate you into coming back to him. He's probably going to kill me for this. But I'm only telling you because I know you love him, too. When you let yourself."

A sob broke open the dam, and Cassidy let her face fall to her hands. "I do love him. But things were so hard. I couldn't do it all. I didn't know what would happen with Mom…" Her throat burned too much to continue making excuses.

"Honey," Darla rubbed her shoulder sympathetically, but her tone was stern. "I think maybe it's time for you to stop hiding behind your mother's problems."

Cassidy raised her head. "She could've killed herself in that car."

"Yes. She could have," Darla acknowledged quietly. "But she's a grown-ass adult. In her sixties. Would it be such a bad thing for you to let her stand on her own two feet instead of always running in to rescue her?"

"She needs me," Cassidy whispered. "She's always needed me." For six years she'd been her mother's caregiver.

"What do you need?"

It hadn't mattered. She made sure she didn't need anything. Or anyone…

Her friend tugged on her hand until Cassidy stood. "I want you to look around this place again, Cass. Picture your life here—your future—without Levi. Is that really what you want? Because you can't have any regrets."

The empty room seemed to double in size. Darla was right. It was cold and lonely with the white walls and the beige carpet. But she could see Levi building a fire in that little fireplace. She could see a goofy picture of them on the mantle. Even with all the risks it posed, Levi would fill her life with happiness and laughter and love. God, he was so good at loving her, even when she'd done her best not to let him.

"I can't picture a life without him." She couldn't imagine it—never hearing that lilt in his voice when he teased her. He didn't use that tone with anyone else. She couldn't imagine never feeling his hand press into the small of her back so intimately. She couldn't imagine never touching her lips to his again, or never having that blinding rush when he slipped his hand into hers.

She bolted for the front door. "We have to go." She had to find him and kiss him and then tell him she needed him. She did. She needed his laugh and his hard-earned wisdom and his wit. She needed him in her life forever.

Chapter Twenty-Five

She looks like me."

Levi gazed down at baby Charlotte, studying the button-point of her nose. She was unbelievably tiny, and every time he held her, he almost feared he'd break her. It was a good fear though. It made him want to protect her forever. He'd never had any interest whatsoever in babies, but ever since Charlotte had been born, he'd started to crave the feel of a warm, weighted bundle snuggled tightly in his arms.

Seeing as how he typically didn't help with the kitchen cleanup, he'd been put on baby duty. It'd become his favorite time of day. "Look at that. She has my nose." Slender and pointed. "Perfect, if I do say so myself. Lucky girl."

"Stop insulting my daughter," Lucas called from the kitchen island, where he was wrapping up the last scraps of the brisket they'd shared for dinner.

Charlotte started to whimper. Levi hadn't quite figured out how to stop that from happening yet.

"Yeah," Lance threw in from where he stood at the sink, doing the dishes, "watch what you say. You made her cry."

"No I didn't," Levi cooed. "Did I? You love your uncle Levi." He bounced her gently until the whimpering settled into a contented sigh. "You're lucky you inherited my genes," he whispered loud enough for his brothers to hear. "Well, mine and your mom's. She's pretty great too." He winked at Naomi, who was resting on the recliner near where Luis and Evie sat on the couch reading a story to Gracie.

"All three of you are spitting images of one another." Jessa always hated to be left out of an argument.

While the three brothers groaned in unison, she dried the platter Lance handed to her.

"It's true!" Jessa looked to Naomi for confirmation. "You all have the same coloring, the same facial structure."

"Definitely," Naomi agreed, resting her head back and closing her eyes as though she was ready for a nap.

"I've been told Charlotte has my chin," Lucas threw in. He strode over and stole his daughter out of Levi's arms.

"Cut me some slack." Levi slumped into a chair. "So I'm hoping my niece has a few of my traits. Someone should. I'll probably never have kids of my own." Not if Cass walked away from him for good. He only wanted her. Her courage and compassion. Her strength. Her hot mountain-biker legs...

She'd completely ruined him for wanting other women.

"Aw, Levi." Naomi lifted her head. "I'm sure Cassidy'll come around."

"I can't believe you're letting her move away." Jessa tossed her dish towel to the counter and came over.

"It's because he loves her." Naomi sighed, her eyes shin-

ing with pride. "I think it's the sweetest thing in the world."
She snatched a Kleenex from the end table.

Gracie giggled. "Mom, are you crying again?"

"Damn hormones," Naomi muttered.

"She wouldn't be happy staying here." That was what
killed him the most. "Not when she was forced to walk away
from an opportunity like that." He's seen it in her eyes the
first time she'd told him about it—that telltale shine. She'd
been ecstatic. How could he let her give up on that?

Jessa trudged to the couch and sat with a heavy sigh. "I
know you did it for her, but we'll miss her so much."

Lucas carefully brought the baby up to his shoulder and
burped her. "Gotta say...I didn't think you had it in you."

"He's whipped," Lance said in disbelief.

Levi didn't deny it. "A lot of good it's do—"

The doorbell rang, and they all traded looks. No one rang
the doorbell at Lance and Jessa's house. Most people walked
right in.

Levi stood. "I'll get it." Since no one else had moved and
he was closest to the door.

Even before he opened it, he knew Cassidy would be
there. He felt it in the hard throb of his heart. He took the
few steps quickly and swung open the door.

She stood a few feet away, her posture tentative.

"Hi." A note of uncertainty gave her voice a breathless
quality.

"Hi." Jesus, she was beautiful. Body humming, he stepped
out onto the porch, but not before Jessa squealed behind him.

"It's *her*!"

With a roll of his eyes, he pulled the door shut.

Cassidy gazed up at him, a smile flickering on her lips.
"You were all talking about me, huh?"

He found it difficult to speak. Didn't want to mess this up. Didn't want to watch her walk away from him again like she had at the hospital. "Uh yeah. Just talking about how much we'll miss you after you move."

"I'm not moving." Her smile stayed brave. "But it's okay. I'm fine with it."

Well, he wasn't. "You have to go." He moved closer to her, not caring anymore if he scared her away. "This is something you've been working toward for years." He couldn't imagine how she'd done it, how she'd gone to school and worked full time, all while trying to support her mom.

"Here's the thing..." She drew in a breath and raised her head, gazing up into his eyes with a steadfast tenacity. "I focused on school and work and my mom for so long because I needed to. I needed the distraction from my own grief." She bit into her lip and seemed to search for more words. "I thought if I finally did this—if I made it into that program—I would be happy. I would feel fulfilled and whole, and I could let the past go. But then it happened..."

Cass paced in front of him, shaking her head as she worked out the sentences. "I got into the program, and I started making plans to leave." With an abrupt pause, she turned back to him. "But then you kissed me that night in the front yard. That's when I felt it. Fulfilled and whole. Not so burdened by the past. And it scared me because that wasn't the plan. I was supposed to leave and keep holding on to my career. I wasn't supposed to need you..." She inched close enough that he could see the faint freckles across her nose, the silvery flecks in her teary eyes.

She made him ache.

"The program isn't enough," she whispered. "I know it won't be enough. Not if it takes me away from you."

Her soft hands clasped his, righting every wrong in his world. He wanted to pull her into his arms, but he simply stood there, holding her hands, running his thumbs over her knuckles. "You don't have to do this." Somehow she'd found out about the money. She had to have, or she wouldn't be here. "I didn't find that program for your mom so you would give up everything you've worked for and come running back to me."

"That's not why I'm here." She shook her head as though frustrated. "I mean, it is. Kind of. Darla told me, but it's more than that. I was looking at this town house, and it was so empty and lonely. Exactly how I felt before you kissed me. I thought about it—really thought about it—and I realized that my life would mean so much more with you in it."

She kissed him lightly, as if she couldn't stop herself, but then she pulled back. "I don't want to live in fear anymore. I want you to be a part of my life."

"I want that too." More than he could ever express to her. He smoothed his hand over her silky hair. "But you don't have to stay in Topaz Falls." No. He should rephrase that. "I don't want you to stay in Topaz Falls. The program will get Lulu on the path to healing." He wasn't stupid enough to think it would fix everything forever, but it would be a good start. "When she comes back to town, we'll all check on her. Jessa said she'll hold the job for her. So you can go." He rubbed his hands up and down her arms, loving the feel of her, loving that she stood here with him, being brave and open. "You *need* to go."

An internal struggle played out in the nervous twitch of her lips. "What about us?"

"It doesn't matter where we are. We'll make it work. It will work. I just know." Nothing had ever been so clear to him. He tightened his hold on her and looked into her eyes, every barrier that had stood between them now in ruins. She was finally his.

"Thank you," she whispered, standing on her tiptoes to kiss him.

He could respond only by opening his mouth to her and losing himself in the force of a shared passion. The power of it flowed through him, making him invincible. Or maybe not him, but his love for her. It would last through anything.

It would be the driving force in his life.

Chapter Twenty-Six

Funny how it could hurt so much to leave a place you never thought you wanted to be.

Cassidy stacked another box near the front door of her cozy house. When she'd bought the place, it had been a move of necessity, prompted by desperation. They were going to lose the house her father had built, and this was all they could afford.

The first time she'd walked through it, the gold shag carpet and the shimmery popcorn ceilings had made her cringe. Now though, glancing around at the 1970s vibe she'd never had the time or money to remedy, those same features brought a smile.

Over the last few days while she'd packed her things, she'd allowed herself to revisit the past more than she had since before Cash's death. She'd allowed herself to let it hurt, and somehow, in the midst of that pain, she'd also found freedom. Cash's death was part of her story—part of what had brought her here to the place where she could walk forward into a new adventure. It was also what had bonded her and Levi's hearts, once she'd finally let it. The same tragedy that had shattered her life was now putting it back together, and that gave her hope for Lulu too.

"I sure hope this is enough for a month," her mother said, dragging her rolling suitcase into the living room. Lulu was still moving slowly, but she'd insisted on leaving for Utah as soon as possible.

"I think they do your laundry for you." Cassidy hurried to relieve her of the suitcase. She parked it next to the tall stack of boxes and turned to her mom. "You're sure about this, right?" She'd asked every day since her mom had told her about the inpatient program. But this was it. Lulu's last chance to bail. Today they would drive down to Denver and drop off some of Cassidy's things at her rented town house before she and Lulu flew to Utah together. She'd insisted on traveling with her mom and staying for a few nights until she'd gotten settled. Then Cassidy would fly back and have one day before the residency program started.

Once again, the details of the plan overwhelmed her with a headache.

Lulu walked over, looking sassy in her jeans and cowgirl boots. "I'm sure," she said, squeezing her daughter's shoulder confidently. "I'm ready. You're starting something new, and I should too."

Cassidy nodded, emotion welling up the same way it had all week when she'd thought about being apart from her mom for so long. "I'll still be here for you. Whenever you need to talk, you can call me." They could FaceTime and Skype. "And I'll come up on my days off. I'll be here as much as I can once you're back home."

"I know you will, honey." Lulu eased down to the couch as though packing had worn her out. "But I want you to love your life in Denver too. You have to promise me that you'll enjoy every moment. I can come down there and visit you. We can go to fancy restaurants and the theater."

"Yes. Oh, that'll be so fun." Though it would take some getting used to—not being her mother's parent anymore. For the first time, maybe they'd simply get to be friends.

"Did someone call for a chauffeur?"

The sound of Levi's voice never failed to weaken Cassidy's knees. She spun and opened the screen door so she could throw herself into his arms. Knowing they'd have to be apart soon, she planned to spend as much time in his arms as she could.

"Hey, baby." He greeted her with a rather suggestive kiss, which she fully indulged in before leading him into the house.

Once they'd stepped inside, he surveyed the stacks of boxes and suitcases. "This is all you're taking?" His tone poked fun at them.

"I'd like to see you pack for a month-long getaway." Lulu stood and hugged him.

Once again, Cassidy's heart melted at the careful way he handled her mother.

"All I need is my boots, my jeans, and my belt buckles," he said, guiding Lulu back to the couch. "But I'm happy to load up a truckload for you ladies."

"And I'm happy to watch." Cassidy loved watching him use that body of his. It was quickly becoming one of her favorite pastimes. Just yesterday, she'd gone out to the corral to watch him train...because she knew she'd have to get used to the idea of him riding bulls. And yes, she'd held her breath when he'd gotten thrown—but she'd also appreciated what his body could do.

Afterward, she'd appreciated what his body could do in the shower too.

Ahem. Before Levi or her mother could tell what she was thinking, Cassidy handed him a box. "Here. This one's pretty light."

A perceptive squint narrowed his eyes. He knew she was moving things along, and he knew why.

"One box?" He bent and lifted a whole stack. "I can easily take four."

Yes he could. Those powerful arms tensed with rippling muscles, proving he could handle that and much, much more.

Cassidy fanned herself as she scooted in front of him and opened the door. "This is better than *Magic Mike*," she said as she followed him outside. He paused and swiveled his hips in a comical little dance before loading the boxes into the back of his truck.

Laughing, she met him at the tailgate. "We need to work on your moves."

"Oh, I have plenty of moves." He nudged her body against the fender of his pickup and swept her hair aside before kissing her neck.

A thrill prickled over her flesh as she draped her arms over his shoulders. "I'm going to miss you. So much."

"Damn, darlin'." He lifted her into a hug that swept her off her feet. "I'm gonna miss you too." His eyes were magic as he rested his forehead against hers. "But that'll make it even better when I see you again." He set her feet back on the ground, though she may as well have still been floating.

"Hey! Hey you guys!" Theo sprinted over from his front porch.

"Theo. My man." Levi gave him a fist bump. "How's it going?"

"Great!" The boy held up his foot in the air to show off his boots. "Look at my spurs! My mom found 'em at the store."

Cassidy and Levi both oohhed and ahhed over the plastic toy spurs.

"I can't wait to come back to the ranch," Theo said. "You're gonna call me when you get back, right Levi?"

"Right. As soon as I roll into town, you'll be the first to hear about it." He took a knee next to the kid. "So you keep on practicing those roping skills. Got it?"

"Got it." Theo looked up at Cassidy. "I'm gonna miss you. Won't be the same around here without you."

"I'll miss you too, buddy." She leaned down to give him a hug, wondering how long it would take her to stop choking up every time someone said goodbye. "But I'll be back to visit a lot. And maybe I'll even bring you some surprises from the city."

His eyes widened. "That would be awesome!" He took off across the yard again. "I gotta go. I'm supposed to be eating lunch. See you guys soon!"

They waved as he disappeared into the house.

"So what surprises are you going to get me in Denver?" Levi asked as he held her hand and led her back toward the house.

"I'm pretty sure they have some good lingerie stores...," she whispered just before they stepped inside.

His puppy dog eyes made it look like she was torturing him.

"You two are cuter than a bug's ear." Lulu was still resting on the couch.

Cassidy glanced at Levi and grinned.

"Sorry." Her mother stood. "I don't mean to make a fuss, but I couldn't be more tickled that my two favorite people in the world have found such happiness together."

"There's a lot of happiness yet to find," Levi told her, hoisting up both of her suitcases. "For you too, Lulu."

"I know." She walked to the window and peered out. Cassidy followed.

One by one, the boxes disappeared as Levi hauled them out to the truck while Cassidy and her mom watched.

"Levi promised to bring Sweetie over right when you get home." While she hated leaving her mom, it helped that she'd have a sweet, furry new roommate. That dog had been so good for Lulu, and Cassidy had no doubt she'd continue to help her heal. Loki, however, would likely not love the new arrangement.

"I'll look forward to that."

"Don't forget to stop by Darla's place a lot. And visit baby Charlotte at the inn." More than anything, she didn't want her mom to ever feel lonely.

"I will." Lulu put an arm around her. "You don't have to worry about me anymore, honey. I'll have everything I need. And knowing you're happy"—she touched her fingers to the corners of her eyes, wiping away tears—"that brings me more joy than you'll ever know."

* * *

"Hey, you okay?"

Cassidy shook herself. She'd been staring out the window, watching the city pass by in a blur of lights. She turned to Levi, trying to smile. "Yeah. I'm fine." She'd gotten used to being fine no matter what. But truthfully, the enormity of what was coming tomorrow had started to overpower her chipper confidence.

After a long flight delay, she'd gotten into Denver four hours late. And she was exhausted. Emotionally, it'd been harder to say goodbye to her mom than she'd thought, even though the treatment center was incredible.

She pressed her fingers to her temple, trying to ward off a headache. "Just a lot on my mind," she said apologetically. She hadn't had time to unpack anything at the town house before they'd left for the airport. Hadn't had time to rearrange the furniture or even sort through her clothes to get everything organized. And she had to be at her first orientation at seven o'clock in the morning. "I'm sorry." She slipped her hand into his. "This is all more overwhelming than I thought it would be."

Levi lifted her hand to his lips and kissed it. "That's why I'm here." He eased the truck into a parallel spot in front of her new rental and cut the engine. "It's all gonna work out. Don't worry. After a little rest, maybe a nice long soak in that new garden tub, you'll feel better."

"Not sure there'll be time for that," she said as she climbed out of the truck. Truthfully she wanted only to fall into bed and sleep. Then maybe wake up in a few hours and make love to Levi before she fell asleep again. But first she had a lot to do.

Together, they walked up the stone pathway that led to her front door. The town house was nice—a stone facade with echoes of the fifties. It was brightly lit, and as Levi had insisted, it was in a very safe neighborhood where she could walk to the grocery store and some fun cafés.

She dug for her keys and unlocked the door, bracing for the mess as she stepped inside. When she flipped on the light, her tired eyes slowly focused.

There was no mess. Not one box. The furniture she'd ordered from Ikea had all been put together and placed around the room in a cozy setup—the small couch and chair clustered around the fireplace. A desk and office chair in the opposite corner. Even the television set had been mounted and hooked up to a cable box...

"Surprise." Levi took her hand and led her farther inside. To the kitchen, where every cupboard had been stocked in a meticulous order. "You even alphabetized the spices," she murmured, opening every door.

"I figured you wouldn't have time to get much done. So I took some creative liberties."

The strength that had buoyed her through the chaotic last couple of days crumbled. A sob hit her in the lungs.

"Whoa." He caught her as she started to deflate under the relief of what he'd done. "Is it okay?" he asked nervously. "I wasn't sure about the spices. But I figured you can't go wrong keeping them organized."

"It's more than okay," she said, crying. She'd cried more in the last five days than she had since Cash's funeral. But according to her mother's new therapist, that was healthy. "It's beautiful. It's the most thoughtful thing anyone has ever done for me." She was already so nervous about her new job. Now she didn't have to think about anything else. She didn't have to make any decisions. "Show me more," she murmured, leaning on him.

"Gladly." With a naughty grin, he led her back to the bedrooms. "This is the guest room." He flicked on the light. Everything was neat and tidy. He'd even made the bed. "But my favorite room is over here." He whisked her across the hall to the master bedroom.

"It's beautiful." She walked around slowly, taking in everything he had done. The walls had been painted a serene cloud blue. Her new queen-sized bed had been put together—complete with a charcoal-gray tufted headboard. The crisp white bedding had been laid out with care, and there were the orange pillows she'd pinned on Pinterest.

On her new dresser, Levi had arranged some pictures—of her family, her parents...and one of her with Levi and Cash in high school. She picked it up. "You thought of everything."

"Well, there is one thing left to do." He eyed her with that hungry gaze as he strode across the room and took the picture from her hands, carefully setting it back on the dresser. "We still need to test out the bed."

Capturing her in his arms, he pulled her down to the soft mattress with him. "Gotta say, it's pretty comfortable."

She rolled onto her side to face him, already working the buttons on his shirt. Suddenly, she wasn't tired anymore. "It won't be nearly as comfortable when I'm in it alone."

He slung a leg over her and urged her closer. "I promise to make up for my absence whenever I come home."

"Home?" Cassidy pushed up to her elbows to get a clear view of his eyes.

"Yeah." He swiped his thumb down her cheek. "Home is you. Here. Or in Topaz Falls. Wherever I can hold you. Kiss you." He lowered his lips to hers. "Make love to you..." The low tenor of his voice shivered through her as he slipped his hands up her shirt.

She shifted onto her back and tugged on his shoulder until his body covered hers. "How did I ever survive without you?" she asked, slipping his unbuttoned shirt off his shoulders.

"You were strong," he murmured, shimmying her shirt over her head.

"But you make me stronger." Her hands brought his face back to hers and she held him there so he could see the gratitude welling up in her eyes. "It won't be easy to be apart. I'll miss you a lot."

"I'll miss you too." He stroked her bare shoulders. "But I promise you, Cassidy Greer, no matter what happens, I'll always come home."

Epilogue

Welcome to Topaz Falls, Colorado
Elevation 7,083 feet
Rodeo Capital of...

The truck blew past the green welcome sign.

Wait a minute. "What did that say?" Cassidy strained her neck to look back over her shoulder.

Levi rested his hand on her thigh. "Aw, Hank added a couple things. You know him."

"What did he add?" She settled against his shoulder again. The large bench seat had plenty of room spread out, but she'd spent the entire drive from Denver attached to Levi's side. Even after a month of seeing him occasionally, she couldn't keep her hands off him.

"It said *Rodeo Capital of the West Central Colorado Rockies*," Levi announced dramatically.

She laughed. "That's quite a specific title."

"Yeah. The only one he could technically claim." He slowed the truck and turned onto Main Street. "You should've been at the town meeting. That was one of the better taglines he proposed. Trust me."

She already did. "It feels like I've been gone forever." And yet everything was the same as when she'd left. The neat sidewalks that lined the downtown shops, the iron lampposts now adorned with fall foliage. Topaz Falls was both nostalgic and welcoming.

A sigh of contentment billowed through her. While she loved Denver, it would never truly be her home.

"I can't wait to see Mom." She'd offered to fly out and escort her mom home, but Lulu had other plans. She'd met a friend at the treatment center, a woman from Vail. The two of them had decided to drive home across the mountains together. To Cassidy, it felt like years had passed since she'd hugged her mom—like they'd both been catapulted into different lives, though they still talked every day.

"She can't wait to see you either." Levi squeezed her thigh. He'd been so great about checking in on Lulu since she'd gotten home the week before. "She looks like a different person, Cass. You'll hardly believe it."

"I'm so glad." Lulu's recovery was ongoing, but Cassidy hadn't heard her sound so positive in years. She'd even joined an AA group in Vail and actually looked forward to attending the meetings. "I really think the treatment program saved her life." She'd thanked Levi a hundred times, but it still felt like the kind of gift you could never pay back.

"The program helped. But she's doing the hard work." Levi turned onto Amethyst Street. It was so cozy and inviting compared to the city. The lawns, the imperfect flower gardens mingled with weeds, the sagging porch furniture where neighbors sat to chat. When the truck pulled up in front of her house, Cassidy gasped. "Oh my god."

Everything was so different. She almost didn't recognize the place. "Levi…" She unbuckled and let herself out of the truck, wandering to the edge of a manicured green lawn. The siding had been replaced and was painted a lovely grayish blue. Brand-new red shutters popped with vibrant color. A new front porch had taken the place of the crumbling concrete steps. And even a beautiful white wooden swing hung in the midst of a dozen potted flower arrangements. It was the grandest house on the block...

"Do you like it?" He snuck up behind her and captured her in his arms, leaning his chin on her shoulder.

"Like it?" Love and admiration for him rose in her throat. "I *love* it. It's beautiful." She faced him. "How did you manage this in between traveling and staying at my place?"

"I had help. Lance and Lucas and I knocked it out in a few days."

"That must've been something to see," she murmured, picturing him shirtless and sweating.

He shot her the grin he saved for their sexy alone-times. "They're all in there. Everyone wanted to be here when you came home. Lucas and Naomi, Lance and Jessa, Dad and Evie." Backing up a step, he took her hands in his. His skin was rougher now that he was back to competing, tarnished with scrapes. She loved the feel of it, of his manly ruggedness against her soft skin.

"You and Lulu are part of our family now. In my heart, you always have been." He dropped to a knee and sent her heart into an upward spiral. "But I want to make it official. I want you to be my wife. I want everyone to know that you hold my soul in your hands."

"Wow. Oh, wow..." A tremble of happiness started in her chest and quickly overtook everything else. Her body sang with it—the unexpected joy that bubbled through her.

"This is the exact spot where I kissed you that first

night," he said. "The night I knew I would never love anyone else."

She closed her eyes, remembering. The emotions that had ripped through her when she'd smashed the bottles in the street. The way he had somehow reached into her deepest pain and held her together.

Levi dug a ring out of his pocket and held it up in the palm of his hand. It was a single solitaire diamond set into a wide gold band.

"It's lovely." So elegant and classic. Not that she cared much about the ring itself. It was the man who held it who had changed her life.

"We don't have to get married this year," Levi said, still on his knees. "I don't care when. I just want you to know I'm committed to you. You're it for me, Cass. It's always been you."

"You're it for me too." She lowered to her knees along with him. Her hand shook hard as he fit the ring on her finger. Steadying it in his own, he kissed her palm. "I love you, darlin'. I always will."

"I love you too." She could barely manage a whisper past the elation that crowded her heart. "Oh my . . . wow . . . we're getting married." She looked at him in wonder.

"She said yes!" The shout came from the direction of the house. Jessa, if she wasn't mistaken. Sure enough, the whole crowd stood framed in the living room's picture window, which had conveniently been left open.

"Of course I said yes," she called, laughing while warm tears streamed down her cheeks. It was the best feeling in the world.

"I told them to keep the curtains closed. Give us some privacy," Levi muttered, pulling her to her feet. But his smile assured her that he forgave them all.

"Pretty sure the word *privacy* doesn't exist in the Cortez Family Dictionary. Especially with Jessa and Naomi in charge." Which was fine by her. Ever since her own family had fallen apart, she'd longed for this. A place to belong. People to enjoy life with. To share the burdens and pains and joys and triumphs.

The door opened, and everyone flooded out onto the lawn.

"I love your family," she told Levi just before she got swept up into the congratulations.

"They're pretty great." He refused to let go of her hand. Together they hugged each person, and Cassidy had a good squeal with Jessa and Naomi. Finally, Lulu broke through the crowd. She did look different. Healthier. Her face was tanned, and she'd put on a little weight.

"Cass-a-frass." She hugged her tight and kissed the top of her head.

"You look amazing, Mom." Cassidy pulled back and let the sight sink in.

"I feel amazing." Happiness danced in her mom's eyes as she looked back and forth between her and Levi. "And I can't wait to plan your wedding."

"I don't think I can wait long either," she admitted with a glance at Levi. Work was intense, but she'd gotten used to the twelve-hour days. And in a few more months, she could likely request a short vacation. "I want it to be a celebration. For all of us." Maybe not the traditional church affair, but more like a party. With country music and a dance floor and cowgirl boots and a huge chocolate cake.

Levi gathered her to his side. "That sounds perfect."

"I don't need perfect." Not when she had him and this crazy, nosy, loud, loving family.

This was enough. It was more than she'd ever dreamed.

See how the Rocky Mountain Riders series began!

What would a big-time rodeo star like Lance Cortez see in a small-town veterinarian like Jessa Mae Love? She has no idea. But once she's inside this rugged cowboy's ranch—and has fallen into his strong cowboy arms—she's too swept away to ask...

An excerpt from *Hometown Cowboy* follows.

Chapter One

Sorry, sir." Jessa Mae Love threw out her arms to block the heavyset man who tried to sit on the stool next to her. "This seat is taken."

He eyed her, the coarseness of his five o'clock shadow giving his face a particularly menacing quality. Still, she held her ground.

"You been sittin' there by yourself for an hour, lady," he pointed out, scratching at his beer belly. "And this is the best spot to watch the game."

"It's true. I have been sitting here for a while." She smiled politely and shimmied her shoulders straighter, lest he think she was intimidated by his bulk. "But my *boyfriend* is meeting me. We have an important date tonight and I know he'll be here any minute." She checked the screen of her cell phone again, the glowing numbers blaring an insult in her face. Seven o'clock. *Seven o'clock?*

Cam was never late. He'd been planning this date for

more than a week. Since she was coming straight from the animal rescue shelter she owned, they'd agreed to meet at the Tumble Inn Bar for a drink before he took her to the new Italian restaurant on Main Street. "He'll be here," she said to the man. "Cam is *very* reliable."

"Whatever," the man grumbled, hunching himself on a stool three down from her.

Signaling to the bartender, she ordered another glass of pinot. "And why don't you go ahead and bring a Bud Light for my boyfriend?" she asked with a squeak of insecurity. But that was silly because Cam would be there. He'd show up and give her a kiss and apologize for being so late because...his car broke down. Or maybe his mother called and he couldn't get off the phone with her.

"He won't let me down," she muttered to cool the heat that rose to her face. He would *never* stand her up in this crowded bar—in front of the whole town.

Everyone considered the Tumble Inn the classiest watering hole in Topaz Falls, Colorado. And that was simply because you weren't allowed to throw peanut shells on the floor. It was nice enough—an old brick auto shop garage that had been converted years ago. They'd restored the original garage doors and in the summer, they opened them to the patio, which was strung with colorful hanging globe lights. Gil Wilson, the owner, had kept up with the times, bringing in modern furniture and decor. He also offered the best happy hour in town, which would explain why it was so crowded on a Wednesday night.

She stole a quick glance over her shoulder. Were people starting to stare?

Plastering on a smile, she called Cam. *Again.*

His voice mail picked up. *Again.*

"Hey, it's me." She lowered her voice. "I'm kind of worried. Maybe I got the time wrong? Did we say we'd meet at six? Or seven? I guess it doesn't matter. I'm here at the bar. Waiting for you…" A deafening silence echoed back in her ear. "Okay. Well I'm sure you're on your way. I'll see you soon."

She set down the phone and took a long sip of wine. Everything was fine. It was true she hadn't had very good luck with men, but Cam was different.

She drummed her fingers against the bar to keep her hand from trembling. Over the past ten years, she'd been *almost* engaged approximately three times. Approximately, because she wasn't all that sure that a twist tie from the high school cafeteria counted as a betrothal, although her seventeen-year-old heart had thought it to be wildly romantic at the time. Little did she know, one year later, her high school sweetheart—the one who'd gotten down on one knee in the middle of the cafeteria to recite one of Shakespeare's sonnets in front of nearly the whole school (did she mention he was in the drama club?)—would go off to college and meet the Phi Beta Kappa sisters who'd splurged on breast implants instead of fashionable new glasses like Jessa's. Breast implants seemed to get you more bang for your buck in college. Who knew?

She pushed her glasses up on her nose and snuck a glance at the big man who'd tried to steal Cam's seat earlier.

"Still no boyfriend, huh?" he asked as though he suspected she'd made up the whole thing.

"He's on his way." Her voice climbed the ladder of desperation. "He'll be here soon."

"Sure he will." The man went back to nursing his beer and tilted his head to see some football game on the television screen across the room.

She was about to flip him off when an incoming text chimed on her phone. From Cam! "It's him," she called, holding up the phone to prove she wasn't delusional.

"Lucky guy," Big Man muttered, rolling his eyes.

"You got that right." She focused on the screen to read the text.

Jessa, I left this morning to move back to Denver.

Wait. *What?* The words blurred. A typo. It must be a typo. Damn that autocorrect.

"What's the word?" Big Man asked. "He comin' or can I take that seat?"

"Um. Uh…" Fear wedged itself into her throat as she scrolled through the rest of the words.

I didn't see a future for me there. In Topaz Falls or with you. Sorry. I know this would've been better in person, but I couldn't do it. You're too nice. I know you'll find the right person. It's just not me.

Yours,

Cam

"Yours? *Yours?*" Ha. That was laughable. Cam had never been hers. Just like the others. Hadn't mattered how *nice* she'd been. She'd been jilted. *Again.* This time by her animal rescue's largest donor. And, yes, the man she'd been sleeping with… because he'd seemed like a good idea at the time. Women had slim pickings around Topaz Falls, population 2,345.

"Is he coming or not?" Big Man asked, still eyeing the empty stool.

"No. He's not coming." A laugh bubbled out, bordering on hysteria. "He broke up with me! By text!"

A hush came over the bar, but who cared? Let them all stare. Poor Jessa. Dumped again.